Praise for *Th...*

"Gabhart sensitively portrays both the challenges of mountain life—poverty, harsh weather, disease—and the heart and warmth of this hardscrabble community. The slow-burn romance between Mira and Gordon adds just the right amount of sweetness. Gabhart's fans will swoon."

Publishers Weekly

"Readers interested in the hardscrabble mountain life will want to add the latest from Gabhart to their TBR lists."

Library Journal

Praise for *In the Shadow of the River*

"Gabhart delivers an atmospheric romance set on an 1890s showboat with plenty of secrets below deck. Supported by a cast of winning characters, this well-wrought mystery skillfully builds intrigue and doesn't let up steam till the satisfying conclusion."

Publishers Weekly

"Gabhart presents another inspiring historical novel. Her masterful storytelling glows with personality and page-turning surprises."

Booklist

"Compelling characters, intriguing history, a sense of adventure, a dose of suspense, and a sweet exploration of what *family* means are all reasons you should pick up *In the Shadow of the River* by Ann H. Gabhart."

Reading Is My Superpower

Praise for *When the Meadow Blooms*

"With its pastoral setting and reflective characters, this cozy read explores the uncertainty present in every new beginning."

Booklist

"An engaging tale of heartache, first loves, and spiritual lessons that leaves the reader entertained and educated."

Interviews & Reviews

"A touching, wholesome story about second chances and the possibility we all have for growth."

Manhattan Book Review

the
PURSUIT
of ELENA
BRADFORD

Books by Ann H. Gabhart

The Song of Sourwood Mountain
In the Shadow of the River
When the Meadow Blooms
Along a Storied Trail
An Appalachian Summer
River to Redemption
These Healing Hills
Words Spoken True
The Outsider
The Believer
The Seeker
The Blessed
The Gifted
Christmas at Harmony Hill
The Innocent
The Refuge

THE HEART OF HOLLYHILL

Scent of Lilacs
Orchard of Hope
Summer of Joy

ROSEY CORNER

Angel Sister
Small Town Girl
Love Comes Home

THE HIDDEN SPRINGS MYSTERIES
AS A. H. GABHART

Murder at the Courthouse
Murder Comes by Mail
Murder Is No Accident

the

PURSUIT

of ELENA

BRADFORD

ANN H. GABHART

Revell

a division of Baker Publishing Group
Grand Rapids, Michigan

© 2025 by Ann H. Gabhart

Published by Revell
a division of Baker Publishing Group
Grand Rapids, Michigan
RevellBooks.com

Printed in the United States of America

Library of Congress Cataloging-in-Publication Data
Names: Gabhart, Ann H., 1947– author.
Title: The pursuit of Elena Bradford / Ann H. Gabhart.
Description: Grand Rapids, Michigan : Revell, a division of Baker Publishing Group, 2025.
Identifiers: LCCN 2024044836 | ISBN 9780800746261 (paper) | ISBN 9780800747084 (casebound) | ISBN 9781493450589 (ebook)
Subjects: LCGFT: Christian fiction. | Detective and mystery fiction. | Novels.
Classification: LCC PS3607.A23 P87 2025 | DDC 813/.6—dc23/eng/20240930
LC record available at https://lccn.loc.gov/2024044836

Scripture used in this book, whether quoted or paraphrased by the characters, is taken from the King James Version of the Bible.

Cover image © Drunaa / Trevillion Images

Published in association with Books & Such Literary Management, www.booksandsuch.com.

Baker Publishing Group publications use paper produced from sustainable forestry practices and postconsumer waste whenever possible.

25 26 27 28 29 30 31   7 6 5 4 3 2 1

To my grandchildren,
who know how to dance like no one is watching.

1

Elena Bradford had yet to meet the man to make her consider marriage.

She would, her mother assured her when Elena was younger.

She should, her mother insisted when Elena turned twenty.

She must, her mother demanded when Elena's father died.

By then Elena was twenty-two. All but relegated to the spinster corner in the minds of most of her acquaintances. She even had the requisite cat. Fortunately for Elena, such a corner didn't seem so terrible when she watched some of her friends chase after a child or two while ballooning out with yet another on the way. They hardly had a moment to themselves that wasn't dominated by a child's whims or a husband's demands.

Elena had no desire to be in their shoes. She rather liked the freedom to go out into her father's rose garden whenever she wanted. Sitting in the first rays of sunshine with her cat twirling around her legs while she sketched a lovely flower seemed a perfect morning.

Now sadness jolted through her as she walked among the

rosebushes exploding with blooms and pulled in a breath of their sweet aromas. Perhaps for the last time. Her cat trailed along behind her.

Her father had a special touch with roses. With any flower, really. That was something the two of them had shared. She loved helping him change a bare spot of ground into a place of beauty. And now, the last rosebushes she had planted were on her father's grave. With the help of their gardener, of course. Jamison promised to keep the bushes watered if the summer turned dry. She imagined those white and pink roses blooming on her father's grave.

Best to let that thought push aside the memory of dropping dirt onto her father's coffin five months ago. How quickly a life could turn. His life ceased in one terrible moment when he clutched his chest and fell. Not here in his garden, where he might have known peace in passing, but at the bank, where he decided who could be trusted to borrow money.

It turned out he wasn't one to be trusted. The dreadful truth of his debts threatened to plunge their family into poverty. She glanced across the wide lawn toward their comfortable brick home on one of the best streets in Lexington, Kentucky. Her mother claimed Elena marrying well was their one hope of avoiding the loss of that house and everything about their life here. What a sad hope that seemed to be since Elena had never entertained a serious suitor.

With a sigh, she moved on through her father's garden, admiring each bloom in its turn. After pinching off a yellow rose turning brown, with its beauty fading, she let the petals flutter from her hand. She supposed she was like the rose. Her beauty fading. She might have laughed at the thought if she hadn't been so overcome with sadness.

Her beauty had never been bright enough to fade. Not that she was ugly. That was such a harsh word. Ugly. A worm spoiling the beauty of a flower, that was ugly. An accidental blob of ink ruining a sketch she'd spent hours creating was ugly.

She was not ruined in such a way as with a bulbous nose adorned with a wart. Her features were ordinary enough. When she smiled, she supposed some might even label her pleasant looking.

Nor did she think of herself as plain, although others had said as much when they didn't think she would overhear. Her mother never defended Elena. Instead, she made no secret of how regrettable she considered the fact that Elena had taken after her father in personality and looks. Both, she had mourned, suited a man much better than a lady.

A lady. Elena let out a long breath as she touched her face. She had strong bones and interesting eyes that never seemed quite sure whether to be blue or green. Her thick, dark-brown hair twisted easily into braids or buns without stray hairs making an escape.

Her beautiful younger sister could never contain her curly blonde hair in the latest styles no matter the number of pins she used. But then at sixteen and lacking patience, Ivy still often let their mother fashion her hair.

The girl was very like their mother in looks with eyes of clearest blue and sweet bow-shaped lips. No one whispered behind their hands that she was plain. But she wasn't like their mother in personality. Or their father either, for that matter. She had surely taken back after some sweet, sainted ancestor long forgotten in their family line.

If only you could be more like your sister. Look more like her. Act more like her. Wasn't that what a younger sister generally heard instead of the older one?

Elena sighed again. What good was it to wallow in regret? Things were as they were. Her father was dead. They had no money. Without someone coming to their rescue, they would lose their house. Her twin brothers would have to leave the academy and find jobs at the tender age of thirteen.

11

No one could expect her mother to ensnare a rich husband so soon after becoming a widow. That would be scandalous. And dear Ivy was too young, too innocent. That left Elena to save them all. At least that was her mother's plan as she had outlined it to Elena days ago after her mother had been informed they would be given only one more extension on the loans. If payment wasn't made by the end of the year, their property would be confiscated by the bank and sold to satisfy the debts.

"What choice do we have, Elena?" Her mother had not waited for her to answer. "It's not as if you are madly in love with anyone."

"I daresay therein lies the problem." Elena glared at her.

Her mother waved away her words. "You are not looking at the situation as you should. If you were in love with someone without the means to support us, then that would be the tragedy. As it is, you are free and able to embrace this plan to choose a husband with the means to pull us out of this precarious situation your father has left us in. Borrowing money he had no way to pay back." She sniffed and touched her nose with her kerchief. Not a tearful sniff. More one of outrage. "And then that horrid Mr. Carter insinuating that—" She clamped her lips together and stopped talking.

"The bank president? What did he say?" Elena knew her mother had conferred with him a few weeks ago.

"Nothing. Nothing at all." She lifted her chin as she turned stern eyes on her. "What Mr. Carter said or didn't say is of no importance. What is important is what happens this summer at Graham Springs." She had narrowed her eyes at Elena. "You must smile more. Demurely. Perhaps attempt a mysterious look. Men are attracted to that."

Graham Springs. People flocked to the famous Springs Hotel in Kentucky to seek cures for various illnesses. If only drinking its spring water could heal their broken finances.

Now, as she continued to stare at the faded rose petals on

the ground, the cat caught her skirt with her claws and mewed. Elena picked her up and rubbed her face in fluffy gray fur to rid her cheeks of the trace of tears. The cat's rumbling purr brought new tears to Elena's eyes.

"Dear Willow, I shall miss you."

Jamison promised to look out for the cat after he returned from taking them to meet the stage to Graham Springs. Willow would be fine. She was a good mouser and had no kittens to feed. Had never had kittens in the four years she had lived in the garden. An implausible spinster cat. Her father said the cat must have some fortunate genetic problem. One cat in a garden was good, but not a dozen cats.

"Elena!" Her mother called her. "We are waiting on you."

When Elena didn't answer, her mother stepped to the garden gate and spoke again, her voice harsher. "Stop dillydallying. It isn't as though you won't see this garden again or that cat. Neither is going anywhere."

But perhaps she would be. Elena might never again sit here among her father's roses to sketch a garden scene while Willow chased grasshoppers. She kissed the cat's head and dropped her. The cat landed on her feet with a soft thud. Cats always landed on their feet. Perhaps Elena could do the same, no matter the fall.

"Coming, Mother." She brushed some cat hair from her black dress, squared her shoulders, and stepped toward her future.

2

Climbing into the stage to go to Graham Springs was every bit as dreadful as Elena had imagined. If her mother's grim face was any indication, she felt the same as they and Ivy squeezed together on one of the bench seats. They had to adjust their skirts to make room for the two gentlemen in the seat across from them. At least, Elena prayed they were gentlemen.

One of them, a pale, slender man who appeared to be not much older than she, seemed a bit unsteady as he settled in a corner of the seat. He clasped his hands together but not before she saw how they trembled, as if the effort to climb into the stagecoach had taken all his energy. The other man's gray mustache indicated he might be her father's age. He had an air of importance about him as he positioned his knees among their ruffles with an irritated frown.

They should have worn their everyday dresses instead of their finest mourning attire. Elena had suggested that. Traveling by stagecoach was notoriously dusty. But her mother claimed they must dress in their finest in order to appear to be in the upper realms of society when they reached Graham Springs.

"As soon as we are settled in, you can forgo the mourning

black," she said as they packed their trunk with party finery. "I, of course, will continue to honor your father's memory for the proper length of time, but he would not want his daughters to wallow in sorrow."

Under her spoken words, Elena heard the truth. Gentlemen might not be attracted to someone wearing the black of sorrow. Her mother appeared to be right if the man's scowl across from them was any indication.

With an icy look, her mother lifted her chin as she always did whenever unpleasantness threatened. A lady had no reason to reveal ill manners even if others did. Ivy, on the other hand, smiled at the man. Her sweet countenance made his scowl disappear like mist in morning sunshine.

"I do apologize for my foul mood, madam. Miss." He looked from Mother to Ivy. A bit of his scowl returned as he eyed Elena, apparently not sure whether to address her as a matron or a miss.

Before he made a decision on that, Mother said, "Think nothing of it. This warm weather can worry anyone into a bad humor."

"Yes." He pulled at his collar and then the sleeves of his jacket.

Elena wanted to tell him that he should consider himself fortunate not to be dressed completely in black as they were. Black had a way of collecting heat and keeping it.

He went on. "My wife is forever admonishing me to remember my manners whilst I am traveling, even if things do not go smoothly." He glanced at the man beside him who kept his head leaned into the corner of the coach with his eyes closed. "If only I could be as ready to sleep through the journey as our companion here."

The other man spoke up without opening his eyes. "Best rest while you can. Once the coach begins moving, it can jostle a person into wakefulness."

His voice was so quiet that Elena barely made out his words above the sound of the thumps and creaks of the coach as things were loaded onto it. She had to wonder if he was unwell and hoped somewhat fervently that if so, he wouldn't convey his illness to his traveling companions.

"You speak truth about that." The older man looked as if he might be worrying about the same as he scooted as far as possible from the other man.

The younger man half opened his eyes to look at them. "Best find a hold to keep your seat, ladies, and be prepared. The drivers like a fast start."

"Again, our companion is right. If you are praying ladies, and I would assume you surely are, I'd suggest a prayer that the jehu brandishing his whip and taking this coach down the road doesn't meet up with another reinsman anxious to prove which of them can be fastest with the mail. All at our expense."

"Jehu?" Ivy looked from one man to the other. "What a perfectly odd name. Are you saying the man driving our coach is Mr. Jehu?"

The older man laughed. "The moniker comes from the Bible. Kings, I believe. King Jehu was reputed to drive his chariot without concern for life or limb. Since the reinsmen of these stagecoaches have the same reputation, they have been given the name."

"Without the title of king." The other man smiled at them. "But I'm sure our travel today will be without incident."

"We can hope," Elena said.

"And pray." Her mother appeared to be doing that already as she closed her eyes and bent her head.

"I can't wait for the stage to start." Ivy bounced in her seat and stared out the square opening that served as a window. Mother touched Ivy's arm to remind her of a lady's conduct.

The young man's smile was fuller now. "It must be your first traveling experience."

"We have not previously had need to travel by coach." Mother touched her eyes with a handkerchief.

Elena wondered how sincere her mother's tears were, but then was ashamed of the thought.

"I do beg your pardon for my lack of understanding." He leaned toward Mother. "Forgive my thoughtlessness and for not introducing myself. Andrew Harper at your service. What little I am able to give."

The older man cleared his throat. "William Taylor here. The same as Mr. Harper, I shall be ready to assist you in any way needed during our travel."

He didn't sound quite as sincere as Mr. Harper, but Mother inclined her head. "Thank you. I am Juanita Bradford and these are my daughters, Elena and Ivy." She motioned toward each in turn. "Your kindness is appreciated."

Mr. Taylor nodded before he grumbled. "Whatever is delaying the start?"

"They must be waiting for someone." Mr. Harper leaned back into his corner and shut his eyes again.

"Stages don't wait for passengers." Mr. Taylor stuck his head out the window to yell at the driver, who shouted something back that was better unheard.

The stagecoach creaked to the side as someone climbed up to the top. Then a man jerked open the coach door and smiled at them. "The jehu says there is room for one more in here."

Mr. Taylor muttered under his breath and made no move to scoot over on the seat. The newcomer didn't let that bother him as he pushed through the flouncy skirts and sank down between the two men.

When he tried to position a square-shaped parcel on his lap, one of the corners poked Mr. Taylor, who shoved the edge away from him. "Watch out, man. You should put that with the baggage."

"No, I couldn't do that." The new passenger adjusted the

parcel that then rested against Mother's small carpetbag in her lap. "From the look of the clouds in the west, it might rain before I get to my destination." He shifted it again and this time poked Elena's knees.

"Sorry." The man flashed a big smile at Elena and her mother but didn't move the bundle away.

Elena was surprised when her mother smiled back at him, but perhaps it wasn't surprising at all. The man's smile was infectious. Elena felt her own lips turning up almost of their own accord, and Ivy put her hand over her mouth to hide a giggle. Of course, Ivy was ready to laugh about almost anything.

Mr. Taylor didn't appear to be taken in by the man's smile. "Perhaps you should give the package your seat if it's that valuable and climb up to ride on top yourself."

"Do not concern yourself, Mr. Taylor. My daughters and I are quite prepared to adjust to accommodate our fellow travelers." Mother looked from the older man to the man causing a stir. "I don't mind the edge of your parcel resting on my carpetbag."

"That is so kind, madam." The new passenger beamed at Mother while he adjusted the package as far from Mr. Taylor as he could. "It is very light, and I promise to keep it balanced."

"Whatever is it? It seems large for a book." Mother touched the edge of the parcel.

"It's a canvas," Elena said.

The new passenger's eyes widened. "How did you know that, miss? Or is it madam?"

"She's an artist." Ivy spoke up. "And a miss."

Elena and Mother both gave Ivy a look that made her shrink back into her seat and fall silent.

"Amazing." The man with the package eyed Elena. "A lovely artist. And what do you like to create with your pens or paint?"

Before Elena could answer, Mother waved her hand in a dismissive gesture. "She merely dabbles in art. Flowers and such."

"As fitting a lady," the man said.

Elena's cheeks heated up, but that would hardly be noticeable in the crowded, overly warm interior of the coach. Her mother did consider her art nothing more than a frivolous waste of time. She often told Elena she would be better served to practice the pianoforte or the art of embroidery.

Mr. Harper opened his eyes as he roused from his corner of the coach to study her. His eyes were the lightest blue Elena had ever seen. Like a sun-washed summer sky. Somehow that added to his pale appearance. He shifted his gaze to the man beside him. "Is she right? About the parcel?"

"As a matter of fact, she is."

"Then it surely must be the art of some master to make it so valuable you are inconveniencing everyone in our coach." Mr. Taylor's frown had not softened.

"Valuable enough. At least to me, since I am the master of the paint spread on this canvas."

"Are you someone I might know were you to say your name?" Elena couldn't stop her words even though they earned her mother's disapproval. Ladies did have to watch their tongues in mixed company, and this company was very mixed. However, in such close quarters with knees practically touching, ladylike behavior seemed next to impossible until they could alight from the coach.

The crack of a whip sounded outside. Hooves pounded against the hard surface of the road. The sudden jerk of the stage knocked Elena back in her seat and slid the parceled canvas toward them. Elena held it away from her mother's middle with one hand and grabbed the edge of her seat with the other.

"Mercy sakes." Mother gripped Elena's arm to steady herself.

When the artist laughed, Elena's mother glared at him. He didn't notice as he leaned across the younger man beside him to peer out at riders and horses scurrying away from the stagecoach.

As they raced past the town's buildings, his brown eyes lit up and he looked ready to cheer.

When Elena's mother shoved the parcel back toward him with enough force to push it against him, he looked around with surprise that changed to contrition. "My apologies, madam. I should have paid attention to my painting as I promised. But I can't seem to help myself when the jehu's whip cracks through the air and the horses thunder down the road, giving way to nothing. There's something exciting about being on the move."

"If you want to go," Mr. Harper murmured. "A fast start is more for the drama of the moment than necessary to our journey."

"Drama enhances the scene," the man said.

"I, for one, am in hopes that our driver doesn't come across another coach that dares him into an even speedier competition." Mr. Taylor brushed off his jacket. The dust rising from the road outside drifted through the window openings. "I find the necessity of going by stagecoach dusty, hot, and decidedly unpleasant."

"The trip is shorter when the jehu hurries the horses along." The still-unnamed artist shrugged when Mr. Taylor made a disgusted snort. "One must take the bad with the good."

"There's truth there, but since we are traveling companions, an exchange of names seems in order." Mr. Harper sat up straighter as he looked at the man beside him. "I am Andrew Harper. These beautiful ladies are Mrs. Juanita Bradford and her daughters, Elena and Ivy." He nodded toward each of them in turn before he went on. "William Taylor sits to your left. And who might you be, sir?"

"A pleasure to meet you all. Kirby Frazier here." The man smiled first at Elena's mother and Ivy and then looked directly at Elena. "And no, I have not yet found the fame that might make my name known to you."

"But you have hopes this painting you are trying to protect from the rigors of travel will bring you that fame?" Elena ignored the jab of her mother's elbow against her side.

Once she reached this husband-hunting paradise land, she would abide by the social rules of timid speak from ladies. But for these last hours before she had to surrender her freedom to save her family from poverty, she would speak her mind without worry that the men across from her might think less of her. These stage travelers were unlikely to be in her future.

"I fear my brushes have not yet painted that canvas, but this one—" Mr. Frazier stroked the parcel he held. "This one might be the key to my future to be the artist I would like to be. Perhaps you, as a fellow artist, can understand the desire to have the freedom to dabble in art by painting whatever thrills one's soul."

"Freedom," Elena breathed the word as her heart felt suddenly heavy. She pulled in a breath and managed a smile. Marrying someone with a fortune would not necessarily mean she had to give up the pleasure of sketching and painting. A man of wealth could assure his wife had the freedom to pursue her own interests. If he so chose.

She would not think of how marriage to whomever she and her mother ensnared in their nuptials trap might mean the end of her artistic pursuits. Marriage could, instead, be a key to a pleasing future. One in which her mother, Ivy, and the twins would be safe. One in which she might even be happy. Might even find love.

Mr. Harper opened his eyes and peered over at Elena. "We all seek freedom in different ways and for different causes. Perhaps freedom from sorrow." His gaze swept to where dust was settling on their black dresses. "Or illness. Or business failures."

"Or freedom to succeed." Mr. Frazier's brow wrinkled as he looked at Mr. Harper. "All does not have to be from something. It can be to something."

"To good instead of from bad." Mr. Harper nodded. "A different perspective. A better one."

"And one surely possible with the Lord's help." Mr. Frazier gave Elena's mother a look that seemed more practiced than sincere, as though he aimed to win her favor so she wouldn't insist the painting be placed with the baggage.

"So, what is it?" Mr. Taylor pointed at the parcel. "This painting that has the power to give a man freedom and the future he seeks?"

Without waiting for the artist to respond, Elena's mother spoke up. "The Lord is the author of our future."

"And he authored sadness in yours?" Mr. Frazier said.

Mr. Harper answered before Mother could. "Sorrows come to all in life at some time or other."

Every line of his face drooped with such a sad expression that Elena had no doubt that more than sympathy for her mother was there. He had surely lost someone he loved not so long ago himself or experienced some sort of sorrow. Perhaps it was good Ivy was the one sitting across from him instead of Elena, for she might not have controlled the urge to touch his hand to let him know she noted his pain.

Ivy didn't even appear to hear his words as she stared out at the countryside rolling past. Ivy was like that. Intent on the new and ready to leave any sort of sadness behind.

Even their father's death had not dampened her spirits for long. In truth, their father had never spent much time with Ivy. She did not share his interests in gardening and reading like Elena had. Ivy had shed copious tears at the funeral, but then Ivy could shed tears over a mouse caught in a trap. She often refused to eat chicken for fear the fowl might be one of the chicks she had once petted on their housekeeper's farm.

She was tenderhearted, their father said. Young, Mother said. Spoiled, Elena thought, but never with any animosity. She loved Ivy the more for her gentle ways. If only she wasn't so beautiful that others noted Elena's lack of the same.

Surely that wouldn't be different at this Graham Springs they were headed toward. Their mother should have considered that and left Ivy with the twins at their cousins' house. That might make it much easier for Elena to attract the proper attention from this as-yet-unknown stranger whom she must convince to marry her. She wouldn't be the least surprised if any man she met would rather woo the younger sister than the older one.

But Ivy was too young. Too romantic to accept a match made for security rather than love. Oh, to have the privilege of such thinking.

Elena was so carried away with her thinking she had almost forgotten what Mr. Taylor had asked the artist until he repeated his question. "How can one painting, that even you yourself do not claim to be a masterpiece, set your future? Give you freedom, as you claim?"

Ivy must have been listening after all, as she turned from the window opening. "Yes, Mr. Frazier, please let us know what you have painted that promises such rewards."

"The subject of the painting is not a secret." The man smiled at Ivy. "It is a hotel with young women as beautiful as you strolling down a tree-lined pathway leading from the hotel to some springs."

"That sounds lovely."

Ivy was no doubt feeling the prod of their mother's elbow in her side to warn her not to be overly friendly to a man they did not know.

"I hope Dr. Graham will think so as well and it will convince him to let me paint more of his Springs for advertisements and also to allow me to do portraits of those staying there."

"You are going to Graham Springs?" Mother asked.

When he nodded, Ivy bounced in her seat and clapped. "So are we."

Mother did lay a hand on her arm then. "Do sit still, dear. The coach wobbles enough without you adding to the jolts."

"Suddenly the destination sounds even more appealing than it did moments ago," Mr. Frazier said.

Beside him, Mr. Harper smiled but didn't speak.

"And so where are you going, Mr. Harper, if you don't mind telling us?" Elena felt no jab of her mother's elbow. She must have given up trying to control this daughter's unseemly behavior.

"That is my destination as well." He smiled slightly. "I've been told a few weeks at the Springs can do wonders for a man."

"Or a woman." Elena's mother gave her a sideways glance.

"Or a woman." Mr. Harper agreed.

Elena didn't stop smiling. At least not with her lips, although she knew the smile had drained from her eyes as she considered the wonders she was expected to make happen at Graham Springs.

Mr. Harper looked from her mother to Elena. Something in his expression made Elena think he had noticed the lack of cheer in her smile. He seemed ready to say something when Ivy spoke in an excited tone.

"Another stagecoach is coming up behind us. Very fast!" She leaned a little way out of the window.

"Best sit back and hold on, miss," Mr. Taylor said. "I fear our jehu is taking the challenge."

Whips cracked through the air as if to prove his words.

"A race!" Mr. Frazier leaned across Mr. Harper again to look out. "May the best coach win, and may that be ours."

Ivy paid no mind to Mr. Taylor's words as she peered out the opening. "There's no room for the coach to pass." She sounded as excited as Mr. Frazier.

3

The mother jerked the girl back into her seat. Dust rolled up around the coach in a cloud as the second coach thundered up even with theirs.

The older man beside Kirby jerked down the shade to cover the other opening. Whether to hide the view of the trees racing by or to block out the dust, Kirby wasn't sure. If it was the last, it was of little use as dust puffed from under the window's curtain as though the coach was smoking a dirt cigar.

The wooden wheels creaked. Hooves pounded the ground. The coach rattled as though about to come apart at the seams. The drivers shouted.

Inside the coach, all was silent except for a few coughs. The man named Harper held a handkerchief over his nose. The ladies seemed afraid to breathe. He had been in two other stagecoaches where the jehus cracked their whips above the horses and pushed them to run without consideration for their passengers or the horses. In one, all had been well, with the horses pulling Kirby's coach past the other team of horses to win the day.

The other had ended with a wheel flying off. The frenzied horses kept going, dragging the coach down the road. Baggage scattered behind them. The coach door flew open and Kirby along with two others tumbled out of the coach. The jehu managed to somehow find his balance on the slanted seat and stop the team before the coach broke apart.

One man's leg ended up bent in a sickening way. A lady was stunned but surprisingly unhurt. Perhaps her multiple petticoats gave her a soft landing. Kirby's wrist was sprained, but fortunately not his painting hand. When he'd gotten back to his quarters, he had sketched the two coaches side by side with the whips whirling in the air above the horses. That picture made the whole adventure, even with a few weeks of soreness, well worth it when it sold to a New York newspaper.

But there was no assurance this one would turn out as well. Kirby pushed the canvas away from him, toward the older woman. He ignored her huffed breath and stood to edge between the young girl and Harper. The man's breath was raspy, but Kirby thought not from fear. More likely the dust.

"Good sakes, man, sit down!" the man named Taylor ordered.

Kirby ignored him as he smiled slightly at the pretty young girl. Her face showed a mixture of fear and excitement as she scooted her knees to the side to give him more room. Then, in spite of her mother's grip on her arm, she leaned back toward the opening, seeming to have the same desire to see as he did.

"The other coach is passing us." She sounded upset.

"Good," Taylor said. "We can hope our man will let it go instead of putting our very lives in danger."

The mother gasped.

The driver kept shouting, not at the other coachman now, but at his horses. The stagecoach didn't slow. It barreled along faster.

Kirby cracked open the door to look out.

"You are apt to fall out." Harper took the handkerchief away from his nose to grab at Kirby's coat.

"Serve him right," Taylor muttered.

Kirby paid no notice to either of them as he grasped the wood over the door and leaned out to see what was happening. Ahead, the road turned sharply to the left. The other coach bounced off the road there and made a wide swing around the bend to disappear from sight. But that coach was smaller and less top-heavy with no baggage secured on its top. Their jehu had surely lacked sense to even think of keeping pace with it.

Kirby pulled his head back inside the coach and tried to shut the door, but it jerked free and swung wide when they hit a dip in the road.

With a glance over his shoulder at the others, Kirby said, "Hang on to whatever you can. We won't make the bend up ahead."

The words were barely out his mouth when the coach swerved and tilted so precariously, the wheels on one side left the road. Kirby fell back on top of his canvas. He groaned. Not from any injury to himself but from how the canvas buckled under his weight.

His head landed in the older daughter's lap. While the mother tried to shove him away, the young woman stared down at his face with surprise mixed with what could only be amusement. Her eyes were a remarkable combination of green and blue, swirled the way he might mix paint on his art palette. While she lacked the sweet prettiness of her sister, those eyes seemed to promise something more than outward beauty.

For a moment, he thought she was going to speak or perhaps laugh, but the jehu shouted out a new oath that sounded of desperation. The woman turned her gaze from him to lift the window covering and peer out.

"The driver, jehu, or whatever has fallen. Poor man." She sounded as though she were safe in a sheltered spot watching a storm crash down instead of right in the midst of the thundering danger.

Taylor leaned to look out too. "We're doomed."

The coach had bounced back on all four wheels as the horses raced on, now completely free of any restraint to their panic.

"Oh, my dears." The mother's voice trembled. The younger girl leaned against her mother's shoulder and began to weep.

"Should we jump from the coach?" the one with the amazing eyes asked as she continued to hold up the shade to peer out.

"Not unless there's a cliff ahead." Kirby supposed he should have picked better words when the mother gasped and the young sister's sobs grew louder.

"Is there?" The woman looked back down at him.

"I have no idea." Kirby raised his head to look at the other men.

"I think not," Taylor said without much certainty. "But there are trees. And ditches. A proper ditch will overturn us."

"Don't panic." Harper sounded choked but calm as he reached out a hand to Kirby to pull him off the canvas and away from the ladies. "The horses will tire and stop of their own accord."

"But soon enough?" Taylor asked.

No one answered. Who could know that? The mother began to whisper a prayer. The younger girl joined in, even as tears streamed down her cheeks. Harper's lips moved in what could have been a prayer as well.

The older daughter, tear-free, reached across her mother's lap to squeeze the other girl's hand. "Shh, Ivy. We're still upright."

Kirby had little faith the Lord would note their prayers. He had long ago stopped expecting the Lord to rescue him from trouble. Not since he was ten and prayed with his whole being for his little sister, Rosie. With no effect. Rosie died. His fault. Kirby didn't deny that, but a loving God would have let her live and if he required a life, taken Kirby's.

Even at that age, Kirby was doing plenty of things to defy

death. Riding horses that were more wild than tame. Skating across ponds on thin ice. Climbing the tallest trees to dare the tops to sway under his weight and pitch him back to the ground. All little Rosie had done was follow him out into the rain and catch a chill. A simple chill. A deadly chill.

Kirby shook away thoughts of Rosie. Time for action, not regrets. He had no desire to look death in the face this day or see these ladies broken and bruised. The stage door had swung closed, but he flung it open again. Then with an apologetic look at Harper, he stepped up on his thighs. Might have been better to use Taylor as a boost up.

"What do you think you're doing?" Taylor demanded.

Kirby had no answer to give him. He wasn't sure what he was doing, but sometimes it was better to simply act. If a man thought about it, he likely would sit down with the ladies and mutter the same useless prayers they were.

Harper didn't protest. He merely grabbed Kirby's legs to steady him as he leaned out the door and grasped the railing along the top of the stagecoach to pull himself up and away from Harper. The man cupped one of Kirby's feet in his hands to lift him more. Lather from the horses spattered Kirby's face.

Then he was boosted even higher. Taylor must have decided to help Harper, or perhaps the daughter with the blue-green eyes. He smiled. Not a bad image to bring to mind. Might make him more determined to live another day to see those eyes again. He twisted around to scramble onto the top of the coach, then crawled to the driver's seat.

The rein ends were caught on the harness of one of the rear horses, but completely out of reach. Kirby kept any sound of panic out of his voice and yelled, "Whoa."

The horses paid the command no notice even though they had to be tiring, as Harper suggested they would. Instead, they galloped on toward disaster either in the bend of the road

ahead or off the road into unseen dangers. If he had hold of
the reins, he might be able to regain control of the team. The
ends flapped tantalizingly on the horse to his right, but far
from his reach.

He pulled back on the brake and shouted again. The wheels
creaked and scooted along the rocky road as the coach bucked
like a wild stallion and shuddered under Kirby's feet. The lever
jerked away from him, and the horses bounded forward with
fresh panic.

Gathering in the reins was the only hope of stopping them.
Before he could think about how foolish it had to be, he leaped
from the stage to sprawl on the back of the horse where the
reins were caught.

He didn't know which of them was the most surprised,
the horse or him. The horse shied sideways, but the harness
held him. Kirby grabbed the horse's mane and pulled up to
a sitting position. Maybe he was wasting his time painting
portraits. He could join the Regiment of Dragoons and be
an Indian scout.

He shook away the foolish thought and reached for the reins.
"Easy, fellow."

Before he could gather them in, the horses bounded over the
ditch beside the road, straight toward a stand of trees. Screams
and shouts came from inside the coach as it bumped along the
rough ground. At any minute the coach could lose a wheel
and crash.

Kirby grasped the reins and pulled back on them. At last,
the horses slowed and a moment later came to a complete stop
a few feet from the trees. The horses heaved but none of them
fell in their traces. One of the front horses reached down to
nibble the grass.

When the horse he was on trembled and shifted uneasily,
Kirby slid to the ground to stare back the way they'd come.

Various bits of baggage showed their trail, but nothing moved. He couldn't see the jehu.

He smoothed away the froth on the necks of the lead horses. The poor beasts needed a rest. A drink as well, but they'd have to wait for the next stage stop for that. He hoped that was close at hand.

"Mr. Frazier, are you all right?" The young woman named Elena yanked up her skirts to climb out of the stage without assistance. She hurried toward him.

"Fine. All in one piece, at any rate. How are those in the coach?"

"Battered a bit, but thanks to you, nothing worse than that."

Taylor climbed down to the ground behind her. "Such recklessness is criminal. We could have all been killed. The stage line will certainly hear from me."

They both ignored him as Elena went on. "Mr. Harper is coughing. The dust, he says. Mother is fanning herself furiously to forestall an episode of the vapors. Ivy can't seem to decide whether to sob or giggle. And as you can hear, Mr. Taylor is little changed by the experience."

"And what of you, Miss Bradford?" He stepped closer to her and wished to be even closer to peer into her eyes again, but he stopped an appropriate distance away.

"Alive and unbroken, thanks to the grace of God and your bravery, sir."

"More foolhardy than brave, but I too am alive to tell the tale. If God had anything to do with it, I hope he chooses someone else to deliver his grace next time."

She frowned slightly, obviously unsure of how to respond to his words. He relieved her uncertainty with a smile. "But then, I suppose the Lord has to call upon whoever is available to save devout followers such as your mother and sister." He stepped closer. Her eyes were more green than blue now. The green of a still pond at sunset. "And you."

"Yes, well, Mother was praying with much desperation."

"And you were not?" He peered at her. "The fear of impending death is an excellent prayer goad."

"It seemed a time for prayer. And for heroes." A smile replaced her puzzled frown, but she still had a look of uncertainty, as if she wondered if she should have stayed inside the coach. The smile disappeared as she went on. "However, I do fear your canvas took more dreadful bounces after your fall upon it. I tried to hold it steady, but we were thrown first this way and then that before the coach stopped."

"Who cares about that parcel?" Taylor wasn't to be ignored forever. "Shouldn't we be on our way?"

The woman frowned at him. "We have to go back for the driver."

"No need for that. Mr. Frazier seems acquainted with handling horses. He can take us on to the next stop. Someone will come along to assist the jehu. If he must wait, that serves him right. He should have let that other coach pass and not given in to the challenge to race. I have a schedule to keep."

"Surely, Mr. Taylor, you can't be so hard-hearted. The driver might be in need of care."

"Are you a nurse, Miss Bradford?" Taylor asked.

"Well, no. But we can take him to a town if he has need of a doctor." The woman glanced back at Kirby. "Can't we?"

"Seems a reasonable thought," Kirby said.

"I suppose you expect me to give him my seat." Taylor snorted. "I paid good money for that."

"That wouldn't be necessary," the lady said. "If he has need of a place in the coach, he can have mine, and I will ride on top. I'd like seeing the countryside from there." She looked around at the coach.

"Perhaps you should reclaim your seat now, Taylor." Kirby went to the front of the team. "I'll walk the horses back. That will let us see if any were injured in their headlong flight."

Taylor swore under his breath and climbed back onto the coach.

"May I walk with you?" The young woman gave the door of the coach a despairing glance. "I have to admit to some dread in getting back inside."

"I don't think you need worry about more runaways. Not from these horses. I just hope they have enough left to get us to the next stop." He led them in a wide circle back to the road going the opposite direction. None appeared to be lame. More of those prayers answered, he supposed.

"How far do you think that will be?"

"I've not been on this route before. So, the same as I didn't know what cliffs might have spelled disaster for us all, I don't know the distance to the next way station. Wherever it is, we can't move it closer by wishing it so."

She walked beside him showing no difficulty keeping pace with him. Nor did she exhibit any concern that the horses behind her were close enough to nibble on the ribbons trailing from her slightly askew hat.

"Elena." The mother stuck her head out the coach's window. "Get back inside here."

"Yes, Mother." She glanced over her shoulder at her mother but kept walking.

"I can stop the horses." Kirby slowed.

"No need. I'll give Mr. Taylor the favor of more knee room for a bit longer."

Kirby resumed his faster pace again. He didn't say anything, but she seemed to hear his unspoken question about her answer to her mother.

Her mouth twisted to one side as though to hide a smile when she looked over at him. "I've always found being agreeable works best with my mother."

"But you're not doing as she asked."

33

"Agreeable and obedient aren't exactly the same." She did smile then.

"Does that make you something of a rebel?" Kirby said.

"Only in small things." The smile melted away. She suddenly looked almost sad.

4

A rebel. If only she could rebel and as easily ignore her mother's plan as she had her mother's words just now. But she would have to be agreeable to the idea of marriage when her mother found a proper suitor for her in this miracle-working place, Graham Springs, reputed to heal whatever ailed a person. Perhaps even a spinster's lack of a husband and a family's lack of a fortune.

Even if Graham Springs was a place of miracles, she, Elena Bradford, with a lack of notable beauty or vivacious personality, was unlikely to be gifted with the miracle her mother hoped to find there. At least not a favorable miracle, such as meeting a man as handsome as the one walking beside her who might have the necessary pockets stuffed with more than cotton lint. And be attracted to her enough to propose. That would be a miracle.

She shook away the thought. A worry for another day. Now she could enjoy walking on this dusty road instead of being dashed about in the coach while fearing death, as they had been mere moments ago. The horses may have tired, as Mr. Harper had claimed, and tragedy been averted without this man by her side stopping them however he had accomplished that. Then again, the coach might have overturned or that cliff might have materialized in front of them. They might be lying beside the road in a heap just as their driver surely was.

Elena straightened her hat to shield her eyes from the sun and peered down the road. "I hope the man was not mortally injured by his fall."

"Perhaps you should get back in the coach before we find him and let Taylor help if there's need."

"You mean in case his condition is not fit for tender eyes." Elena looked over at him. "I promise not to faint. I leave such vapors to my mother."

"And sister?"

"Ivy is very tenderhearted."

"And lovely."

"Yes. Yes, she is."

"And very young."

"Do you have sisters and brothers, Mr. Frazier?" Elena kept her eyes on the road.

"No."

His answer was so abrupt—almost angry—that she stepped to the side, all at once very aware of the horses behind her. Walking with a man she had just met in front of a team of horses slowly pulling a stagecoach suddenly seemed too odd. Perhaps, as her mother would tell her, something a lady should not do. This man, this artist, probably thought the same and that she should have stayed in the coach.

"I think I see our trunk." She hurried ahead to where it had landed after tumbling from the coach, glad to have a reason to move away from him.

Thanks to the strong belts her mother had insisted they clasp around it, the trunk had not spilled out their clothes. The party dresses that were to make her an attractive catch would be unharmed inside. She wasn't as concerned about the finery as she was about the sketch pad and art supplies she had slipped under the dresses in the trunk. At this magical Springs Hotel they were going to, there would be gardens where Elena could attempt to capture beauty on paper. Every moment wouldn't be taken up with dances and flirtation. Heaven only knew she would be better at sketching flowers and trees than charming the gentlemen.

At least she would still have the ball gowns to give her the illusion of beauty. Perhaps that would be enough to catch the notice of a man as desperate for a wife as her mother had determined Elena was for a husband. Of course, he also needed to have the required fortune.

She wasn't going to think about that now. She would simply be glad their unmentionables weren't strewn hither and thither across the road. Other parcels and valises were scattered about, and farther down the road, the coachman sat against a tree. When he saw them, he got to his feet and started toward them. Unsteady but without evident injury.

Elena perched on their trunk and left whatever happened next to Mr. Frazier. She studied the coach and the horses while the men talked. The way the horses' heads drooped made Elena doubt they could run a step now. The other two men climbed down from the coach, and this time when Elena's mother motioned impatiently at her, Elena stood and got back in the coach to squeeze in place as an obedient daughter.

She pulled up the curtain over the window opening to watch Mr. Harper gather up the valises. She could have helped with that. Mr. Taylor grumbled as he helped Mr. Frazier reload the trunks.

At last, the jehu climbed back onto the driver's seat. Mr. Frazier climbed up beside him while the others got back inside the coach. At the way station, fresh horses were harnessed to the coach, and they went on toward Graham Springs. When Mr. Taylor chose to find another way to get to his destination, the remainder of their travel was without incident or complaint.

Mr. Harper appeared to sleep most of the ride while Ivy chattered about the sights they were passing. Mother looked as if one of her headaches was coming on as she gripped her valise. Elena held Mr. Frazier's canvas and wished the packaging had been torn away when he fell on it so she could see the painting. But the ripped paper only exposed a few trees.

Mr. Frazier hadn't climbed back inside the coach at the way station but instead stayed with the jehu. Perhaps to make sure he didn't get dizzy and fall again. Now and then when they were on a smoother stretch of road, a few of their words would float down to her ears, but not enough to make sense of their conversation. She swayed from wishing she was riding on top of the stagecoach with the wind cooling her face to wishing the artist had climbed back into the stagecoach to talk about being the master of this painting.

Hours later, the stagecoach turned from the public road to go down a long lane between towering trees to Graham Springs. At the end of the driveway, a grand hotel stood four stories high with windows like dots along its walls. A chimney rose from each corner of the building.

Bedraggled and exhausted, they alighted from the coach as daylight ebbed. Mr. Harper politely wished them good day and headed toward the hotel. He moved up the steps to the entrance with no sign of eagerness to be there. Her mother leaned on Elena while their trunk was lifted down from the stagecoach. Ivy whirled first one way and then another, taking in everything.

In the soft late-afternoon light, couples strolled across the green lawns. Music wafted through the air. Elena glanced around and saw some men on a raised platform with instruments.

People sat in chairs along the veranda. The murmur of their voices sounded something like a creek sliding over rocks. A few men came to the porch railing for a better look at the stagecoach and those who alighted from it.

Elena ignored them as she gave her skirt a shake in a vain attempt to get rid of the road's dust before she followed her mother and Ivy toward the entrance. She wasn't about to start looking at every man she saw to wonder if he would be someone her mother would consider favorable.

The entrance door opened to let out a burst of more music and voices. Ivy grabbed Elena's arm. "Isn't this going to be the most wonderful adventure ever?" Her eyes sparkled in her glowing face.

"I think we've had enough adventure for one day," Elena said.

"But I've been told they have a grand ball almost every night. Do you think we will have time to dress for that?" Ivy shoved a stray blonde curl behind her ear. "I can't wait to wear one of the dresses Mother ordered from New Orleans. That's all the fashion now, you know."

Mr. Frazier stepped up behind them, carrying his canvas. "Of course, you must go to the dance, Miss Ivy. You will be the belle of the ball." His gaze slid over to Elena. "As will you, Miss Bradford. Beautiful dance partners are much desired at a place like this."

"Will you be there, Mr. Frazier?" Ivy looked ready to start dancing right there.

"That remains to be seen." He hoisted the now-unwrapped canvas a little higher to look at it. The back was facing them. "According to how valuable this painting turns out to be." A shadow of worry crossed his face.

"May we see it?" Elena asked.

"Only if you promise to flood it with praises. As a fellow artist, you must know how tender our feelings can be about our work." With a somewhat tentative look on his face he turned the canvas toward them.

Elena knew at once that it was a scene much like the one they had seen moments ago, except instead of daylight ebbing as it was now, the hotel, the trees, and the people on the walkways were bathed in sunlight. The stretched tear in the middle from Mr. Frazier's fall didn't take from the peace of the scene.

"How lovely." Ivy sounded breathless.

"Thank you." Mr. Frazier smiled at Ivy before he turned his gaze back to Elena. "But what of you, the artist in the family?"

"When one looks at it, you are so certain the people in the picture are having such a wonderful time that you want to be in the scene yourself. It gives one a feeling of joy in the moment." Elena lifted her gaze from the picture to Mr. Frazier's face. "Is one of the people you?"

He shook his head. "No. I'm one, like you, on the outside looking in."

Elena frowned a little. "Why do you say that?"

"About you?" He didn't wait for her to respond. "Does it make you uncomfortable?"

"Uncomfortable?" Elena met his intense look. For a moment, they seemed to be the only two in this room full of people as the bustling noise around them faded. "I can't imagine what you mean."

"That I do not believe, my lady. You do imagine. Many things. All artists do." A smile came into his eyes then.

"I fear I am not the artist you are, sir. As my mother said, I merely dabble in paints." She didn't know why she said that. The words stabbed her even though she had uttered them herself. Was she afraid to admit to this man, to anyone, how the desire to draw burned inside her and how much she feared losing that?

He reached to touch her hand. "There are times I feel the same. Only a dabbler, but then another sun rises and another scene beckons me. Keep looking for that next sunrise, Elena."

The use of her given name shocked her. And then Ivy was shaking her arm, saying her name as well.

"Elena, Mother wants us to go with her."

The noise of the hotel rushed back, with people moving past them as if they were rocks in a river. Elena pulled her gaze away from him to look at Ivy and then at her mother motioning to them from across the room.

"Go on and see what she wants. I'll be along in a minute."

Ivy moved off without argument. Elena should have followed her. Nothing was holding her there with Mr. Frazier. Nothing but the way he was looking at her, as if she wasn't as plain as she'd always thought.

She was still searching for the proper words of parting when the stream of noise died away again. Not because of Mr. Frazier looking at her with that hint of a smile she wasn't sure whether she found charming or irritating. Instead, a man's voice boomed out to draw the attention of everyone within hearing range.

"Andrew! Come, let me look at you. Your grandfather sent word that I should expect you today."

The man speaking had white hair and a long white beard. Something about his bearing gave him a presence that made it plain he was in charge. He came across the lobby, straight toward Mr. Harper as if he'd been waiting for him for days.

Mr. Frazier turned from Elena to watch. "Looks as if our Mr. Harper has found a proper welcome. And from the man who rules this place. Had I known Harper was so well known here, I would have tried harder to find a way to earn his favor."

"You did stop the runaway horses, Mr. Frazier."

"Oh, please call me Kirby. After the day we've had, I think we can skip past the formalities and be friends," Mr. Frazier said.

"I don't think Mother would approve of that."

"Your mother is on the other side of the room."

"Yes, and frowning my way already. But as to earning your fellow coach passengers' favor, due to your daring, the stage-coach didn't overturn and we didn't run off that cliff."

"The supposed cliff that wasn't in our path after all," he said. "Since no pesky cliffs materialized, our Mr. Harper was probably right in saying the horses would tire and stop running without any heroics."

"What heroics did you do, other than daring to climb out of the stagecoach up onto the roof to reach the horses?"

"A true hero never has to boast about his own deeds." He shook his head and looked down at his canvas. "I will need to brag on my art to convince the man there to let me spend the summer here as an artist for hire." He raised his head to stare at the man still talking with Mr. Harper.

"Who is he?" Elena asked.

"Dr. Christopher Columbus Graham, the owner and operator of this place. Have you not heard of him?"

"Should I have?"

"Not necessarily, but I wouldn't be surprised if you had. He's a man of many talents and much experience."

"An artist?"

"If so, I've never heard it said, but that too wouldn't surprise me. He's a doctor. An author. A soldier who has marched into war. A man reputed to be acquainted with every person worth knowing since the 1700s. A champion sharpshooter who shows off his skills here with his rifle club. And of course, he champions his spring water as a cure for almost anything."

"I see." Elena studied the man talking animatedly with Mr. Harper.

"Even poverty." Mr. Frazier murmured those last words as if he'd almost forgotten she was there.

Her gaze flew back to Mr. Frazier, but he showed no sign that he had guessed about her family's need. Elena's mother must not be the only one looking for monetary miracles in this place. If only Elena could find her miracle with a sketch pad and paints as he must hope to do.

42

5

Kirby watched Elena Bradford walk across the room toward her mother and sister. He shouldn't have called her by her given name. Not so soon. But she liked it. He could tell. He knew women. He should after the many portraits he'd done of ladies over the last few years. He knew how to keep the women happy and coin in his pockets. But he had long since tired of such sketching and painting.

Perhaps he should never have gone west with that surveying team to chart their discoveries in maps and illustrations when he was eighteen. Being there had buried a desire in him to go west again with his paints and pencils to capture the beauty of that rugged land. He would go again. It was simply a matter of time. And money.

He could have already been on his way or nearly so if not for the hotel fire that had destroyed all his sketches and finished paintings. Their sale was to have bankrolled his westward trip. He wondered now if he should have trusted in fate and used his last bit of money to buy a ticket west instead of to Graham Springs. But fate had never been very kind to him.

Seemed best to take a safer course and come to this Springs

Hotel, convince the owner to hire him as an artist in residence for a few months. Wealthy women would be here. Such women wanted to be portrayed as beautiful, and he knew how to make that happen. A slight altering of the chin line, a shading here and there to make wrinkles disappear. A sweet smile. He could always find some beauty to bring out in a portrait no matter the lady's age or looks.

Even better, he had a way of talking to his subjects that made them feel lovely. He'd been doing it for years in this town or that ever since he left home. Some accused him of being a charlatan, but if the intention was to make someone happy, what was the harm in it? Surely it was more a favor than a pretense.

The fact was, to his artist's eye, very few women were truly ugly or truly beautiful. The right expression could light up a plain face. The wrong one could steal the shine of a pretty one.

He looked back at the woman who had joined her mother and sister on the other side of the room. Elena. He sensed she thought she lacked beauty. Perhaps because of her sweet little sister with her curly blonde hair, blue eyes, and easy smile. The sister probably never even thought about her looks. Her pleasing appearance was as natural to her as breathing.

Next to her, Elena must feel plain. Perhaps she embraced such a look. That could be why her dark hair was tightly caught up in buns with no chance of strands escaping to soften the severity of the style. Nor did her smile come easy like her sister's did. Instead her smiles would have to be earned. And yet she had those eyes that had grabbed his notice. She had beauty there, but she obviously glanced over the loveliness of their blue-green color without notice whenever she looked into a mirror.

If he wanted to marry a woman to finance his artistic dreams, why not Elena Bradford? She was at the Springs with her mother and sister. That indicated money. The black dresses made him think her father had recently died. That left no man to doubt Kirby's true motives. And what was wrong with the motive of marrying a lady and being a faithful husband? He could do that. Give her a good life while she enabled him to live his dream.

The woman might even have backbone enough to go west with him. After all, she had brazenly ignored her mother and walked with him in front of the horses to look for the fallen jehu. The color in her cheeks hadn't been only from the heat. She had wanted to know him better.

Perhaps just the artist and not the man, but he thought not. She could be the best of two worlds. A well-to-do woman who might understand the artistic urge to capture something with pen and paint. She wasn't simply the dabbler she had claimed to be. Her expression when the words were spoken had revealed that. Even more telling was how she had seen at once what he had tried to convey on the canvas he held.

No time for courting her now. He might never have that time if he couldn't convince the man smiling so broadly at his guests to let him stay. But those were guests with money. Like Harper must be. Like Elena and her mother had to be.

He wished Elena had stayed by his side while he approached Christopher Graham. If she shared her feeling that his painting conveyed joy and made mention of what she called his heroics on the stagecoach, that might tip Dr. Graham's consideration of Kirby as an onsite artist toward favorable.

He didn't know if Harper would think the same about the stagecoach adventure. The man had been amenable enough when they were gathering the scattered baggage. But he had that look in his eyes Kirby had seen so often from those with no worry about money and no sympathy for those who lacked such riches. Harper looked to be born to money, as if that made him better than a man like Kirby raised on a poor dirt farm with nothing but his own cunning and hard work to bring him good fortune.

Kirby shoved those thoughts out of his mind. Graham was

a self-made man himself, and look at him now with this resort that was the talk of the country. The Saratoga of the West it was said.

With a last glance at his painting for confidence, he started toward where the doctor was still talking with Harper.

"I was sorry to hear about Gloria." The man clutched Harper's shoulder with such firmness that the younger man looked unsteady for a moment.

A closer look at Harper's face made Kirby think the words were what staggered him as much as the force of Graham's hand.

"Yes, well." Harper dropped his gaze to the floor as though he couldn't bear the sight of the sympathy evident in the older man's face. "Thank you."

"Don't worry, son." This time the doctor gave Harper a little shake. "Your grandfather has sent you to the right place. We will have you ready to get back to living the good life in no time at all. One can't dwell on what cannot be changed."

Harper raised his head, but instead of looking at Graham, he let his gaze slide past the man. When he spotted Kirby, he looked relieved, as though glad for something, anything, to keep the other man from saying more about this Gloria.

"Frazier." He moved back away from Graham's hand on his shoulder and motioned to Kirby. "Come meet Dr. Graham. Let us see that painting we carried along on the stagecoach."

Kirby heard the forced camaraderie in Harper's voice, but he appreciated the man's effort to sound friendly and wasted no time taking advantage of this introduction.

Harper turned back to Dr. Graham. "We had an incident on the trip here today. Our driver foolishly tried to race with another coach and ended up being thrown off. The horses panicked." Harper smiled at Kirby. "But Frazier here somehow managed to climb out of the stagecoach up onto the roof, where he must have crawled over to rein in the team and avert tragedy to the horses and, more importantly, to those of us in the coach, including those lovely ladies across the room."

Harper nodded toward the three women in black. The mother and the younger sister didn't notice, but the older sister appeared to have been waiting for them to look her way. She nodded slightly toward the canvas Kirby held as her lips twitched in a slight smile.

"That sounds like quite a feat," Graham said. "Welcome to our establishment. Have you come for the waters?"

"No, sir." Kirby turned back toward the doctor. "I'm an artist and I hoped to find employment here as such. Perhaps to fashion advertisements for your brochures or to add entertainment for your guests by sketching or painting their portraits."

The man's face lost its smile as he studied Kirby. "I see."

Kirby could tell Graham wasn't a man to be flattered or conned into hiring him. He didn't know what he'd do if the doctor ordered him gone. Make the long walk back to the town, he supposed, but he hadn't been ordered away yet. He squared his shoulders and turned the canvas around toward Graham.

"I brought a sample of my work with the intention of giving it to you, should you like it," Kirby said. "But sadly, it got damaged on the way here."

"Hmm." Graham stroked his beard and stared at the painting.

Harper spoke up. "Too bad you fell on it when the stagecoach was bouncing around."

Graham frowned. "I thought you said he was climbing up to stop the horses."

"This was just before. The same bump that threw Mr. Frazier down on his canvas unseated our driver. Stagecoaches are rough rides even on the smoothest roads with the properly pacing horses, Doctor. You know that."

"True enough." He looked from the canvas to Kirby. "I like it. There's something happy about it. Not sure what, but it's a feeling I like." He still wasn't smiling as he continued to stare at Kirby for a long moment. Then he turned to Harper. "Will you vouch for this man?"

Harper only hesitated a second. "For his courage and daring. For his geniality. And from this example, for his art. Yes, I can."

"For his honesty?" Graham raised his eyebrows even as he kept his gaze on Harper and not Kirby.

"That I cannot say for certain, but I have no reason to doubt it. He might be the one to answer that."

Graham leaned toward Kirby. "I won't have a shyster taking advantage of my guests." His voice was barely audible now instead of booming as before.

Kirby kept his voice low but firm as he answered him. "I always have the greatest respect for the subjects of any portrait I do. Fair pay for my work, if it meets with the person's satisfaction, is all I ask. Any sketch or painting I might do for you in regard to your establishment here would have to meet with your approval, although I would appreciate room and boarding."

The man lifted his chin and was silent for a moment before he spoke in a normal tone, not booming or quiet now. "You must know how to handle horses."

"Sir?" The change in the direction of their conversation rattled Kirby.

"You stopped the runaway stage."

"Oh. My father had a contrary mule I had to deal with at plowing time on our farm." When Graham smiled, Kirby hurried on. "Then a few years ago I went west with a survey team as a cartographer, but I had to pitch in with everything on the trip. One of the men taught me about handling horses and driving a team."

"Good skills to have and that proved to be fortunate for young Harper here." He turned toward Harper. "Best go find your room, Andrew. Dinner will be served soon, and then there's the ball."

"I thought to skip the dance," Harper said.

"No, no." Graham's booming voice returned. "Can't allow that. Dancing is part of the treatment here."

Harper didn't look pleased, but he inclined his head slightly before he turned to Kirby. "I look forward to seeing more of your work."

As Harper walked away, Graham spoke almost as if talking to himself. "A shame how a bad experience in love can wreck a man."

Kirby stayed where he was, still holding the canvas. He hadn't been dismissed or ordered to leave. Yet. He could do nothing but wait for the man's verdict.

"But once you've lived as many years as I have, you know that almost anything can be defeated with strong will and proper living."

"And taking the waters at the best Springs Hotel."

With a laugh, Graham jerked his attention back to Kirby. "Another skill is knowing what to say and when to say it. It appears you may be as gifted in that as you are with your brush."

"That's something that a man on his own has to master, but I've heard in the case of Graham Springs that partaking of the waters does have a reviving effect."

"True enough." The laugh gone, Graham studied Kirby with narrowed eyes.

Kirby didn't say anything. There were times to speak and times to be silent. With this man, he figured there were more times to listen than to speak.

"Tell you what. You repair that canvas." The doctor pointed to Kirby's painting. "I'll take that in exchange for two weeks' lodging."

"I can't mend the tear." Kirby looked down at the rent in the canvas.

"Then work it into the whole. That's what we have to do

when we are surprised with unexpected catastrophes in life. Work them into the fabric of life."

"All right," Kirby said. "But after the two weeks?"

"Let's see how things go. Whether you can show your worth to the clients here. They come for healing but also for a good time. Will your presence add to their pleasure?"

"I have no doubt of that," Kirby said. "Most enjoy seeing likenesses of themselves."

"True enough if such likenesses show them in the best light."

"I always find the best light."

Graham smiled again at that. "For the right price?"

"That can help the light be brighter."

"No signs with prices. But you can accept whatever any subjects of those likenesses offer you in payment."

"Very well."

"You can start by coming out to the rifle club to sketch some of the gentlemen displaying their marksmanship." An amused look came into the doctor's eyes. "You might do well to remember they do have guns and thus leave off the evident warts and scars."

"Such can make a man look stronger at times."

"True, but perhaps not more generous." He clapped Kirby on the back with such force, he had to take a step to keep his balance. "And as there were a variety of duties on that westward trek you went on, so it is here too. Can you dance?"

"I can."

"Then I expect you to be at the dances and make a willing partner to the ladies regardless of their beauty." Again, the man's eyes narrowed. "But without leading the naïve on. No romantic nonsense."

"It looks a place for romance."

"Not for my workers. I'll not have a handsome fellow like you leaving a trail of broken hearts in your path."

Kirby looked straight into the older man's eyes. "I'll draw

their pictures. I'll whirl them around the dance floor. I'll make them smile, but I'll leave their hearts intact."

He had no problem making that promise. If he enticed an heiress such as Elena Bradford to fall in love with him, no heart would be broken. He would give her his own heart. At least as much of it not already owned by his art and his dream of the west. He could make a woman happy.

6

vy peeled off her black dress and, with it, the gloom of death it represented. She worried that might be disrespectful to her father, but she couldn't see why wearing black was such a requirement of grief. She could grieve her father in blue or pink just as well. Besides, he never wanted any of his girls to shed tears. Or the twins either, for that matter.

Papa liked them all to be happy. Even Elena. Well, especially Elena. She had always been his favorite. That didn't bother Ivy. She was the girl in the middle. Elena was the oldest. The twins were not only the babies, but they were like bonus prizes to her mother and father. Two boys. Every man wanted sons. Every woman wanted to give her husband sons. A daughter was fine, but a son was vital to carrying on the family name.

Ivy loved her little brothers. She couldn't remember before they were born. Elena could. Elena could remember before Ivy was born. At least, she said she could. Sometimes she sounded like she wouldn't mind going back to that time. That didn't bother Ivy either. Hardly anything did. Well, other than wearing shoes that pinched her toes or a corset pulled so tight it made breathing next to impossible.

But she could put up with such minor nuisances tonight as she pulled on the rose dress her mother ordered from New Orleans. She had never had such a beautiful organdy dress with a tiny waist and a flowing skirt. The silken petticoats under the skirt made the most tantalizing rustling sound.

"Isn't this the most exciting thing ever?" Ivy swished her skirts back and forth in front of a gilt-framed mirror that was almost as tall as she was.

"Shh." Elena motioned to their mother, who was resting in one of the beds with a damp cloth over her eyes. One of her headaches.

"Oh, sorry, Mother," she whispered.

Her mother lifted her hand and waved away her apology.

Elena didn't seem upset with Ivy either as she fastened her hair into a tight bun. Ivy wanted to tell her to let a few tresses curl around her face, but she didn't. Elena never listened to her advice about anything like that. Well, about anything.

At least she didn't look cross as she smiled at Ivy in the mirror and spoke softly. "More exciting than a runaway stage-coach?"

"A different kind of excitement. That was dreadful." Ivy felt breathless and not because of her corset. Her heart did a little stutter when she thought about how sure she'd been that their coach would break apart as it bounced along the rough road. Keeping her mother's headache in mind, she went on in a near whisper. "Wasn't Mr. Frazier a wonder climbing out of the coach to stop the horses? He has the most amazing smile. Like he has never seen anything he didn't like. Or anyone. But that Mr. Taylor. I don't think he knew how to smile. I'm glad he didn't come here."

"I'm sure there will be some Mr. Taylors here." Elena turned her head one way and then the other to check her hair.

"No, there couldn't be. How could one be grouchy in such a place as this?" She swirled her skirts again before she slipped on her shoes. Not the pinching ones, even if they were a better match to the dress. She wanted nothing to take away from the pleasure of the dance. She hadn't been to a dance in months. So no pinched toes tonight.

"What about Mr. Harper? Smiles didn't seem to come easy for him either," Elena said.

"I know. Poor man. He was so sad. The kind of sad that makes smiling difficult."

"Sad?" Elena's forehead wrinkled in a slight frown as she handed the comb to Ivy. "I rather wondered if he has some health problem and that is why he came to the Springs."

"That could be. He did seem very concerned about how the dust made him cough." The swipes Ivy made at her curls simply made them more wayward. "So yes, ill, but sad first."

"I thought him very nice."

"Being sad doesn't keep one from being nice." Ivy tapped the comb on her cheek. "Do you think terrible people feel sad?"

"I would think being terrible might make a person very sad."

"Oh, I don't know about that. I doubt truly terrible people feel much remorse about anything."

"How many truly terrible people do you know?" Elena asked.

Ivy shrugged to pretend she wasn't bothered by that look Elena gave her, as if Ivy was still a child who couldn't know anything about anything. She tried to gather her hair back into a bun on top of her head, but strands escaped her comb and fingers to spring out in all directions.

She looked toward the bed, wishing her mother would offer to dress her hair. But she appeared to be asleep. She sighed. She couldn't wake her. Sleep always helped her headaches go away. She made another attempt at corralling her hair.

Elena laughed and reached for the comb. "Here. Sit on the stool there and let me."

"Oh, thank you, Elena. I despair of ever learning to properly fix my hair." She peeked up at her in the mirror as Elena combed back her curls into an efficient bun. "I do like a few curls loose around my face."

"Worry not, little sister. There are no pins strong enough to capture your every curl. You will have plenty of loose curls to entrance your dance partners."

"Do you think anyone will ask me to dance?"

"I think every man there will ask you to dance. You do need to remember to not let them talk you into stepping out into the dark with them."

"You mean to steal a kiss." The thought made Ivy grin.

"No kissing allowed for you." Elena tapped Ivy's head with the comb.

"How about for you?"

"Only if they are very rich and have just asked me to marry them."

Ivy thought Elena meant the words to be teasing, but unease sounded in her voice. What their mother expected to come from this trip to the Springs was no secret. Nor was it a secret that Elena had not embraced the plan with enthusiasm.

"You won't have to say yes. Or let them have a kiss either."

"A worry for another day," Elena said.

Ivy watched her in the mirror a few seconds before she said, "Have you ever been kissed, Elena? By a boy."

"I guess I'm past the kiss-the-boys stage. Remember the part about somebody proposing?"

Ivy didn't bother asking her again. The way she avoided answering proved she hadn't kissed any boys. Or men. Poor Elena. She never gave any suitor a chance.

Elena spoke again before Ivy could decide what to say next. "Have you?"

Ivy hesitated as she let her gaze drift toward her mother in the bed. She was snoring softly, but Ivy had known other times when she thought her mother couldn't hear but she did.

"Why, Ivy, I do believe you're blushing." Elena leaned around Ivy to peer at her face.

Ivy fanned herself with her hand. "It's so hot in here. I don't know why Mother didn't want us to raise the window."

She didn't really mind telling Elena about Jacob. She didn't mind telling anybody about Jacob. Except she knew what they would all say. *You are too young. It's nothing but puppy love.* But they were all wrong. She and Jacob did know what love was about. They were going to get married as soon as Jacob finished school. And yes, they had kissed. More than once.

"I think my little sister has secrets." Elena finished pinning up Ivy's hair and handed her the comb to fix the stray strands however she wished.

Ivy concentrated on twisting a curl around her finger and releasing it to tickle her ear. "Everybody has secrets, don't you think?"

"Sisters shouldn't have secrets from each other."

Elena had never shared a secret with her, or hardly anything, but Ivy wasn't going to mention that. She wanted to believe they could be sisters who shared everything, even their deepest secrets. From the time Ivy could remember, she had wanted to be more like Elena. So sure of herself and able to do everything well. She never spilled her drink or tripped over her own feet.

She seemed to glide through her days unruffled by the most upsetting problems. She simply figured out what should be done next. Even their mother looked to Elena to find ways to cope. Just like when their father died so suddenly. Ivy struggled for days to even believe it had truly happened, and Mother had taken to her bed. Elena had been the one to talk to the undertaker and their preacher. She had kept them all together. Ivy had no doubt she would continue to do so, whatever it might take.

Ivy took another quick look at her mother before she whispered, "How I feel about Jacob is hardly a secret."

"Jacob? That Pennington boy who used to climb the trees in our yard to shake down water on you after a rain? I thought that infuriated you."

"He's grown up since then. He's two years older than I am, you know. Well, almost. He'll be eighteen next month." Ivy twirled another strand of hair around her finger with great care before she released the curl. She wished Jacob was waiting down in the ballroom. She would dance every dance with him.

"Eighteen. I did see him at Father's funeral. I hardly knew him, he had gotten so tall, but I don't remember him visiting you for a while."

"He was away at school. In the east. And yes, he is very tall and handsome." A smile flickered across Ivy's face. "He has the most wonderful brown eyes that seem to capture sunlight."

"He does, does he?" Elena raised her eyebrows as she watched Ivy in the mirror.

"Didn't you notice?"

"Obviously I should have, but I suppose I was too busy that day at Father's funeral." Elena kept her gaze fixed on a ruffle she was straightening on her skirt as she asked, "And you have let him kiss you?"

Elena didn't sound all that interested. She, the same as everyone else, was probably sure what Ivy felt for Jacob was nothing but a childish infatuation. Even so, she seemed to be waiting for Ivy to answer.

"Only a time or two."

Ivy tried to sound a little cavalier while, in truth, she could recall every detail of the four times Jacob had kissed her. The first was a sweet peck when they were mere children. Two were stolen in the shadows, one of them a so-very-gentle kiss after her father's funeral. Jacob had so much love in his eyes for her that day.

The last, well the last was not one she liked to think on as much. The kiss was fine, but then after Ivy told him they were leaving for Graham Springs, Jacob had been upset. He had only the day before returned to Lexington from the school in the east.

"Tell your mother you refuse to go," he'd said.

"I can't do that."

"You could. If you really cared for me. I thought we would see each other more this summer before I have to return to school." His voice changed from demanding to pleading. "You could stay with a friend."

"Mother wants me to go. She says I have to help Elena find a husband."

"But what if you are the one to fall in love?" He had looked so very worried then as he held her hands and stared into her eyes. "With someone else."

At the time, she had wanted to find a way to do as he asked. She had even mentioned to her mother that she could stay in the city, but her mother had brushed away the idea as foolish. Ivy had ended up writing Jacob to assure him no one could ever replace him in her heart. Two months wasn't forever. Actually, her mother said it was a very short time for Elena to be properly matched with a suitor.

"I see." Elena's words brought Ivy back to the present. She turned away from the mirror. "Come. We are as ready as we are going to be. Time to go find the ballroom."

7

Elena followed Ivy out into the hall and quietly shut the door behind them. Finding the ballroom would not be hard. Dancing all night with this or that man perhaps stepping on her toes might be. But she couldn't put it off. Dance she must.

First, she wanted to talk to Ivy without being overheard. Their mother's breathing had been calm and even as though she were asleep, but Elena thought Mother might have been pretending in order to hear more once kisses were mentioned. Ivy's kisses. It could be they both had not noticed Ivy becoming a young woman or this neighbor boy a man.

Elena did remember Jacob. A sweet boy despite his tendency to mischief. He was from a good family. She thought his father was a teacher. Perhaps a professor at the local college. Yes, that sounded right. There were brothers and maybe a sister. All older, Elena thought. One of the brothers was about her age, but they were never the friends Ivy and Jacob were.

Try as she might, she could come up with no memory of Mrs. Pennington. She shrugged. Mother would know. If she knew about the romantic feelings between Ivy and Jacob, this trip to Graham Springs might have another purpose in addition to Elena finding a suitable husband. Her mother might hope the separation would cure Ivy of thinking she was in love.

Thinking she was. Who was Elena to judge whether Ivy's love was merely a young girl's fancy or something that would truly last for a lifetime? Just because she had never sought or been surprised by love didn't mean Ivy had followed the same path. Elena's path was not the expected or normal one. Girls fell in love. Young women wanted to marry.

She needed to keep that in her thoughts now and try to awaken that normal desire in her heart. Thoughts of Kirby Frazier popped into her mind. The man interested her. An artist with obvious talent. A man of daring. Of good looks. The kind of man Elena could imagine falling in love with. But was he the kind of man who could save her family from poverty? She doubted that since he was so nervous about his damaged canvas. The canvas he had to depend on to convince the owner of the Springs to let him stay.

She pushed those thoughts away. One problem at a time. She considered Ivy walking beside her. The hallway was empty. Perhaps everyone else had already found the ballroom. She did think she heard music, but then there had been music around them ever since they climbed down from the stagecoach, except when they were in their room. And then, if their mother had allowed them to open the windows, they might have still heard music from somewhere.

"What does Mother think about Jacob and you?" Elena kept her voice light as they continued down the hall.

"I don't know." Ivy kept her head down, staring at the floor.

"Look at me." Elena stopped in the middle of the hall and caught Ivy's arm to stop her. "Does Mother know you have a romantic interest in the Pennington boy?"

"He's not a boy." Ivy faced her and lifted her chin. "But

Mother thinks he is. She thinks I'm still a child. You probably do too."

"You are only sixteen."

"Plenty of girls fall in love at sixteen. Two girls I know married at that age, and very few are not either married or at least betrothed by the time they are twenty." Ivy jerked away from Elena and rubbed her arm. "You are the odd one out here. Not me. Just because you couldn't find somebody to love doesn't mean I couldn't." Her eyes flashed with defiance, then just as quickly filled with tears.

Elena took a breath and touched Ivy's cheek. "Shh. You don't want to have tear streaks on your face. I'm sure Jacob is a wonderful young man."

Ivy sniffed and swiped a tear from the corner of one of her eyes. "He is wonderful. But he didn't want me to come here." She blinked as more tears threatened. "He's upset with me. But I really had to come. Mother wouldn't let me stay home."

"Of course not." Especially if she knew Ivy had romantic trysts planned with a young man. "You did have to come. And now you need to stop worrying about Jacob and enjoy our time here. True love will survive a few weeks apart."

"How do you know?"

"Obviously not from personal experience, as you aptly pointed out."

Ivy ducked her head. "I'm sorry. That wasn't nice of me."

"Truth is truth. But don't you think your love can survive time apart? It seems if Jacob has been away at school that it already has."

"But he didn't have any choice about going away to school."

"And you didn't have any choice about coming here. We are here, and I think whatever happens with Mother's grand plans for me finding the proper husband, being here and taking the waters will be good for her. Perhaps it will cure her of those dreadful headaches." Elena put her arm around Ivy's waist to turn her back toward the stairway. "Now, come along. Let's go enjoy the music. I think I hear it already."

In an instant, Ivy was smiling. "Oh, I do too. Thank you, Elena. You always know what's best. I'm so fortunate to have you for my sister." She moved away from Elena, almost dancing already.

Elena couldn't keep from smiling. If only she could be as enthusiastic. After a moment, she followed, even though she would rather have gone the other direction. Out the door into the night, where she would surely find a garden of flowers. Perhaps even roses. Not kisses. She had no interest in romance in the moonlight.

She sighed. Tonight she couldn't chase after peace among the flowers. She had to dance. And keep an eye on Ivy to be sure she didn't dance her way into trouble. That thought brought back memories of when the twins were born.

Ivy was three and Elena was nine. Because the twins needed so much care and their mother's recovery from the birth was slow, Elena was tasked with watching Ivy most of the day. She had resented the loss of her own freedom to read and draw. At times, she even had to miss school to see to Ivy.

She hadn't wanted to do it, but she hadn't shirked the responsibility put upon her young shoulders. She did what was expected. She always did what was expected. Except, she supposed, being married or betrothed by the age of twenty. Now, it might have been better if she had followed that normal, expected path. Then she could be in her own home, tucking in a sweet baby girl or boy instead of being ready to forgo love for the security of her family.

With a sigh, she trailed Ivy down the winding stairs to a room glowing with light and sounding of music. Couples swirled around the dance floor. A few older ladies sat around tables and sipped drinks, obviously not inclined to dance with the many available partners. Men outnumbered the ladies two to one. They stood around the walls, eyeing the dancers as though choosing which they would hurry toward before the next song.

Three men spotted Ivy and jostled for position in front of her when she stepped onto the ballroom floor. She laughed, peeked back at Elena on the stairs behind her, and took the hand of the closest gentleman. At least, Elena hoped he was a gentleman. She hoped they were all gentlemen.

If the man second in line was disappointed to not win the dance with Ivy and instead was left with Elena, he didn't show it. He bowed slightly. "Would you honor me with this dance, miss?"

And so, the dancing began. A different partner each time the music changed. Some young. Some old. Many of them of that age where one could not be sure of their years. She wondered, as she smiled and worked to keep her toes out from under their feet, if she looked the same to them. Of indeterminate age. If so, none of her dance partners had been gauche enough to ask.

She smiled at the thought. She was only twenty-two. That was hardly old enough for gray to streak her hair or wrinkles to crease her face. She had looked decent enough in the mirror in their room. The blue of her dress brought out the blue in her eyes. Her hair was a nice, rich brown. Her waist was trim.

It was only seeing Ivy in the mirror beside her that made her feel old. The girl sparkled with beauty and youth. Elena looked over her partner's shoulder to seek out Ivy among the dancers. She hadn't stopped dancing since they got to the ballroom. As soon as she parted from one man, another was by her side.

Elena supposed the same could be said about her. The difference was inside Elena. Her cheeks might be flushed but merely from the heat in the room and the exertion of the dances. Not the glow of excitement that had Ivy's eyes sparkling and a smile ready on her lips. But perhaps that was only obvious to Elena.

The man guiding her around the dance floor looked down

at her. "You and your sister have added beauty to our dance floor this night, Miss Bradford."

"How kind of you to say."

She searched her mind for his name. He had told her, but all the names of this man and that had become a jumble in her mind. Johnson, or was it Thompson? Or had he merely stated his given name? No, she thought not. He appeared too formal for that. He might be in his forties. He did have the air of success about him. That surely meant he was well to do. He wasn't exactly handsome, but pleasant enough looking. A person wouldn't cringe to see him across from her every morning at the breakfast table.

A flush at her wayward thoughts warmed her face. The man could very well already be married. Probably was. A man only looking for a dance partner, not a wife. However would her mother determine which ones Elena should keep her best smiles for? The ones who met her mother's criteria for a son-in-law.

The more she thought about her mother's plan, the less chance she thought it had of success. All they were doing was frittering away money they could ill afford to spend. A chancy gamble when the stake on the table was Elena's hand in marriage.

She kept her smile bright as the man—Mr. Thompson, she decided—spoke about all the wonders of the Springs.

"Dr. Graham has spared no expense making this the Saratoga of the West."

"We arrived late today with no time to look around before dinner," Elena said.

"I am confident you will find everything to your liking. This isn't my first visit. Taking the waters can cure miseries of the body and mind."

"That's wonderful to know." Should she tell this man she had no such miseries that needed a cure, even as she wondered what he might have in need of healing? "My mother is hoping for relief from headaches she has at times. I'm simply along in support of her needs."

Needs in more ways than one, but she wasn't telling this man that. Or any man there. At least not until progress was made on their true purpose.

She was glad when the music ended. Glad to have the man go seek another partner. Just the thought of whether he might meet her mother's requirements for a suitor made Elena wish to never see him again. She needed to put such thoughts from her mind. Nobody was seeking her hand in marriage this evening. They were merely asking for a dance.

"Your smile appears to lack enthusiasm." Kirby Frazier held a cup of punch out to her. "Is the song not to your liking?"

He looked very dashing in his waistcoat and evening jacket. She had seen him dancing with other women. He appeared to be very light on his feet, and his partners had all been smiling.

"No, no. It's a lovely song. I suppose I'm just a wallflower for this number." Elena took a sip of the lemony drink. She held the cup up. "Thank you for this. Very refreshing."

He took a drink from his own glass. "It has been a long day for some of us."

"And an eventful one." Her smile came easy. "I trust your talk went well with Dr. Graham and that he liked your painting. He seems a man of great enthusiasm." She looked out at the dancers. The doctor had convinced one of the older ladies to take a spin around the dance floor with him.

"The man appears to think dancing, shooting, and his spring water can heal anything that ails you."

"Shooting?" Elena frowned slightly.

"Target shooting. I've been told the good doctor is the country's best shot. No contest. He has a rifle club here, but should you hear the guns, don't be concerned. It's all for fun."

"My dance partners have been telling me that most everything here is for fun. Even the healing waters."

"Do you need healing?"

She wasn't sure if his question was serious or in jest. Did she look as if she needed the healing powers of this spring water?

"I suppose we all need healing in some way." She kept her tone light.

"True enough." He took her cup to set on the tray of a passing servant. "Come, dance with me, and heal my need for a beautiful partner."

When he held out his hand, she took it with a smile. "You haven't seemed to have any problem finding those this evening."

"There is beauty and then there is beauty. Surely you as an artist know that." He peered down at her as he led her back out onto the dance floor.

Elena had no fear for her toes as they moved smoothly into the dance steps. Under her hand, his shoulder felt muscular and young in comparison to some of her earlier dance partners. A man like this would be easy to love. And had he really indicated he saw some kind of beauty when he looked at her? She pushed that thought aside. That was obviously no more than a glib line to tickle her ears, and in fact, it was sweet to hear whether she thought it true or not.

Perhaps she had finally met a man who might convince her marriage could be a good thing. Not that she could allow herself to fall in love with him. She was fairly certain his pockets weren't stuffed with money.

8

ndrew Harper stood against the wall in the shadows. He didn't want to be here. Not here watching the dancers. Not here at Graham Springs. But he couldn't say no to his grandfather. He had never been able to say no to him. Even if he had, Grandfather Scott would have run roughshod over his no, and Andrew would have still ended up at the Springs, where the party went into the night and the waters were supposed to heal whatever ailed a person.

He could use some healing, but he had no confidence that drinking mineral spring water or bathing in it would help him. The healing he truly needed had nothing to do with the health of his body.

Dust did make him cough. Always had. A sickly child, he had often had the croup that made breathing a struggle at times. His three brothers, all much older than him, had been strong and hardy. They could have spent the night outside in a blizzard and suffered no more than a red nose from the cold. By the time Andrew was seven, the brothers had all left home to seek their fortunes. Brave, strong, ready for adventure.

Andrew was not strong or adventuresome. His mother coddled him. His father, disdainful of a son who failed to show the Harper strength, gave Andrew over to her as the useless last child born to him.

More than once, his father accused his mother of bearing another man's child. He only said it when he'd had too many drinks, but the words landed like coals of fire on Andrew's heart. Little wonder that his father's death when Andrew was ten caused him more relief than grief. Something that left a stain of shame. If he had been a son such as his brothers, then he might have felt cleansing sorrow.

Since the older brothers had long since moved on to their own lives, he and his mother had gone to live with her father. His grandfather had not coddled Andrew. He had pushed him to do more, to be more, but with love and acceptance of his failings. He became the loving father Andrew needed.

That was why Andrew had no way of refusing to come to Graham Springs when Grandfather Scott said he must. For his health, he claimed, but Andrew knew his underlying aim. Grandfather thought if he came to the Springs, Dr. Graham would have Andrew dancing, hiking, shooting, playing yard games, and regaining his appetite for food and fun. Most of all, though he didn't say it out loud, Grandfather was sure Andrew would meet someone new to take his mind off Gloria.

But Gloria was a barb in his heart that couldn't be softened by games or the smiles of other women, no matter how lovely they were as they swirled around the dance floor. When some of the ladies gave him hopeful looks, he kept his eyes away from theirs.

A few times, he caught sight of the two young women he'd met on the stagecoach. Shed of their grieving black, they were dressed much like every other woman there. The rosy pink suited the youngest, a mere girl, who practically sparkled with the joy of the dance. The older sister looked lovely in a dress the rich blue of an evening sky. Like her sister, she had no lack of partners, but her smile appeared to be more practiced, as if the same as learning the steps of the dance, she had learned the socially correct expressions.

He would surely be the same were he to step out on the floor with one of the ladies. But instead, he clung to the shadows and wished to be in his room with one of the books he had brought along. Even better would be back on his grandfather's horse farm planting a new flower garden to attract the bees and birds. The gardens were the only place he could find a measure of peace after Gloria.

He pushed aside thoughts of Gloria. He would put in the expected time here at the Springs. He would eat the fine food and gain a few pounds. Perhaps the waters would ease his problem with dust. For certain, no superfluous dust would be floating in the air in this beautiful place with servants to scrub it clean every day.

"Why aren't you out there on the dance floor?" Dr. Graham demanded in his overlarge voice. Dr. Graham had a zest for life that he insisted everyone around him share.

"I'm enjoying the sight of all the dancers." Andrew forced a smile.

"Observing, are you?" The doctor frowned. "That will not do. You must join in, get your feet moving."

"The ladies already have an abundance of willing partners."

"And you should be one of them." Dr. Graham poked his finger at him. "Men twice your age are out there courting the ladies' favors."

"And stumbling along, stepping on their toes." Andrew backed away from the doctor, who laughed.

"True enough. Age can make us less fleet of foot. But I'm thinking you might be more adept with your dancing moves." Dr. Graham looked around. "This song is winding down. Step out and choose a lady to make her smile."

"They all look to be smiling already." Andrew made no move to leave his spot in the shadows.

"Ah, but they will beam brighter when a handsome young man such as yourself begs a dance from them." Dr. Graham studied the dancers. "There is a lively young dancer." He motioned toward the young sister who had come on the stagecoach with Andrew. "Her smile is contagious, don't you think?"

Andrew watched the girl dance past them. "She is very pretty. And very young."

"A dance is not a marriage proposal, Andrew. And you are very young too."

"Not so young at twenty-six."

Again the doctor laughed. "That sounds very young to me. Just the cusp of life. But if you fear her youth, you can choose her sister. She seems to be gliding along with that artist friend of yours."

"He's not my friend exactly." Andrew felt the need to make that clear. "I just met him on the stagecoach."

"So you said, and that he was the man who answered the need of the moment with your runaway horses."

"Yes." Andrew glanced out at Frazier. "I see you didn't send him away."

"Why would I do that?" The doctor stroked his beard. "A man ready to risk life and limb to keep others safe. Plus, the painting he offered was fine enough to earn him a chance. The ladies will be entertained by his good looks and talents."

"With the bonus of a willing dancing partner." Andrew managed an easier smile this time. "That's better than me."

"He is a hired hand. You are a guest. But I did promise your grandfather I would see that you had a good time." The doctor gripped Andrew's upper arm and urged him toward the dance floor. "Dancing with a lovely lady is a good time. I can attest to that from my many years of life. It is good exercise. It makes a lady happy. Moving to the rhythm of music can make you happy."

"It has in the past." He wanted to jerk away from the man, but he didn't.

"And it will again. Maybe tonight. Maybe next week. And whether it happens now or then or later, a man doesn't want to get out of practice."

The song ended, and the dancers started off the floor to find the next round of partners. Dr. Graham let go of Andrew and stepped out in front of Frazier and Miss Bradford. Frazier smiled, gave the lady a little bow, and went his way before the doctor led the woman over to Andrew. It appeared Andrew was going to dance whether he wanted to or not.

He hadn't been on a dance floor since Gloria was in his arms. A year. What a long time to dwell in sorrow. He pushed a smile out on his face. This young woman had no part in his pain. Besides, the good doctor meant for Andrew to dance whether he wanted to or not. So, dance he must.

· · · ·

Andrew Harper smiled when Dr. Graham ushered Elena over to him, but it looked a little forced. Perhaps the same as hers. But a lady didn't let her smile fade no matter how tired she was of dancing or how her feet might hurt. A pretend smile was better than a frown.

She rather doubted Dr. Graham allowed anyone to frown for long in his presence. He appeared to be determined all enjoy themselves or . . . A sincere smile came to her lips as she tried to imagine the penalty of pretending happiness in this garden of wonders.

She might be packed on the next stagecoach away from here. She might have to turn in her dancing shoes. She might be forced to dance every song with the old gentleman who had stepped on her toes more than once. General Dawson. She could remember his name. He had told her at least three times while regaling her with stories of his army days.

Nothing at all like dancing with Mr. Frazier. With him, she

seemed to be floating on air. Nothing had been forced about his smiles or hers as he stared into her eyes and talked of paint colors and brushstrokes, one artist to another.

She did hope she would have the chance of another dance with him if the music kept playing, but she might claim the vapors if the general headed her way. A laugh bubbled up inside her at the thought of placing the back of her hand against her forehead and swooning. She must make sure a chair was near to hand.

"You seem amused about something, Miss Bradford." Mr. Harper leaned a little away from her as he capably moved her into the dance. "I hope it's not my lack of footwork skill. I confess to being out of practice."

"Oh no." Elena brought her thoughts back to her dance partner.

While somewhat withdrawn, he had been exceedingly nice during their stagecoach ride. He had either slept or pretended to most of the way except, of course, when they appeared headed for disaster after the horses panicked. Even then, he hadn't seemed overly concerned, assuring everyone the horses would tire and stop. At the time, she hadn't been sure if he actually believed they would come to no harm or if he simply hadn't cared. She thought now about Ivy being so sure sadness was afflicting him more than illness.

He continued to look at her now as if waiting for her to say more. Why not tell the truth? "I was thinking about how I might feign exhaustion if a certain gentleman asks me to dance again."

"Mr. Frazier?" He sounded surprised.

"Not at all. Mr. Frazier has the same grace as you." That should reassure him that she hadn't been laughing at his dancing skill. "But one of my earlier partners must have stepped on my toes six times and my dress hem once. I do hope it is not ripped." Her cheeks warmed as she mentioned her dress. That wasn't proper conversation with a man she barely knew.

His polite smile changed to one that lightened the blue of his eyes. "It sounds as if your reluctance has merit."

"I shouldn't have mentioned it though. He seemed a nice man and eager for the pleasure of the dance."

"I shall hope that, should I get to the age of General Dawson, I will be sensible enough to not subject my clumsy feet to any unfortunate ladies. With age comes wisdom, I'm told. But perhaps not to those loving to dance."

Elena flinched. "Now I am truly embarrassed. And contrite that you have guessed the gentleman about whom I spoke such unflattering words." She lowered her gaze.

He laughed. "I have been watching the dancers. I didn't need your testimony to know that the general should have given up dancing years ago, but he is an interesting character. I'm sure he told you all about his army heroics."

"You know him?" She looked back up at him. With the energy of the dance, his cheeks had gained a little color. The smile on his lips and in his eyes turned his somber face pleasant and made her realize he was better looking than she had thought. Perhaps not as vibrant as Mr. Frazier, who the same as demanded one notice his good looks, but very nice-looking all the same.

"He is an acquaintance of my grandfather's."

"Then please don't share my ill-advised words. I would not want to injure General Dawson's feelings."

"I doubt you could. He's a tough old bird, but worry not. Your honest appraisal is the same as forgotten."

"Thank you. In the future, you can be sure I will attempt to be kinder in my words."

"Sometimes it is kinder to be truthful than to continue a lie." His smile faded then. He looked as he had in the coach, withdrawn and wishing to be alone.

Elena kept her smile as the music ended and they walked toward the edge of the dance floor.

"Thank you for the pleasure of the dance."

While his polite words seemed to lack conviction, she thought it had little to do with her and more with whatever memory his thoughts of lies had brought to mind. She searched for a response that might bring back some of the ease they'd shared while dancing.

"I think Dr. Graham must have insisted you choose me for a partner, but since my toes were quite safe, I am glad he did so."

When she gave him her best smile, he seemed to come away from whatever gloom had enveloped him. He leaned closer and spoke in a near whisper. "Don't look now, but I think the general is coming your way."

She laughed. "I fear it is no doubt my due for my unkind thoughts. However, I do think after the day my sister and I have had, with an early rising and a runaway stagecoach and dancing until the midnight hour, that we can slip away quietly into the night."

He looked out at the other dancers beginning to partner up again. "I'm not sure you will talk your sister into going."

"Do they dance all the night long here?"

"I'm not sure. This is my first visit, but I think, as you say, that we both can slip away without shame after such an eventful day. So, good evening. I will look forward to seeing you again." Then with a nod, he turned and headed toward the stairs, away from the ballroom.

Elena didn't make as good an escape and could not avoid another round on the dance floor with General Dawson, who really wasn't so bad. But before that could be repeated, she found Ivy, paid no attention to her dismay at leaving, and led her back to their room.

9

A couple of weeks passed, one pleasant day after another. Elena danced at night with a parade of partners. At least once with Kirby Frazier and once with Andrew Harper. And always twice with General Dawson. She had become more adept at keeping her toes away from the general's feet and actually began to enjoy the stories the old man liked to tell. He seemed to come up with a new one for every dance.

Ivy didn't share Elena's patience with the general. As they shed their finery after Thursday's dance, she rubbed her feet. "My poor toes. I wasn't able to avoid old General Dawson tonight. I'll have to soak my feet in Dr. Graham's mineral water." She looked up at Elena. "You danced with him twice. I don't know how you do it. You should feign illness when he heads your way. You can be sure I'll do that next time he wants to dance with me."

"But how will you explain a fast recovery that allows you to dance with the next gentleman who asks? I notice you rarely sit out a dance." Elena looked at her with raised eyebrows.

"He's so old he'd probably never notice. Besides, I think you are his favorite partner." Ivy smiled up at Elena.

"You should be nice to him. The poor man doesn't intend

to trample your toes, and he always has a great story to tell. He's had an amazing life."

"Because he's ancient," Ivy said.

Their mother looked around from the mirror where she was undoing her hair bun before bed. "Really, Ivy. He's not that much older than I am. Do you think I'm ancient too?"

Ivy stared down at her feet as she muttered, "Of course not, Mother."

Mother sighed with a smile. "I think that means you do, but life isn't over simply because one passes fifty, although I think General Dawson might be closer to sixty. Anyway, he seems to have plenty of life yet. I'm told the general lost his wife a couple of years ago and has stayed here at the Springs as much as possible since then. Lonely, I suppose. Some say he's thinking of remarrying." She peered over at Elena. "It's good that he has taken to you, dear, and you to him."

Elena was too stunned to speak for a moment. She swallowed hard and found her voice. "You can't mean you've put him on your list." Her mother had been making a list of potential marriage candidates.

"Not my list. Your list."

"You can't be serious, Mother." Elena stared at her mother. "He is, as Ivy just pointed out, old."

"But he is very comfortably well off. One of the richest men here, I've been told."

Elena sank down on the bed. It was one thing to agree to marriage as a way to shore up their family finances when it was naught but words and one could imagine a potentially strong husband like Kirby Frazier. Romance could be part of such a match. But General Dawson?

"He's old enough to be my grandfather." Elena's voice was faint.

Ivy sat on the bed and put an arm around Elena. "Mother can't mean for you to entertain him as a suitor."

Mother continued to brush out her hair. "I don't know why the two of you sound so upset. May-December weddings often work out famously. And at any rate, if the man is so tottering old and such a union was formed between you and the general, the marriage might not last long." She looked over at Elena again. "Once he passes away, you would be free to marry whomever you liked with the security of a generous inheritance." Bitterness crept into her voice. "Unlike how your father left me."

"Mother, you can't expect Elena to—"

"That's quite enough." Mother cut off Ivy's words. "I can and do expect much from both you and Elena. I don't think either of you has grasped the severity of our situation. It is time to forget your foolish romantic notions and face reality." She pointed her brush at Ivy. "And that includes your dalliance with that Pennington boy."

Ivy gasped and stiffened beside Elena. "It's not a dalliance. We love each other."

"Love is for those who can afford it. Or for those who care nothing about having the finer things of life." She dropped her brush on the bureau with a clatter and came to stand in front of them. "Jacob's father has gone deeply in debt to send his boys to those eastern schools. They are in as precarious a situation as we are. Your father told me so after I noted you slipping away to meet that boy. I should have put an end to your relationship months ago, but with your father's death, I let things slide. Obviously, a mistake on my part."

Tears streamed down Ivy's face. "I don't care about what you call 'the finer things.' Not if it means I have to forget Jacob."

"Shh." Elena pulled her closer to her side.

Mother reached out and touched Ivy's face. "I know you believe that now. But I've seen you this week. You enjoy the good life here. You are attracting attention from the right sort of suitors the way flowers attract bees. Use your beauty to your advantage."

"You mean your advantage," Ivy shot back at her.

"Our advantage." Mother's voice softened. "And if Elena does as she has promised and finds a suitable match, perhaps you will be able to follow your heart."

As she has promised. The word stabbed through Elena. Had she promised? To marry a man like General Dawson? She couldn't have promised that. But she had been as naïve as Ivy. What hadn't been promised by anyone was romantic love.

"Did you never love Father?" Elena asked.

Her mother didn't look angry about Elena's question. More sad. "I had your father's children. I kept his household orderly. I did my best." She paused and then went on. "We had love. Perhaps not the earthshaking love that you and Ivy seem to think is the only kind of love worth having, but we did have love. The truth is, your father didn't trust that love. He thought he had to buy it."

"And he didn't?" Elena wanted to add that it seemed she had to buy her mother's love now.

"Of course not. But it wasn't my love he sought with money we didn't have. It was yours and Ivy's and the boys' love."

"He knew I loved him." Elena was sure of that.

"Yes, no doubt he did." Mother dropped down in a chair beside the bed.

She was still an attractive woman, but with her hair down, the gray overtaking the blonde was more evident. Without her normal commanding expression, the wrinkles around her eyes and mouth appeared deeper. How old she looked stabbed at Elena. Somehow she hadn't noticed age creeping up on her mother, perhaps because she was usually so firmly put together that she held the years at bay. Now seeing her so vulnerable took away whatever protests Elena thought to make.

Her mother went on, her voice sad. "But poor man never felt he had enough or did enough. Perhaps that was my fault, as you are surely thinking, Elena, but I don't know what more

I could have done other than be a faithful wife. I never wanted him to take advantage of his position at the bank."

"You don't think he did anything dishonest."

"Not intentionally dishonest." Mother waved away her words with an impatient gesture. "But he did things he shouldn't have. He approved loans for himself that he knew or should have known he couldn't repay. He did the same for others. He could be taken in by any hard-luck story. A sick child, a farmer's dead mule, a woman in tears, any man's business venture, however unlikely of success, whatever. Your father handed out money without the necessary assurance the bank would be repaid."

"He is not liable for those bad loans," Elena said.

"No, only his own." Her mother shook her head. "Only his own. There was collateral for those. Our home. Add the expense of your father's funeral."

"And of this summer here at the Springs."

A ghost of a smile touched Mother's lips. "This is an investment."

"One as risky as any of Father's ill-advised loans." Elena pushed that truth at her mother. "Even if I were to attract a suitor, you couldn't expect him to propose marriage after knowing me only weeks."

"You underestimate your appeal, my daughter, and a man's desire for a wife. Certain men, anyway."

"If only I had the desire for a husband."

"Whether the desire or the need, you must entertain the possibilities open to you here." Mother leaned toward Elena, stressing her words. "The atmosphere is perfect for romance."

"I thought you had ruled out romance as an option."

"Not at all. You must awaken the romance in someone. The right someone." She turned to Ivy, who still had tears on her cheeks. She stood and handed her a handkerchief. "Enough of tears. The sun will come up in the morning on a new day. All I ask is that you explore the possibilities, my dear Ivy. And that you, Elena, do the same. Do I have that promise from you both?"

Ivy nodded and got up to hug her mother. Elena turned away from them both and slipped into bed. She pulled the light cover up to shield the lamplight and the sight of her mother's face. She had already promised too much. She was not about to promise to entertain the possibility of marrying a man old enough to be her grandfather. At least not tonight.

After Mother extinguished the light, Ivy crawled under the covers beside Elena. She scooted close and whispered, "Mother is simply having one of her worrying times. We must be patient with her. Things will work out."

Elena made no answer.

"We will both pray. Doesn't the Bible say the Lord will give us the desires of our heart? He knows how I love Jacob." Ivy patted Elena's shoulder before turning away. Minutes later, she was asleep.

If only she could have Ivy's optimism, but unlike her sister, Elena no longer believed in fairy-tale endings where a prince fought through briars and killed dragons to kiss a princess and set the world to rights.

Oh, to be so young to believe love could conquer all. But Elena was almost sure that if she ended up having to kiss a frog, he wouldn't magically turn into a prince.

Not that the general was a frog. The problem was, she might rather kiss a frog.

Perhaps she should do as Ivy suggested. Pray. The Lord did love his children and want to give them good gifts. The Bible said to ask and it would be given and to seek and whatever was needed could be found.

Since a child, she had said the expected prayers. She shot thankful prayers up silently at times when she saw a rose bejeweled with dew in her father's garden or when a sunset lit up the western sky, but she hadn't truly prayed with purpose since she was nine and the twins were born.

At the memory of those prayers, she shifted uneasily in the bed. They had been centered on what she wanted—her mother to recover from the birth so Elena wouldn't have to see to Ivy. That the twins would stop crying so much. That her father would stop looking frazzled and would sit in his easy chair and share stories from his evening paper the way he had before the boys were born.

Would her prayers now be as selfishly motivated? *Let me fall in love with the man of my choice with no thought of my mother. Of my sister and brothers.* Surely a better prayer would be to let a man she could love be the answer to her prayers. To her mother's prayers.

Many men were at the Springs. She could ask the Lord to place the right one in front of her and not give credence to her mother's thoughts that perhaps he already had. To give her a chance at love. But hadn't she avoided chances for love in the past? Not avoided exactly. Rather, never known. No boy when she was younger, no man now, had ever truly pursued her. Or was it that she had never given love a chance?

What was love? As a child, the very first Bible verse she learned was *God is love.* She did believe the Lord loved her, loved the world enough to sacrifice himself for whoever believed in him, as John 3:16 said. Did she have any of that kind of sacrificial love for her family?

As she searched her heart for an answer, the dark of the night pressed down on her. Then another Bible verse came to mind. One her father had sometimes quoted to her mother when she, as Ivy said, was in one of her worrying times. *Take therefore no thought for the morrow: for the morrow shall take thought for the things of itself.*

She couldn't solve her problems tonight. Tomorrow would bring whatever it brought, and she would face it with the Lord's help. With his love. She pulled the thought of that love up over her like a blanket and slept.

At first light, she awoke almost as if someone had shaken her shoulder. She slipped out of bed to keep from waking Ivy. As quietly as possible she washed her face in the basin with the water the maid brought last night. She pulled on her dress and, without bothering to look in the mirror, brushed back her hair and tied it at the nape of her neck. She didn't worry about containing every strand as she usually did. With the sun not yet up, she doubted she would meet anyone in the hallways. Once outside, she planned to find an isolated spot in a beautiful place to await the sun.

With her sketchbook and pencil case in hand, she crept out the door. Idly, she wondered if Kirby Frazier would be out before the sun to capture a scene on canvas. She doubted it. Sunsets seemed more to his liking. The sun was generally well up before he set up his easel by the lake, the place he'd chosen to do portraits of the Springs' guests.

Elena had walked through the gardens in the daytime. She appreciated the skill of the placement of the trees and flowers and the benches that might give those strolling around the grounds wonderful places to stop and rest or simply admire the surroundings.

Now as she made her way to one of the rose gardens, she was glad the pathways were empty. She wanted to be alone. At the garden, she breathed in the sweet-scented air, and memories of her father flooded through her. They didn't bring tears but smiles as she thought of how he often went out at this same time of day to clip one of the rosebuds to put in a vase for her mother.

He never cut a rose for Elena. Instead, he would leave a note about a particularly beautiful bloom. *The white rose with the red blush in the far corner of the garden is ready to pose for you this morning.* She always went out to sketch the rose and commit its shadings to memory to paint it later.

Her father loved everything she drew or painted. At least those he saw. She never showed him the portrait of him tending his roses. It was far from perfect, but somehow she had caught the care with which he tended the roses in his contented smile.

When she walked through the gardens on the previous days, she hadn't even considered sitting down to do a sketch. She had always drawn and painted in the privacy of her father's garden. Her art meant so much to her, she feared giving others the chance to ridicule her efforts.

Yet she had brought her sketchbook and hadn't completely denied her desire to paint when Ivy told Kirby Frazier she was an artist. At the time, she'd had no idea he was also on the way to Graham Springs.

That he hadn't laughed at the idea of her being an artist had made her immediately like him. Still, it could be she should tell Ivy not to share her artistic hopes with whomever she met. Ivy was not prone to silence.

Elena wouldn't be totally surprised if she blurted out that they were at the Springs to find her practically spinster sister a husband. Elena sighed. She probably didn't have to. Their mother was doing a fair job of that as she compiled her potential husband list.

The paths through the roses were deserted now, but as soon as the morning meal was done and the waters taken, people would be strolling about the grounds. Elena didn't mind missing breakfast or the taking of the spring water. Spring water sounded so refreshing, but this mineral water rising up from underground streams carried with it the unpleasant flavor of something deep in the earth. Whatever that was gave it the healing properties many sought, but Elena had no chronic illness to defeat. She would sip the medicinal waters on another day when not so many troubling thoughts had her seeking solitude.

Sketching sometimes could make her worries slide away. Some of those problems marched through her thoughts. General

Dawson. The very idea of marrying at all. How Kirby Frazier looking down at her while they danced caused her heart to beat too fast. Ivy so in love that she was embracing the thought of marriage at her very young age. Her mother's lack of consideration of Elena's happiness. Andrew Harper's sad eyes.

The last thought popping into her mind surprised her. Why should Andrew Harper's unhappy look trouble her thoughts? Ivy might have even been completely wrong about him, but then she had heard Dr. Graham offer condolences about someone named Gloria. He could have been grieving the loss of a loved one. Perhaps that was what made him look so unhappy. A sorrow of the heart.

She shook away thoughts about him. She was here to forget her worries. Not add new ones. She found the perfect bench near a yellow climbing rose so fully in bloom that the bush practically glowed. A pink blush touched the inner petals.

After studying the bush for a moment, she focused on one particular rose that seemed to lift its petals toward the first rays of the sun and began to draw. The pencil in her hand became a connection between the rosebush and her sketch as a cascade of the blooms spilled across her paper. The lines were mere black marks, but in her mind they exploded with color the same as the roses in front of her as the sun rose higher to bathe the bush in its light.

"This is the day the Lord hath made. Let us rejoice and be glad in it."

With a start, Elena looked around at Andrew Harper.

10

I apologize," Andrew said. "I didn't mean to startle you."

He shouldn't have said anything at all but simply moved away without her ever knowing he was there. And then to quote a Bible verse as though he was some kind of preacher. He wasn't that, but the verse had spilled out because that was often the first thing his grandfather said each morning. Especially on a morning when the sun was coming up after being heralded by a blush of pink across the eastern horizon.

When his grandfather said it, Andrew always felt the sun shine a little brighter. But that was before Gloria. He wondered if he'd ever quoted the verse to her. Surely he had, but he couldn't remember doing so. Perhaps he had never been with her as the first rays of sun spread light into the world. She was not an early riser. Said sunrises were for roosters and maids. They shared more evening moments before she decided to share her moments with someone else.

He shook away the thought. He needed to stop dwelling on Gloria.

"What a lovely thought to begin the day." Elena Bradford smiled but didn't look particularly glad to see him.

"Forgive me for intruding on your solitude."

"Don't concern yourself. The gardens are for everyone." She kept her smile but tilted her drawing away from him. "Were you hoping for solitude yourself in the beauty of the morning?"

"Not at all. Just out for an early walk. I generally awaken early since back on my grandfather's farm, I need to be up at daylight to help exercise the horses." He stepped a little closer to her.

"That sounds interesting." She hesitated a moment before she scooted over on the bench. "Would you like to sit a moment?"

He wasn't sure if she wanted him to stay or wished he would go. But what did he want? He was surprised to realize he wasn't anxious to walk away. He wanted to sit on the bench beside her and enjoy the rising of the sun.

"If you're sure you don't mind."

"Please, sit. The beauty of the day is something to share." After she closed her sketchbook, she gathered her skirt to the side to give him more room. "And as you said, to rejoice in. Although I suppose that verse indicates one should rejoice in every day whether there is sunshine or clouds."

"My grandfather often quotes that verse in the morning. When I was younger, I sometimes wanted to put a pillow over my head in hopes he would go away."

That made her laugh. A nice laugh. They had danced together every evening, but while they talked easily as they circled the floor, she had never laughed. He had the feeling that while her sister bubbled over with merriment, this sister was less free with her unpracticed smiles and laughter.

"I'm sure I used to be the same, but now I like being up early," she said. "And here, it seems a shame not to enjoy every moment of the day."

"You are a guest after Dr. Graham's heart. He doesn't believe in wasting a moment of life. My grandfather has plenty of stories to tell about the things the man has done. One, building the Springs here into such a remarkable place to take the waters that people come from everywhere."

"Where are you from, Mr. Harper, if I may be so bold to ask?"

"Not far. Bourbon County."

"Is that where you work with horses?"

"Yes." He answered without elaboration since he wasn't sure if she was genuinely interested or only being polite.

"I have two younger brothers who love horses. They have been begging my father to buy them one for several years." Her smile stiffened. "Poor boys have little hope of getting that horse now. Not that we had any property to keep a horse anyway, with only a yard and a rose garden."

He remembered they had been wearing black on the stage-coach because of her father's death. "I can attest that a horse can make it hard on roses. One of my grandfather's horses found a gate accidentally left open and made short work of one of our prettiest rosebushes."

"You like roses?" Her face lit up with sincere interest now.

"Who doesn't like roses? Especially those as beautiful as the Lady Banks here." He nodded toward the yellow roses. "It seems to capture the sunlight in its petals." He stood and clipped off a rose for her. "I don't think the bush will mind sharing a bloom with you."

"Lady Banks," she murmured as she sniffed the rose's light fragrance. "I didn't know roses had names like that. My father loved planting them, but he generally said he had a red one or a yellow one. He often got starts from neighbors or from someone he met at the bank where he worked."

"Red, yellow, pink can describe them well." Andrew smiled and sat back down. "Grandfather Scott takes pride in his roses. He planted a garden in memory of my grandmother many years ago. I only have the vaguest memory of her, but Grandfather finds a new rose variety to add to the garden each year to mark her birthday. He says he likes to imagine the roses' fragrance wafting up to heaven to let her know he has never forgotten their love."

"How romantic. My father loved gifting my mother with a rose from his gardens, and I—" She stopped as if she had almost said something she might wish unsaid. She went on. "And I admired them all."

"But you were about to say something else, weren't you?" He peered toward the book she had overturned in her lap. "That you like to draw them and that's what brought you out here so early this morning?"

"That is one of the reasons."

"Are there more?"

"Sometimes it's hard to know exactly why we choose to do this instead of that." She shrugged. "A momentary impulse to steal a few moments alone before the busyness of the day. A pause to think or not to think."

"And then someone bumbles along to spoil that."

"No, no." She touched his arm. "I had my alone moments. It's good now to have someone here to share the day's beautiful beginning. Your grandfather's verse has me paying more notice of that gift."

Could he say the same? How many weeks and months had slid by without him seeing beauty in anything? Maybe she was right. It could be time for him to pause and not think of his wounded heart but only of the current moment. And the pleasure of sharing that with the lady beside him.

"That would make my grandfather glad," he said.

They both fell silent as sunlight spread around them. As if on cue, a black swallowtail butterfly fluttered around the roses.

After a moment, she spoke not much above a whisper. "Would you like to see my sketch?"

Her cheeks were flushed and her fingers trembled slightly as she held the square book in her lap. A few strands of hair were loose around her face. Her gaze skittered from him to the roses and then to her hands on the sketchbook.

When he didn't answer right away, she went on. "Oh dear, I've put you in the awkward position of not knowing whether to say you do or don't. You are probably thinking that you won't have the words if you see the sketch and think it's horrid. I shouldn't have asked." She started to gather up her pencils.

"Wait." Now he touched her arm. "I would like to see what you've drawn. I can't imagine it being horrid."

"But you don't know. It might be. It's not perfect. Far from it." She didn't open her book to reveal the drawing. "I don't know why I even thought you would want to see it. Mere dabbling." Those last words looked as if they were sour in her mouth.

"Hardly anything is ever perfect, but I would like to see your work."

She looked straight at him then as if to judge if he were being truthful or perhaps if she could trust him. He didn't look away but met her gaze. He hadn't given her looks much thought when he first saw her on the stagecoach. He had noted the younger sister was very pretty with a charming innocence. This sister, Elena, was not pretty in that way, but as he looked into the depths of her striking eyes, he wanted to know more about her.

. . . .

Elena studied the man's face. He did look not only kind but honestly interested in what he had called her *work*. Had she ever even used that word herself? She said her *art*, which had seemed to be claiming too much. But work? That was what an artist like Kirby Frazier did.

She had no idea why she had offered to show him her sketch. She hadn't even given the sketch an assessing look herself. And now the idea of revealing her drawing seemed something like revealing her heart.

She should stand up, tuck her sketchbook under her arm, and go back to her room. She should, but at the same time, she realized she did want to know what he might say about the roses she had drawn. Still, she hesitated.

"It's just that I've never shown my drawings to anyone other than my parents. Oh, and my sister. But of course, Ivy likes everything. My father was somewhat the same and so full of praise that I felt most of his comments about my paintings or sketches were shaded by his love for me."

"And your mother?"

"Mother thinks my drawings are lines on paper that are a waste of time."

"But what do you think?"

"I don't know if anyone can look at their own efforts with an unbiased eye. You want it to be good, but Mother is right. Even if the sketches are capable, what good are they? What profit?"

"The profit might be in how you feel or how others might feel if you shared the sketches. I think our stagecoach hero, Mr. Frazier, has made those he has sketched happy with their likenesses."

"That's his purpose as he wants his subjects ready to reward him with coin for a favorable portrait." She looked from Mr. Harper's face back at the roses. "I don't think these roses care whether I have drawn them well or not."

The swallowtail butterfly landed on first one bloom then another, and Elena's fingers itched to take up her pencil to add it to her sketch. She stared at it to memorize its beauty. She could add it later.

Now she needed to open up her sketchbook to her drawing and end this embarrassing situation for both Mr. Harper and her. What difference would it make what he might say?

She hardly knew him and in a few more weeks, after they left this place, might never see him again. She would be headed down the path her mother chose for her, and he would be going back to his grandfather's farm where they knew the names of roses.

With trembling hands, she opened the book to her sketch. She could tell herself it didn't matter what anyone else thought of what she drew, but in ways, the sketch was part of her. A tender part that wasn't immune to words that could injure.

She stared down at the cascade of roses across the page. Two dozen blooms, at least, with the trailing vines and leaves. To her eyes, it did lack perfection, as she had told the man beside her, but at the same time she felt she'd captured the beauty of the roses. She noted a perfect place to add the butterfly.

Then again, she could be seeing only what she wanted to see. She dared a glance up at Mr. Harper's face. He was studying the sketch with what appeared to be great concentration.

"It is, as my mother says, only dark lines on paper." Elena's heart sank as she braced herself for whatever he might say.

"True, the lines are there." He didn't look up at her but continued to stare at the sketch. "But somehow those lines are disappearing in front of my eyes, and all I see are beautiful roses. They are even taking on the sunlit yellow in my mind's eye." He glanced from the sketch to the roses spilling over the trellis. "I will never look at these roses the same. Now, in my mind, they will forever be Elena's roses."

A blush of pleasure warmed her cheeks. "That is so kind of you, Mr. Harper. Thank you."

He looked at her then. "Would you think me too forward if I suggest we be friends while we are here at the Springs? If so, I would consider it a sign of that friendship should you call me Andrew and give me the pleasure of calling you by your given name and that of the roses." He smiled. "Elena."

"I'd like that." She hesitated before she added, "Andrew."

He picked up the rose he had given her earlier from the bench where she had placed it between them. He held it out in the sunlight. The butterfly fluttered away from the bush to hover over it and then settle on the petals.

"Butterflies are flowers on wing." He very slowly moved the rose with the butterfly closer to Elena. Its wings trembled but it didn't lift off the bloom. "Do you want to add him to your sketch?"

Without thinking, she picked up her pencil and quickly drew the butterfly's shape. "I'm always amazed by the underside of butterflies. I would think it would just be black or brown like any bug, but look at the white spots that match the spots on its wings."

"I hadn't noticed that before. The wings got all of my attention." The butterfly fluttered up into the air to circle the rose trestle again before lighting on a bloom. "It can be enlightening to see things through another's eyes. Especially an artist's eyes."

An artist. She could claim that even if she never expected her paintings to hang in a museum or anyone's home other than her own. That didn't mean she couldn't continue to enjoy art, no matter who ended up sharing her life with.

Andrew blew out a breath and pushed up from the bench. "As nice as it is here and as unpleasant as Dr. Graham's famous mineral water is, it is time I swallow down some of it. The doctor will frown on me if I don't and no doubt inform my grandfather I didn't embrace the cure."

She wanted to ask what illness he had that needed a cure, but she bit back the words. Even if he had claimed to want friendship, some things couldn't be mentioned until closer connections were made. But ill or not, his eyes didn't look as sad when he looked down at her.

"Thank you for allowing me to share this sunrise with you,

Elena. Perhaps we can do it on more days. The good doctor has many gardens to enjoy in this paradise he's made."

"That would be nice." Elena held up her sketchbook. "I have more empty pages to fill."

"Pages to fill with beauty." His face changed as his smile faded. "Do you ever draw that which is not beautiful?"

She frowned. "What do you mean?"

"There are snakes in the garden as well as butterflies." He looked from the ground toward the sky. "And buzzards as well as songbirds."

"True." Above them, a buzzard floated in easy circles on the wind. "I suppose everything has its purpose in God's world and its own beauty. But no, I've not drawn a snake or a buzzard. So far none has come close to pose for me."

His gaze came back to her then. "I pray they never do."

She had the feeling he was talking about something other than a garden snake or the buzzard above them. Before she could come up with what she thought might be a proper response, he turned and without another word walked quickly away.

She watched him out of sight and then studied the grass around the rosebush. A snake could be hiding there the same as the buzzard circling overhead. Would she be frightened if it crawled out where she could see it? Startled perhaps, but an artist should want to see every part of the world around her. She was sure Mr. Frazier would be more than ready to add a snake to his paintings were he to think it fit the scene.

She picked up one of her pencils and sketched in a snake at the bottom of the roses. Staring at its twisting form, she started to cover it with a cascade of fallen petals.

But no, while not beautiful to Elena's eyes, the Lord had created the snake as well as the butterfly. Perhaps she was the one out of step. She traced the lines of the snake with her finger before she packed her pencils back in their case.

While she would avoid the taking of the waters this morning, she nevertheless needed to leave the beauty of the garden and seek out her mother to see what was planned for the day.

As she followed the path back to the hotel, she thought again of Andrew Harper asking if they could be friends while they were at the Springs. Friends who loved the beauty of roses and the sunrise, but would they share more than that?

His visage had changed when he spoke of snakes in the gardens. The snake he spoke of wasn't one in the grass but something different. Something that had caused the sadness Ivy had noted to come back into his eyes before he turned and walked away from her.

He might never share the reason for that, but they could still enjoy time together among the flowers here. For a moment, she wondered how deep his pockets might be. She shook away the thought. She would not spoil her chance to have a friend who appreciated her art by thinking of money.

The crack of gunfire gave her a start. The rifle club's shooting range must be close by. Another shot sounded, and she turned to head away from the sound. Perhaps because he had warned her of the noise of rifles, Kirby Frazier came to mind. He would be there with the men. Taking part in the shooting perhaps or maybe sketching the others.

It could be that Andrew Harper had chosen the beauty of a sunrise over a shooting match. She doubted Kirby Frazier would have done the same. Two very different men, but no matter how her summer ended here, perhaps on the way to being married to a man more than twice her age, she was glad to have danced with both of them.

11

Kirby yawned as he made his way from the hotel kitchen where he'd charmed one of the maids into bringing him a plate of eggs and bacon. He'd had no desire to go to the dining area at the assigned breakfasting time.

All the young, pretty girls would be sleeping in after the dance the same as he wished he could do. And while he might consider charming one of the older ladies breakfasting at this early hour into parting with some of her money to have him by her side, he had more appealing choices in mind to try first.

Elena Bradford, with those fetching eyes and her love of art, seemed extra glad whenever he invited her to dance. Another potential target, Madeline Southworth, lacked beauty and grace, but she wore a continual blush and clung to him when they danced. She did have an attentive father who might make Kirby's pursuit of his daughter difficult. Worse, he struggled to imagine the development of the slightest attraction for her. Elena was another matter. She drew his interest.

If he did plan to do right for whichever woman he convinced to marry him—and he did—a chance for affection for the girl would be best. Else the years he pledged to a wife would be long and tedious and perhaps make it hard to keep his marital promises.

He was to do Madeline's portrait this very afternoon. Alone with her by the lake, he might see more to admire about her than a rich father. Elena's rich father would not be a stumbling block on a romantic path since he had passed on. He had obviously left them well off in order for them to come to a place like Graham Springs not for a week but for the summer.

He would need to win the mother over. It could be she had yet to forgive him for the way his painting had poked her on the stagecoach or worse, that her daughter had ignored her commands and climbed down from the coach to walk with him after the runaway crisis was averted.

One thing at a time. Right now, he needed to make sure to stay on Dr. Graham's good side. That was why at sunrise he was packing his easel and art supplies with him toward the firing range. He had missed a few days sketching those in the Boone Rifle Club, and the good doctor had let him know that wasn't acceptable. He was to be available all through the day with his paints and pencils to capture the likenesses of the guests.

If he thought finding beauty in every lady's face he painted tiresome, doing the same with men past their prime but wanting to believe that wasn't true was considerably worse. At least he had no problem with the portrait of Christopher Columbus Graham. His white hair and beard showed he was nearing sixty, but he was the picture of health with the body of a man much younger. He had to be his own best advertisement for his mineral water here at the Springs. Perhaps Kirby should ignore the unpleasant taste and drink more of the water.

Angry voices suddenly rose from a grove of trees along the pathway in front of him. Not the doctor's voice taking a worker to task. Two men. Kirby stopped and stepped off the path behind a pine tree as the voices grew louder.

"We had a deal. Time to pay up." The man's words weren't shouted but spoken with cold determination. "Or else."

"Don't you threaten me." The other voice was loud with rage. "I owe you nothing. Nothing, you hear?"

"I beg to differ, and I will be paid one way or another. If not . . ." The first man let his voice trail off.

"I'm not frightened of you."

"That could be a mistake on your part." The man sounded as if he spoke of nothing more important than the weather. After a moment of silence in which Kirby imagined he could hear both men breathing, the voice went on. "You have a lovely daughter."

A strangled oath was followed by the sound of a scuffle. Kirby turned away from the tree to find a different path to the rifle range. He had learned years ago to see nothing and hear nothing in a conflict that was of no concern to him.

Nevertheless, once he was on the firing range with men milling around before starting to practice their shooting abilities, he did watch to see if he could determine which two he'd overheard. A man might not want to be involved in the scuffle, but information could sometimes be turned to one's advantage. Kirby wasn't above storing away those sorts of nuggets whether he ever used them or not.

He set up his easel a little distance from where the men lined up to fire their rifles and got his paints ready. From much practice, he could turn out a reasonable likeness of the scene before him in a few strokes of his brush.

Kirby's eyes sharpened as a man came out of the trees, adjusted his hat, and tugged down his vest as he moved toward the other men. After a few steps in the open, he glanced back at the trees and then walked faster. He was younger than most at the firing range. Kirby had heard he was related to Dr. Graham in some way. A nephew or cousin. A couple of mornings earlier, he had grunted a brusque refusal to Kirby's offer to paint his likeness. No one else emerged from the trees behind him.

"Where you been, Sanderson?" one of the men asked when the man reached the rifle range. "Sleeping in this morning, were you?"

Sanderson shrugged with a grin. "Shooting isn't the only sport to occupy a man in this place."

His voice was that of the man making the threats. Kirby gave him a closer look.

"Uh-oh. I'm thinking you might have been hitting the shuttle-cock over the net with some pretty young thing before the dew dried on the battledore court."

"Do I look like a man who would play and tell?"

That brought some laughter from the men around them.

"Here, here, men." Dr. Graham silenced them. "Enough of that. We're here to practice our shooting. Later you can finesse your aim of romancing the ladies."

The doctor looked over at Kirby. "Our artist is here if any of you would like to strike a pose for him."

The man who had poked at Sanderson changed targets to Kirby. "Hey, artist man. Can you operate anything other than a paintbrush?"

"It seems to be my weapon of choice." Kirby waved the brush at him.

"Weapon?" the man laughed.

Kirby thought it might be pleasurable to use the weapons of his hands to knock the man flat. He was short with a paunch straining the fabric of his shirt. Perkins. That was his name. Bertram Perkins. He had to be forty or more with the appearance of a man who had never had to work a day in his life. No growing up on a farm for him. Inherited wealth.

With an easy smile, Kirby said, "You know what they say. The pen is mightier than the sword."

That seemed to throw down the gauntlet to Perkins. He

lifted up on his toes to stare at Kirby. "Tell you what, man. Let's have a shooting match. Just the two of us, and we'll see what is mightier."

"Sorry, but I don't have a rifle. Just this brush."

"I have an extra rifle. We want to see what you can do with a man's weapon." Perkins looked around at the other men. "Maybe some of you others want to get in on the action." He brought his gaze back to Kirby. "We can sweeten it with a little wager."

"Couldn't do that." Kirby shook his head. "My pockets are too empty to risk losing a wager to a shooting champion like you."

He really couldn't recall seeing the man shoot on the other mornings he'd been at the firing range. Looking as if he couldn't walk to the outhouse and back without getting out of breath had no bearing on whether he could sight in a target. Even so, Kirby knew better than to bet money he didn't have.

He took a look over at Sanderson. Maybe that was what had happened between him and the man he was threatening in the trees. A bad wager. But he had said "deal." What kind of deal could make the man subtly threaten a young woman? Maybe he should mention what he'd overheard to Dr. Graham, but in his experience, talebearers nearly always came out the worse for their efforts to keep the peace. Especially when the tale was about a relative.

Sanderson had moved to the back of the group, appearing uninterested in whether Perkins could goad Kirby into taking up the challenge or not.

Kirby waited for Dr. Graham to put a stop to the man's nonsense, but he kept his silence and watched as if amused.

"Tell you what," Perkins offered. "You win, I'll give you a fiver. I win, you paint my portrait for nothing."

The men around him whistled. One of them said, "Wow, Perkins. Your pockets are going to be lighter if you lose."

"No chance of that." Perkins turned back to Kirby. "So? You game?"

"I would do your portrait for nothing anyway," Kirby said.

"Then it's a can't-lose opportunity for you. And these others"—Perkins glanced around again—"these others can do some wagering on their own. Make things interesting if they can find anybody willing to take a bet picking a painter over a rifleman." The scorn was plain in the man's voice.

When Kirby didn't take him up on the offer right away, he went on. "Unless you're afraid of being humiliated."

Kirby put down his paintbrush and moved away from his easel. "Do I get to choose which rifle?"

"He's onto you, Perkins. Worried you know one of your rifles is apt to be off," one of the men said. "Didn't you say that old flintlock of yours needs the barrel cleaned out?"

"Those are fighting words, Haskell." Perkins flared up. "I don't need to cheat to beat a man who makes his living with a paintbrush."

Dr. Graham moved forward to take control. "To make the contest fair, you can use two of my rifles." He looked straight at Kirby. "How long since you've done any shooting?"

"A while. But some things you don't forget how to do."

"True." The doctor studied him a moment. "But a man's skills can get rusty without practice."

"I suppose that will give Mr. Perkins an advantage, but it will be a pleasure having the opportunity to shoot one of your rifles."

Kirby tried to read the doctor's face. Did the man want him to back out or maybe make sure Perkins, the paying guest, won? He wasn't going to back out. Not now. As for who won, Perkins winning might have nothing to do with Kirby trying to miss the targets. As he told the doctor, he hadn't done any offhand rifle shooting for a while.

But besides learning how to drive a team of horses on that

trip out west, he'd done plenty of shooting. Not with guns as fine as Dr. Graham's, but he'd watched the men loading and shooting when he was sketching on the other mornings he'd been at the shooting range. He had confidence he could hit the metal targets on at least a couple of shots.

When he'd seen men enter into a challenge with one another, they loaded and shot four times, or tried to, in a two-minute time frame. That was where practice truly mattered. A man needed to have economy of movement while loading.

The details were arranged. Somebody was picked as timer. Another man would watch the targets, a row of five metal circles hanging down from a horizontal pole.

Perkins balked at using one of Dr. Graham's rifles. "A man knows his own gun. It's nothing to do with me if this artist man hasn't one of his own."

"What say you, Mr. Frazier?" Dr. Graham asked.

"Makes no difference to me." Kirby took the rifle Graham held out to him. A finer piece than he had ever handled. With one hand under the midpoint of the gun, he held it out to let it sweetly balance in the air. He stroked the wooden stock and hefted it to his shoulder to sight down the barrel. Win or lose, a man could enjoy the moment.

"Wagers all set," Dr. Graham announced.

Kirby looked around. He couldn't believe anybody had put money on him as a winner. They must be wagering on how many he'd miss. Didn't matter to him. As Perkins had said when he insisted on the challenge, he had nothing to lose.

12

"Mr. Perkins, as the challenger, you can draw a straw." Dr. Graham held out his hand with two straws sticking up between his thumb and forefinger. "Short straw shoots first."

Perkins pulled the short straw. "I'll make quick work of this." As he stepped up to the line, he peered over at Kirby. "Watch how it's done by an expert, artist man. Maybe you will learn something."

"I can hope so." Kirby kept his voice mild.

He looked around at the men watching. It would be best if they thought he had simply accepted the challenge for the fun of the competition. He spotted General Dawson. That old man could have probably given him some good tips. Madeline Southworth's father had his eyes fixed on Kirby. Win or lose, he might make some points with him. Even Sanderson had come forward to show interest.

Perkins laughed, but his bluster seemed forced as the timer counted off the seconds before he shouted "Start." A little powder spilled as the man poured it into the muzzle. His fingers appeared to have a tremble when he positioned the patch and the ball on the muzzle's opening before he rammed it home. Last, he poured a bit of powder in the flashpan, pulled back the cock, and positioned the gun against his shoulder.

His first shot went wide. The targets shivered in the slight breeze across the range. Beads of sweat popped out on the man's face as he loaded again. This time the shot pinged into the target. The third shot did as well, but the final shot he got off just as the man called time was high. Some of the men groaned. A few laughed.

Perkins's face went red. "Two out of four is better than most of you can do."

Kirby stepped up to the firing line. The rifle felt as though it belonged in his hands. He was surprised at how his muscles remembered the moves to load and fire the same as when he was hunting for food on the western trip. Then, it was a matter of eating meat or corn pones. A man had to be quick to stop a jackrabbit in its tracks.

The powder flashed up a puff of smoke on the first shot. The ping of the ball hitting the metal target sounded good. He breathed in the smell of powder as he loaded again. The smoke drifted away as he aimed and fired again. Another satisfying ping. The rifle was really a sweet piece.

As if to remind him not to get too cocky, on the third load, the powder in the pan flashed but didn't set off the shot. Kirby poured more powder in the pan, set the full cock again, and pulled the trigger. The gun fired this time and another target pinged.

For the first time, he noticed the men yelling behind him as he loaded for the last shot. He'd won already. He didn't even have to take the last shot. He had no doubt he could hit the target again, but he needed to let most of these men think they could outshoot him. Even Perkins, who would find an excuse for missing the target twice.

Kirby hadn't wanted to lose. A five dollar note in his pocket was nothing to sneeze at, but perfection wasn't necessary. Better for the men around him to feel generous when he did a portrait of them or their wives and daughters. Kirby let the rifle dip slightly. The shot went low.

A few cheers went up, along with some groans from those who must have lost their wagers.

Kirby ignored them as he handed the rifle back to Dr. Graham. "A fine piece. Thank you for letting me fire it. Would you like me to clean the barrel?"

"No, no. I'll see to it." The doctor stroked the carving on the rifle's stock. "You appear to be a man of many talents, Frazier. Handling horses. Marksmanship. Painting."

"Each of those just takes a confident hand," Kirby said.

"And skill." A slight smile slid across Dr. Graham's face as he went on. "A shame you missed the last shot."

"Such happens. I suppose my lack of practice showed. My arms tired." Kirby rubbed his arms.

"Or you deliberately dipped the barrel." The doctor's eyes sharpened on him.

Kirby looked around to be sure no one was listening before he shrugged. "Or that."

"Another talent, I suppose. Reading the feel of the men around you."

"Knowing the mood of my subjects is always helpful when I'm doing a portrait." He wasn't sure if the doctor thought that was a good talent or one to guard against, but he met the man's gaze without flinching. "And a talent that I have no doubt you share, Doctor."

"Yes, well, such can be useful in the medical profession to treat a patient's ills and anxieties. And in keeping my guests happy here at the Springs. Be sure you keep doing that, Frazier." Dr. Graham smiled broadly then as he slapped Kirby on the shoulder. "Looks like Perkins is coming to pay up."

"Going first is always bad in a shooting match," Perkins

grumbled as he handed Kirby a bank note. "I think I might have been hoodwinked with you using the doctor's rifle. He always has the best. You do know he's the nation's champion offhand rifle marksman."

"I'm not surprised. I saw him shooting a couple of days ago."

"If I were you, I wouldn't get too full of yourself and challenge him. We, the Boone Club, sent out a notice all across the country promising ten thousand dollars to any challenger who could beat him. Nobody even dared try."

"Smart of them." Kirby folded the money and put it in his pocket. "I can still do a portrait for you."

"One of me losing to you?" The man shook his head. "I don't think so."

"In a portrait, the rest of the story after the pose can go any way you want it to go."

"True enough. But I best wait until I get over the sting of letting an artist man outshoot me." He did have the grace to smile slightly. "But tell you what. I can send my wife around, or even better, my niece. My brother says she needs something to cheer her up. She's been drooping around ever since they got here. Some kind of romantic troubles, but when did girls that age ever have anything else?"

"What's her name?"

"Wynona."

"Tell her to hunt me up." Kirby went back to his easel and picked up his paintbrush. "I'm ready to use my weapon of choice any time."

The men went back to taking turns at the target until the air was full of smoke and the smell of powder. None of them came over to pose for him or to ask him to sketch them shooting. So Kirby gave up on the paints and sketched the whole scene with pencils and chalk. He picked out a few men to include.

Perkins, of course. And Dr. Graham in his shooting stance. He drew in Sanderson before he slipped away from the group.

If the man he'd argued with ever joined the men, Sanderson showed no sign of it. Nor did any other man look uneasy around him. None of his concern, Kirby reminded himself as he began packing up his things when the men started to drift away to other pursuits. No doubt to chairs in the shade on the hotel's veranda.

General Dawson stepped up behind him to survey the sketch on his easel.

"You do all right with your pen and pencil too." The old man pointed toward the likeness of himself in the drawing. "You could have made me look younger."

"A true man embraces his years and the wisdom he's gained and the adventures seen," Kirby said.

"Hmm." General Dawson stepped back and studied the drawing a moment before he said, "If C.C. doesn't want this, I'll buy it from you if you're done with it."

"This is only a sketch. It needs some finishing up, some shading here and there." Kirby pointed with his pencil to places on the sketch. "I could copy it on a millboard canvas for something more lasting than a paper sketch."

"You do that, son, and I'll hand over the money I made on you today. A tidy little sum. Seems most of the men thought backing Perkins was a sure thing."

"I admit to being surprised anybody was willing to take their wagers."

"The men wanted to put their money down. Made it more exciting for them. Me letting them win some money was my contribution to the fun. Have to admit I didn't think I'd be collecting any winnings, but that didn't keep me from calling in the bets." The old man laughed.

"That explains it. I wondered who would bet on the artist."

The general eyed him. "Now that I've talked to you, I'm thinking it might never be smart to bet against the artist. There's more to you than a paintbrush and a pencil."

"I don't know about that. From the time I was a kid, I've never wanted to do anything except capture pictures." Kirby closed the sketchbook and folded up his easel.

"Could be other men ready to challenge you to shooting matches."

"I'd have to turn them down. Too much chance of an accident with the powder blowing up and taking off a finger." Kirby held his hands up and flexed his fingers. "I don't aim to do any more shooting unless I get hungry and need a rabbit for my dinner."

"Then it could be you shouldn't have missed that last shot. Made you look beatable."

"Everyone is beatable." Kirby smiled. "Except, I hear, Dr. Graham."

"You have the truth there. C.C. doesn't miss." The general gave him a look. "Unless it's on purpose, the way you did. You should join the army and use your skills for the country."

"Not unless they need an artist." Kirby laughed and picked up his supplies.

When he started away, the general stayed in step with him. "Tell me. C.C. says you came in on the stage with those Bradford ladies."

"I did." The change in topic surprised Kirby.

"What did you think of them? I've always been of the opinion that a man can tell a lot about the people he spends hours with on a stagecoach."

"I was only in the coach a little while. I rode up with the jehu most of the way."

"I heard about that too. The runaway horses. But the women. Did they fall apart when the stagecoach was bouncing around?"

"The mother and the younger sister did some praying, I think."

"A good time for prayer. Those coaches turn over, things can go bad." The old man nodded. "The older sister wasn't praying?"

"I couldn't say for sure. She might have been."

"Screaming?" The general pitched out the word quietly as he stared down at his feet.

Kirby gave him a curious look, but he didn't see any reason not to answer. "I heard some shouts and screams. Nothing more than expected. I might have squeaked out a few alarms myself. But I couldn't say who was doing what since I was out of the coach trying to stop the horses by then."

"I see." The general slowed down his pace as he stared down at his feet.

Kirby slowed beside him. "What makes you ask?"

The man looked up at him with a smile. "Well, it's like this. My wife died a couple of years ago. I'm thinking on recruiting some company for my final years."

"You have someone in mind? One of those ladies?" Kirby's heart jolted at the thought it might be Elena, and who else would it be? Ivy wasn't much more than a child. He might need to get his bid in first with Elena, but surely she wouldn't agree to marry a man old enough to be her grandfather.

"Just surveying the battlefield. Never good to head unaware into an ambush."

"Spoken like a true soldier," Kirby said.

"Never been anything else. You get that painting done, I'll hand over my winnings. Haven't counted it yet, but wouldn't be surprised if it tops what Perkins gave you."

"Do you want me to make you look younger?"

"Draw it the way you see it, son. That's always the best way." The old soldier smiled before he turned down a different path and left Kirby behind.

13

By the time Elena got back to the hotel, the sun was well up and shining fully on her bare head. She had paused more than once in the gardens to lift her face toward its warmth. The feel of her hair sweeping across her back was somehow freeing too. All she needed was her cat, Willow, to make the morning perfect.

But of course, Willow was not in the Graham Springs gardens, and Elena was not in her father's rose garden with the freedom to wear her hair down and let the sun touch her nose.

Now, unless she could slip up to their room without her mother seeing her, she was in for a lecture. Her mother might even have a fit of the vapors at the sight of her bohemian daughter. Elena sighed as she approached the hotel entrance. Nothing for it but to face her mother's wrath if she was still in their room. Thank the heavens, Elena spending so much time hidden away among the roses with Andrew Harper could remain a secret.

The thought made her smile. Andrew. A friend who shared her passion for roses. A friend who said kind words about her sketch. She wondered whether Kirby Frazier would have been as kind. More likely he would laugh at her amateur efforts, especially if she tried sketching something other than flowers. Say, his portrait. She couldn't imagine asking him to pose for her, but still, she might attempt it in private. She could bring up his face in her memory.

She could do Andrew's too. He might even consent to posing for her some early morning in one of the gardens. And why not? He would be kind even if her sketch looked nothing like him.

On the stairs up to their room, Elena thought about the lines of both Kirby's and Andrew's faces. So different. The men were every bit as different. Andrew quiet with a kind of confident assurance, even though Ivy was right. Something had hurt him deeply and left the visage of sadness behind. On the other hand, Kirby could never go unnoticed in the background. No sadness veiled his eyes. Determination hardened the lines of his face.

And yet, there was something else, too, that she hadn't quite figured out. She shook her head. She didn't have to try to figure everyone out. Except perhaps those her mother was putting on the potential husband list. Kirby Frazier would not be listed there. His pockets definitely weren't the deep ones her mother was after.

"Elena, where have you been?" Ivy rushed down a couple of steps to meet her. "Mother is beside herself."

"I went for a walk in the gardens." Elena shifted her sketchbook in her arms. "To do some sketching."

"Mother feared it was so. She says you should have never brought your art supplies with you."

"Why ever not? I can surely have a few minutes to myself in between husband hunting."

"Shh." Ivy looked around. "You don't want someone overhearing you. That sounds so . . . so . . . I don't know. So unromantic."

"It is unromantic."

110

Ivy sighed. "I suppose you're right, but don't you think it better to pretend it is?"

"I don't think pretending will make it any different. I'm the same as up for sale."

"Really, Elena. It isn't as bad as that." Ivy looked near tears. "Is it?"

Elena took pity on her and made her voice cheerful. "No, of course not. I may yet meet my prince. I have weeks and weeks to find him." She managed a smile. "But that doesn't mean I can't go out in the mornings to sketch some of the beauties of this place."

"Oh, I think you should. I don't know why Mother would be bothered by that. It's the evenings where you can charm the men." Ivy held out a straw bonnet bedecked with flowers she'd been hiding behind her skirts. "But here. I noticed you forgot your bonnet this morning. You should put this on before we go to the room to keep Mother from knowing you went out without anything to shield your face from the sun. You know how Mother is about freckling."

"My skin doesn't freckle the way yours does."

"Yes, but I don't think Mother trusts that to be true."

"You are right and a dear to smuggle out a bonnet for me." At the top of the stairs, Elena put down her art supplies and took the bonnet. She tucked up her hair and tied the ribbons under her chin. Maybe, thanks to her sister, she could avoid the lecture after all. "Thank you, Ivy. That was thoughtful of you."

"I love you and Mother so much, and I hate it when either of you is upset."

"How about when you are upset?"

"I hate that too." Ivy's face drooped into sadness. "Mother says I can't write to Jacob. He will think I've forgotten him."

Elena started to tell her that was exactly what their mother was hoping, but she didn't let out the words. Ivy was upset enough as it was. "He will understand when you explain."

"But what if he finds someone else this summer?"

"Then he surely isn't the prince you deserve." When Ivy looked ready to tear up again, Elena gave her a hug. "But that hasn't happened. And I doubt it will. He'd never find another girl as sweet and beautiful as you."

"But I promised I'd write."

"Write your letter. Perhaps we will find some pennies on the pathways to pay the delivery charge. Most of those here are so well off they probably wouldn't pick up a coin if they dropped it." Elena smiled as she retrieved her pencil box and sketchbook. "Especially if it was one of us ladies with our waists whittled down so tight. However could anyone expect us to lean over to pick anything up?"

Ivy frowned. "Then how can we get the pennies were we to see them?"

Elena's smile turned to a laugh. "Some of us rebel at times and wear a dress that lets us breathe." She took Ivy's hand to make her touch her midsection.

Ivy's eyes widened. "You don't have on a corset."

"I didn't think the roses would mind, and it's such a struggle to properly adjust if you or Mother don't pull the laces tight."

"But what if someone had seen you?"

"Then I wouldn't have let them touch my waist so that they wouldn't mind either."

"You are wicked, Elena." With a smile, Ivy shook her head. "Come on. Let's hurry to the room. Oh, and a lady moved in next to us this morning. She came by coach very early. Did you see her when you went out?"

"No. The hallways were empty. You've already talked to her?"

"I did. A while ago. She seems very nice. She came all alone."

"A lady coming here alone seems a little strange. The three of us being here without a male relative to keep watch over us is unusual enough."

"Vanessa says her father, a judge in Louisville, has been delayed but will be joining her soon."

"Vanessa. You are on a first-name basis with her already. You make friends so easily, dear sister."

"She didn't say her family name. Was that odd as well, you think?" Ivy answered her own question. "I don't think so. We were just two girls meeting in the hallway, although I guessed her several years older than me. She had that certain grace about her that I don't think I'll ever have no matter how old I am. Anyway, I didn't say my family name either. But we talked awhile. She seemed glad to make an acquaintance here."

"So, what else did you find out about her?"

"I didn't question her." Ivy frowned slightly. "I'd never do that. But she is very beautiful. Blonde hair neatly styled and lovely eyes. A pure blue. Skin very pale as is so fashionable right now."

"To stay that way, she best keep her bonnet on." Elena moved her head to one side and then the other. "Even if it does limit what a woman can see. You know what? A bear could sneak up on me and I'd have absolutely no chance of escape. But then how could a woman run in a full skirt and petticoats with the air squeezed out of her by a corset? It would be hopeless."

"Oh, Elena." Ivy giggled. "I'm sure Vanessa faithfully wears a bonnet, but she didn't have one on when I met her. She must have heard me in the hallway and came out to meet me. Anyway, when I told her I was looking for my sister, she said she would love to meet you. She seemed impressed that you had gone out for a stroll by yourself so early in the morning."

"I can't see why that would have impressed her since she came all the way from Louisville on her own. That would seem to take more courage than simply going out to enjoy a sunrise."

Ivy shrugged. "I don't know, but I'm sure you would like her."

"Once I am suitably outfitted with corsets and have my hair

twisted into the proper buns, I will grab a parasol and knock on her door to introduce myself." Elena looked toward their own room with some reluctance. "But first, I suppose I best face Mother."

"You won't argue with her, will you?"

"I would if it would help, but since it won't, I'll meekly listen to what she has to say and agree to it all."

Ivy sighed. "And then do whatever you want."

If only that were possible, Elena thought, as she followed Ivy into their room. Her mother delivered her upbraiding quietly, obviously aware of neighbors close enough to hear angry voices. Elena said nothing in her own defense and did as she had told Ivy, nodding at all the right places but saying little. She could agree without capitulating. After all, she was not a child.

"I am sure that anyone who saw you out so early thought you were no more than a common maid going to clean the guest rooms."

"It's honorable work that someone has to do," Elena said.

Her mother's eyes tightened. "And work you may have to do if we fail in this grand adventure we've undertaken." She sank down into the chair and put her head in her hands. "I don't know what I've done to deserve such a rebellious daughter."

"I'm sorry, Mother. I wanted to see the gardens at sunrise. Is that so awful?"

"A lady has to guard her reputation. Think of the example you are setting for your sister."

"A woman willing to marry for money rather than love is hardly a lady. Nor is it a path I would wish my sister to follow me down."

"Not money. Security." Her mother stared up at her. "And to keep from falling into a hard life of cleaning and cooking for others. Being that maid I mentioned a moment ago. You can't want that for your sister."

"Of course not."

Elena glanced over at Ivy wringing her hands as she watched them. Such a gentle soul. Even if Elena did take up the broom and mop of a maid's job, she couldn't make enough to support her mother and Ivy or her brothers.

Perhaps she could get some other job. She could teach art. For a moment, a spark of hope flickered, but then it went out. Artists were notoriously poverty stricken. Her mother's grand adventure—rather, scheme—was the best answer. What Elena needed to do was find the right man, one she could imagine living with for the rest of his or her life.

Everyone always thought she would end up a spinster. A marriage without love wouldn't be very much different. Except . . . well, she wouldn't think about the *except* right now. She couldn't think of what would be expected. If only there was a prince somewhere out there who would turn this sentence of marriage into a promise of actual love.

"Dear Father in heaven," she whispered after Ivy and her mother left to take the waters. "If there is a man like that here, please let me meet him. One I can love as a wife should love her husband. I realize I've done nothing to deserve love, but love isn't something to earn. It just is."

She pitched the bonnet onto the bed, scooted the chair over close to the window and raised the sash. Then without the first thought to arranging her hair into the proper style or squeezing herself into a corset, she opened her sketchbook and finished drawing the butterfly.

She held her hand over it the way the butterfly had hovered over the roses before it alighted on the rose Andrew held. That had let her get the best look at its wings and the small white spots on its body. She was glad Andrew hadn't pinched its wings to keep it there but had allowed it to stay or fly away.

How wonderful to be allowed to stay or fly away.

14

Vanessa was every bit as beautiful as Ivy said. When Elena, properly corseted and with hair in neat buns, knocked on the door next to theirs, the woman opened it at once as though standing there waiting. Without the slightest hesitation, she slipped out into the hallway and pulled the door shut, not giving Elena so much as a glimpse of the room behind her.

She wore a light-blue patterned morning dress with a lacy white shawl draped around her shoulders and a bonnet adorned with blue ribbons. Its wide brim at least allowed her to see more of her surroundings. Elena had left her bonnet on the bed and carried a pink-and-white parasol as defense against the sun instead. The color didn't match her yellow dress, but she didn't care. She wanted to see around her.

"You must be Elena." The woman spoke in a breathless rush before Elena could say a word. "I'm Vanessa, but I'm sure your sister told you that. I am so glad you knocked. I was just considering if I should venture out on my own, but it will be ever so much more enjoyable with a companion. And less worrying."

"I'm sure you would have been fine." Elena wasn't sure why she would be worried.

"You can never be certain with so many men around." She went on in a near whisper. "Not all—even those claiming to be—are gentlemen. A lady alone must be vigilant."

"I suppose that is best."

"But Ivy said you went out early this morning. By yourself. She didn't seem surprised at that. She says you are very independent." Vanessa adjusted her bonnet. "It must have been very early, before I arrived."

"I wanted to be in the gardens when the sun rose."

"The sunrise was lovely. I saw the rosy glow of the eastern horizon as I arrived. Such a gift." A full smile lit up the woman's face and made her even more beautiful.

Any men they met along their walk would not even notice Elena beside Vanessa. Not that Elena cared if they did or not. "A gift?"

"Did you not think it such when you walked in the gardens?" Without giving Elena time to answer, she went on. "You must have. The first rays touching the flowers. Were there roses?"

"Many roses," Elena said.

"And bees and butterflies flying about them?"

"There was a black-and-blue swallowtail butterfly."

"Oh, I do hope I see one today. And a hummingbird. Don't you simply love hummingbirds?"

"I didn't see one this morning." Elena could add one to her drawing though.

Almost as if she read Elena's mind, Vanessa said, "Your sister told me you are an artist. That you paint beautiful things." She looked at Elena as they went outside. "Do you paint portraits? I would ever so much love to have a portrait of myself."

"I'm not that accomplished with faces." Elena hesitated a moment before she went on. "But there is an artist here. I could introduce you."

She didn't know why she hesitated. Kirby Frazier was doing portraits of women more beautiful than Elena every day. And what did she care if he did? Even if her pulse did speed up a bit when they were dancing, that hardly meant his did. Besides, what did she really know about him? Except that he was handsome. Brave. And a talented artist.

"That would be delightful." Vanessa rose up on her toes and clapped her hands. "Do you think he could do it today? I'm not sure how long I will be here."

"We can ask him."

"But don't portraits take days? Even weeks?"

"Perhaps some do, but Mr. Frazier works very fast with his brushes and pens and chalk." She had watched him a couple of days before. Not close behind him but from a distance. He'd had a small board on his easel and had filled the space with alacrity. When he gave her the painting, the lady appeared to be excited. Elena had waited for her along the walkway to the hotel to ask to see the portrait. The woman had been more than happy to oblige.

Elena had looked from the painting to the lady's face. It looked like her but at the same time didn't. She was not a young woman, every bit as old as Elena's mother. But Mr. Frazier had used a slight shading to erase some of her years and given her soft and generous lips to contrast her patrician forehead. With an economy of brushstrokes he'd copied her hairstyle and silvered only a few streaks through the brown.

What might he change or not change about a truly beautiful woman like Vanessa? Elena hoped he would do the woman's portrait since that would give her the opportunity to watch him work close at hand without seeming too forward. She would be with her new friend.

They found him at his easel down by the lake. The water was nearly as blue as the sky and glittered in the sunshine when a light wind slipped across its surface. A few ducks floated on the far side. Another place of beauty here at the Springs.

Elena wondered if the lovely grounds might do as much healing as Dr. Graham's spring water. If she somehow enticed a wealthy man into marrying her, she might also entice him into coming back to this place every summer. She should attempt to number the advantages of her mother's grand scheme as well as the disadvantages. Money would be an advantage.

She studied the woman beside her as they walked toward the lake. She must have money to have made a trip alone to this place. Her hair was elaborately coiffed, her dress the latest fashion. Her waist was so narrow, she had to be wearing a corset tightly tied, but Ivy had said nothing about her arriving with a lady's maid. And no sister or mother to take the place of one, like Elena had.

Elena touched her own waist that was almost as small. One could manage the corsets if the laces were long enough to tie in the front. Not as tightly as her mother jerked them but tight enough.

"Elena." Mr. Frazier looked up from positioning his paint box. "I hope you have come to let me capture your beauty on my canvas."

Elena felt her cheeks flush with pleasure at the man's words and how he used her given name. "I fear not, Mr. Frazier. My mother would never approve."

"Please, can't we be friends enough for you to call me Kirby?"

In one day she had two men asking to be friends. Perhaps there was some sort of magic in this place. "Another thing my mother would not approve."

He moved closer to her. Close enough to touch. Her heart pounded up in her ears. "Didn't you once tell me that while you might always listen to your mother, you then set your own course?"

If only a man like Kirby Frazier would have those deep pockets her mother desired. She took a breath to steady herself. "I can at least agree to call you Kirby since you seem determined to speak my name."

He did reach out and touch her cheek very lightly then. It was good she wasn't the type to swoon. Instead, she very sensibly stepped back and motioned toward Vanessa, who had lagged behind as though shy of being seen. "I've brought a friend who wishes to have a likeness of her face."

"Oh?" He turned his gaze from Elena to Vanessa.

"This is Vanessa." Elena hesitated and looked at the woman. "I'm sorry, I don't think you mentioned your last name. Not that it matters to Mr. Frazier, er, Kirby. He seems to prefer a more familiar address."

"So I do." Kirby smiled at Vanessa. "An artist needs to see beyond names to the spirit of the person. But it's good to know a name as well."

"Hasting," Vanessa said quickly. "Vanessa Hasting."

"Vanessa. Your name matches your beauty. Beauty I would love to attempt to capture on my canvas board since our Elena doesn't seem ready to pose for me."

Our Elena. She needed to get her emotions under control. She was not his Elena and could never be, even if his touch had sent shivers through her. Perhaps she had at long last met a man who would make her look favorably upon marriage. What a trick of life. A man she could not entertain as a suitor, even if his words were more than simply a way to charm her into posing for a portrait for which he would expect payment.

Now his focus was entirely on Vanessa, who stepped closer to him. "Oh yes. If you have the time to do so."

"Time stops for no man, but if it did, I'm sure it would stop to soak in your lovely visage, Miss Vanessa Hasting." He shot a look back at Elena as though to make sure she knew he hadn't forgotten her. "Two beautiful women to make this day even finer."

He led Vanessa over to a bench in the shade. "The light will be better here. This close to midday the sun can be too bright."

Once she settled on the bench with her skirt straightened, he adjusted her shoulders slightly at a slant. Then with his hand under her chin, he turned her face toward him. Elena could almost feel his fingers under her own chin tilting her head to find the perfect light. She brushed the idea away. She was there to observe his technique with his brush or pencils, not to wish for his touch.

"Do you think you can sit like this for a little while?" Kirby kept one finger under Vanessa's chin.

"If that is what needs to be done."

"Then we are all set as soon as I mix some paints." He moved back to his easel to take a couple of tiny bottles out of his box. He looked at Elena as he made sure the lids were tight and shook them. "You should have brought your sketchbook." He turned back to Vanessa. "Our Elena is an artist too."

"So her sister told me." Vanessa spoke the words stiffly without moving her head. "Elena was out today at sunrise to catch the beauty of the morning."

"Impressive."

Kirby murmured the word, but Elena couldn't tell if he was responding to Vanessa's comment or to the sight of the woman on the bench with the lake behind her. He picked up a brush but stood without moving for a long moment as he studied Vanessa.

Elena started to ask if he would be bothered by her watching over his shoulder, but she didn't. She somehow knew he might not even hear her, that he was scarcely aware of her being there at all. He was lost in the vision he wanted to capture with his brush. She had felt something the same that morning as the sketch of the roses had flowed from her pencil. But roses were one thing. A person's face another.

With the confidence of a professional, he made a few swift brushstrokes to form the shape of a face. At first it could have been anyone's face, but then with a few deft lines, Vanessa began to appear. Once, then twice, he made a mark with the brush that seemed wrong, but he quickly adjusted with a little shading.

Once he had the outline of the face, he took a brush that made lines as precise as a pen to paint the eyes. That was the part of a face Elena always struggled to capture truly when she tried to do a portrait. Kirby's brush brought the eyes to life in a few strokes. Not any eyes, but Vanessa's. It made Elena wish she could pose for a portrait by him.

Perhaps if she could find enough coins on the ground, she could ask him to do her portrait. A silly thought. That wouldn't happen. She would be fortunate to find any pennies for Ivy. She had simply been trying to give her hope.

Ivy deserved her chance with Jacob. What they had might not last, but then again, it might. Elena's heart was softening to the idea of romantic love now that she had doubts she would ever have the chance to embrace such feelings. But perhaps her sister could.

There seemed to be romance in Kirby Frazier's movements as he painted. She moved a little to the side to see his face. She had thought he would be too engrossed in his art to notice, but he smiled over at her while still moving his brush as though he didn't even need to see what he was doing.

He did pause then to ask, "What do you think, my artist friend?"

"That your brushes are miraculous."

"My brushes?" He had a teasing look as he put one down on the easel stand. "They don't seem to be doing much now."

"My mistake. Not the brushes. The hand holding the brushes, the eyes seeing the picture."

"Oh, please, may I come look?" Vanessa asked.

"Certainly not," Kirby said. "Not until I'm finished. You must stay where you are, Miss Vanessa, until I say you can move. Until then, you will have to trust our Elena's word that it is becoming a passable likeness."

There he was with *our Elena* again. She should tell him not to say that. She wasn't anybody's Elena. At least not yet. She did sort of like it, but at the same time she was aware that Kirby was performing and making her a part of the show he was putting on as he painted Vanessa's portrait. He made some flamboyant moves with the brush, but she noticed that none of those movements ended with lines or colors across his canvas.

Others had gathered around to watch, perhaps drawn as much by the beautiful woman on the bench as to Kirby's painting. Or perhaps not. Kirby was just as attractive in his manly way as Vanessa was in her womanly one. His shirt stretched tight across his broad shoulders, and his curly hair dipped down onto his forehead. As he stepped back to eye his canvas and then Vanessa, he almost looked as if he were dancing to music only he could hear. The music of his art.

Elena pulled her gaze away from Kirby to look around at those drawn to the artist's show. She was surprised to see General Dawson among them. Somehow she hadn't expected an old soldier like him to be drawn to the arts.

She turned away quickly when he noticed her looking at him, but too late. He started making his way over to her. Maybe she should do as Ivy suggested and feign illness. But no, she wouldn't make a spectacle of fainting, and she had no intention of leaving here until she saw Vanessa's finished portrait.

She could talk to General Dawson. What she couldn't imagine was standing at a marriage altar with him. Her gaze slid to Kirby.

On the other hand, matching up with a man like Kirby Frazier didn't take much imagination at all. Ah, if that were only possible, romance might truly be singing in the air.

15

Andrew stood among the willows by the lake and watched Elena Bradford watch Kirby Frazier paint a portrait. Not Elena's but that of a lady who seemed to be a friend of hers. He had never seen the woman posing for the artist. Perhaps a new arrival. Perhaps a relation of Elena's.

He could go ask. Leave the shadow of the willows and join the group that had assembled to watch Frazier. If Dr. Graham had told the man to be entertaining, he had taken it to heart. He was putting on a show with elaborate sweeps through the air with his brush and a stream of words that had the people around him smiling and laughing.

Elena too. She appeared to be entranced by the man. She hadn't even noticed Andrew when he walked past them and around the lake to the shade of the willows. In the shadows again. He had been watching for her after their talk among the roses. Had even planned to ask if she wanted to play a game of battledore. It had been so nice sitting with her as the sun came up.

But then he had left her without properly saying goodbye. Instead, he had allowed thoughts of Gloria to darken the pleasure of their time together. Talking of snakes and buzzards as though he wanted to remind her that all was not beauty in their world. He wouldn't be surprised if Elena ran in the opposite direction when next she saw him instead of smiling a welcome.

For certain, Frazier wouldn't be bringing snakes and buzzards into the conversation, although Andrew wouldn't be surprised if the man had added a few such things to his paintings now and again.

Maybe the artist was the snake in the grass, with a place here because of Andrew's words to Dr. Graham. Andrew shook his head. He was being ridiculous. The man seemed nice enough, affable. What was souring Andrew's mind was what he'd heard as he'd walked past those under the big oak where the man had chosen to place his easel.

Our Elena. Who was Frazier to be claiming Elena as his? He had only met her on the stagecoach traveling to the Springs the same as Andrew. Had promises been made in other meetings here? Perhaps Andrew wasn't the only one Elena met in the gardens to share her sketches.

He tamped down his runaway thoughts. It wasn't as if it mattered if that was true. She wasn't *his* Elena either. He had simply suggested friendship to her. She had simply accepted that suggestion. People came to this place to enjoy the beauty, to dance and be healed, to meet new acquaintances. Elena had seemed glad to accept his friendship. That didn't mean she couldn't enjoy other friendships as well.

But there was something about Frazier that bothered Andrew. He wasn't sure the man could be trusted. True, he had acted courageously on the stagecoach, or perhaps foolishly. The horses would have tired and stopped of their own accord without his heroics. Some men had to continually prove how brave, how strong they were.

His friend Zachary was like that. Never satisfied with doing things the simple way. He was forever daring more than necessary.

If they were riding across a field, he didn't want to go a few extra yards to a gate. He would jump the fence with no regard to his mount. The higher the fence, the better.

That could be why he had taken off in the middle of the night with Gloria. The daring of it. He could have gotten any girl he wanted, but stealing his best friend's bride-to-be practically on the eve of that friend's wedding must have been a challenge he couldn't resist.

Andrew shook his head and almost smiled. Zachary could do that to him. Infuriate him and make him laugh at the same time.

Somehow—who knew why—he had never blamed Zachary for his heartache. He'd given Gloria all the blame. He never doubted she had been the instigator of his friend's betrayal, of her own betrayal. Even now, trying to look at it clearly as he stared at the blue of the lake, he still felt that way. Zachary would have probably brought Gloria back before dawn and acted as though it was all some silly prank and no harm done.

But they hadn't come back. Gloria must have wanted the adventure Zachary promised over the settled life she thought Andrew offered. Had he offered that? A life devoid of excitement and challenge?

Perhaps so. He didn't like courting disaster. He saw no need in tackling fences so tall his horse might be permanently lamed and his own head fractured.

Instead, his heart had been fractured by Gloria's betrayal. He hadn't gone after them. He had accepted Gloria's choice. His father, had he still been living, would have said Andrew wasn't man enough to chase after them.

His grandfather hadn't said that. He hadn't said anything, but if he had, Andrew knew it would have been good riddance to the both of them. Zachary for being a danger to his horses and Gloria for being a danger to Andrew.

"It was bound to happen sooner or later. Better that it was sooner." Grandfather Scott hadn't said that to Andrew but to

the guests that had to be told the wedding was off. He hadn't seemed to care that Andrew overheard him.

Neither he nor Andrew's mother had taken to Gloria.

They would both like Elena Bradford. Why had that thought slipped into his head? Unless they decided to come for a night at the Springs themselves before the summer was over, it was unlikely they would ever even meet Elena.

It would be nice if they could join him for a summer week-end. Maybe he should write his mother and suggest that. He could tell her about meeting a female artist. He was sure Grandfather Scott would find a way to get reports from Dr. Graham about Andrew's progress of shedding his melancholy. In some ways his grandfather was the same as his father. *"Buck up and face whatever life hands you."* It was the love behind his grandfather's words that made the difference.

He could almost hear his grandfather telling him to stop hiding in the willows and go join the group watching Frazier. Step up beside Elena and be that friend he had offered to be, but instead Andrew turned and walked the other way.

Something about Elena drew him. He did want to know her better, but he might be foolhardy to risk his heart again.

Perhaps tomorrow morning he would feel more daring and seek her out among the flowers again. At sunrise. On a new day the Lord made.

16

The sight of the old general coming up beside Elena made Kirby jerk his paintbrush to make an unwanted mark. He would have to add a flower or a feather to the lady's hairstyle to cover it up. Most women were pleased to have a little extra added to their portraits.

This Vanessa would be no different. She did seem more than eager to sit for her portrait and was staying very still without complaint. He wouldn't care if she did move. He had captured her image with no need to search for a way to make her look more attractive. She had beauty cornered.

That should have made the portrait an easy task, but oddly enough, it wasn't. He was distracted by Elena watching him.

He had come on too strong with his familiarity. Not that she didn't like him using her given name. She did. But he shouldn't have claimed her as his Elena, even if he had tried to include her new friend in with his *our*.

That friend wouldn't mind him saying *our* Vanessa. Madeline coming later wouldn't mind him claiming her either, even if she did appear to be a timid little bird. He could probably waltz her off to the altar without the slightest struggle as long as her father didn't interfere.

Yet Elena was the one who kept coming to mind. While she might not have the same beauty perfection as this woman posing for him, those eyes of hers looked as deep as one of the bottomless lakes he'd seen in the west. She was a woman a man could live with for a lifetime. She wouldn't put hobbles on him. He could even imagine actually falling in love with her. He hadn't, but he was almost sure he could if he made up his mind to do so.

Then General Dawson came limping along to stir trouble into Kirby's plans. The old man couldn't really be courting Elena. Kirby pulled his brush away from the canvas before he made another stray mark that would add extra time to doing the portrait. This wasn't a true portrait. Merely a sketch in paints to make the lady happy.

He needed to finish it. Move on to someone else. The more paintings he did, the more money in his pockets. Perhaps that was why the old general was here. To see if he had finished the Boone Club one. Kirby had thought to do a few more touch-ups, but it was good enough that he could hand it over and move on to something new.

Move on. That was what he needed to think about doing. Moving on with one of these ladies. He peeked over his shoulder. Elena was smiling at the general as if glad to see him. She must not know the old codger had designs on her or she wouldn't keep smiling like that. She was probably thinking about him as a friend of her father's. Or her grandfather's.

Kirby pulled his attention back to Vanessa and his sketch. There was something a little different about the woman. She had the looks to make her a self-assured princess, but instead she acted a little too eager. She made him think of a girl invited to a party where she hadn't thought she'd be welcome. Women who looked like Vanessa were generally accustomed to others doing their bidding at the bare lift of a finger.

But this lady seemed unsure of herself. Before he had told her to hold the pose, she had glanced over her shoulder more than once as if worried someone might be watching. Perhaps he should ask Elena about her. They seemed to be friends.

Or ask Vanessa about Elena. That might serve him better.

He finished off a purple feather in the woman's hair to hide his stray mark and stood back to give his work an assessing look. Not bad.

"All right, Miss Vanessa. You may come look now."

The woman jumped up, then sank back down on the bench and fanned herself with her bonnet. Elena rushed toward her. "Are you all right?"

"It's nothing." Vanessa waved her away. "In my excitement, I stood too suddenly. I'll be fine in a minute." She put her bonnet on and with slow precision tied the ribbons under her chin. "Go, look at it and tell me what you think."

"You judge my efforts, Elena, while I assist Miss Vanessa." Kirby moved past Elena to offer a hand to Vanessa. "I apologize for having you sit so motionless. That could be what made you dizzy."

"I'm sure you are right." She stood more slowly this time and took Kirby's arm.

The woman still seemed a little pale as she leaned against him. Probably hadn't eaten all day to keep her slender waist, and then wearing a mountain of petticoats in the warmth of the day. Fashion was a hard taskmaster for ladies. But Elena didn't seem ready to have the vapors. Another thing in her favor.

"You are certain to be pleased, Vanessa." Elena stood in front of the portrait. The old general stood behind her, close enough to touch. "Mr. Frazier has captured your beauty with his brush."

Mr. Frazier again. Not Kirby as she had said earlier. He needed to catch her alone. Find a way to charm her. But that didn't seem possible right now with the general and the others who had been drawn to the show he'd put on while doing the portrait. He had himself to blame for that, but Dr. Graham had made sure Kirby understood he was to be an entertainment for the guests.

In due time he would have the freedom to do what he wanted. To stop having to be a show and simply be the artist he wished to be. A favorable marriage would hurry that day along.

"Elena, your words are too kind." Vanessa turned loose of Kirby's arm and without looking at the portrait covered her eyes. "I'm almost afraid to look."

"No need to fear, fair lady," General Dawson said. "Our artist has done a credible job and, as Miss Elena says, has portrayed your beauty."

Vanessa peeked out through her fingers. Then she did a little hop of pleasure and clapped her hands. "You have flattered me. Thank you so much, Mr. Frazier." A blush colored her cheeks as she lowered her voice. "But I fear you will have to wait until my father arrives for payment."

"Worry not about that." He managed to keep any disappointment from his voice. Often the ladies did not come prepared to offer payment for a portrait, a definite problem with no sign indicating payment was expected. "It was simply a pleasure to portray your beauty with my paintbrush."

"May I take it now?" She reached toward it.

"Not yet." He blocked her hands. "It needs to cure a little since I used paints and not just pencil and chalk."

"Oh." Vanessa looked disappointed.

"The artist knows best." General Dawson gazed at the painting before he looked over at Kirby. "You've outdone yourself on this one, young man." He stepped closer to Kirby and stuffed something into his pocket. "That is for the one we spoke of earlier with a bit extra to help Miss Vanessa here." He smiled. "I think I'm becoming a patron of the arts."

"Thank you, sir." Kirby was glad enough for the heft of the money in his pocket, but he couldn't help wishing the general had waited until later to come pay him. He was definitely spoiling Kirby's chance for any private words with Elena.

General Dawson gave Vanessa a little bow. "I'm General Dawson, and Miss Elena was kind enough to share your name, Miss Hasting. I'm very pleased to meet you."

"And I the same, General." Vanessa answered his bow with a little curtsy.

"Very well, ladies." He looked from her to Elena. "Shall we go find some midday refreshments? One of the servants can fetch your painting later and take it to your room, Miss Hasting."

"I did miss eating this morning," Vanessa said. "And I believe Elena did as well."

"Dear ladies, you must not go without proper nourishment," the general said. "Let me escort you to the dining area. I am almost certain Dr. Graham will have ordered the kitchen to have a variety of food available along with some sweet goodies. I'm told even ice cream may be in the offing today. Then we can check out the lawn bowling."

"Ice cream?" Elena seemed to have no hesitation in slipping her hand under the general's elbow. "How in the world could there be ice anything in the summertime?"

"The doctor has his ways," the man said.

"That sounds delightful," Vanessa said. "This day is turning out the best."

The general patted Elena's hand and offered his other arm to Vanessa. "I think I am the one to win the prize this day. A thorn between two roses." He nodded at Kirby. "Good day to you."

The old fellow had a spring in his step as he led the two women away. The others who had been watching Kirby paint the portrait drifted away too. He should have tried to entice someone among them to be his next model. He wasn't in top form. He was letting his emotions overpower his good sense. Elena Bradford wasn't the only woman at the Springs who might entertain his attentions.

From the time he began drawing again after his little sister's death, he had not let feelings get in the way of his plans. When Rosie died, his grief had nearly snuffed out something inside him. Something he hadn't wanted to lose but nearly had.

He sat down on the stool in front of his easel and turned to a fresh page in his sketchbook. Rosie filled his mind and the scene around him disappeared. He was ten and she was four when she caught a fever.

His mother lost two babies before Rosie came along to become a beam of sunshine in their rough cabin. Kirby loved her so much. She followed him around like a puppy dog and could sit for an hour watching him make pictures. He didn't have paper and pen then. No paints, but he saw things and had the urge to draw them. He scratched out pictures on rocks and in the mud. With ink made from poke berries, he painted with his fingers. He carved pictures in fence posts and the logs of the barn.

That was what he was doing on a cold, rainy day in November. He didn't know she had followed him outside. He wasn't thinking about anything but some free time to carve out a picture somewhere in the barn. When he was creating his pictures, the vision in his head blocked out everything else.

He remembered the image in his head. His mother had told him a Bible story about an apple tree in the Garden of Eden. Adam and Eve were told by God not to eat the apples, but Eve had been tempted by the serpent. He aimed to draw the tree. He knew what an apple tree looked like. They had three in the backyard.

When he stepped back to consider the carving and how he could put Eve ready to pluck an apple, Rosie sniffed and jerked him away from his vision of the Garden of Eden. He had no idea how long she might have been watching him without a word. She had her arms clutched around her body to keep warm, but her lips were turning blue from the cold. He forgot his picture and wrapped her in his arms to try to stop her shivers and teeth chattering.

After he hurried her in by the fire, she seemed fine, but a couple of days later she came down with a fever. The doctor asked if she'd had a chill. His words were like a knife twisting in Kirby's heart.

He prayed and prayed, but the Lord turned away from Kirby. Away from Rosie. Her coughs shook her small body until after a week, she went still. Her death broke his mother. She went about her chores like a ghost. His father changed too. Grew morose and stern. Nothing Kirby did could please him.

Kirby quit drawing. Anything. It seemed wrong to do something to give him joy when he was the reason Rosie was gone. Dark days turned into weeks, then months. But the sun kept coming up each morning.

Early one spring day, as he walked the mule to the pond before they hitched him to the plow, the sun edged up over the horizon and shot rays across the field. Sparkling jewels seemed to be scattered through the frosty grass. When he pictured how he and the mule looked walking through that glitter, he wanted, more than anything, to stop and find something to use to capture that image.

He didn't. His pa would have never understood that. Instead, he went on to the field to follow the mule as the plow turned over the ground. But the sunlit jewels had awakened his yearning to draw and do more than follow a mule the rest of his life. Not long after that, a teacher opened up a school close by. His pa said he was too old to go, but Kirby went anyway.

One day while the other boys played marbles on the bare schoolyard ground, he picked up a stick and drew in the dirt. The picture wouldn't last. Some kid would run through it, the wind would shift the dirt, or rain would wash it away. But something inside him came to life again after almost two years of pushing away the itch to draw.

When the teacher rang the bell to end their dinner recess, Kirby didn't hear it. He didn't notice the other kids going inside. He was part of the picture he was making of Rosie. It was hard to make her sweet face in the dirt, but he smoothed out the dust, found different size sticks, and almost captured his memory of her. Then he drew daisies and kittens around her. He wanted to think heaven was full of things like those that she loved.

The teacher came to look for him. A woman teacher, older than his parents. When she spoke behind him, he was startled. He swiped his hand across the dirt to erase the picture. The teacher didn't say he shouldn't have. She didn't say anything, but the next day she gave him a bound book of rough paper and a bottle of ink and asked him to draw the picture she'd seen in the dust again. When he did as the teacher asked, he could feel Rosie smiling at him. And he needed smiles.

He had toughened up since then. He needed money more than smiles. Money to do what he wanted and not have to be forever working to please some vain woman with a sketch she wouldn't accept if it showed her wrinkles or double chin.

Kirby looked down at the sketch he'd done almost without thinking about the lines he was making. A little girl holding a kitten. The girl's head was bent over the kitten. Her hair hung down to hide her face, but it was Rosie. He stared at the drawing for a long moment before he turned the page.

Madeline Southworth was walking toward him. Time to keep his focus on his goal to go west and capture the wonders there with his brush. That was what was important. He wouldn't let the foolish emotion of love get in his way. If Madeline Southworth was the one to finance his dream instead of the fetching Elena Bradford, so be it.

Right now he would dance between his options until the picture came clear. He did that with his art. He could do that with his life too.

17

Elena was not there when Ivy went back to the room after she and Mother had been to the baths. While Ivy had to force down drinks of the spring water, she liked soaking in the baths with rose petals floating around her to give the mineral water a more pleasant scent. Robes and towels were always within reach. The baths gave her a glow through and through, and she stayed in the tub until the tips of her fingers wrinkled.

Her mother had already left the bathhouse to enjoy the June breezes on the veranda. Ivy offered to join her there, but her mother had other orders for her and Elena. "No need in that, my dear. Such relaxing is for us older folk. Go find Elena and the two of you walk around the grounds. How does she expect to meet any possible suitors if she keeps hiding out in the gardens with that silly sketchbook?"

"I'll ask her, Mother."

"Do more than ask. Tell her in no uncertain terms that I said so. And perhaps that new lady you spoke to earlier today can join the two of you in a stroll." Her mother had frowned. "Whoever heard of such a thing? A young woman without a proper escort."

Ivy heard the echo of Elena's words that they were in almost the same situation, but she would never repeat them to Mother, even if she could see the truth in what Elena said. They were there without a male escort. At least Vanessa had a father coming later.

That thought brought moisture to Ivy's eyes. Her poor father couldn't be coming. Even if he had done little more than pat her head now and again, she loved him. Of course she did. He was her father.

If only he hadn't died so suddenly. He would have found a way to lift them out of this awful situation they were in. Surely Elena's marriage possibilities couldn't be all that stood between them and poverty.

Her mother did have a way of always seeing the dark side of things. It wasn't fair for her to expect Elena to pick a husband with the only consideration his fortune and no thought of love. She talked as though love didn't matter at all.

That must be why she thought their weeks here at the Springs would make Ivy forget Jacob. That couldn't happen. Dancing with a thousand men wouldn't make her forget Jacob.

Ivy would do as her mother said and find Elena for that walk after she wrote to Jacob. She had promised. She needed to have a letter ready to send if—no, when—she figured out a way to have it delivered to Lexington. Her love for Jacob was true and right. The Lord would open up a way for her to send a missive to him.

Ever since she could remember, she had felt a comfort in prayer. Afraid of the dark? In her mind, she would see the Lord beside her with a candle. Someone at school made her cry with unkind words? She would remember the words, "For God so loved the world." She was one of those in the world. The Lord loved her.

There was also the verse, "Honor thy father and mother." She did that. Slipping a sheet of her mother's writing paper from her case wasn't dishonoring her mother. Or stealing. Her mother would give her the paper if she asked.

Still, her fingers trembled and she looked over her shoulder toward the door as she pulled out her mother's writing case. When she opened it, a few coins stared up at her. She could take one, maybe two, of these to pay someone to deliver her letter. Her mother might never miss them.

Ivy stared at the coins for a long moment before she slipped out a sheet of paper and firmly closed the case. She would not take the money. If she needed a coin to get her letter to Jacob, one would appear along her path. That would be a sign the Lord did not want her to forget Jacob.

Her heart was racing as if she had danced five times in a row without stopping for a second's rest. She fanned her face with the sheet of paper, then pushed open one of the windows to lean out and pull in a breath of fresh air.

The hotel was four stories high, and while her mother complained about the stairs, Ivy loved their bird's-eye view here on the top floor. Music floated up to Ivy, and she caught the scent of magnolias. This did have to be one of the loveliest places on earth. If only Jacob was here with her. She turned from the window to sit at the writing desk. She dipped the pen nib into the ink and tried to think of the perfect words to write.

Dear Jacob,

Graham Springs is a beautiful place with flowers and trees and the nicest people. Music floats in the air as servants sing and play guitars, fiddles, harmonicas, and who knows what else all day long. That keeps everyone in the sweetest of moods. Plus, there's an artist we met on the stagecoach. He paints the ladies' portraits. Well, not mine. Mother would never allow that.

She looked at what she had written and shook her head. This sounded as though she were having such a wonderful time that she didn't miss him at all.

She dipped the pen nib in the ink again.

I wish you were here.

That was better. What she wanted to write.

If you were, then the summer days would be perfect. We could walk in the gardens or play lawn bowling or battledore in the daytime and dance away the nights. Dr. Graham, the man who owns the Springs, insists on everyone dancing. He says exercise is almost as good as his spring water tonics, and dancing is certainly splendid exercise. He also insists everyone imbibe his spring water. I do, even though it does have a most dreadful taste. Elena avoids more than a sip. Mother drinks it willingly in hopes it will cure her headaches.

She had veered away from what she wanted to write again. She sighed and turned back toward the window. If only she were artistic like Mr. Frazier or Elena. Then she could send him a drawing of her alone with tears on her cheeks. It didn't matter that she wasn't alone all the time or that she hadn't actually dissolved into tears. He wouldn't be alone all the time either.

She gripped her pen tighter. That Melba Smith was probably finding ways to be wherever Jacob was. She had been after him forever. Hot blood rushed to her face as she pictured Melba making eyes at Jacob, practically asking him to kiss her.

Slow down. She could almost hear Elena's voice in her ear. Elena had a way of being so calm, always in control. Even on the stagecoach when they could have all been killed, she had sat silent while protecting Mr. Frazier's painting as though she had been assigned the task.

What would she do now? Better yet, what would she tell Ivy to do? Get control of her thoughts. Stop imagining things that probably would not happen. Ivy pulled in a breath and held it a moment as she looked out the window again. Birds were singing. A little wind rustled through the oak leaves. Voices and laughter drifted up to her along with the music.

She took another deep breath and imagined Jacob's arms around her. She was the one he wanted to kiss. Not Melba.

Ivy halted her runaway imagination and stared down at the words she'd written. The page was almost covered, but if she wrote small, she would have room for a few more sentences. What would Elena tell her to write? But no, these last words needed to be Ivy's to Jacob.

She shut her eyes to picture him. For a second, she could see nothing but his angry face when she'd told him she had to come here with her mother. She squeezed her eyes tighter to get rid of that image and picture him smiling at her instead. A sad smile, since she was here and he was there.

Tears slid down her cheeks. One of them dripped off her cheek onto the letter to smudge a few of the words. He would see that and know the tear was because she missed him so much. She dipped the pen into the ink and began to write.

I love you. I miss you. I will be home soon and we will have time to be together before the end of summer. Know that whenever I have to dance with someone, I imagine it is you. Only you.

Love forever, Ivy

She read over the last lines. She had spilled out her heart in those words. She folded the letter into a neat square and wrote his name and address on it. She blew on it to dry the ink before she slipped it deep into her pocket with a little prayer that she would find a way to send it to him.

As she put the cork back in the ink bottle and waved the

pen around to dry its nib, she could almost feel her mother's disapproving eyes watching her. She hurried out of the room and practically ran down the stairs to get away from the guilt chasing after her. She stepped out of the hotel into the sunshine and felt better at once as she looked around. No sign of Elena.

When her mother waved from the veranda, the letter burned in Ivy's pocket as she hurried away from the hotel to find Elena the way her mother had told her to. But where should she look? Elena could be in any of a dozen flower gardens with her sketchbook or inside reading or who knew where.

Maybe Mr. Frazier had seen her. She might even be watching him paint down beside the lake. That sounded like something Elena might do.

Ivy kept her eyes on the path as she walked and could hardly believe it when she saw the sparkle of metal. She stooped to pick it up. Not a dollar or half-dollar. Only a cent piece, but it felt like a sign that she would find a way to send her letter to Jacob.

By the time she got to the lake, her steps were light, her guilty feelings forgotten. She couldn't wait to tell Elena about the coin.

18

M r. Frazier was at his easel, but Elena wasn't anywhere in sight. A lady Ivy hadn't met sat on a bench beside the lake, her bonnet in her lap with the ribbons spread out just so as she posed for the artist.

Behind the woman, ducks floated calmly on the clear-blue water. The drooping branches of a few willows brushed the green lawn along the far side of the lake. Two trees with small white blossoms released a sweet scent into the air. Here and there some bushes were covered with clusters of pink blooms. Ivy had never seen any like them before, but she did know the hollyhocks that brightened the scene with their colorful flowers. The woman on the bench didn't appear to share the peace of the scene as she fidgeted with her lace collar and then smoothed her hair.

"My dear Miss Madeline, if you can stay still a few moments longer, I only lack a few brushstrokes to capture your visage." Mr. Frazier stepped away from his easel to speak to the woman. His smile seemed a little stiff.

"It's been forever already. This bench is horribly uncomfortable." Miss Madeline frowned at him and then looked over her shoulder. "And those horrid ducks keep quacking at me."

"They must be attracted by your beauty." The artist's voice was smooth. "I'm sure they are harmless."

When he moved back to his painting, he noticed Ivy there. "Miss Ivy, are you here to have your portrait done?"

"That would be lovely, but not today," Ivy said. "I'm looking for Elena. Have you seen her?"

"She was here earlier. She brought a friend for me to do her portrait." He pointed to a canvas leaning against a tree. "But they left to find some refreshments."

"Oh." Ivy should go back to look for them at the hotel. She'd promised her mother, but she could linger here a few minutes to watch Mr. Frazier paint.

Suddenly the woman by the lake shrieked and jumped up when a duck came out of the water beside her.

"Just shoo it back to the lake, Miss Madeline." Mr. Frazier turned back toward the woman.

"It might peck me," she screamed as she backed away from the duck.

The artist looked unsure of what to do as he held his palette in one hand and his brush in the other. He looked over at Ivy. "Miss Ivy, are you afraid of ducks?"

"No." Ivy hesitated before she added, "I like ducks." She didn't want to make this Madeline feel bad since she obviously did not like ducks. The woman flapped her bonnet at the duck that appeared to be unbothered.

"Then could you go nicely ask the duck to leave Miss Madeline alone so I can finish her portrait?" He winked at Ivy. "Please?"

Miss Madeline swiped at the duck again with her bonnet and looked ready to climb up on the bench. The duck waddled closer as if it thought she might be throwing breadcrumbs.

The lady danced a few feet away and threw her reticule at

the duck. Instead of scaring it away, the duck quacked louder. Several of its companions followed it out of the water onto the bank. The woman put her hand to her chest and appeared ready to faint.

Ivy lifted her skirts and ran toward them. She was almost sure Mr. Frazier chuckled as she went past him.

"They won't hurt you," Ivy assured the woman. "They must think you are feeding them."

Miss Madeline's eyes widened even more as she shook her head slightly. Ivy twisted her mouth to hide her smile as she shooed the ducks away from the woman. With disgusted quacks, they waddled away to slide smoothly out onto the lake's surface.

All seemed well until the woman shrieked again and pointed to her bag on the ground. "My reticule."

Ivy picked it up. "I fear it might have a bit of dirt on it." Dirt seemed better to say than duck droppings as she held it out toward the woman.

"You cannot expect me to touch that. It's—it's got duck stuff on it." The woman shrank back from Ivy. "This whole afternoon has been nothing but dreadful. Him thinking I can sit like a stone forever." She glared at Mr. Frazier as she jammed her bonnet down on her head. "Ducks attacking me. And now my best reticule ruined." Tears rolled down her cheeks. "Ruined."

"It will be fine once you clean it off," Ivy said.

"I can't." Her voice was shaky as she swiped tears from her cheeks. "Would you do that for me?"

She sounded so pitiful that Ivy felt sorry for her. She went to the edge of the lake and wet her handkerchief to swipe away the worst of the duck droppings before she held it out to the woman again.

Without a word of thanks, the woman took it and held it at arm's length as she started away.

When Ivy turned back to the lake to rinse out her hankie, she spotted several coins that must have fallen out of the reticule. One looked to be a half-dollar piece, along with several five-cent coins and pennies.

"Wait," Ivy called to the woman. "You lost some coins."

Madeline made a face as she looked back at Ivy. "Eww. If you want to pick them up out of duck dung, you can have them."

An answer to prayer. Ivy could hardly believe it as she picked up the coins. The Lord blessed fully and greatly.

. . . .

Madeline rushed by Kirby without even a peek toward him. These young women born to a life of privilege and ease were exasperating. He watched her out of sight before he turned back to his easel. She could have at least stopped long enough to give her portrait a look after he had performed the next thing to magic and made her look halfway attractive. A little fluff up of the hair and a few well-placed shadows to transform her weak chin line.

He sighed. Two portraits without the promise of so much as a coin for either of them. That wasn't exactly true for the Vanessa portrait. He touched his pocket that felt nicely full of the banknotes and coins the general had stuffed in it.

The old codger wasn't so bad even if he did appear to have designs on Elena. If Madeline Southworth had been lost as a potential marriage target, as it surely seemed she had with her hurry to leave the lake and him behind, there was still Elena. A much more inviting prospect than Miss Southworth. A man the age of General Dawson wouldn't be able to knock him out of the picture. Plus, somehow he doubted he would have to save her from ducks.

Perhaps if he had put his paintbrush down to rescue Miss Madeline, he would have stayed in her good graces. But afraid of a duck. What could a duck do to her? There was the spoiling of her reticule. Kirby smiled as he remembered the woman's face when she took her bag from Ivy. Now that would make a picture.

That duck might have done him a favor. He wasn't sure any amount of money would be worth being tied to a woman like Madeline Southworth for life. If the duck wasn't what had helped him escape such a fate, then pretty Miss Ivy had done so by showing up to chase away the duck. If she hadn't, he supposed he would have had to put down his palette and go to the rescue. The woman might have ended up in his arms, full of gratitude.

A slight turn of events could make a lifetime of difference. The appearance of Elena's little sister at that perfectly opportune moment might have been another of those slight turns he could use to his advantage.

At the lake's edge, the girl presented a lovely picture. Afternoon sunlight glimmered on the water behind her while a slight breeze riffled the willows on the other side of the lake. But it was her smile that lit up the scene. She looked from the coins she'd picked up off the ground to the sky and suddenly whirled once around without so much as a glance down to be sure her skirt hem wouldn't find some of the duck leavings. She looked the picture of joy.

"Miss Ivy," he called to her. "Thank you for chasing away that army of ducks coming ashore to attack. I will be forever grateful, as I'm sure Miss Southworth will be as well when she recovers from her state of unease."

"She did seem very upset." The girl shoved the coins into a pocket on her full skirt and came toward him. "May I look at her portrait?"

"I wish you would. Miss Southworth showed no interest in seeing it." He gestured toward the portrait with the paintbrush he still held.

She stepped over to the easel to study it for a long moment.

"You are very quiet. I'm not sure that is good." He always felt a little nervous when a person assessed one of his paintings, even these sketches that he did so quickly and without great care.

"Oh, but it is. I am completely in awe of how you captured the lady's face. And made her so pretty." She looked a little shamefaced as she glanced over at him. "Not that the lady wasn't attractive. I'm sure I didn't see her at her best." She turned back to the painting. "But you've made her lovely."

"Ladies do prefer their portraits to compliment them." He moved up beside Ivy and pointed his brush toward the bottom of the canvas. "What do you think? Should I paint a little duck here in the corner?"

"That's wicked of you, Mr. Frazier." Ivy put her fingers over her mouth, but that didn't hide her giggle. "I really don't think your Miss Madeline would like that very much."

"Ahh, alas, I rather fear she's far from my Miss Madeline."

"Did you want her to be?"

"To be what?"

"Your Miss Madeline." Ivy turned to look directly at him for a second before a flush bloomed in her cheeks. She dropped her gaze to the ground. "Do forgive me. I shouldn't have asked that. I am not usually so nosy."

"It could be that we could all get along better if we said what we think instead of beating about the bush, don't you think?" Kirby smiled at her. She had such a youthful freshness that his fingers itched to capture her image.

"I don't think Mother would agree."

"And Elena?"

"Elena nearly always says what she thinks. Or at least she did before our father passed away." Sadness flashed across her face. "That has changed so much."

"I am sorry."

She looked up and around. "I do need to find her. You said they went for refreshments. Did you mean Elena and Vanessa?"

"And General Dawson."

"Poor Elena." She frowned a little. "I tell her she should feign illness whenever he wants to dance, but she doesn't. I suppose I don't either, but I do try to grab another partner when I see him heading my way."

"That bad, eh?"

"I shouldn't have said that. The general can't help being old."

She looked chagrined as a blush colored her cheeks and made her face even more appealing as a subject for a painting. He touched her chin with his brush. "It looks as if I have no more willing customers this afternoon to sit for a portrait. Would you let me make a sketch of you? Not paint, but pen or charcoal. I can capture your beauty among the ducks."

"But I'm not among ducks now."

"A man has an imagination."

"That does sound delightful, but my mother would not approve nor be willing to pay for such a drawing."

"Worry not about payment. This will be a mere sketch." He put down his palette and brush to pick up his sketchbook. "Something fun to draw."

"I don't know." She sounded hesitant but at the same time interested.

"Come. Humor the artist in me. I'll sit on the bench, and you can stand by the lake and perhaps entice the ducks back over to you." He grabbed his charcoal pencil and chalk box. "I will not take no for an answer."

"Then I suppose I can't refuse." She practically skipped back to the lakeside.

He followed her. He wasn't sure how this would help him with Elena, but the girl had a special sparkle he wanted to capture on paper. And who knew? Perhaps someday he could sell the drawing if he was able to make the idea come to life.

She stood where he posed her with the willows in the background. "Perfect." He took a seat on the bench.

"Will it bother your concentration if I ask you something?"

"Not at all. Ask away." He made the first quick lines to position her on the paper.

"Have you ever been in love?"

That did make him look up from the sketch.

"Is that something I shouldn't have asked?" She looked a little worried.

"Not at all. Just a question I wasn't expecting." He smiled to set her at ease and began drawing again. "I expected you might ask about how or why I draw."

"I suppose those would be good questions. Elena says she can't imagine not drawing things. That it seems to be part of her, a yearning inside to make pictures. Do you feel like that?"

"I do. Like now. Wanting to draw you among the ducks."

"But no ducks are coming over to me."

The ducks were on the far side of the lake now. "Don't concern yourself. I can draw a duck without it posing for me."

"All right." She quietly kept the pose a moment before she went on. "Are you going to answer my question?"

"About being in love?" He stilled his pencil and looked up at her. "All right. Love has never taken a strong hold on me, but I am hopeful it will someday."

"Aren't you old to have never been in love?"

"I'm not all that old yet." He laughed. "Love may still find me."

"Do you think you will know when it does?"

"I'm sure I will."

"But what if you didn't know?" She sighed. "What if you thought you were but weren't or thought you weren't but were?"

"Now you are talking in riddles, Miss Ivy."

"I guess so. But you say you've never been truly in love, but if you were, how would you know it was true?"

"Hmm." He drew without saying anything for a moment before he went on. "I suppose if I thought about the other person all the time. If my heart felt lighter when I was with her. If I went all atremble inside when the person I loved touched me. If I didn't think I could live without her."

He wasn't sure he should have answered her with such detail, but she obviously thought he was too old to hold any love interest for her. No one was near enough to overhear if the talk was inappropriate. And he was getting a great sketch. That was what could make him sometimes feel raw and trembly inside.

"All that sounds right."

"If you know that, you must be in love, Miss Ivy."

"Or, just as you with drawing a duck, girls can have imagination too."

"And imagine a great many things, I am sure." He looked up at her. "Almost finished. You are an excellent model."

"You will let me see the finished sketch, won't you?"

"Of course."

She was quiet for several moments. When she spoke again, it wasn't about love. "Do you know anyone who might be going to Lexington from here?"

"Are you trying to find a ride away from us?"

"I have a letter I need to send a friend there."

"A special friend?"

She didn't exactly answer him. "I promised him I would write, but I don't know how to send a letter from here. Also, even if I did, Elena says the person who receives the mail has to pay for the delivery and what if they wouldn't."

"That is a dilemma." Kirby quickly drew some ducks around Ivy's skirt. "But I might be able to help you out. Dr. Graham is sending a servant to Lexington for supplies, and he has agreed to have the man pick up some things for me. I'm sure for a slight fee he would deliver your letter."

A smile exploded on her face as she clapped her hands. "Oh, that is wonderful."

Kirby had to laugh. If ducks had actually been around her, she would have scared them all back onto the lake. This girl had him laughing more than anyone had for years. She would make a delightful sister-in-law.

19

General Dawson escorted Elena and Vanessa into the dining area, where he called the servants by name and within minutes had an array of fruit, sandwiches, and delightful cakes on the table in front of them.

He seemed to know everyone they met and had a story about them all. Usually one that had Vanessa and Elena smiling.

"General," Vanessa said. "You are going to have to stop this. Elena and I won't be able to look any of these gentlemen in the face when they ask us to dance."

"Then I suppose you will have to dance every dance with me." When he smiled, he didn't look so old.

"How are you going to dance with both of us every dance?" Elena asked.

"That could be a challenge, but it's one I'm ready to take on now that the good Dr. Graham's spring water is easing my rheumatism." He popped one of the small ham biscuits into his mouth. He eyed them while he chewed and swallowed before he went on. "Are you ladies taking advantage of the waters?"

"I only arrived this morning and it's been such a swirl ever since," Vanessa said. "And I don't think Elena did this morning since her sister said she was out at sunrise to do some sketching."

"Sketching?" The general raised his bushy eyebrows. "Are you an artist such as Mr. Frazier?"

"I can't compare to him, sir." Elena wished Vanessa hadn't told him about her sketching. She assumed the general would be like her mother and think it a frivolous waste of time, but he surprised her by showing true interest.

"It is as hard to compare art as it is to compare grapes with peaches." He pointed toward the fruit on the table. "Both are fruit, for a certainty, but much different. The good Lord makes us all unique with a variety of talents. I hope you will show me some of your sketches. Perhaps you could even do a sketch of this old man."

"Oh no. I need more practice on drawing people."

"I can supply the subject for your practice. What about you, Miss Vanessa? Willing to sit for another artist?"

"Perhaps on a different day. I fear I couldn't face sitting that still again today. You cannot imagine how much I wanted to touch my face." Vanessa rubbed her nose as if even the thought of it was causing an itch now.

"That's very kind of you both." Elena shook her head. "But I had best practice on roses for a while longer or perhaps birds." She started to mention the snake she'd drawn among the roses that morning but didn't. The general might think a woman drawing a snake extremely odd, and even the thought of a snake might frighten Vanessa. Something about her made Elena think she might be prone to the vapors.

"Before the summer is over, then," General Dawson said. "Your mother did tell me you were staying until August."

"You've spoken with my mother?" Elena felt a sudden drop in her spirits. What must her mother have said to make him so ready to escort them to the dining room?

"Yes. A delightful woman. My sympathies for the loss of your father."

"Thank you." Elena looked down at the petit four on her plate. She had lost her appetite.

She pulled in a steadying breath. No need to imagine the worst. Her mother surely wouldn't have hinted at anything about marriage. Elena needed to think as positively as she could. Perhaps the old gentleman had a son. General Dawson might make a very nice father-in-law. At any rate, she was ready to switch the conversation away from her art.

"Do you have children, General?" she asked.

"No, I fear I am all alone. Delores, my dear wife, died a couple of years ago. We did have three children. The two girls succumbed to fevers at very young ages. Such happened much too often to babies in those days, and our son took pneumonia and died while he was out west in the army."

"How sad." Vanessa touched her eyes with her handkerchief.

"Yes." Elena echoed her sympathy.

"None of those sad faces now." He waved away their words. "That all happened years ago. Not that the death of a child ever loses its sting, but one does find a way to go on. My wife and I had many good years together. But since she passed, I have been lonely. That's why I spend as much time as I can here among these good people. Besides the palliative effect of the springs, I get to meet lovely ladies like you."

"You are too kind." Elena took a bite of her small cake. No son. That was disappointing.

Vanessa leaned forward across the table toward the general. "Have you considered marrying again?"

This line of conversation was worse than her art. Elena took a sip of her tea before managing a smile.

"As a matter of fact, I have been seriously considering such a move." The general's smile looked more sincere than Elena's felt. "While to you youngsters, I may seem to be older than dirt,

I have plenty of life still in me. What about you? Either of you married or considering such a move?"

Elena's mouth went dry, and she took another sip of her tea. It had a very odd taste. Perhaps made with the spring water.

Vanessa appeared to be as unsettled by the question as she was. She looked over her shoulder as though expecting someone watching to make sure she told the truth. "No, no. Much to a father's distress."

"That's right. Your father is Judge Hasting in Louisville." General Dawson's forehead tightened in a frown. "I have met him at some political events in the past, but I don't think he mentioned having such a lovely daughter. You weren't with him, were you?"

"He rarely took my sister and I along with him to business gatherings." She shifted in her seat as though she'd suddenly noticed the chair lacked comfort.

"Fortunate for you. Those gatherings are always very dull." General Dawson turned to Elena. "And what about you, Miss Elena? Marriage plans?"

"Someday, I hope." Elena kept her smile steady. "If I meet the right person."

"Ahh, the right person is always best." He twirled his glass. "Do you have someone in mind? That right person."

"I fear not. I'm not sure but what my younger sister might beat me to the altar."

"She is a lovely girl," Vanessa said. "So full of enthusiasm."

"That's Ivy. But we are still mourning our father. So, she might have to temper her enthusiasm for marital bliss." Elena hoped that kept her from looking so available.

"Yes. I suppose that would be a consideration." The general looked from his glass to Elena. "How long since your father died? If I may ask."

"He died in January, right after the holidays."

"I see."

Elena imagined him counting off the months. Five months. Was there an official period of proper mourning time before a daughter could marry? Or did that only matter for the widow? Her mother had allowed them to put away the black dresses. Not just allowed. Insisted.

Elena looked down at her cream-colored skirt with lilac flowers scattered in bunches on the material. Lace and ruffles adorned her collar and sleeves. There was nothing to show Elena was in mourning except a black ribbon around her wrist. Her father deserved some remembrance from her. But her mother still wore the black signature of grief even though it made her stand out here at the Springs amidst all the fashionable colors.

Elena had overheard a few whispers about how a widow still in mourning should not be basking in the pleasure of a place like the Springs. As if a widow couldn't have health needs that could be improved by taking the waters the same as any other person. That wasn't why they were here, but it could be. Other whisperers noted how aware her mother obviously was that widow's weeds happened to be a perfect color to flatter her blonde hair and pale skin.

As always, Elena stood in the shadow of the beauty of both her sister and her mother. Yet she was supposed to attract a suitor to save them all. Perhaps this man across the table from her. At least spending time with him let her see him in a different light than she had when they first arrived at Graham Springs. He came across as a caring person and was not nearly as ancient as she originally thought. Perhaps the spring water did have rejuvenation properties.

Now, as if being outshone by her sister and mother was not enough, here she was with this beautiful young woman. Vanessa could outshine anyone in her light blue dress with sleeves slightly puffed from elbow to wrist. She wore a bonnet bedecked with flowers. Her tiny waist gave proof that she was properly corseted, just as Elena was now after slipping out in the early morning free of the dreadful undergarment.

"And so, Miss Vanessa?" General Dawson turned his attention to the other woman. "Has your father sent you here to find romance?"

Color stained her cheeks as the young woman touched her lips with her napkin. All of a sudden, she seemed a little out of breath. Her corset perhaps. The garments had a way of depriving a lady of air if she moved too quickly or ate more than a tidbit of food.

She recovered enough to answer. "I'm sure my father would be thrilled if that were to happen."

"Would you be thrilled as well?" the general asked.

"Romance is always thrilling." Vanessa appeared to be recovered from her breathlessness. "Don't you agree, Elena?"

"My sister certainly would." Elena tried to think of a way to shift the conversation away from romance. She picked up one of the little cakes. "These are delicious, aren't they?"

General Dawson laughed. "I do believe Miss Elena is not interested in talking about romance. Does that mean you have a young man waiting for you at home?"

There was nothing for it but to answer. "Regretfully not. Most of my friends think I am fated to be a spinster."

"Dedicated to your art, perhaps." Vanessa took a nibble of her petit four. She seemed as ready to leave the romantic talking behind as Elena was.

"My dear ladies, romance is the very flower of life." General Dawson picked up one of the little cakes.

"Did you keep the romance alive in your marriage?" Vanessa asked.

"I did try. Did you have that example with your parents?" He took a bite of the cake.

Vanessa stared down at her plate a moment before she said, "Sometimes romance has a way of dying out."

"That is a sorrow. One I hope you never experience." The general turned his gaze on Elena. "Of course, Miss Elena, you are observing a time of sorrow along with your mother, but I doubt your father would wish either of you to embrace that sorrow overlong."

"I'm sure you are right. Father did want us to be happy," Elena said. "However, my mother feels at least a year is the proper bereavement period, but I wonder how such can be settled on as this or that number of days and months. How long were you in mourning for your wife, General Dawson?"

"The loss of my Delores will always be a sorrow in my heart. In many ways, I will forever be in mourning for her. At the same time, I have room in my heart for more love. I think your mother might be the same. She could find a new companion just as I intend to do. I think Delores would want that for me, and although I didn't know your father, I feel he would surely think the same for your mother. In time, when she is ready to think of such a future."

"In time." Time was what Elena did not have if they were to pay her father's debts. Their debts now. Perhaps she should embrace the idea of marrying an older man like General Dawson. While he wasn't a prince, he wasn't a frog either. Besides, she was hardly a princess.

An image of Kirby Frazier flashed through her mind. His broad shoulders, his expressive hands, his warm brown eyes. His empty pockets. As her mother kept telling her, she had to face up to the truth that she couldn't keep hiding out in gardens while imagining romantic encounters with the wrong men. Her morning with Andrew came to mind, but that was merely the meeting of two who thought to be friends.

Her mother was right. She needed to commit to the plan and dance to the music whether she had a chance for love or not.

The general put his hands down on the table and pushed his

chair back. "But enough about love lost and yet to be found. Why don't we go see if we can find a lawn bowling game? Have either of you ladies played before?"

Both Elena and Vanessa stood up. Vanessa said, "Is it a game a lady can play?"

"Indeed. A very easy game. One merely has to roll a ball to see how close you can get it to the target ball without hitting it. Even at my age, I can defeat all comers." He smiled at them. "However, if we can find an empty green, I'll go easy on you ladies."

"That sounds like delightful fun. Don't you agree, Elena?" Vanessa hooked her arm in Elena's. "I don't know when I've had a better day. Meeting new friends. Having my portrait done. Enjoying some repast with two such wonderful people. Thank you both for being so welcoming to a lonely lady."

"Lonely? I can't imagine you ever lacking for friends," Elena said.

For an instant, Vanessa looked almost sad before she smiled brightly. "I certainly never imagined a place as beautiful as this."

The general stepped between them to take both their arms again as he had at the lake. "Don't forget about the dance tonight and how you've both promised me every dance."

"Come, General, other gentlemen will be in line to secure a dance with our newest guest," Elena said.

"Oh, very well." The man chuckled. "I will be happy with two dances with each of you."

"That will just make the day even more wonderful," Vanessa said. "I love to dance."

20

That evening after Kirby donned his blue waistcoat and coat with tails, he tied his cravat, smoothed down his hair, and studied his reflection in the mirror. He had the looks. Women were attracted to him. Men dismissed him for being an artist, but at times, they learned that being able to wield a paintbrush didn't mean he couldn't do other things considered manlier.

A good number had learned that lesson earlier on this day. Thanks to the old general, Kirby had profited even more than the wager Perkins had insisted on making. He glanced at the banknotes and coins he had pulled out of his pocket and counted when he got back to his room. Not a bad day's work, even if he never got payment for the portraits of the two ladies, Vanessa and Madeline.

A servant had carried the portraits to their rooms. He had no reason to keep them, although Vanessa's might make a good face for a magazine advertisement. Somehow, he didn't think she would agree to that, and in good conscience, he would need her permission to sell her portrait. On the other hand, he might paint another similar portrait with enough changed about her looks to sell it later on.

As for Madeline Southworth's, he was glad enough for the girl to have it whether he was paid or not. He hoped she would be happy with his portrayal of her when she got over being so upset by the duck fiasco. But he never knew what a woman would think of the portraits he did. Some that he thought were the best were not that well received. A person often saw themselves much differently than others did.

He had refrained from adding ducks along the bottom of Madeline's portrait. At least, none the girl would notice. He had penciled in a very, very tiny sideways duck in one of the corners. It seemed so necessary and had made Ivy laugh. He had insisted she never share the secret of that duck. If she did, he would be out the gate here at the Springs and have to find another way to finance his westward dream.

"You, sir, don't always exhibit good sense." He pointed at his image in the mirror but smiled as he shook his head. He did have a way of taking foolish risks. Like jumping onto a runaway horse. Like drawing one very tiny duck that could spoil his great start here at the Springs simply to make sweet Ivy laugh. She became a picture of happiness when she laughed.

He wondered if her sister was as transformed by her laughter as Ivy. He had seen Elena smile but never laugh. She was ever serious. Sometimes almost looking sad, but he supposed she was still grieving her father. If Ivy was, she did not show it as readily, but she was very young.

The sketch he had done of her and the ducks was one reason he was feeling so good this night. He had not given it to her. He would not give it to her. That sketch was sure to bring him money someday. He might make a small copy for her if he had the time in the next few days. She deserved that for being such a wonderful model.

Then again, he had agreed to see that her letter found its way on the morning stagecoach to her sweetheart. She had given him the coins that had spilled out of Madeline Southworth's reticule. That should be enough to encourage the man going for the supplies to make his way to the address on the folded letter. If not, Kirby could add another coin or two.

The mother must be tight with their money. That might not bode well for Kirby's future plans, but given time, he could surely charm the mother the same as the daughters.

Besides, he would only need their money to get him started. Once he was in the west, he could make his own way selling his paintings and sketches. How great to never have to do another portrait unless he chose the subject, as he had with the young sister. He had sketched her whole figure standing with her head partially turned toward the lake to capture the innocence of her youth. Sometimes the images he made with quick charcoal lines surprised even him when they turned out to be more than he expected or even hoped. Those moments were the best, and the sketch of Ivy and the ducks had done that.

He put down his comb, straightened his cravat, and brushed a speck of lint from his jacket. Tonight he would be sure to dance with not only Elena but also her mother if she were willing to take a turn around the dance floor. And of course, Ivy would be ready to dance, especially if she saw General Dawson starting her way. Kirby laughed out loud, hid the money in his artist bag, and went out of the room.

The night held promise.

• • • •

Ivy sat on the stool in front of the mirror as her mother worked her magic on her wayward curls. Mr. Frazier had done some magic of his own when he was sketching her by the lake with ducks around her even though none swam over to them. Drawing in the ducks hadn't been the magic. That had been somehow making Ivy's curls springing loose from their pins look as though they were meant to be that way.

She wished he had given her the sketch, but it was probably better that he hadn't. She had no idea what her mother might say about her posing for the artist. Kirby Frazier had not won Mother over. She had nothing good to say about him despite how he had saved them by stopping the runaway stagecoach horses.

"You appear to be in a better mood this evening, Elena." Her mother looked at Elena in the mirror as she fastened another pin in Ivy's hair. "That's good to see."

"It's easy to be in a good mood in such a beautiful place." Elena threaded a ribbon into her own hair. Ivy was happy to see that she had not pulled her hair back so tightly and left a few waves to soften her look.

"Oh, it is," Ivy agreed. "Did I tell you about watching Mr. Frazier paint a portrait of a woman named Madeline? Can you believe the woman was afraid of a few ducks coming up on the bank next to her? I thought she might faint before I could chase them away."

She stopped herself before she blabbed about the thrown reticule and the found coins. Best her mother did not know anything about that either. When she and Elena were alone later, she could tell her the whole story. She would be glad Ivy had found a way to send a letter to Jacob. Ivy could hardly believe it had turned out to be so simple. Perhaps simple wasn't the right way to think about it. More an answer to prayer.

"I'm surprised you didn't try to pet the ducks instead of chasing them." Elena peered over at her.

Ivy giggled. "I might have, but Mr. Frazier asked me to scare them away. Besides, the poor woman was near hysterics. She kept waving her bonnet at them. I think the ducks thought she had breadcrumbs."

"It seems that artist man should have chased them away

himself." Her mother pulled Ivy's hair tighter. "And not expect a girl to do it. I do hope you didn't ruin your dress."

"I was careful to keep my skirt out of the lake water." She thought it best not to mention the duck droppings. "Mr. Frazier had his hands full with his palette and brush, and I didn't mind helping the lady."

"I saw him painting a couple of days ago. He does put on quite a show." She tapped the top of Ivy's head with the comb. "But not one you should spend your time watching." She looked over at Elena. "Either of you."

"Why not?" Elena didn't look at Mother. "He merely puts on a theatrical act to attract more prospective subjects. Perhaps you should have a portrait done, Mother. The one he did of Vanessa was wonderful. He always makes the ladies look beautiful."

"I'm quite satisfied with my looks. I don't need the flattery of an artist's brush. And you both need to keep in mind that we do not have money to waste on such foolishness as that." She pointed the comb at Elena's reflection. "Besides, I saw this Vanessa. Any capable artist could capture her beauty in a painting."

"She is so pretty. And nice too." Ivy hoped getting her mother to think about Vanessa instead of the artist would stop her from yanking Ivy's hair so hard. It didn't work.

"A woman coming here all alone. There's something strange there." Her mother frowned and jerked a tress of Ivy's hair through her fingers to smooth out some of the curl. Ivy flinched and bit her lip to keep from making a protest.

"She enjoyed herself so much today," Elena said.

"I saw the two of you with General Dawson." Mother finally smiled. "I hope you were properly ladylike, Elena."

"Of course. I only nibbled on my petit four and made sure to dip down curtsy-style to roll the lawn balls. I was dreadful at it. So was Vanessa, but the general politely did not make fun of our efforts," Elena said. "He can be very entertaining. Vanessa liked him very much, and he seemed to be quite taken with her."

Ivy knew Elena put that last in to poke her mother, who huffed out a breath. She sneaked a look at Elena in the mirror and caught her smile. Thank goodness Mother did not.

"How old do you think he is?" Elena tucked a jeweled comb into her hair. She looked as pretty as Ivy had ever seen her.

Mother put one last pin in Ivy's hair and stepped back to survey her work. "Clive says he is fifty-seven."

Elena whirled around to stare at Mother. "Clive?"

"General Dawson." Mother stepped closer to the mirror to smooth her eyebrows.

"You know the general's given name?" Ivy said.

"Well, certainly." Mother licked her finger and ran it over her eyebrows again. "Surely you didn't think his name was General?"

"I thought it might be." Ivy shrugged with a little laugh, but neither her mother nor Elena seemed to hear her. Her mother turned from the mirror to sort through combs and jewelry on the table while Elena kept staring at her.

"He did say he had talked with you." Elena raised her eyebrows. "And does he call you Juanita?"

"He has a very friendly manner. I am sure he called you Elena and your new friend Vanessa."

"Miss Elena. Miss Vanessa."

"He may have said Miss Juanita, but I don't know why you are being so curious about it." Mother turned to look straight at her. They both ignored Ivy. "I have made friends with quite a few of the older crowd out on the veranda. It has been very helpful in knowing which men might be attracted to you. General Dawson is definitely one of them."

"Perhaps I am not the one he's attracted to," Elena said.

"Are you saying it's that Vanessa? I suspect she has a man she's planning to meet here."

"I didn't mean Vanessa. He did ask me how long it had been since Father died."

"Don't be ridiculous, Elena. You are the one to consider all possibilities."

Elena turned away from her mother. "I intend to find a possibility that is not old enough to be my grandfather."

"That is wonderful as long as you remember the reason you need to make a match. You cannot let your emotions get in the way."

"I can't very well ask every man I meet how much is in his bank account."

"You leave that part to me," Mother said. "But I am serious about that artist. Stay away from him. I hear he grew up on a poor dirt farm and hasn't a dime to his name."

"I will do what I want, Mother."

"Very well. Just make sure you want to do what you should."

Ivy stood up and rustled her skirt. She was almost ready to tell about Mr. Frazier sneaking a duck into Madeline's portrait simply to lighten the mood. But that might not work since her mother did not seem to have any fondness for him, and she had promised Mr. Frazier to never divulge that secret. Perhaps talking of Vanessa would be better.

"Did Vanessa say if she wanted to walk down with us? I could go tell her we're ready."

"She didn't say," Elena said.

"I daresay she can find the ballroom without our help." Mother went into the hallway, and they followed her. She pointed toward the door next to theirs. "Check with her if you like."

When Ivy tapped on the door, Vanessa opened it a crack. "Oh, Ivy. You look beautiful, but I'm not quite ready. I will be down very soon. Don't get all the men tired of dancing before I get there." Then without waiting for Ivy to say anything, she closed the door.

Mother frowned. "Has she got something hidden in there?"

"She probably wasn't dressed yet. Or maybe the room was a mess." Ivy made excuses for her, but it did seem odd that she seemed so secretive when she opened her door. Not that she needed to see the room. It would be identical to theirs. Ivy turned back to Elena and Mother. She grabbed Elena's hands and laughed as she swirled her around.

"Let the dance begin." Elena laughed with her.

Even their mother laughed.

21

Ivy's enthusiasm was contagious. Elena danced with her down the hallway without the first worry that somebody might see and think they were acting silly. She supposed they were, but she didn't care.

Whatever else came from their summer at the Springs, Elena was glad for how sharing the hotel room forced her to spend more time with Ivy. At home in Lexington, their paths always seemed to be away from one another. That was her fault. She had been the one to keep the distance between them. She had been the one to spend hours in the garden painting or in her room reading. She had been the one to discourage Ivy whenever she tried to step closer.

Ever since she had been tasked with watching Ivy when they were children, she had nursed an unreasonable resentment. She knew it wasn't Ivy's fault. She had only been three, but Elena, at nine, had been a child too. Then Ivy was so much prettier than Elena could ever hope to be. And had such a sweet nature. It was only natural for everyone to look past Elena to admire Ivy.

Elena had become the sour older sister, something like the older brother in the Bible story about the prodigal son. Not that Ivy was like the younger son. She wasn't. But Elena had never been ready to celebrate a party for her sister, even when she deserved one. That made her ashamed, and she wanted to find ways to make it up to her little sister.

After she and Ivy did another whirl in the hallway, Elena peeked back at her mother to see if she was frowning at their silliness. But no, she was smiling, not looking bothered at all. That was Ivy. She had a way of bringing sunshine wherever she was. Elena hoped some of that would rub off on her now that she was ready to leave her resentment behind.

Music floated up the stairway to them. It was no wonder General Dawson came here to escape his loneliness. Such a wonderful place that aimed to make a person healthy and happy. When they reached the ballroom, she wasn't surprised to see him coming to meet them.

He gave a little bow. "Ladies, I've been watching for you because I knew you would all three be a treat for these old eyes."

Ivy smiled with a quick nod to acknowledge the compliment, then slipped away before the old gentleman could ask her to dance. Elena looked at her mother. Was that flush on her cheeks from their walk down to the ballroom or from the general's greeting?

Whether her mother was right about his intentions to court Elena or Elena right about his possible interest in her mother didn't really matter on this night. She was there to dance. She would keep a smile on her face, pleasant words on her lips, and let tomorrow take care of itself.

"Since it seems young Miss Ivy has rushed away to find a better dancing partner, which of you lovely ladies will agree to take a round of the dance floor with me?" He smiled at Mother, then Elena.

"Why don't you take the first dance, Mother? The song they are playing is one you like and with a slow tempo."

"The very kind of dance that is best for a man like me." The general held out his hand toward Mother. "Come, Juanita. Won't you dance with me?"

No *Miss* or *Mrs.* there, Elena noted.

"I couldn't, General." Mother whipped out a fan from some unseen pocket and unfolded it. She fluttered it in front of her face. "It wouldn't be proper in my state of bereavement."

"Very well," he said. "Then I will circle the floor with your lovely daughter and afterwards, if you will allow me, come sit a spell with you. I want to hear more about those twin boys you say love horses."

Elena didn't shrink away from his hand as he reached toward her. She didn't even want to. "I did promise you a dance."

He was old but such a gentleman that she no longer had any aversion to dancing with him as she had on that first night at the Springs. It helped that she had learned how to keep her toes away from his feet.

"If I remember correctly, you may have promised me two dances."

Elena laughed. "Perhaps I did."

They moved out onto the dance floor among the other dancers. "Where is your friend, Miss Vanessa?"

"She will be down soon."

"Good. She promised me dances too." He looked very pleased with himself.

"So she did. You may be the most popular man on the dance floor tonight."

"The most envied, for a certainty." He smiled at her.

They chatted about their lawn bowling adventures as they moved to the music. While Elena listened and smiled, she did notice Kirby Frazier when he moved past them with one of the older women. That was part of Dr. Graham's instructions for him if he wanted to continue here at the Springs, or so he told her on the first night. He was not only to paint the ladies' portraits but also be a willing partner at the balls. The doctor didn't want any of his guests feeling like unhappy wallflowers, whatever their age or appearance.

She smiled. Perhaps that was the reason he danced with her. Not that she'd had to worry about being a wallflower. Not with the men so outnumbering the ladies.

Ivy rolled her eyes at her and grinned when she swept by with one of the young men who seemed to always be in the line to dance with her. When Elena had asked her his name, Ivy had shrugged. "I don't know. Aaron or Adam. Something with an A, I think. He's a good dancer, but not much of a talker."

"He surely told you his name."

"I'm sure he did on the first night we were here, but so many names circled in my head that night, I couldn't possibly remember them all. And now, since he is forever saying 'Miss Ivy' this, 'Miss Bradford' that, I can't very well let him know that I forgot his, now, can I?"

"I'm sure Mother could find out for you."

"I don't care what his name is, and I certainly don't want Mother deciding he might be a good match for me when I'm already matched with Jacob."

Yes, Jacob. Elena should have talked to Ivy about how to get a letter to him. The general would no doubt know someone headed back to Lexington who could take it. That might have made Ivy stop running away whenever she saw General Dawson coming to ask for a dance.

Kirby danced past again and winked at her. She was almost sure he did. It made her forget to listen for a moment to General Dawson's story about his horse coming up lame somewhere in the west years ago and the miles he had to walk. But she nodded. He really didn't need very much encouragement to continue his stories.

As the music ended, they started off the floor to where her mother had found a seat.

"Who is that?" one of the men close to them asked his companion.

A murmur went through the dancers as they seemed to turn as one toward the stairway down into the ballroom.

"I think our beautiful new friend, Miss Vanessa, has arrived." The general looked practically mischievous. "And can you imagine what all these young fellows are going to think when she gives me her first dance? And after I just danced with another beauty."

"You are too kind, General." Whether it was true or not, the words were nice to hear.

"Truth doesn't take kindness, but let us go welcome Miss Vanessa. She looks a little flustered by the attention."

He led the way over to where Vanessa did indeed look as though she might turn and run back up the steps. Relief flooded her face when she saw them.

"Oh, Elena, I am so glad to see you. And you too, General." She sounded slightly breathless. "Why is everyone staring at me?"

"Because of how you look in that evening dress," Elena said.

Vanessa would grab the notice of every man at the dance no matter what she wore, but her silvery pink dress with darker pink bows tracing a line down the shimmering skirt left no doubt that she was the princess of the ball.

Vanessa touched the low bodice that revealed her pale shoulders and then fingered the ribbons on the off-the-shoulder sleeves. "Is something wrong with my dress?"

"Only that it is so beautiful, it has astounded everyone here," the general said. "And if I recall correctly from our earlier conversation, you promised to dance with me."

A smile pushed away her concerned look. "I love to dance."

"Then you have come to the right place." General Dawson looked from Vanessa to Elena as she freed her hand from his arm. "Thank you for the lovely dance, my dear. We will dance again before the night is through, but now I will surrender you to others. I must get Miss Vanessa off on the right foot." He waggled his bushy eyebrows at Vanessa as he took her hand. "I hope Miss Elena warned you to watch your toes."

Vanessa laughed and stepped out onto the dance floor with the general. The band struck up a new song, and when another man extended a hand to Elena, she took it.

The dance went on, but the whispers did as well. She wondered if there had been as many whispers when Ivy, her mother, and she first came to the ballroom. If so, perhaps she had been too nervous to notice. Then again, something a bit mysterious seemed to hover around Vanessa, a young woman alone.

· · · ·

In the shadows next to a window, Andrew leaned against the wall. The room was very warm with the lit candelabras and the crowd of people. Sheer curtains covered the windows to keep out the moths and other insects drawn to the candlelight while allowing some cooler outside air to flow in.

He pulled at his cravat and wished he could be outside in that cooler air. Earlier he had danced with a couple of ladies. That should keep Dr. Graham happy. Andrew didn't mind dancing. In fact, at one time he had loved waltzing, but that was with Gloria.

The memory of their last dance, when he had thought all was well between them, came to mind, but the stab of the memory wasn't as sharp as it had been days ago. Perhaps his grandfather was right to insist he come to the Springs to take the waters.

Not that drinking any kind of water could heal a fractured heart. But this place with its beauty and multiple entertainments, from rifle shooting to battledore to backgammon and bridge, had a way of keeping him too busy to sink into sorrowful reverie.

Gloria had made her choice. He was not that choice. She had gone with another. Not man enough to keep her. That was what his father would have said, but what his father thought or said no longer mattered. So what if he liked roses? Grandfather Scott liked roses, and he had been a captain in the army. While Andrew had no desire to be a soldier like his grandfather, he had learned plenty of other things from him. He had taught Andrew how to train a horse and how to appreciate the beauty of roses.

Thinking of roses brought Elena to mind. Only a few moments before, she had danced past him with General Dawson. Andrew smiled and had to give the old gentleman credit. He always seemed to get the loveliest girls at the ball to dance with him.

Elena. She had looked so lovely, so natural, among the roses that morning. He had enjoyed watching her and, in fact, had watched her for a while before he made himself known to her.

He had liked watching her dance by with the general too. She actually looked as if she enjoyed dancing with the old soldier. And why not? General Dawson had always been full of entertaining stories whenever he visited the farm. He had made a fortune in land investments and owned two of Grandfather Scott's best horses. The rumor going around was that the general was tired of the widower's lonely life and was looking to find a new wife. He didn't look lonely now, but the season at the Springs didn't last through the year. In the winter months, sunshine could be scant and the world gray.

A lady to sit by the fire with him would surely brighten up a winter day. Could the old man be thinking to capture a wife as young as Elena? Andrew frowned at the thought. He didn't like picturing Elena in that other chair in front of the general's fireplace.

With a little shake of his head, he pushed those feelings aside. He barely knew the woman. What she did or didn't do was hardly any concern to him, but telling himself that didn't keep him from hoping General Dawson had no plans to pursue Elena as a wife.

When Elena's dance with the general had ended and the dancers were moving off the floor, a murmur had swept through the room.

The young woman Andrew had seen having her portrait done earlier had come into the ballroom. She looked like Cinderella appearing at the prince's ball, but if she wore glass slippers, her long ball gown hid them.

The general, with Elena still at his side, had hurried to greet her. Andrew had to smile when the woman's face lit up as she had let the old gentleman lead her onto the dance floor.

Perhaps he should ask the general to share his magic with the women. The old fellow would probably say magic had nothing to do with it. That a man simply had to ask. And why not?

As Andrew made his way around the floor to be ready to capture the next dance with Elena, he felt lighter on his feet somehow. Perhaps the doctor's spring water did truly have healing properties. Or perhaps his grandfather had been right that all he needed was to stop hiding out on the farm. Gloria was gone. It was time for him to start living again.

22

The band played two more songs before Andrew managed to be first in line to request a dance with Elena.

"Andrew, I hoped you would ask me to dance." She took his hand. "I looked for you earlier but didn't see you."

"You were too busy dancing."

"And what were you doing? Surely, it didn't take Dr. Graham to coerce you into dancing with me." She smiled. "Don't answer that. I would be humiliated if it were true, and as you said this morning, friends can't lie to one another."

"Did I say that?"

"I think so. I do know you said we should rejoice in the day the Lord had made."

He shook his head. "You probably thought that odd."

"Not at all. I liked it. But the Lord makes the nights too. Do you think he minds if we are dancing?"

"Who, the Lord?" When she nodded, he went on. "I think King David and some others did some dancing in the Bible."

"Different kinds of dances, I'm sure."

"True, but as Dr. Graham is fond of saying, dancing is fine exercise, which he will be the first to tell you is every bit as necessary to good health as his spring water."

"I see. That's a relief." Elena lowered her voice. "Please don't tell him, but I have only taken one sip of his spring water."

Andrew laughed. "It will remain our secret. Friends can have secrets, can they not?"

"From others, I suppose, but not from each other."

"Everyone has secrets, even from those dearest to them." He looked down at her. She did have lovely eyes. "I'm sure you have secrets you haven't shared with even your little sister."

"Should I have any secrets, I'd be afraid to tell them to Ivy. If I did, they wouldn't be secret long. She struggles to not tell all she knows."

He nodded toward the girl dancing by them. "It's no secret she loves to dance. And the new lady seems to as well."

"Vanessa did say that is true." Elena peered over his shoulder. "There she is. You should have seen some of the men's faces when she gave her first dance to General Dawson."

"The old gentleman has a way with the ladies. I saw you dancing with him earlier."

"We both promised him a dance earlier today. He taught Vanessa and me how to lawn bowl, although we weren't very good at getting the balls to roll where we wanted them to. Have you ever played?"

"I have, but I wouldn't want to play against General Dawson. He has a way of always winning." He felt an odd pang at the words and frowned. They were only talking about a yard game. It hardly mattered who won at lawn bowling.

"I don't think he had to try very hard to outdo us, but we had the most laughs."

"Is Vanessa a relation or friend of yours? You seem to already know her while everyone else is buzzing with curiosity."

"A very new friend. She's in the room next to ours. Ivy was in the hallway when Vanessa arrived this morning. And as Ivy does, she made friends with her immediately."

"Did anyone come with her?" Andrew asked.

"Ivy didn't see anyone."

"So, she is a mystery woman."

"Why do you say that?"

"No family with her. No one here seems to know her. A regular Cinderella to the ball." Andrew smiled. "Should we look outside to see if she has a coach pulled by mice?"

"They wouldn't be mice again until midnight." Elena laughed. "Besides, who is the prince who will fall madly in love with her?"

"I don't think there are any princes here. But I wouldn't doubt several infatuated men might be ready to chase after her."

"Will you be one of them?" She gave him a teasing smile.

"Hardly." He kept his voice casual.

"You should dance with her. She's a perfectly delightful girl. Still, it's interesting that you mention Cinderella. I have the feeling this is all new to Vanessa. She seems as tentative about being here as I imagine Cinderella might have been when she entered the prince's ball."

"You don't think she is accustomed to dancing and being admired as she is this evening?"

"I don't know." Elena hesitated before going on. "She surely is, but she did act so excited about everything today as though she had been given a dozen surprises to open on Christmas morning. Each thing was like a never-seen-before gift."

"It does seem strange that she is here alone."

"My mother thinks so, but Vanessa says her father, a judge in Louisville, couldn't get away yesterday to come with her. Legal duties, I suppose."

"A judge? Did she mention his name?"

"Her last name is Hasting. I assume her father would be Judge Hasting."

"Judge Hasting," Andrew repeated with a frown. "I know Judge Hasting. He owns one of the horses stabled at our farm."

"Then you do need to get in line for a dance with her. She will be thrilled that you know her family."

"I think I will ask her for a dance."

Among the dancers, he caught sight of the mystery woman again. He definitely would. The Judge Hasting he knew had no daughters. There must be a mistake in the name. He pushed the thought aside as the song came to an end. He looked down into Elena's eyes and wanted to delay their parting. "Are you going to be out among the roses again tomorrow morning?"

"I hope so. At least somewhere in the gardens. There are so many beautiful places to explore here." When she smiled, her eyes became even lovelier. "How about you? An early morning for you again?"

"Perhaps. If I could have the hope of finding an artist at work amongst the flowers."

A blush he was almost sure had nothing to do with the warmth in the room colored her cheeks. She lowered her gaze a moment, then seemed amused when she looked back up at him. "Hide-and-seek in the gardens. I hadn't heard about that game here at the Springs."

"Sounds like one I might like to play." He laughed. "As long as someone didn't hide so well I never found her."

"I guess that remains to be seen." She twisted her lips to the side to hide her smile and raised her eyebrows.

"Yes, in the morning."

The music stopped, but they stayed where they were as though waiting for a new song to begin as the other dancers moved past them off the floor. Finally, Elena said, "Thank you for the dance."

"The pleasure was all mine." Then as she began to turn away from him, he reached out to catch her arm. "If I don't have that pleasure again this evening, I better tell you now."

"Tell me?" She cocked her head to the side and looked up at him. "What is that?"

"When daylight comes again, ready or not, here I come."

• • • •

Elena had to laugh. She'd heard that yelled many times when the neighborhood children were playing in their yard, but never had it felt as if it was meant only for finding her.

She moved toward the tables where her mother sat with General Dawson. Andrew didn't follow her. That was all right. Tomorrow morning they could talk as the sun came up. If he could find her.

"You are looking very pleased, lovely Elena." Kirby Frazier stepped in front of her. "Is it because you saw me heading your way to beg a dance from you?"

"That could be." As Elena took his hand, she looked behind her, but she couldn't see Andrew. No doubt he had already found a new partner for the next dance.

"Looking for someone? Perhaps General Dawson?"

"No one in particular." Elena turned her attention back to Kirby. "But I do owe the general another dance. But he says it can't be a quadrille."

"Seems the band is playing more waltzes and two-step numbers this evening." Kirby put an arm loosely around her waist as the music started up. "We seem to be in luck with another waltz."

They moved out with the other dancers all turning and whirling the same way. They must look like a spinning wheel of pastel dresses and dark suits. She wondered if that was something she might paint. She wouldn't have to draw faces that distinctly. Just the dancing figures and swirling skirts.

"I think the quadrilles are fun," Elena said.

"They are, but they make conversation difficult as one goes back and forth between partners as the moves are called."

"That may be why General Dawson doesn't like them. He prefers a captive audience for his stories."

She looked up at Kirby. He and Andrew were so different.

If she didn't know better, she would pick Andrew as the artist and Kirby as the horseman. But then, Andrew had said he
cultivated roses too, and hadn't Kirby handled the stagecoach
horses? It wasn't good to judge a person on looks alone. Or on
the money in their pockets.

"Those stories do appear to attract the beautiful ladies."
Kirby smiled. "Your friend Vanessa gave him her first dance."

"Have you danced with her?" Was that why Kirby was glad
for the waltz to give them a chance to talk? Did he want to know
more about Vanessa?

"I did."

"She appears to have no lack of willing partners." Elena
smiled as she spotted Vanessa moving past them. "Your portrait
of her was wonderful."

"I could paint your portrait." He tightened his arm a bit
against her back to pull her closer to him. "Although I'm not
sure I could ever properly capture your eyes in paint."

She resisted enough to keep an appropriate distance between
them, but she wondered how it would be to surrender to an
embrace in his strong arms. She pushed away the thought as
his words played back through her mind. "My eyes? There's
nothing that special about my eyes."

"Have you never looked in a mirror?" He sounded surprised.

"All the time." He probably had some such compliment for
all his dance partners. It meant nothing. "Ivy is the beauty in
our family."

"She is very pretty. She posed for me today."

"She did? I don't think Mother would approve of that."

"It wasn't a portrait but a sketch of a girl with ducks." He
laughed. "Did she tell you about the ducks and Miss Southworth? I rather think I shan't get Miss Southworth to agree
to a dance this evening." He didn't look as though that disappointed him.

"That's too bad. Ivy did mention chasing ducks away from

the lady, but she didn't tell us about posing with ducks." Elena raised her eyebrows. "I'm surprised she was capable of keeping that secret."

"And can you keep secrets, Miss Elena?"

"I don't think I have any to keep."

"That I don't believe." He peered down at her with a searching look. "I see secrets hidden in the depths of your remarkable eyes."

A tingle went up her back. The man did have a way with words. She was glad when the tempo of the song picked up and left little breath for talking as they moved faster to stay in step. She supposed she did have secrets, as they pretended to be here at the Springs only to take the waters instead of attempting to take a husband. A wealthy husband to keep their future secure.

She thought of the other dancers as they circled the dance floor in unison. How many others here had secrets they couldn't share? This man she was dancing with had some of his own. She was sure of that the same as she'd been sure Andrew had things he did not want to speak aloud. Even General Dawson, who seemed ready to tell every story in his past, no doubt had things he would never share.

Then there was Vanessa with her dramatic entrance this evening. Why would a judge's daughter, who surely had been to many balls, look so uncertain? She had to know she was beautiful. Mirrors would reveal that to her.

Mirrors? Hadn't Kirby just said the same about mirrors to her? But those were simply flattering words. Her eyes were, well, her eyes. The color shifting from blue to green could sometimes look a little different, but that wasn't remarkable. Merely odd. She shouldn't start believing a silver-tongued artist.

But then hadn't Andrew said something the same? She gave herself a mental shake. She needed to concentrate on moving her feet and making sure not to step on the hem of her dress when she dipped down a bit.

She caught sight of herself in one of the long mirrors that were spaced here and there along the walls. And then there was Vanessa, smiling and laughing. Andrew was right about her being the Cinderella of the ball, but where was Prince Charming?

Who was her Prince Charming? Once, a long time ago, she'd read that love matches were made in the stars. She simply had to wait until she found him or he found her. Everything else about the book was long forgotten, but that romantic idea had taken root in her mind. She had never been ready to settle for any but the very right one. The one written in the stars. Then when she never met anyone glittering with stardust, she had stopped entertaining such foolishness.

The band began playing even faster and Elena missed a step and nearly tripped. Kirby gripped her waist and lifted her with ease to keep pace with the music and in step with him. For a moment she felt as though she were dancing on air.

Laughter along with a few sighs of relief rippled through the dancers when the music stopped. With the sound of her heart pounding in her ears, Elena tried to catch her breath. Whether she was breathless from the dance or from Kirby being slow to release her, she dared not try to determine.

Kirby looked over her head toward the band. "The fiddler tried to set his bow on fire with that one. If he'd played any faster, we'd have been flying, but there is no one I'd rather be flying with." He captured her hand and, before she knew what he meant to do, lifted it to kiss her fingers. "Don't forget to come see me at the lake. I'm already thinking of the paints I must mix to capture those eyes of yours."

"I'm not sure that can happen." She pulled her hand away from his.

"But it must. Some things are meant to be. Us in the same stagecoach. Dancing together to that particular song."

She nodded at him with a noncommittal smile as the band

called out a new number. A quadrille. "The dance goes on, and it's time to change partners."

"So it is, but we will have many opportunities to dance again."

An older lady grabbed his arm, and he was gone without a backward glance.

That was good. Better for her not to see stardust on him, for that would be a trail she couldn't follow.

General Dawson stepped up beside her. "I think this dance is mine, Miss Elena."

"It's a quadrille, General," Elena said.

"With you helping me remember the steps, I will be fine."

She smiled and the two of them lined up with three other couples to begin the dance. Certainly no stardust clung to General Dawson, but that didn't mean she couldn't enjoy a dance with the old gentleman. Besides, she needed to brush away the idea of stardust and forget Prince Charming fairy tales.

23

Midnight found the dance floor less crowded as some guests had left the ballroom. Elena's mother claimed the music was giving her a headache and went to their room an hour before. For once, Elena hadn't wanted to accompany her.

Even now, with the clock striking twelve, the night felt young. She stepped to the end of the room for a cup of punch and one of the sweet confections to await the next dance.

Ivy, her cheeks flushed and her curls escaping their pins, came over to gulp down a cup of the fruity drink. "Isn't this the most fun ever? I could dance all night."

"I think we already have." Elena looked out to where the men and women were milling around waiting for the music to start again.

"Look, there's Vanessa. I think she's danced with every man here." When Ivy waved at her, the woman came over to them carrying a drink.

"Are you having a good time?" Elena asked.

"It is so wonderful. I love dancing, and the music is perfect."

She sipped her drink. "And this punch is divine. I hope this night never ends."

Just then, the bandleader called out that they were playing the last song of the evening. Always a waltz. A scattering of protests went around the room.

The man held up a hand. "Every dance must end. Whether you have run out of steps or not, we are running out of notes. So find your favorite partner and go around one last time this evening before we must say good night."

"Uh-oh, here comes the general." Ivy put down her cup. "I'm not finishing the night with him."

She was gone to be captured by the young man who was obviously entranced with her. Elena had found out his name was Aubrey. From the smile on Ivy's face as she followed him out on the dance floor, she wondered if Ivy even cared about sending that letter to Jacob anymore.

"I'll dance with him," Elena told Vanessa.

"No, no." Vanessa took another quick drink before giving her cup to one of the servants passing by with a tray. "Let me. I promised him two dances. I know you did too, but you've already had the two dances. I saw you doing the quadrille with him. He was so nice to us today."

"Whatever you want." Elena shrugged.

"You will be able to find another partner, won't you? Of course you will. Everyone wants to dance with you."

"And you."

Vanessa pulled a handkerchief from some fold of her dress to dab against her forehead. "Have they closed the windows? It seems so warm in here all of a sudden."

"Are you all right, Miss Vanessa?" The general looked concerned as he stepped up beside them.

"Oh yes. I am fine and hoping you have come to ask me for this last dance." She smiled and tucked away her handkerchief.

"The last dance. I would be honored." General Dawson nodded at Elena and led Vanessa out onto the floor as the music started.

For a few seconds, Elena thought she might be left without a partner, until Andrew appeared in front of her and held out his hand in invitation.

"Ready or not?" Elena took his hand. "You seem to have found me before the morning."

"I couldn't let the prettiest girl at the ball miss the last dance."

Whether his words were true or not, they made her smile as she let him lead her out onto the dance floor. "That's very kind of you, sir."

"Kindness has nothing to do with it."

"Then the good doctor must have insisted you get more dancing exercise."

"He will be smiling for certain."

"I saw you dancing with Vanessa. Was she surprised that you knew her father?"

"You could say that." A shadow swept across his face. "We didn't dance long. She said she felt ill and needed a rest. But I noticed she was back on the floor with another man before I found a spot by the windows. I think I was what was making her feel ill."

"You?" Elena frowned. "What would make you think that? Perhaps she only needed a moment to catch her breath."

"That could be. She was a little pale. Perhaps our Cinderella is not accustomed to so much dancing. Or perhaps her glass slippers were pinching her toes."

"The clock has struck midnight, and she doesn't seem to have changed from a princess back to a servant girl." Elena caught sight of Vanessa and General Dawson. They were at the edge of the floor and appeared to be moving very slowly and no longer in time with the music.

"Miss Elena, Andrew," the general called when they danced closer. "Miss Vanessa is feeling faint. I fear I may not be able to assist her to a chair quickly enough."

Even as he spoke, Vanessa slumped against him and the old gentleman staggered back. Andrew covered the few feet between them and caught Vanessa before both she and the general fell. He lowered her gently to the floor.

Elena knelt beside her. "Vanessa, what's wrong?"

The woman grabbed at her chest.

"Get the doctor, Andrew," General Dawson ordered. "Elena, loosen her stays."

Andrew headed across the dance floor to find Dr. Graham. The general went for water.

Elena felt for buttons, but Vanessa pushed her hands away. "Too late," she whispered.

"Don't say that." Elena touched the woman's face. Her skin was clammy.

"We had such fun." Her body stiffened as she gasped for air.

"We'll have more fun tomorrow. Relax and try to breathe."

Vanessa clutched Elena's arm. "No one will ever know . . ." Her words trailed off too faint for Elena to hear.

"What?"

Her answer was a mere whisper of breath. "Why" or maybe "who."

"Shh. You can tell me later."

A smile touched her lips when General Dawson crouched down beside her with a cup of water. "I hear music."

Her hand went limp on Elena's arm.

"Vanessa!" Elena grabbed her shoulders to shake her.

The general put down the water and took Elena's hands. "She's gone, dear."

"Gone? What do you mean?" Elena jerked her hands free. She couldn't take in his words. "She can't be gone. Minutes ago she was dancing. She was fine."

Everything about Vanessa looked perfect. The general had to be wrong. She couldn't be gone. Not dead.

The music stopped. A sudden hush fell over the ballroom.

"There's nothing we can do for her now." General Dawson stroked Vanessa's arm.

Elena stared at Vanessa's face, which was pale as moonlight. The vibrant blue of her eyes dulled. Behind them, Dr. Graham was telling people to stay back as he made his way toward them. A buzz of questions followed him.

"What has happened?" Dr. Graham helped General Dawson to his feet, then knelt in his place beside Elena.

"The general says she's gone." Elena sat back as the doctor placed his fingers to the side of Vanessa's neck to feel for a pulse.

Elena pressed her fist against her lips to hold back a sob when the doctor lowered his head and muttered a prayer before he gently pushed the young woman's eyelids closed.

Strong hands reached down to pull Elena to her feet. Andrew wrapped his arms around her. "I'm so sorry, Elena."

She leaned against him. "How can she have died like this? We were drinking punch together only moments ago before the music started for the last dance."

"I don't know." Andrew rubbed his hand up and down her back. The buzz in the room grew louder as some people pressed forward to see what was happening.

Dr. Graham stood and took control. "Please, everyone. Stay back. One of our young ladies has had a medical issue. We will be caring for her, but please, I must ask the rest of you to go on to your rooms. The ball is over."

"Is she dead?" a man shouted.

The doctor didn't answer him. "I will let everyone know in the morning about the lady's condition."

"Does that mean she's still alive? That there is hope?" Elena whispered.

Andrew leaned his head down close to her ear to answer. "I think not. Dr. Graham simply wants everyone to leave before he does whatever else needs to be done."

"I can't believe it." She started to turn her head to look at

Vanessa again, but Andrew stopped her with a gentle hand against her cheek.

"Remember her the way she was earlier. Not there with the life gone."

"Is it that new woman? The one none of us knew?" another voice, a woman's this time, demanded.

"Vanessa?" From somewhere among the dancers, Ivy let out a little scream.

Elena stepped back from Andrew to look for her. Ivy pushed through the people to stop in front of her.

"You've been crying." Her voice sounded accusing. "Is she all right? Vanessa?"

Elena shook her head slightly and pulled Ivy closer. "Don't make a scene. Let Dr. Graham do what he thinks is best."

"But Elena." Ivy peered past Elena. "Why aren't they helping her?"

"Shh." Elena touched Ivy's cheek. "We can talk when we go to our room."

She started away with Ivy, but the doctor stopped her. "Please, stay here, Miss Bradford. I will need to talk to you and Andrew. And to General Dawson after we clear the ballroom. Andrew, get the ladies chairs."

Some of the people in the room headed for the stairs out of the ballroom, but others continued to mill around.

Dr. Graham spotted Kirby among them. "Frazier, escort any who might need assistance to their rooms." Then he motioned to some servants behind them. "Help clear the room. But first bring a tablecloth."

Andrew brought the chairs. Elena sat down but wished she could still be leaning against Andrew. He had looked almost frail when she first saw him on the stagecoach, but a moment ago, he had felt like a wall of strength. She watched him help the doctor cover Vanessa with the cloth a servant brought.

General Dawson came over to Elena's chair. His face was

gray, and the sparkle in his eyes was quenched by sadness. He looked shakier on his feet than he had that first night she danced with him.

She stood up. "Here, General. Take my chair."

He hesitated. "I wouldn't normally agree to sit when a lady has to stand, but this is making me feel my years." He sank down into the chair.

Ivy jumped to her feet. "Take my chair, Elena. I don't think I can sit still anyway." Her gaze went to the shape of Vanessa's body under the tablecloth. But then after Elena sat down, she dropped to the floor beside her in a cloud of organza and petticoats. She scooted close to Elena's chair. Elena started to warn her that she would get her dress dirty, but then it didn't seem to really matter.

She ran her fingers down Ivy's cheek. "You could go on to the room. Dr. Graham didn't say you needed to stay."

"Please, don't make me go." Ivy's eyes beseeched her. "Mother will already be asleep, and I can't bear to be alone."

"All right."

"What happened to her?"

"I don't know. She was dancing with General Dawson and just collapsed."

"What did he do to her?"

Beside Elena, the general pulled in a breath but didn't say anything.

Elena put a hand on his arm. "She didn't mean that. She's upset. We are all upset."

"Yes," he said softly as he covered her hand with his. His fingers were cold despite the warmth of the room. She felt a tremble, but she wasn't sure whether it was his hand or hers that was shaking.

Elena turned her attention back to Ivy. "The general was dancing with her, Ivy. He would have never done anything to hurt her." The general gave her hand a little squeeze.

"I know." Ivy peeked around Elena's skirt at General Dawson. "I'm sorry, sir."

"Understandable, child." His voice broke.

"I can't believe this." Tears filled Ivy's eyes. "We were just talking to her."

Elena slid her hand away from the general to pull Ivy's head over into her lap and smooth down her curls. They had escaped from the pins meant to keep the elaborate style their mother had fashioned for Ivy. Elena wondered if her own hair looked as unkempt, but she didn't reach up to check. What difference did a stray strand of hair make now with death stealing one so young?

She stared at Vanessa's body. She had been full of a joyous wonder all day long and had danced as if she never wanted the music to end. But the music had ended.

24

Kirby had to tamp down his temper when Dr. Graham ordered him around as though he were a servant. He wanted to tell him to clear his own room, but instead he started ushering people away from the group around the doctor and toward the stairway. What choice did he have? As yet, he hadn't accomplished what he came to Graham Springs to do.

Now wasn't the time to think about that. Whatever was happening across the room looked serious.

Elena was there. So was General Dawson. Kirby still couldn't imagine the old man trying to court Elena, even if he had heard gossip about him looking for a bride.

Kirby didn't want any gossip like that about him, but he was doing the same. Looking for a bride. A bride like Elena Bradford. She intrigued him. Not that he was falling in love with her. He had no intention of being caught in a net of love.

Elena appeared to be trying to comfort her sister, who had sunk to the floor beside her. Whatever could be wrong? And why was that Andrew Harper hovering around them? From the talk going around, Harper was suffering from melancholy, the result of a broken engagement. Too bad about that. The man needed to pull himself together and stay out of Kirby's way. He wasn't about to let anybody rob him of his chance with Elena.

He moved over behind her. "Are you ladies all right?"

Ivy scrambled up off the floor to grab his arms. "Oh, Mr. Frazier. It's awful. Terrible. Vanessa." She choked on the name and didn't seem able to go on.

He saw the body in front of them then. The woman's upper body was covered, but enough of the silvery pink dress showed below the cloth to let him know it was Vanessa Hasting.

Before Kirby could put his arms around Ivy to comfort her, Elena stood and turned her away from him.

"Take a deep breath, Ivy, and get control of your emotions." Elena grabbed the girl's hands.

Ivy sniffed and pulled away from Elena to rub her wet cheeks. "I need a handkerchief."

That Harper guy had his handkerchief to her before Kirby could reach for his pocket. What was he doing here anyway? Why hadn't he been cleared out with the others?

"Thank you, Andrew," Elena said.

Andrew. That didn't sound good. She not only used his first name, but she did it without hesitation. Hadn't she still called him Mr. Frazier today when she brought her friend to pose for a portrait? The friend who lay on the floor with her body covered now.

He reached for Elena's hand, but she didn't appear to notice. She sat down with her back to him. Harper was there almost at once with another chair for Ivy. He seemed to be one step ahead with whatever was needed.

Elena put an arm around Ivy and didn't even glance back at Kirby. He supposed that was to be expected in this kind of situation. It had to be a shock to be sitting by a friend's body, but the same as when the stagecoach horses had run away, she wasn't falling apart.

It was a shock to all of them. General Dawson looked stunned.

Kirby wouldn't be surprised if the old man fell out of his chair to join the poor girl on the floor. Oddly enough for a man suffering from melancholy, Harper looked composed. Then again, he, the same as Elena, had kept his composure on the stagecoach.

Near an outside door, Dr. Graham talked with one of his men before he came back to where they waited as if they were on trial. Harper was there with a chair for him too.

Dr. Graham frowned at Kirby. "Why are you still here, Frazier? I told everyone to clear the room other than Miss Bradford, Andrew, and the general." He spared a glance at Ivy. "I can see that young Miss Bradford is in need of her sister's support."

"Thank you, Doctor," Elena said softly as Ivy dabbed her eyes with Harper's handkerchief.

"Frazier?" The doctor stared at him.

General Dawson spoke up. "You best let him stay, C.C. He was with the deceased as much as any of us, except perhaps Miss Elena."

"Very well." The doctor looked down at his hands.

"Have you sent for the sheriff?" General Dawson asked.

"I have, even though I have no reason to think it necessary. The poor girl appears to have perhaps danced too energetically, such as to make her heart give out."

"Is such a thing possible?" Ivy's eyes were wide.

"No worry, miss. While possible, it is very, very rare. Miss Hasting must have had a weakness of the heart muscle." The doctor gave her a comforting look before he turned his gaze to Elena. "Now, tell me, Miss Bradford, what you know about this lady."

"I just met her today. Ivy"—she nodded toward her sister—"she met Vanessa early this morning after she arrived by coach."

The doctor's eyes went back to Ivy. "I see. Who was with her?"

"I didn't see anyone else. She looked so terribly alone. That's why I spoke to her. Of course, I would have spoken to her anyway since I was there in the hallway when she came up the steps. I always speak to everyone."

"The two of you talked?"

"A little."

"What did she say?"

Ivy looked thoughtful. "She told me her name, and I told her mine. She wanted to know what I was doing, and I said I was watching for my sister to come back from the gardens, where I thought she might have been doing some sketching."

"Dr. Graham only needs to know about Vanessa, Ivy," Elena said.

"Yes, sorry." Ivy looked at Elena, then back at Dr. Graham. "I don't really know anything else. I went on toward the stairs. She went into the room next to ours. When Elena and I returned to our room, the hallway was empty, but I told Elena about Vanessa and how she'd like to meet her."

"Which I assume you did, Miss Elena." The doctor turned his attention to Elena.

"Not then, but later. When I went back out, I knocked on her door to introduce myself."

"Was anyone in the room with her?"

"I wouldn't know. She slipped out into the hall without opening the door wide enough to see past her."

"Didn't that seem odd to you?" Dr. Graham asked.

"Not really. I assumed she was on the verge of leaving her room when I knocked."

"I see. And then what did you do?"

"When we started down the stairs together, she asked if I could do her portrait. That morning Ivy had told her I had been out early to do some sketching." A little blush rose up in Elena's cheeks as if she was embarrassed by the admission. "I told her I lacked that ability, but since she seemed especially excited about having her portrait done, I took her to see Mr. Frazier."

She did finally glance back at him.

"And so, Mr. Frazier, you painted her portrait." Dr. Graham looked at Kirby.

"I did."

"Did she seem ill? Her hands shaking? Anything at all out of the ordinary?"

"Nothing to make me think she wasn't well, even though she did have a dizzy moment when she stood up after sitting for the portrait. Nothing too unusual about that after one has been still for so long." Kirby said. "She was very excited about having her portrait done."

"Yes." General Dawson spoke up. "She acted thrilled to be here as though she had never before experienced anything like things here at the Springs. I saw the two ladies, Miss Elena and Miss Vanessa, at the lake with Mr. Frazier, and since he had finished painting her likeness, I invited them to go with me to the dining room. After we ate, I showed them how to lawn bowl until time for dinner and the dance."

"The dance." Dr. Graham stared down at his hands spread out on his knees for a moment before he looked up at General Dawson. "You were dancing with her."

"I was. She had sweetly promised me dances and allowed me to be her first partner when she came to the ballroom."

"I saw that." Dr. Graham smiled. "You still have the old charm, Clive." His smile faded. "And she was well then?"

"She seemed so."

Dr. Graham looked at Kirby, then Harper. "The two of you danced with her?"

Kirby answered first. "I did. A quadrille."

"And did she talk about anything while you danced?"

"She had to concentrate on the moves. The dance seemed to be one she wasn't as familiar with." Kirby didn't know what the doctor was trying to prove, but whatever it was, he didn't want any blame to cast a shadow on him. "She did say she liked the portrait I'd sent to her room."

"Still there, I guess." Dr. Graham looked at Harper. "And you, Andrew?"

"I did." Harper seemed a little uneasy. "But the music had hardly begun when she claimed to not be feeling well, and I escorted her off the dance floor. There she had a fast recovery since a moment later she was dancing with someone else."

The doctor raised his eyebrows at Harper. "Did you do something to upset her?"

"I might have." Harper shifted on his feet and sent a quick glance toward Elena. "Miss Bradford told me that the lady's father was a judge in Louisville. I think the fact that I was acquainted with Judge Hasting made her uncomfortable."

"Why would that be?" Dr. Graham's eyes narrowed on Harper.

"Judge Hasting has no daughters."

"You are sure of that?"

"I am." Harper sounded very sure.

"Perhaps there are other judges by the same name." Dr. Graham looked thoughtful.

"That could be, but before I could ask the lady about that possibility, she claimed to feel faint."

"You say 'claimed.' Did you not believe her?"

Harper looked even more bothered. "I don't want to speak unkindly about the lady."

The doctor cut into his answer. "It's past time to worry about that. We need to know more about this woman and why she fell dead on my dance floor."

"Then I will say I think she pretended to be ill so I wouldn't ask her more about her father. I don't think she wanted her subterfuge to be found out."

"Subterfuge. An interesting choice of words." The doctor let out a long sigh as he stood up. "Whether you are right or not,

Andrew, I will have to contact Judge Hasting. Perhaps you are wrong about him having no daughters. Or she could be some other relation to him and simply claimed him as her father for some unknown reason." He looked at Elena. "Miss Bradford, is there anything more you can tell us about her? Perhaps whether she showed any sign of illness while you were together today."

"Like Mr. Frazier said, she did get dizzy when she stood up after sitting for her portrait, but she waved it off as nothing. She hadn't eaten, and with the excitement and the midday heat and . . ."

When Elena's voice trailed away, the doctor nodded. "Such can cause difficulties for ladies."

"Yes, but she seemed fine while we were lawn bowling this afternoon," Elena said. "She was bothered by the heat tonight and complained about the warmth of the room while we drank some punch before the music started again."

"You were all drinking punch?" the doctor asked. When both Elena and Ivy nodded, he went on. "Where did you get the punch?"

"A servant came around with trays of drinks," Elena said.

"But that's not where Vanessa got hers." Ivy spoke up. "A man brought her a drink. I assumed it was her last dancing partner. A couple of the gentlemen have done that for me."

The doctor's eyes sharpened on Ivy. "Who was the man?"

Ivy shrank back in her chair. "I didn't pay that much attention. Everyone was milling around, and then the band announced it was the last dance. We were talking with Vanessa, and General Dawson was coming over. I left to find a partner. I didn't want to miss the last dance."

"I see." Dr. Graham turned toward Elena. "Is that the way you remember it as well, Miss Bradford?"

"Yes, except I didn't see Vanessa get her drink. After Ivy left, Vanessa drank the rest of her punch. That's when she complained about the heat. Her face was flushed, and when General

Dawson came up to us, he asked if she felt all right." Elena glanced at the general, who nodded. "But she brushed aside his concerns and took his arm to go out on the dance floor."

"Did you see where she put the glass when she finished her drink?"

"She gave it to one of the servants."

When the doctor's eyes tightened in thought, General Dawson spoke up. "You don't think someone poisoned her, do you, C.C.?"

"No, no, of course not. We don't have those sorts of guests here. The poor girl's heart must have simply given out from too much exertion. A dreadful shame, but such things can happen." He shook his head sadly.

Kirby suddenly remembered the argument he had heard that morning before he went to the rifle range and the threats Sanderson made about the other man's daughter. But that could have nothing to do with this woman. She wasn't even at the Springs until today. He couldn't see any reason to mention it now. Especially since Sanderson was the doctor's nephew.

Dr. Graham went on. "I'm sure more answers will surface on the morrow. Until then, please try to get some sleep. We will think of her in heaven and at peace."

Kirby moved to offer to see Ivy and Elena to their room, but before he could, General Dawson grabbed his arm. "Sorry, Mr. Frazier, but I seem to be a little unsteady on my feet."

"That's to be expected." Dr. Graham looked at Kirby. "Frazier, accompany the general to his room."

"I had thought to escort the two ladies to theirs," Kirby said.

"Andrew can do that. You see to the general," the doctor ordered.

"I would be most grateful for your help, young man." The general tightened his grip on Kirby's arm.

In the general's look at Kirby was the memory of the money he'd stuffed in his pocket earlier. There was also something more. Perhaps an intentional block of his chance to talk to Elena.

"Of course, General. Whatever you need me to do." Kirby had no other choice.

At least he got a smile from Elena, although a wan one, before she turned to go with Harper.

"Such a tragedy," General Dawson said.

"It must have been a shock to you when she collapsed as you were dancing."

"Very much so." The man didn't seem all that unsteady on his feet now.

"I am sure. Odd, don't you think, that she would pretend to be someone she was not?"

"We don't know that for sure."

"That Harper fellow seemed sure."

"That will easily be determined as true or not, but I can't imagine why she would have come under a false name."

"She could have been running away from something. A demanding father or husband, perhaps. Do you think they could have tracked her down here to give her a drink of poison?"

"The doctor would know about that if it were so. I'm sure it's just as he says and that the unfortunate lady had a weak heart. I am sorry to have been her last dance." The old man was quiet a moment before he went on. "But I suppose we all have a last dance at some time."

"I'm not ready to dance my last one just yet."

"I'm sure Miss Vanessa was thinking the same and yet . . ." The man's voice faded away.

"She did." Kirby finished the thought for him.

"None of us are promised tomorrow," the general said.

Kirby didn't say anything as the words echoed in his head. His mother had said that after Rosie died. It had been no comfort to Kirby then, and he couldn't imagine it being a comfort to this woman's family either. Whoever that family was.

The man went on. "But we all expect to see the sun come up on another day. Even an old codger like me. Tonight we can hope that sunrise in a few hours will bring us a better day."

Kirby left him in front of his door. As he headed to his own room, he thought again of the cup of punch someone gave the woman before that last dance and then the argument he'd heard that morning. This woman was not that unknown man's daughter, but then it appeared she wasn't the daughter of the man she claimed was her father either. Not if Harper knew what he was talking about.

He tightened his fists as he went in his room. The smell of paint and the sight of the canvas of the morning's shooting contest on his easel helped him focus. Melancholy Andrew Harper was no more of a challenge to him than the old general.

But even if he were, other women were here at the Springs. Kirby didn't have to capture Elena's favor. He opened up his blue and green paints and took out a dab of each to mix on his palette. He found a small canvas, only five by five, and with fast strokes had two eyes in a face's shape. He carefully dotted the mixed blue and green in the eyes.

Still not right. Would he never get everything right?

25

At their door, Elena thanked Andrew for escorting them to their room.

"Think nothing of it," Andrew said. "If there's anything else I can do for you, please let me know. After all, that's what friends are for."

"Yes, friends." Elena echoed his words.

Ivy smiled slightly and slipped through the door, but Elena watched Andrew walk down the hallway. He was such a nice man. So thoughtful and kind. It was good to count him as a friend.

They shed their party dresses in the moonlight drifting in the windows to keep from waking Mother. Morning would be soon enough to talk about death. The problem was Elena couldn't forget. Nor could Ivy.

After they were in bed, Ivy whispered one question after another, but Elena had no answers. Did Elena see Vanessa fall? Did she think she seemed ill? Could she have been poisoned by the man who brought her punch? And how horrible that would be to consider. What if they had danced with that very man? A murderer. Ivy trembled when she said the word.

Elena put her fingers over Ivy's lips. "Dr. Graham will find the answers. We need to go to sleep."

"I don't know if I can. I keep seeing her lying there with her face covered."

"I know, but we did only know her one day. We can be sad but hardly distraught."

"Seems only right to be distraught over such a sad death whether we knew her well or not." When Ivy's voice rose, their mother shifted in the other bed.

After Elena hushed her, Ivy was silent for a moment before she went on in a whisper. "And we were going to be famous friends. I'm sure we were."

"It did seem that might be, but there is no changing what has happened." Elena kissed Ivy's forehead. "Now turn over and try to sleep."

Ivy did as Elena said. In the silence that fell over the room, Elena heard a whippoorwill call from somewhere. The sound was somehow so sad she had to fight to keep back tears.

"Do you think it was Vanessa's time?" Ivy broke the silence. "The way Mother said it was Father's time? To die, I mean."

"I don't know."

"I don't think it was. Maybe Father's but not Vanessa's. She was too young."

"Babies and children sometimes die," Elena said. "At very young ages."

"Not while they are dancing." Ivy sounded very certain. "I think she was poisoned. That wouldn't be something meant to be."

"We don't know that she was poisoned."

Ivy ignored her words. "That man must have done it. The one I saw give her a drink. I will watch for him. I'm sure I can recognize him."

Fear clutched Elena's heart. "No, Ivy."

Ivy twisted around to peer at Elena. In the moonlight filtering in through the windows, her face looked determined. "I have to."

"No," Elena repeated. "We don't even know that her drink was poisoned."

Without saying anything, Ivy rolled over, away from Elena.

"Promise me you won't do anything to put yourself in danger, Ivy." Elena kept her voice firm.

Ivy's silence pounded against Elena's ears. She repeated her words. "You have to promise!"

"I promise that if I do see the man, I'll tell Dr. Graham. I would never be foolish enough to confront someone who might be a murderer."

Elena wished that made her feel better, but it didn't. She had no trouble imagining Ivy going around peering suspiciously at every man she met. If one of those men had actually poisoned the punch Vanessa drank, he would not hesitate to do more to guard against discovery. Tomorrow she would push that truth at Ivy when she could look the girl fully in the face to make her understand.

Right now, Ivy's body was stiff under Elena's arm. Her own body felt as tense. She pulled in a long breath and let it out slowly. She rubbed her hand up and down Ivy's back and tried to think of something to move them away from thinking about Vanessa no longer in the room next to theirs.

"Did you write your letter?"

"Oh, I haven't told you, have I?" Ivy pushed up off the bed to peer over at Mother. "She's really asleep, don't you think?"

"I think so."

Ivy scooted lower in the bed and jerked Elena down with her. She pulled the coverlet over their heads.

"We might suffocate." Elena pushed up the cover to make a little tent over them. All she could see was the glitter of Ivy's eyes.

"I'll talk fast. Mr. Frazier said Dr. Graham was sending one of his men to Lexington for supplies and had agreed to get some more painting supplies for him. He is going to ask the man to deliver my letter. Mr. Frazier is so nice. And I know he likes you. You two would make a wonderful couple."

"Don't be silly. Mr. Frazier is not on Mother's list of potential husbands. The man is as poor as we are."

"Mother and her plans. She needs to pray and trust the Lord."

"What? To rain down money on us?"

Ivy actually giggled. "That's what he did for me. Sort of, anyway."

"What in the world are you talking about?" The air was moist under the cover. Elena lifted a corner of the cover to take a breath.

Ivy didn't seem bothered by the absence of fresh air. "You know how you said I might find a coin on the pathways? Well, I did. A one-cent piece. It seemed a sign. And then when I chased those ducks away from that lady at the lake, she had dropped her reticule and some coins spilled out. I told her about them, but she said she didn't want them. That they might have duck droppings on them and I could have them. An answer to prayer. Mr. Frazier said it would be enough to pay the man to take the—" She hesitated and took a peek out from under the cover toward Mother before she went on. "Well, the you-know-what to you-know-who."

"You are a wonder, Ivy." Elena had to smile.

"It's the Lord who did a wonder for me." Her voice went to sad again. "But not for Vanessa. Do you think we should pray for her? For her family?"

"That would be nice. And pray for us that we can get some sleep."

Ivy threw back the coverlet and settled down on her pillow. She murmured some prayers, and then her breathing became soft and regular as she surrendered to sleep.

Elena tried to do the same. Send up prayers for peace and the ease of sleep, but instead she stared at the dark air over the bed and wished she was in her father's rose garden with her cat, Willow, winding back and forth around her legs.

She could enjoy rose gardens here, but there were also men she was supposed to entice to marry her. How did a woman do that? And there was a woman—a beautiful young woman— lying dead in the ballroom. One who might have sipped a cup of poison. If that was true, her sister could be in danger if anyone thought she saw whoever gave Vanessa the drink.

So many worries. Perhaps her mother would be willing to go back to Lexington when she found out about Vanessa. They could sell the house. They didn't need such a large house. The boys didn't have to go to the schools in the east. Ivy could marry Jacob. She, Elena, could be the spinster she always thought she was meant to be.

She slipped out of bed and went to the open window. The whippoorwill's call was somehow comforting despite its lonesome sound. Lonesome. That was surely the life of an unmarried woman. Strange, she had always thought spinsterhood would not be so dreadful. A woman could do what she wanted without the demands of a husband and children. But such a woman did need to find a way to support herself or be forever in the debt of whichever relatives allowed her a corner in their household.

She had known such women but never thought of herself in the same way. At times a person could filter out the unpleasantness of truth. Besides, since she'd been here at the Springs, she had a different feeling about the institution of marriage. She'd watched the couples promenading along the paths. Newly married ones and those married many years. Most looked happy, but then why wouldn't they in such a beautiful place with all their needs met by servants?

If she married a man like General Dawson, she would have servants at her beck and call. But would she have love?

In the past, she often thought she had never met a man to make her consider marriage, but had that changed since she came to Graham Springs? Did the very air here reek of romance, or was it meeting Kirby Frazier that had changed her ideas of love? And then there was Andrew with his gentle ways and kindness. Could she love him? Might she even learn to love General Dawson if he turned out to be her fate?

Her fate. She should be grieving for Vanessa's fate as Ivy had said. Not a fate she could have imagined as they enjoyed the day together.

With a sigh, Elena went back to bed. She pushed her jumbled thoughts aside and concentrated on the whippoorwill singing its name over and over. She didn't realize when she fell asleep, but the next thing she knew, dawn's light was seeping through the sheer curtains.

As she had the morning before, she slipped from bed to dress as quietly as possible. She left off her corset again but did arrange her hair properly. She didn't pick up her sketchbook. She had no heart for drawing today. But she did remember to take her straw bonnet.

She looked at Ivy as she went to the door. She should stay with her to share the sorrowful news about their beautiful neighbor with Mother, but the urge to be out in the early morning air was too strong.

Besides, she had the same as promised to meet Andrew in one of the gardens. If he could find her. That was before the terrible ending to the night. He might not even remember speaking about it. But the flowers would still be there. The sun would be coming up. The air would be fresh.

The same as the day before, the pathways were empty except for a few servants hurrying to their morning duties. Elena put on her bonnet and tied the ribbons below her chin. The bonnet restricted her vision to seeing only straight ahead unless she turned her head, but she could hear the birds singing. No whippoorwill now. It was a night bird, and with the glow along the eastern horizon promising the sun, now was the time for morning birds.

She didn't go to the rose garden where she'd met Andrew the day before. Instead, she found a stone bench among a cluster of wine-red, white, and pink hollyhocks. Since she was mostly hidden from view, she took off her bonnet to enjoy the first rays of sunshine shooting up over the border of trees along the horizon.

It was good to see another sunrise. She hadn't thought about that before. She had taken each new sunrise for granted, but Vanessa would not see this sunrise.

Elena reached to touch one of the white hollyhock flowers. The leaves that touched her arm were rough, but the petals were like silk. Pollen drifted down from the tuft in the middle of the flower. She pulled her hand away as a bee buzzed into the bloom.

A cat came out of the hollyhock stalks. With no sign of being startled to find Elena there, it rubbed against her legs, much as Willow did back in her father's garden.

"Good morning, kitty cat." The silvery light-gray cat was gorgeous with a smudge of darker gray across its face as if it had nosed around in an ash bucket. She held out her hand for the cat to sniff before she stroked it head to tail.

Purring, the cat looked up at Elena with the most remarkable blue eyes. Eyes the same blue as Vanessa's. Elena's hand stilled for a moment. The cat meowed and pushed its head into Elena's hand to keep her stroking it. Then without invitation, the cat jumped onto her lap and did a halfway circle before settling down contentedly.

"Well, make yourself comfortable, my friend." Elena laughed softly as she continued to rub the cat. "And what might be your name? Smoky? No, I don't think so. Or Misty? No, that's not fancy enough for you. Sapphire. How does that sound? Princess, perhaps. You do look like a princess among cats."

"Cinderella." Andrew stepped around the hollyhocks and gave the cat a look. "I think that would be the perfect name."

26

"C inderella?" Elena looked up at Andrew with sad eyes. "That's what we called Vanessa when she came to the dance." Her voice sounded faint.

Andrew kicked himself. Why in the world had he suggested that name for the cat? How could he have let it slip his mind that they had talked about the mystery lady being like Cinderella? Even the cat gave him an accusing look.

"Forgive me." He squatted down in front of Elena. "That was thoughtless of me. The smudge on the cat's face made me think it had been nosing around in a fireplace's cinders."

He supposed he could blame his lack of tact on very little sleep. He'd gotten up at first light to watch for Elena in case she went out to the gardens as she had promised before the tragic happening at the dance. He hadn't slept well. He kept seeing the lifeless woman on the dance floor and worried that his asking about her father had upset her enough to add to her heart failure, if that was what had taken her from life.

Not really her father. No matter that Dr. Graham said Andrew might be wrong, he wasn't. Judge Hasting didn't have a daughter. Of that, Andrew was certain. But he shouldn't have confronted the woman about it. What difference did it make if she wanted to pretend to be someone she wasn't? She wasn't doing any harm. Simply having a great time dancing. If Dr. Graham didn't get paid for her stay, he'd hardly notice with all his other paying guests.

But why had she come? And how could someone with so much energy for dancing die so suddenly? Could she really have been poisoned? Intentionally? The doctor should have been able to tell that, and he said not. Then again, he wouldn't want word of a murder at his resort to get around. The Springs was a place for healing, not dying.

All those impossible-to-answer questions about the woman had spun through his mind all the night through. They might never know her story now. Perhaps that would be for the best.

He had pushed all that aside when he went out on the veranda to watch for Elena. The sun had yet to rise, but light crawled over the horizon to push back the gray of night while he waited.

He wasn't sure she would go out to the gardens after last night. She and her sister might stay in their room trying to make sense of it all. Not that there was any sense to be made of the woman's death.

A guest for a day.

But Elena had come out of the hotel, and he followed her. She looked so lovely there among the hollyhocks, and then the cat had wound past him as it made its way to her. He, too, wanted to make his way to Elena. Something about her drew him.

Now he had carelessly made her sad. He touched the cat's head. At least it accepted his touch without spitting at him.

Elena accepted his apology too. "The name is perfect. I was calling her Princess. And Cinderella was a princess."

"After she married Prince Charming."

"Do you think Vanessa was searching for a Prince Charming at the dance last night?"

"Since she gave her first and last dance to General Dawson, I somehow doubt it, but that's something we will never know." He sat down on the walkway. The rocks were damp with dew, but his trousers would dry.

"I could move over and make room on the bench."

"This is·fine. I wouldn't want to disturb Princess Cat." He smiled at her. The truth was he liked sitting where he could see her face. "She looks very settled in your lap. You must have a way with cats."

"I have a garden cat at home."

"I suppose this is a garden cat too." Andrew could hear the rumble of the cat's purr as Elena stroked it.

After a moment, she said, "Did you note her eyes?"

"The cat's?" When she nodded, he peered closer at the cat. "They are a very vivid blue."

"The same color as Vanessa's eyes."

"And as your sister's eyes."

"But more like Vanessa's." She looked down at the cat. "Did you know there were cats here at the Springs?"

"I hadn't seen any, but it's not surprising. Cats are pretty much everywhere."

"Do you like cats?"

Andrew shrugged. "We have several barn cats at the farm." He smiled as he remembered one of them. "When I was eleven or twelve, a cat made friends with one of our horses. That cat would crawl up on the stall door and perch there. Grandfather said the cat and the horse were talking. I asked him what they were saying."

"Did your grandfather know?"

"He claimed to." Andrew shook his head. "Sometimes he would say they were discussing the weather. Other times, the horse would be asking the cat to go for a ride or the cat would be wondering if the horse had seen any mice. Silly things."

"Did the cat ever go for a ride?"

"I asked Grandfather that once, and he was sure it did but only during the secret midnight hours when no one would see." Andrew laughed. He hadn't thought about that for a long time.

"Your grandfather sounds nice. Is he still living?"

"Very much so. Still riding horses."

"In the secret midnight hours?"

"I wouldn't be surprised." When she smiled at him, a little thrill swept through him. He could talk to her the way he'd never been able to talk to any girl before. Not even Gloria.

"The midnight hour wasn't so good last night." Her smile disappeared as she looked down at the cat. "After you went to get the doctor, Vanessa said something before she died."

"Oh?"

Elena nodded. "She said, 'No one will ever know.'"

"What?"

"I asked her that, but her answer was little more than a breath of air. It might have been 'why' or maybe 'who.'" Elena kept stroking the cat. "She sounded so sad."

"But she chose to claim a name that wasn't true," Andrew said.

"Why would she? What secret could she have been guarding?"

"As she said, that's something we may never know."

"It's all so odd." Elena sighed. "She seemed such a sweet person and took such joy in everything we did yesterday. With no sign of illness."

"You or your sister had never met her before?"

"No, but sometimes you can feel an instant bond with someone."

"True." Wasn't he sitting there feeling that kind of connection with her? He'd danced with her at Dr. Graham's insistence that first night at the Springs and then more willingly on other nights. He'd enjoyed those dances and their ballroom chatter but finding her among the roses the day before had made him see her in a different light. Now just looking at her with the

213

first rays of the sun lighting up her face made his heart feel warm somehow.

He wanted to know more about her. He'd heard a rumor that her mother was here to find her a husband. As if Elena couldn't attract suitors on her own. That couldn't be true. She radiated an inner beauty. Maybe there was some broken heart in her past as there was in his. If so, that hadn't become part of the stories going around about her.

A person couldn't pay attention to rumors at a place like this, where some liked to watch and whisper behind their hands about others. In that kind of gossip fest, the truth could sometimes be hard to discern. Who knew what they might be saying about him? A man whose fiancée had left him days before they were to marry. With his best friend.

That was the truth, but not one he had to wallow in. It was past time for him to stop thinking about Gloria. She was gone, no longer part of his life. His grandfather was right to insist on him coming here where he could meet new people. Like Elena.

And whether she had known Vanessa long or not, the woman's death was a shock to her. A shock to all of them. It would be all the talk on this day.

"I should go back to the hotel. I shouldn't have left Ivy alone to tell Mother about Vanessa." Elena looked worried. "Do you think someone could have given her . . ." She didn't finish her thought, as if it was too horrible to consider.

"It seems unlikely. Nobody here even knew her. Why would anyone want to hurt her?"

"Sometimes things aren't what they seem. If the judge she claimed for a father didn't have a daughter, Vanessa obviously wasn't what or who she wanted us to believe."

"So it seems." Andrew wished Elena would look up at him, but she kept her eyes on the cat.

"Are we all just pretending? Playing a game here in this beautiful place?" She didn't give him time to answer before she asked another question. "Do you believe?"

"Believe?" Andrew frowned a little.

"In the Lord. That he watches over us?" She looked up then at the sunrise. "That he sends us blessings each and every day?"

"I think on some days we have to keep our eyes open to see those blessings. This might be one of those times."

"But he sent this cat. I've been here a few weeks now without seeing a cat anywhere. Then this morning when I needed a reason to smile, this cat comes out of the hollyhocks to look at me with eyes the same blue as Vanessa's. It's like the Lord sent the cat as a gift." She stared down at the cat in her lap.

If she got comfort from that thought, Andrew didn't want to spoil it for her, even if he couldn't fully embrace her idea of the Lord sending the cat. Then again, all at once, something that happened last summer after Gloria left him came to mind. He was so full of resentment at the time that he had waved away his grandfather's words that it was proof the Lord still had blessings for him. But now, with Elena suggesting the cat was a gift, he wondered if his grandfather was right.

Before he could decide if he should tell her about it, she murmured, "You probably think that's a foolish thought."

"No, no," he said quickly. "It's a nice thought. In fact, something similar may have happened during a bad time for me."

"Oh?" She kept her head down.

He hesitated. He didn't like talking about Gloria's betrayal, but he took a breath and let the words out into the air between them. "I was supposed to get married last year, but a few days before the wedding, my intended left with another man."

"That had to be terrible for you." Her gaze flew up to his face then.

"I'm not telling you this to get your sympathy, but you talking about the cat being a gift from the Lord made me remember something that happened then. Grandfather has this rosebush that he planted the first year after my grandmother died. It never has more than one or two blooms even though Grandfather treats it with special care. But a few days after everything fell apart for me, Grandfather asked me to go check on the roses. When I did, I had a hard time believing my eyes. That bush, the one that blooms so scantily every year, had a dozen blooms. Maybe more."

"That had to be a good sight." She shut her eyes. "I'm picturing pink roses."

"They were white with a pink tint. My grandmother's favorite. I think Grandfather knew the bush had bloomed, but he wanted me to be surprised by the sight."

"Were you?" She opened her eyes and studied him.

"I was. My grandfather and I had often talked about how the bush was such a stingy bloomer."

"A stingy bloomer." She looked thoughtful. "I wonder if a person can be a stingy bloomer. Never mind that." She shook her head. "Did it make you feel better to see the rosebush with all the blooms?"

"Did it make you feel better to see the cat?"

"It did." A smile touched her lips and then was gone as she gave him a sympathetic look. "But as sad as I am about Vanessa's death, I hardly knew her. Your loss had to be so much more upsetting. Your whole life must have felt in shambles."

"True, but that didn't mean I shouldn't have noted the wonder of that rosebush blooming as it never had before. Instead of clinging to my misery, I should have embraced what my grandfather was trying to tell me."

"What was that?"

"He wanted me to think about the roses as a message that my life would flower again."

"What a nice thought. And that your life wouldn't be a stingy bloomer." She looked over at the hollyhocks. "Maybe in time, it will bloom in many colors."

"How about you, Elena? What are you hoping for?"

"I don't know." The question seemed to puzzle her for a moment, but then she went on. "The best. I'm simply hoping for the best."

"The best? The best of what?"

"The best cat to purr in my lap." Her smile was quick this time when she looked straight at him. "A friend when I need one. And here you are."

"A friend."

He echoed her words and then surprised himself by reaching out his hand to her. Without hesitation, she took it. At her touch, a jolt went through him. Her eyes widened a bit as if she might have felt the same. He tightened his fingers around hers. She didn't pull away.

A bee buzzed past his head to one of the hollyhock flowers. A mockingbird began singing in a tree not far from them. The cat stood up and bumped its head into their hands. Andrew let go and laughed as the cat glared at him. It did have the bluest eyes.

The cat worked its paws up and down in Elena's lap as it looked up at her. Elena's cheeks flushed. Whether with pleasure or not, he couldn't be sure as she dropped her gaze back to the cat.

She picked up the cat and gently put it down on the path. "Goodbye, Princess Cinderella, I hope I see you again." She brushed off her skirt and reached to put on her bonnet. As she tied the ribbons below her chin, she peeked out from under the bonnet's brim with a surprising shyness. "Both of you."

He scrambled to his feet. His sudden movements made the cat disappear into the hollyhocks. He stepped in front of Elena before she could disappear as well. "I will find you again later."

"More hide-and-seek?" She smiled again. "Perhaps I will be the one seeking you next time."

"That would be even better." He moved off the path then to let her pass. He watched her move away and wasn't surprised when she stopped beside a rosebush to sniff the fragrance of one of the blooms.

The cat came back out of the flowers then to wind its way around his legs before it ran off as if it had just spotted a mouse. The cat with eyes the color of Vanessa's. Yesterday, she had embraced all life offered here at the Springs. What a sorrow that she would never feel the morning sunshine on her face again.

That sunshine felt especially good to him right now as he stepped out of the shadow of his lost love. As he started back toward the hotel, he smiled and flexed his fingers when he remembered holding Elena's hand. He would have every chance to see her again and again in the days ahead.

At the hotel, he stopped on the veranda to watch a coach come up the driveway. Maybe it would bring someone who knew the mystery woman. She wouldn't stay a mystery. Someone was sure to know who she was and why she had come to Graham Springs. Perhaps the more important thing to know was why she died.

While questions about the woman played through his mind, the private coach came to a stop and the driver jumped down to open the door for his passengers to alight.

A lady climbed out, her head lowered and her face not visible under her straw bonnet. Another woman alone, it seemed, when the coach driver shut the door behind her. He fervently hoped she would have a more fortunate stay than the lone woman who had come yesterday morning.

He watched her speak to the driver. Something was familiar about the woman. His heart lurched as she turned to look up at the hotel entrance.

"Gloria."

He breathed out her name in little more than a whisper. She couldn't have heard him, but she looked up at him and smiled as though they had just parted yesterday.

27

A *stingy bloomer.* The words followed Elena all the way back through the gardens that were blooming so lavishly. Was that what she was? A stingy bloomer, or worse, a no bloomer.

Andrew had been talking about roses, not people. Yet his words had poked her. Just as the cat might have appeared as a comfort for her sadness, his words could be the nudge she needed to change her attitude about her mother's plans for her.

She had spent too much time hiding in her father's rose garden. Even here at the Springs, she was still trying to disappear among the flowers, a place where she felt safe. But then Andrew had found her there. Ready or not, he had said while they were dancing. She had been ready and hopeful that he would seek her out this morning.

Among the hollyhocks with the first rays of the sun touching her face, she found it so easy to talk to him. Whatever happened from this trip to Graham Springs, she was glad to have met him.

Her fingers tingled as she thought about him taking her hand. A friendship gesture. Surely nothing more, but when their hands touched, she'd felt a surprising connection. Her heart had dipped a little and then started beating faster as he tightened his fingers around hers.

Had she ever had such a friend? No, because she seemed to fear blooming. She hadn't even been a good friend to her sister. Instead, Ivy had always seemed a responsibility she didn't want. How silly that seemed now. Another way she hadn't bloomed. Being stingy with her time and with her love. No wonder everyone was so sure she would end up a spinster.

She supposed that could still happen despite her mother's plans. She thought of General Dawson. He had looked so upset last night. After she talked to Ivy and her mother, she would look for him. Perhaps she could find a way to make him feel better.

Odd how a person's ideas about someone could change so quickly when one got to know them better. The general was such a nice man. Still old, but if her future lay with him, that didn't seem quite as dire as it had when they first got to the Springs.

She had changed. She liked making new friends, especially when one of those friends turned out to be her own sister. And now Andrew. And the general. Perhaps she could even count Kirby Frazier as a friend. She had to smile when she thought of the three so very different men she had come to know here. None were the best marriage possibilities. The general was too old. Kirby was too poor, and Andrew too heartbroken. Kirby would not be on her mother's list, but General Dawson seemed to be.

She had no idea what her mother thought about Andrew. Elena didn't really care. She was glad he'd found her among the flowers. Perhaps a heartbroken man needed a friend. She couldn't imagine how any woman could have treated him so badly after promising to marry him.

If she ever said yes to a proposal, she wouldn't back out at the last moment. Of course, love wasn't the main purpose in her securing that proposal. That didn't mean she couldn't imagine how much better it would be to fall in love before she stepped to the marriage altar. Even better if the one she fell in love with was the one waiting at the altar.

She almost laughed as she went up the steps and into the hotel. Perhaps whenever the music started playing again for a new dance, she would meet the perfect man and find love in this place. She could bloom.

What a lovely dream, but no time to think about that now. She had to make sure Ivy didn't do anything foolish to find the man she thought had given Vanessa a poisoned drink. As Andrew said, nobody even knew who she was. The mystery woman. And now she might forever stay the mystery woman. *"No one will ever know."*

But what if someone did know? Perhaps not whatever Vanessa was hiding but that Ivy had seen him give her that last cup of punch.

As she climbed the four flights of stairs to their floor, her mind swirled from one idea to another. Finding a husband. Saving their home. Giving up on the whole idea and going back to Lexington to find another way. If they left right away, at least Ivy would be safe.

When she saw the door to Vanessa's room open, she peered in. Dr. Graham and a maid were inside.

When he saw Elena, he gestured toward her. "Miss Bradford, perhaps you can be of help."

She stepped over the threshold into the room a little hesitantly. "Have you heard from her family?"

He shook his head. "I fear young Andrew was right about that. The sheriff confirms what he said. He knows Judge Hasting well and says the man has no daughters. Nevertheless, we have sent a messenger to the judge in case he does know something about this poor woman."

The doctor dropped down in one of the chairs while the maid

straightened the room. There was little out of place. Little to show that anyone had even been in the room except a small carpetbag and the dress Vanessa had worn the day before spread out on the neatly made bed. The portrait Kirby had done of her was propped on the small writing desk.

Dr. Graham must have noticed her staring at it. "The man is an excellent artist. The portrait captures her beauty."

"Yes," Elena said. "She was so happy with it."

"You say she was excited about having a portrait done." The doctor stroked his beard as he looked at the canvas. "Wonder why."

It wasn't really a question, but Elena answered it anyway. "Perhaps to prove to herself her attractiveness."

"She had a mirror for that. She had to know she was beautiful."

"One would think so, but we don't always see ourselves as others do." Elena thought of how she had never felt attractive. Yet Kirby wanted to paint her portrait, and Andrew had called her a pretty woman among the flowers.

"That is true. I've known many women with blind eyes to their own beauty or worth." He raised his hand and waved toward the dress on the bed. "Tell me, Miss Bradford. Do you think it normal for a woman to travel with only a party dress besides what she was wearing when she arrived?"

"There's nothing else?" Elena looked around again.

Dr. Graham shook his head. "A brush. A comb. A few hair pins, but not even a nightdress."

"Surely she had something in her reticule." Elena looked around.

"There wasn't one here in her room. Did she carry one when you were together yesterday?"

Elena shook her head. "We neither one did. It didn't seem necessary, but I do have one here."

"It appears Miss Vanessa did not. Nothing but a carpetbag."

He pointed. "It's empty except for a few coins. No letters. No books of poetry or a diary. Don't all young women have such things with them?" He blew out a breath of air. "It's as if she came knowing she would only be here the one day."

"She couldn't have known that." Elena frowned. "Could she?"

"Not unless she poisoned her own drink." He seemed sorry for his words immediately as he rushed on. "That didn't happen. Her drink wasn't poisoned. Her heart simply gave out from overexertion."

Elena didn't say anything. From the look on the doctor's face, silence seemed best.

"You didn't hear anything unusual from this room?"

"We weren't in our room very long during the day. Just in and out. Later, when we came back to get ready for the dance, she would have been more likely to hear the three of us while we got dressed."

"I see." Dr. Graham pushed up from the chair. The same as General Dawson, the death of the young woman appeared to have him feeling his age. "I have to wonder if someone else was with her that you didn't see. That might explain why she was so secretive and careful to not open her door wider when you knocked. Perhaps he took off in the night with whatever money or personal items she might have had."

Elena looked at the maid dusting here and there while they talked. "What about your maid? Did she see anyone?"

"She hadn't been in the room yet." He dismissed that possibility. "Not until now. Well, she brought water in the early afternoon, but the rooms are nearly always empty at that time of the day. Isn't that right, Betty?"

"Yes, sir. No one about. Ceptin' the young sister in the next room." The maid looked at Elena and then away. "So I waited until later to see to that room. But no, sir, nobody was in this room at all, but I didn't pay mind to what the guest might have brung with her."

It was obvious she'd already answered these questions for the doctor. She pointed toward the bed and went on. "She did have her dancing dress all laid out on the counterpane like as how this dress here is now." She pointed at the bed. "Would you be wanting me to fold it up and pack everything outta here, sir?"

"No. Leave things as they are right now. You can be on about your other tasks." The maid scurried out as if she felt Vanessa's ghost chasing her.

Elena didn't sense any kind of presence. The room just felt empty. Very empty.

"Thank you, Miss Bradford." Dr. Graham motioned her toward the door. "You've been very helpful."

"It is so sad." Elena gave the room another look. "What will you do if no family comes for her body?"

"Don't let that concern you. We intend to give her a proper burial here at the Springs." He took her arm to escort her out into the hallway and then shut the door firmly behind them.

"That will be kind of you." Elena started to move away toward their room.

"Wait, Miss Bradford."

When she turned back toward him, he said, "It would be better if we don't say anything about what the young lady might have drunk last night. Or about the oddities in her room. At least until we have more concise information. You know how rumors can spread and be added to and changed until it is impossible to know the truth or have false assumptions corrected. It can be like shaking out a pillow tick full of feathers. There would never be a way to gather all the feathers that blew away on the wind of our words."

She lifted her chin and stared straight at him. "I am not in the habit of gossiping."

"Good." He met her look. "Might I suggest you instruct your young sister to be the same?"

She inclined her head in agreement. She had no reason to

take offense. The doctor was merely reinforcing what she had intended to tell Ivy anyway. But what about the maid and the other servants that had been in the ballroom while they had talked the night before? She had a sinking feeling that some of those gossip feathers had already escaped into the air.

28

"A ndy!"

That was what Gloria always called him, even though he told her he hated his name shortened. "But it's my special pet name for you," she would say.

He stared at her now, not sure he could believe his eyes. Where was Zachary? He thought they had married months ago. He had just shrugged off some of the hurt of her betrayal and now here she was.

She lifted her skirts and rushed up the steps and out onto the veranda where he still stood frozen. "I just knew you would be the first person I saw when I got here. That you would somehow sense I was coming and be watching for me." Her face lit up as she grabbed his hands.

He didn't pull his hands away, but he wanted to. "Where's Zachary?"

"Oh, him." She gave his hands an irritated shake. "Let's not spoil this moment talking about him."

He did free his hands then and shoved them in his pockets. "I thought you got married."

She gave him the fetching smile that had always gotten him

to agree to whatever she wanted in the past. But this was no longer the past.

"Don't look so glum, Andy. Marriages don't have to be forever. Not when they weren't meant to be. We were the ones meant to be forever." She put her hand through his elbow. "Come. Help carry my things to my room." She snuggled up close against his side and whispered, "Unless you want to get married right away so we can share a room."

His head was spinning. Gloria had always affected him this way, pushing him to do whatever she wanted. He'd never tried to resist, and he didn't now. He took his hands out of his pockets and walked with her down the steps to the carriage where the driver waited.

"Be a darling and pay the driver." She motioned toward the man before she picked up a hatbox.

He felt as though he'd stepped back in time as he reached into his pocket and did as she said. This was what he wanted, wasn't it? Gloria by his side. They were to have married almost a year ago. Except she had married someone else. A storm of emotions swept in and knocked him off-kilter. A storm named Gloria.

He thought about how pleasant it had been with Elena among the hollyhocks moments ago. Even when they were talking about Vanessa, there was an underlying calm, a feeling that somehow everything would work out all right. With Gloria chattering in his ear, he wondered if that kind of peace was now lost to him forever.

It didn't have to be. He could tell her to get someone else to carry her luggage. He could walk away. But did he want to? He had planned to spend the rest of his life pleasing her. Had that changed?

One thing he was sure had not changed was that she would make a scene if he did walk away. That would be an entertaining spectacle for those watching from the veranda. He glanced up at the men along the railing. Even a few women had deserted their seats to see what was happening. They weren't even pretending to hide their curiosity.

The talk of the day would be this new woman showing up to claim him. Not that he had been paired with anyone else here. Not yet. Again, Elena came to mind. She had said she might hunt him in the gardens next. Would she now, after she heard about Gloria?

"Please don't dawdle so, Andy. The travel here was exhausting. I need to freshen up before you show me around." She gave him the hatbox. "I know we will have such a good time together here."

He took the box and then picked up a bag. Servants would carry her trunk to whatever room she was given. For certain, that was not going to be his room. He needed time to think. Time away from her.

"How did you know I was here? Did Grandfather tell you?"

"Don't be silly, dear. Your grandfather would not tell me to take shelter if the sky was falling. Or your mother either. They have always tried to keep us apart. You know that." She pulled a long face. "I can't imagine why they can't see how perfectly matched we are."

"Then how did you know where I was?"

She handed him another small case before she led the way up the steps. "Our friends have been keeping me informed about your sad state. Melancholy, they said. They were quite upset with me." She turned to pat his cheek. "But I'm here to make it up to you. It will all be wonderful."

"And Zachary?"

She frowned and stomped her foot. "I told you I didn't want to talk about him. It was perfectly awful what he did. Enticing me away from you."

He didn't say anything more then. Just followed along behind her, feeling all the eyes watching them. Even the couples along the paths toward the spring had stopped to watch. Gloria held her head high. He couldn't see her face, but he had no doubt she was smiling and enjoying being the center of attention.

She was very aware of her beauty. Nothing at all like that beautiful girl who had died the night before. Vanessa had arrived at the Springs without fanfare. She had come to the ball in that Cinderella dress seeming to have no awareness of the entrance she was making.

Gloria wouldn't be like that whenever Dr. Graham arranged a new ball. She would expect admiration and would get it. She was stunningly flamboyant in her beauty. He didn't have to check to know every man within sight had their gazes glued to her. Every one except him.

He stared down at the steps as he followed her. He just felt tired, as if the melancholy that had lifted in the last few days was settling back down on him. He wished he could move over into the shadows again and let life pass him by.

At the top of the steps, he did look around. He was glad not to see Elena.

General Dawson was hurrying toward them. "Andrew."

Gloria gave the old man a dismissive look and went on into the hotel.

Andrew balanced Gloria's bags and stopped to speak to him. "Good morning, General. How are you today?" The man looked better than he had last night after the mystery woman died in his arms.

"I am still somewhat in shock about it all. You have to know that I've seen many people die in battle and even on the home front. My daughters. My wife. But to have such a vibrant, beautiful woman die while dancing with me . . ." He paused a moment as if struggling to find the proper words. Words he didn't find. "Well, it's not something a man would ever expect or know how to prevent."

"I don't suppose there was anything you or anyone else could have done."

"Of course, you are right. Still." The general's shoulders drooped.

"Dr. Graham says it had to be her heart."

"Have you talked with him this morning? Has he found out anything more about her?"

"I haven't seen him," Andrew said. "I would assume he will discover more when he checks her room."

"You are sure she wasn't Judge Hasting's daughter?"

"I am." Andrew saw no reason to avoid that truth now.

"Interesting. Such a sweet girl. She and Miss Elena were perfect companions yesterday when we were lawn bowling." The general looked at the door, then back at Andrew. "Have you seen Miss Elena today?"

Gloria pushed open the door in time to hear General Dawson's question. Before Andrew could say anything, she frowned at him, again ignoring the general. "Andy, what is taking you so long?"

"I stopped to talk to General Dawson. You remember him from when he visited the farm, don't you, Gloria?"

She pulled up some manners. "I don't believe I do, but I was meeting so many new people then as we planned the wedding. Forgive me."

"Quite understandable, Miss Collins. Interesting to see you here." There was a hard edge to the general's voice.

Gloria's eyes flashed. She knew what the general found interesting. Her smile lacked sincerity. "Yes, so interesting to see you too." She gave Andrew a sweet look. "Are you coming, Andy?"

"I'll be along in a minute." Andrew turned from her to the general. "About Elena, yes, I saw her in the garden this morning."

Gloria huffed out a breath and let the door close behind her.

General Dawson's face stayed impassive. "I trust she was all right?"

"Sad and puzzled about it as we all are. She was concerned about her sister."

"The younger one wears her feelings on her sleeve." The general smiled. "Both lovely girls." His smile slid away as he looked at the door. "You best go on in. Miss Collins will want her luggage."

"Yes." Andrew shifted the cases and the hatbox to reach for the door handle.

General Dawson stepped closer to open it for him. "Just remember, son. A man is free to do what he wants until he says 'I do.'"

"I haven't said 'I do.'" Andrew shoved his shoulder against the door.

"And it's a wise man who thinks long and hard before he does." The old man turned and went back toward the veranda.

Gloria waited inside the door. Andrew could see her foot tapping under the edge of her skirt. "What did that old codger want? And who is this Elena?"

"Not now, Gloria. Get your room so you can settle in."

Her expression changed. "You're going to do it for me, aren't you?" She pushed out her lips in a little pout.

"Sorry, no. Not unless you have Grandfather's permission to add onto his bill." He met her stare straight on.

"Very well. I see you are holding a grudge." She tossed her head, and a few of her honey-brown curls slipped out from her bonnet.

He watched her flounce away. Was he? Holding a grudge? Could being upset by her leaving with his best friend practically on the eve of their wedding be watered down to merely holding a grudge?

He sighed and watched her smiling at the desk clerk, no doubt charming him into a lower price or a better room. She was the same, the very same as she'd been last summer when he wanted to marry her. Demanding. Infuriating. Lovely. She hadn't changed, but perhaps he had. Perhaps spring water actually could cure a broken heart.

Kirby Frazier stepped up beside him. He was as loaded down as Andrew with his painting supplies.

He looked over at Gloria. "Your lady friend is a looker. You should let me do a portrait of her. Of both of you together if you like." He turned his gaze back to Andrew. "You make a great couple."

"Who said we were a couple?" Andrew didn't like the man's knowing smile.

"Aren't you? Or are you just a pack mule?"

Andrew considered dropping Gloria's things to punch the man in the nose, but he tamped down his temper. "You're packing plenty yourself." Andrew nodded toward his load.

"The life of an artist. A working man." The man looked at Gloria coming toward them. "But it can be pleasant work when I have such beautiful subjects the way I have here. Like Vanessa, poor girl. Such a shame." As he started to move away, he said, "If you see Elena, tell her I am looking for her. You will see her, won't you? Elena?"

Without waiting for an answer or to be introduced to Gloria, he smiled before he went on out the door.

Andrew didn't have an answering smile. He didn't feel much like smiling at anyone and especially not Kirby Frazier, who looked entirely too smug as though he knew more than he could.

"Who was he?" Gloria asked but didn't wait for Andrew to answer before she asked a different question. "And who is Elena?"

"A friend."

"A friend?" Gloria eyed him. "I don't think I like that."

"There's nothing not to like." Andrew shrugged slightly.

"I think I need to know more about this Elena."

Andrew could tell her more he was sure she would like even less. Especially that right now Andrew wished he was in the garden with Elena instead of following Gloria like that pack mule Frazier had called him.

29

Her mother dismissed Elena's suggestion that they leave the Springs with an impatient wave of her hand.

"This girl dying is sad, but the two of you are making it into more than it is." She looked at Elena, then Ivy. "No one poisoned her. She must have been sick when she got here and then was foolish not to realize she should rest."

"But she seemed fine yesterday when I met her," Ivy insisted.

"Seeming and being are two different things. I can't believe you two. We haven't achieved what we came to do." She stared straight at Elena. "We are going to lose everything. Everything. I will have to see if my cousin in Mississippi will give me a place in his house. You and Ivy will need to find positions as maids. The boys—" She sank down in the chair next to the desk and dabbed her eyes. "The boys will have to become street sweepers."

"Street sweepers? What in the world, Mother?" Elena frowned.

Her mother jumped up from the chair and got right in Elena's face. "Street sweepers. Day laborers. Farm hands. They will lose their opportunity to be anything else. We will never be a family again. You don't realize what your father did to us with his unwise debts."

With a strangled sob, Ivy sank down to the floor beside the bed.

Their mother glanced at her but didn't move to comfort her. "Your sister will never be able to marry that boy she foolishly thinks she loves."

"I do love him." Ivy began crying harder.

Mother ignored her as she turned back to Elena. "This is our chance. You are our chance." Her shoulders slumped and she dropped down in the chair again. She put her face in her hands. Her next words were muffled but each of them stabbed Elena. "Life will never be the same for us if we can't make this work."

Elena pulled in a shaky breath. Either way, life would never be the same for her. Even so, her mother was right. It was time to face reality. She could do as her mother said. Find a husband. Keep the family from the poorhouse. But could she keep Ivy safe if Vanessa had actually been poisoned and whoever gave her that poison knew Ivy saw him?

"But Ivy could be in danger. Let her go back to Lexington." Elena moved to put her hand on Ivy's shoulder.

"And stay alone in our house? With that Pennington boy wanting to come court her? I think not."

"You could go with her, then."

"You are panicking over something you don't even know happened. You just told us that Dr. Graham doesn't think the lady was poisoned. Even if she was, Ivy didn't recognize whoever gave the drink to her. But to stay completely safe, Ivy cannot drink anything someone offers her and only take the drinks the servants pass around."

"What if one of the servants poisoned the drink?" Elena said.

"You are being ridiculous, Elena. I do not want to hear another word about this. That girl died of some natural cause the same as your father did. Hearts stop. People die. Such is tragic and sad, but we are staying. You will find a proper suitor."

"I can't force a man to consider marrying me."

"Leave that to me." She pointed her finger at Elena. "I will find you the right man. The right man for all of us. It certainly will not be that artist."

"Kirby Frazier has no romantic interest in me." Elena ignored Ivy brushing away her tears and staring up at her.

"I saw you dancing with him last night." Mother's eyes narrowed. "The man is little more than a huckster talking women into those portraits."

"He's an outstanding artist." Elena took up for him. "The portrait he did of Vanessa is incredible."

"It is." Ivy echoed her.

"A lot that matters to the girl now."

"Her family might treasure it." Ivy still had tears in her voice.

"If anyone shows up to claim kinship. If I understand what you are saying, nobody even knows who she really was. She might have pulled the name Vanessa out of a hat the same as she did Hasting. Claiming to be someone she wasn't."

"We are doing the same," Elena spoke up. "Pretending to be who we aren't."

"That is nothing of the sort. The two of you are respectable young ladies. We aren't making up names or pretending anything. I've made no secret of my desire to see you both well settled. I've even asked for help to know about the eligible men here." She shook her finger at Elena again. "And you will look with favor on whichever match I arrange for you."

"I don't know how you can arrange any kind of match for me. We don't have anything to offer."

"You sell yourself short, my dear. You will make some fortunate man a wonderful wife."

"I've already said I will do whatever you want, Mother. But

tell Ivy not to go around staring at men to try to find whomever she saw."

"Of course, you are not to do anything so unladylike, Ivy. You are no longer a child. Now wash your face and you and Elena go out and do something." Mother put her hand to her forehead. "You've given me a headache."

Elena was glad to step out into the hallway with Ivy and be away from her mother's expectations. They weren't gone, but for a while she could push them aside. They both stopped and stared at the closed door to the room beside them. It was locked. Ivy tried the knob to be sure despite Elena telling her not to.

Nobody was listening to her today. She wasn't sure anybody had ever listened to her. But then she thought of talking with Andrew that morning and how intently he had watched her as she tried to explain how she felt the Lord had sent the cat to comfort her. Princess Cinderella. Elena smiled at the memory of the name. Somehow it fit.

"Are you smiling?" Ivy frowned at her.

"That's not a crime." She let her smile slide off her face.

"But now? As we are right here in front of Vanessa's room? You don't think her body is in there, do you?"

"No. I told you I saw Dr. Graham in her room a little while ago. The only thing there was the dress Vanessa wore yesterday. Not her party dress, but the day dress. That's all."

"I think I would like to travel like that. Without a lot of extra baggage. Just a dress and a bonnet."

"We may both find out exactly how that feels. When we are forced to hire on as maids."

Ivy turned wide eyes on Elena. "You don't think that really is going to happen, do you?"

"No, not for you." Elena saw no reason to make Ivy miserable. If or when their situation became that dire would be soon enough to face such an unsavory future. "You will marry your

Jacob. He will become a lawyer or a professor or a business tycoon, and you will have maids instead of being one."

"But Mother says his family is poor too. Like us."

"He might not stay poor. Men become successes all the time without their families having money. All the time."

"But not women?"

"Do you know any female business tycoons?"

Ivy smiled for the first time then. "No, but I think you could be the first."

"If only." Elena had to laugh. "What kind of business do you suppose I could run?"

"Oh, I don't know." Ivy stopped to study Elena. A smile continued to twitch her lips. "You could propagate roses. Write poems. Come up with a better paintbrush. Write a bestselling book. You could use your initials, E. R. Bradford, and everyone would think you were a man."

"You are a funny girl, Ivy Mae, and the one with the imagination. You will have to be the one to write that bestselling book." Elena reached over and gave her a hug. Then she gripped her shoulders to stare straight into her eyes. "Promise you will not try to find this man."

"But—"

"No buts. Just a promise. I've not been the best sister to you, and I'm sorry about that now."

Ivy interrupted her with a protest. "You have always been a wonderful sister."

"That's not true and you know it. I've ignored you, resented you, and never shown you the love you deserved. I can't change how I was before, but from now on, I want to be here for you. And if Mother can pull off this amazing feat of finding a rich man willing to marry me, I will step up to the marriage altar and say 'I do.'"

"Even if you don't love him."

"I can pray he will be a nice man and someone I can like."

"I think you should marry Mr. Frazier."

"Kirby Frazier doesn't seem the marrying kind." Elena turned away from Ivy to start down the stairs.

"That's not true. I've heard he is looking for a wife."

"He's looking for a wife. General Dawson is looking for a wife. Everybody is looking for a wife." Elena thought of Andrew. What if he was looking for a wife? A flare of hope went through her. But then it burned out. She shouldn't clutch at straws.

"Not everybody." Ivy giggled. "I think Mother is looking for a husband. For you."

"If only she were looking for a husband for herself."

Ivy looked surprised. "Do you think she would be? With Father only gone these few months? She's still wearing black."

"She could stop wearing black."

"Isn't there some kind of rule that you have to wait a certain amount of time before marrying again after your husband dies?"

"Only rules people make for themselves." Elena shrugged. "Widows remarry all the time. Mother is an attractive woman. She could probably find a husband for herself easier than finding someone interested in me."

"Oh, Elena. You are beautiful. Any man would be glad to have you as his wife." Ivy grabbed her arm. "Come on. Let's go see one of them. He wants to paint your portrait. I know he does."

"I don't have any money to give him in payment." Even if she did, she wouldn't spend it on a portrait.

"He doesn't charge for his portraits."

"But he expects some coin for his work." That was true even if he had claimed to want to paint what he called her remarkable eyes. Was that the kind of word people used when beautiful didn't fit?

"He might expect something different from you." Ivy's eyes

lit up. "We can make it a test. If he offers to do your portrait, that will prove he wants to get to know you better."

"And if he doesn't have time for such foolishness?"

"We won't tell him what we're doing." Ivy grinned. "If he knew, it wouldn't be a true test. But if he seems too busy for you, for us, then we won't have time for him." She lifted her chin in the air with a disdainful look.

"You are so silly." Elena had to smile. "But why not? I like to watch him work."

"You'll be posing. Not watching."

Elena shook her head but let Ivy tug her toward the lake. At least this way she could keep an eye on the girl and make sure she didn't start trying to find whichever man had given Vanessa her last cup of punch.

Sadness tugged at her heart. Yesterday she had hurried this way with Vanessa. They had laughed. The day had been good. Elena never dreamed it would be the young woman's last day of life.

She looked over at a flower garden a little way off the walkway and wished she could go looking for the cat. Or for Andrew. Hadn't she promised that she might be the one to seek him out next time? A smile came unbidden to her face. They had talked so easily that morning among the hollyhocks.

"Have you seen any cats since you've been here?" she asked Ivy.

"Cats?"

"One found me in the gardens this morning. It had the most amazing blue eyes. Like Vanessa's."

"A cat with blue eyes. Don't most cats have green eyes?"

Elena shrugged. "Some cats have blue eyes. At least this one did." She stepped a little ahead of Ivy to peer around her bonnet brim at her eyes. They were very blue but a bit darker than Vanessa's and the cat's. "As do you. Lovely blue eyes."

Ivy waved away her words. "They're just blue. Plain blue. I've always wished I had eyes like yours that change from blue to green according to what you are wearing or your mood. Much more interesting."

"Why do we always seem to want to look somehow different than we do? You with your blue eyes and curly blonde hair. Me with my dark brown hair and eyes that don't know what color they want to be. Wonder if Vanessa was that way too. Unaware of how pretty she was."

"She did seem so, but she had to know her dress was beautiful. Do you think they will bury her in it?" Ivy answered her own question. "They should. They definitely should."

"I suppose that will be up to her family."

"But you said no one knows her family."

"That doesn't mean the doctor won't find someone who does. She had to have family. Friends."

"She had us." Ivy looked sad. "For one day."

"Ladies. What is with the sad faces?" Kirby came toward them.

Elena had been staring down at the pathway as she thought about Vanessa and hadn't realized they were so close to the lake.

"We were thinking about Vanessa," Ivy said.

"A good reason for sad faces. I'm sure it's all the talk here at the Springs and perhaps why no one has come to ask for a portrait this morning. But that is good."

"Good? I wouldn't think that would be good for you," Elena said.

"But it is. I've been mixing colors for days to find the perfect tint for your eyes. This morning I think I have finally found the right combination." He reached out and took her hand to pull her toward him. "So, you cannot say no. You must let me paint your portrait."

Ivy clapped her hands and did an excited little jump. "I told you, Elena."

Elena looked at her and then back at Kirby. She should pull

her hand free, but instead, she let him lead her into the shade of the huge oak tree where he had his easel. He seemed so strong and in control.

Somehow that was comforting. To let someone else decide what she should do. What could it hurt to let him paint her portrait? Still, she couldn't let him think he would receive payment.

"No, I can't let you do that. My mother wouldn't approve, and I have nothing to pay you."

"Worry not about that. Think only of art," he said. "Surely, you can understand how there are simply some subjects an artist must try to capture. Your face is one of those. A must."

"Please, Elena," Ivy said. "Mother doesn't have to know."

"But that wouldn't be fair to Mr. Frazier."

"Come, come. I thought we were friends. Call me Kirby. Don't worry about any kind of recompense. Your beautiful sister posed for my 'Girl and Ducks' sketch yesterday. I will be able to sell that to a magazine."

"Really?" Ivy's eyes widened. "Think of it, Elena. I might be in a magazine."

"A good possibility." He smiled at Ivy. "You and those ducks could sell hundreds of magazines."

"I'd like to see it," Elena said.

"That could be arranged." He gave her a teasing look. "If you agree to let me paint your portrait."

"Please, Elena. You have to let him." Ivy circled around Elena. "You have to."

"Very well." She finally pulled her hand away from his, but the warmth of his touch stayed with her. "But if some other lady shows up wanting a portrait, I will step aside."

"That won't happen. I'll hang up a closed sign."

"You don't have anywhere to hang a sign." Elena looked around at the open space under the tree.

"Then Ivy can scare them off by telling them about the lake's attack ducks." He smiled over at Ivy. "She did tell you about our duck adventure, didn't she?"

"Attack ducks?" Elena smiled remembering Ivy's story about the lady afraid of the ducks. "Then they might attack me if I sit on the bench by the lake."

"Never fear." Ivy held up her fists. "I'll protect you from the ducks."

Elena had to laugh. All at once, the idea of posing for Kirby seemed like a lark and, oddly enough, a way to remember Vanessa. She had so enjoyed sitting for her portrait.

Plus it felt good to defy her mother in this small way. That wasn't proper behavior for a daughter, but a little rebellion before she gave up her life surely couldn't hurt.

30

"Forget those ducks. I want you to sit right here. Close enough to see your eyes."

Kirby grabbed the stool he had in front of his easel and set it in a spot of dappled shade. This was going well. First seeing Andrew Harper with his demanding lady friend, which appeared to take him out of competition for Elena, and now here she was with her sister to let him paint her portrait. Laughing, glad to be there with him.

After she perched on the stool, he said, "But you have to remove your bonnet."

"Mother won't like it if she gets freckles," Ivy said.

"I don't freckle." Elena untied the ribbons of her bonnet. "My hair may look dreadful though."

"My dear lady, there is no way you could ever look dreadful, but don't worry. If a few strands are out of place, I will make things right with my paintbrush."

He smiled down at her as she removed the bonnet. Then he surprised himself by cupping her cheek with his hand. Her eyes widened, but she didn't jerk back from his touch. Those eyes captured him. He stayed frozen as his heart seemed to melt inside him.

What was the matter with him? He pulled in a breath to steady himself as he tried to turn the near caress into something necessary for posing for the portrait. He slid his fingers down under her chin and tipped up her face the slightest bit. "That makes the light better on your face."

He was relieved his voice didn't sound as shaky as he suddenly felt. Something about this woman was making him forget to keep his emotions under control. If not for her sister standing beside him, he might have bent down to cover her lips with his.

He had kissed other women. Plenty of them. But those kisses had always been to please the women. The thought of kissing Elena would be to please him. She gave no indication she wanted to be kissed. She was merely sitting for her portrait.

That didn't mean she wasn't attracted to him. Hadn't she gotten out of the stagecoach to walk with him even though her mother was calling her back? Didn't her eyes warm with a different glow when she looked at him? He expected women to be attracted to him. Elena was a woman.

He hadn't intended to be attracted to her. At least not yet. He must get that under control. Finding the right woman to marry was a business prospect. He had no intention of letting love spoil his chances of getting the monetary stake he needed. But some attraction could be a nice plus if Elena turned out to be his answer.

Certainly those ducks had done him a favor chasing away that Southworth girl. No attraction there for him. He could have made it work, but that was what it would have been. Work. Making Elena happy wouldn't be work, only pleasure. With a little more time, he could convince her they belonged together. He took a breath to focus on her portrait. The tremble in his fingers surprised him. He couldn't remember the last time he was nervous about making the first touches of color on a canvas.

The brush in his hand often seemed to make the lines without his conscious thought. The shape of the face, the nose, the lips, the eyes.

He was almost glad when Ivy spoke to break his concentration.

"Elena, I think I should go see how Mother is feeling. It takes a while to do a portrait, doesn't it?" The girl looked at Kirby.

"Art takes time." Kirby pushed a smile out on his face. Normally he'd be well along with a portrait by now, but this one needed to be exactly right.

"I know. I can't wait to see it. Keep looking beautiful, Elena. I will be back." She hurried up the path away from the lake.

Elena didn't turn to watch her. She was holding the pose he'd suggested. "How long do you think it will be?" she asked.

"Not all that long. An hour or so."

• • • •

An hour? Or so? Elena didn't remember it being that long when she was watching Kirby paint Vanessa's portrait the day before. But then she hadn't been the one holding a pose. She shouldn't have agreed to let him paint her. A sketch maybe. That wouldn't have taken so long. A few pen strokes by a man who knew how to capture a face on paper.

She was curious about how he would make her look. Would she cringe when she was confronted with his vision of her? But at least, in his portraits, he always found a way to make the women attractive. That could be why he seemed hesitant to begin. Perhaps he wasn't sure he could do that for her. She didn't care about that. She knew she wasn't a beauty like Vanessa. Or Ivy. A person was however the Lord made her. True beauty was more than outward appearance anyway. Pretty is as pretty does. She'd heard those words often, as did most little girls.

She hadn't always taken them to heart and done as she should to make that inward beauty glow. But she could do more to change the inner her than the outer one.

So what if she had her father's nose? It did what a nose was supposed to do. To prove it, she pulled in a deep breath and caught the scent of a nearby flowering bush.

So what if her hair was dark and straight instead of blonde and curly and her skin lacked the pale beauty of her mother and her sister? She reached to smooth down any stray hairs. She rather liked her dark brown hair and the fact that she truly didn't have to worry about the curse of freckles if she shed her bonnet. But Ivy was right. Her mother would be aghast to see Elena holding her face up to the sun, even in this partial shade.

She pushed away thoughts about how she looked. However Kirby portrayed her in the painting, she would thank him sincerely. She wasn't sure why he had volunteered to do her portrait.

Now that Ivy was no longer there with them and no one else had come to watch him paint as sometimes happened, a strained feeling settled between them. She tried to think of something to say, but she wasn't sure she should speak. Surely she didn't have to sit stock-still for an hour. Or so. Already her neck and shoulders felt stiff.

At least she could watch Kirby work. He wasn't being as flamboyant as he usually was when others watched him produce a painting. And she did want to know more about him. They had no chance for anything romantic between them, even if Ivy was right and he was looking for a wife. Perhaps he hoped to find a rich wife just as her mother was looking for someone with unlimited resources to marry Elena.

Marriages weren't always made in heaven. Sometimes they were made in the line to the bank. She sighed. Romance was good in stories where love could conquer all. But here in the real world, where her mother wanted her to marry a man like General Dawson, storybook romance needed to be forgotten.

She should have looked for the general before she came here to get stuck on a stool while Kirby painted a portrait she could not keep. The poor old man had been so upset. He could be ill. She mentally shook away that thought. The general was tough. He had surely handled much worse than Vanessa dying in his arms.

The silence kept building under the oak tree until it practically twanged in her ears. She had to find something to end it. "Does it bother you to talk while you're painting, Kirby?"

That couldn't be true. He had talked the whole time he was doing Vanessa's portrait. But then he'd had an audience. Today there was only her.

"Forgive me. I am being uncharacteristically quiet, aren't I?" He smiled over at her. "I'm concentrating on making the lines, your lines, right. Have you ever tried to draw someone's face?"

"I did a portrait of my father once. At least, I tried. I'm not sure anyone would have recognized my efforts. Not even Father."

"The person you are capturing with your pen or brush is generally the last to recognize themselves in their portraits. Few of us see ourselves as others do."

"I suppose you are right." She thought a moment before she went on. "I should have drawn him from the back, clipping one of his roses."

"You still can." When she gave him a puzzled frown, he went on. "You have that picture in your mind. You can draw it from memory. Just as I could draw your portrait without you posing for it."

"Then why am I posing?"

"I could do a fair job from memory, but it is always better to have a visual in front of my eyes."

"How is it coming? It seems as though it's been an hour already."

"Hardly, my dear. More like a quarter of an hour. But you don't have to sit totally still. Feel free to move if you want."

She did twist her head from side to side before she assumed the pose again. "Thank you for being so kind to my sister. She loved posing for the picture with the ducks. And she said you helped get the letter to her friend in Lexington."

"She was excited about that. And about finding the coins Miss Southworth didn't want for fear they might have fallen among some duck droppings." He laughed. "Your sister didn't have any qualms about picking them up."

"Ivy isn't afraid to go after what she wants."

"And you?" He peered over his easel at her. "Are you the same?"

She fiddled with the ribbons of her bonnet a moment before she answered, "I don't think I've ever been as sure about what I want as she is. Life can be complicated."

"I suppose so." He looked from her back to the painting as he went on. "But let's make it simpler. Think about last summer. What were you dreaming of doing then?"

"Last summer." She sighed. "I don't think I was dreaming of anything. My life already seemed settled into a quiet little spinster corner."

"Spinster!" He jerked his head up to stare at her. "Surely you jest."

"Not at all. I spent many days in my father's rose garden, sketching and painting. No suitors showed up at my door."

"Would you have opened it if they had knocked?"

"Perhaps." Elena smiled slightly. "I'm not sure. But this summer I am no longer hiding in my father's garden."

In some ways she supposed she was still finding gardens to hide in here. Her smile settled in a comfortable spot inside her as she remembered someone seeking her out in those hiding spots. She wished Kirby would finish the portrait. She wanted to go in search of Princess the cat. And Andrew.

"You have come out of the garden to charm everyone you meet. You are in much demand at the ball."

"Only because the gentlemen need partners for the dance."

"Everyone needs a partner, and here at the Springs, where romance seems to always be in the air, partners can be found."

"Are you looking for romance, Kirby?" Her cheeks warmed. She couldn't believe she said that out loud.

"An artist thrives on romance." He smiled at her and then made a flourishing swipe with his paintbrush. "Are you ready to see your portrait?"

She stood up and looked around, not sure she wanted to see how he saw her. "Oh look, here comes Ivy. And General Dawson."

"That old man knows how to keep a pretty girl on his arm." Kirby didn't sound happy to see him coming.

Elena wasn't glad to see them coming either. Now she wouldn't be able to slip away to find Andrew.

"Don't you want to look at your portrait?" Kirby said.

"I'm not sure. As you said earlier, we don't always see ourselves as others see us."

He took her arm. "Come. Look at it before they get here." He pulled her around to the easel. "You might like it."

Elena stared at the face in the painting. It wasn't her. It couldn't be her. She touched her hair. Her buns on each side of her face felt tightly wound, the way they always were. But in the painting, the woman's hair was loosely tied back with a few strands falling around her face. The woman's eyes were a mixture of green and blue. And her nose didn't look too big at all. This woman was actually remarkably attractive, even pretty.

"That's not me."

"I did change your hair." He traced one of the strands with the brush he still held. "Freed it from its buns and pins."

She looked at him and then back at the painting. "My eyes and nose are different as well."

"No, this is you. Have you never looked in a mirror? Really looked."

Ivy and the general came up behind them. Ivy clapped her hands. "Oh, Elena. It is wonderful."

"It doesn't look like me," Elena said.

"But it does. Except for the hair." She turned to General Dawson. "Doesn't it, General?"

"It is a good likeness." The general looked from the portrait to Elena and then Kirby. "Are you giving the portrait to Miss Elena, Mr. Frazier?"

"She says she doesn't want it. She simply graciously allowed me to practice my art on her."

"Then I'll buy it," General Dawson said.

Kirby shook his head. "It's not for sale."

"I see." The older man's eyes tightened as he looked at Kirby.

Elena frowned at the two men. She hadn't expected the general to offer to buy her portrait, but Kirby's refusal to sell it to him was even more surprising.

She decided to ignore them and turned to Ivy, still studying the painting. "You really think it looks like me, Ivy?"

"Of course. He captured you. It's even better than the one he did of Vanessa." Ivy's smile vanished as she blinked back tears. "General Dawson says they are going to have a funeral for Vanessa later today. He thought we would want to know."

"No family came?" Elena looked at the general.

"No," he said. "Dr. Graham thinks it is best to honor her with a funeral and burial here on the grounds. He has his men digging the grave."

"I can't stand it." Ivy sniffled. "To think about her under the ground. It's just so awful."

Elena put an arm around her. "Shh. We will remember her the way she was yesterday."

"We have to go to the funeral."

"Of course. When is it?"

"Not for a few hours." The general spoke up. "So, come along, ladies. We will see what the dining room is offering for a midday snack."

"Would you like to come with us, Mr. Frazier?" Ivy looked around. "I don't see anyone waiting to have their portrait done right now."

"You would be welcome." The general's smile seemed a little stiff. "However, Dr. Graham asked me to tell you he wants you to bring your paints and find him at the hotel. I think he wants you to do a last portrait of the unfortunate young lady before her funeral."

Kirby's face hardened. "I don't do funeral portraits."

"Then I suggest you let the doctor know that." The general might have said "suggest," but his voice had the sound of command. "Come along, ladies, before we grow faint with hunger."

Elena took another peek at the painting before she followed the general. Could she really look anything like that? She turned toward Kirby. "Thank you for doing my portrait."

"My pleasure. If you change your mind about wanting it, you only have to say so."

"I told you I couldn't pay you anything."

"And I told you no payment was needed."

"If General Dawson wants it, you should sell it to him." Elena glanced at the general. Wanting the painting must mean he was serious about considering her as a bride. She wouldn't think about that right now.

"I could make it worth your time," General Dawson said.

"Not for sale."

Kirby turned back to the painting to trace one of the strands along the face, her face, with his paintbrush. Elena could almost feel his touch. She put on her bonnet and tied the ribbons. When General Dawson offered her his arm, she took it. Ivy hesitated and then took his other arm.

As they headed toward the hotel, Elena looked at the walkway that wound up toward the rose garden where she had talked to Andrew that first morning. He might be waiting for her there now. But she had to go with Ivy and the general. She would find Andrew later.

31

People gathered at the edge of the lawn in front of the hotel for Vanessa's funeral. Elena didn't know whether that was from curiosity or genuine sympathy for a young woman dying in such a strange way during the last dance at a ball. Whichever it was, every Springs guest must have been gathered around the burial site.

The place Dr. Graham had chosen for his servants to dig a grave was lovely. The spring blooms on the redbud trees along one side were long gone, but their heart-shaped leaves seemed perfect. Hydrangeas bloomed on the other side. No clouds disturbed the blue of the late afternoon sky.

General Dawson was waiting for them when they arrived. He insisted that Elena, her mother, and Ivy move to the front of the onlookers. It seemed only right that they act as family for Vanessa, and Elena was glad she and Ivy had decided to wear their mourning dresses to match their mother.

Elena wondered if somewhere a mother or sister, some loved one, would watch for Vanessa to return home, wherever that was, and grieve when she didn't come. They might never know what became of her.

Not that Dr. Graham couldn't still locate her family. He had the portrait Kirby had done to show anyone who might come looking for a missing daughter or friend. Perhaps he would also have a painting of her death face if Kirby had complied with the doctor's wishes.

Surely he had, for how could he refuse, even though it had been more than apparent he wanted nothing to do with painting Vanessa after death stole her smile? She didn't blame him for that. She thought it best to remember a person in life. That was why she had avoided looking at her father in his casket.

But she had seen Vanessa in death. She had knelt beside her, heard her whispered words. *"No one will ever know."* Elena needed to forget those words and remember her last ones as life left her. *"I hear music."* Then Vanessa was gone. Nothing but the shell of her body was left there on the dance floor.

Elena pushed aside that vision and followed her mother and Ivy as they threaded through the crowd. All at once, her ears picked up the sound of their name. She held her breath and listened as intently as she could.

"There is that Bradford girl who saw someone give the poor departed her last drink." A woman's voice.

Another voice answered. "Poisoned, they say."

"What else would cause her to die so suddenly?"

When Elena looked around, two women shifted their eyes swiftly away from her. She shouldn't have turned her head. Better to pretend not to hear.

She let her gaze stray to others in the crowd, and there at last was Andrew. She had managed to slip away from the general and Ivy long enough to take a round through the gardens after the midday meal, but he had been nowhere to be found.

She smiled and started to motion for him to come stand with them. A beautiful woman grabbed his arm and stepped very close to Andrew. Elena's hand froze in midair. Somehow she knew without anyone telling her that the woman was Gloria, his intended bride last summer. The one who had left him. The one who now had come back.

She didn't look away quickly enough. Andrew saw her and his face changed. Not a smile. Not a friendly wave. Nothing. She whipped her gaze from him and hurried to take her place between Ivy and her mother at the front of the gathered people.

Tears pricked her eyes as the musicians began to play the same song they were playing for the last dance the night before. The dance she had with Andrew. She gave herself a mental shake and blinked away her tears. She was being ridiculous. Andrew had offered her casual friendship. Nothing more. But it had felt so right talking with him in the garden and then while they were dancing. Until this very moment, she hadn't even realized she had entertained the idea of something more than friendship with him.

That was all he'd offered. She was the one imagining more. How silly she'd become since being here at the Springs. Being attracted to Kirby and now to Andrew. Her head was spinning. She needed to forget romance. Forget falling in love. That was for others, like the beautiful woman clinging to Andrew. Not for her.

Tears filled her eyes and spilled over to moisten her cheeks. Everybody would think she was weeping for Vanessa. Shedding tears for the young woman was only proper. Her death was tragic. There was nothing tragic about Andrew being reunited with the woman he wanted to marry. Elena should be happy for him. Happy for both of them.

She dabbed her eyes with her handkerchief as more tears spilled over. She needed to stop thinking about Andrew. Think instead about Vanessa as the song ended and a singer stepped forward to bring new tears to Elena's eyes as he sang "Amazing Grace."

She'd heard the song many times in church. Had even hummed or sung it when she was in her father's rose garden, but the words had never touched her heart quite the way they did now.

Grace. She hoped Vanessa had embraced the grace that could take one through dangers, toils, and snares. Grace would help Elena get through whatever lay ahead for her too. She would forget the feeling that had been awakening in her heart for Andrew. She would refuse to think about Kirby and how he had painted her portrait with beauty. With the grace of the Lord, she would find her way along whatever path opened to her.

While she might never know what dangers and snares Vanessa had tried to avoid by taking an assumed name and coming to the Springs, she could still think about her in heaven basking in the bright shining light as she sang the Lord's praises. After all, she had said she heard music.

Elena wiped away a few more tears. At least these were for Vanessa instead of herself as the last words of the song drifted away.

Dr. Graham stepped to the front then to speak about Vanessa's beauty and her zest for life exhibited by her love of the dance. "No one who saw this young woman spinning around the ballroom last night expected anything but that she would be dancing again this evening. Instead, we are witnesses to the brevity of life. None of us are promised a tomorrow. So we must instead live as this young woman did, with joy in each day, since we never know which day might be our last. We knew Miss Vanessa for only a brief moment in time, but her loss is still a sorrow in our hearts."

He gestured toward the wooden casket covered with a cascade of freshly cut roses. A green rug covered the waiting grave. When Ivy's sniffles became a sob, Elena wrapped an arm around her. Ivy turned to hide her face against Elena's shoulder. Tears slid down Elena's cheeks too. Even their mother was blinking back tears.

General Dawson patted Mother's shoulder before he joined

Dr. Graham in front of them. He shared about Vanessa's day at the Springs and how she looked like a princess when she came down the stairs into the ballroom.

He opened a Bible but didn't look down at it as he recited Psalm 23. His voice deepened but trembled slightly as he spoke. "Yea, though I walk through the valley of the shadow of death, I will fear no evil: for thou art with me; thy rod and thy staff they comfort me."

His voice got stronger as he went on to the next verse and then finished with a sound of victory that made Elena wonder if he'd once been a preacher as well as an army general. "Surely goodness and mercy shall follow me all the days of my life: and I will dwell in the house of the LORD for ever." He closed his Bible. "And that is where our young friend is on this day and forevermore."

When he stepped back beside Mother, she reached for his hand. He whispered something in her ear before he gave her his handkerchief.

"There's no more to add to that," Dr. Graham said. "We shall always remember this young lady who spent her last day on earth among us. Thank all of you for coming. We will have no dance tonight, but tomorrow evening the ballroom will be open again. I'm sure Miss Vanessa would be the first to tell us to continue to dance with joy."

Elena turned to go back to the hotel. She did not want to see Andrew and the woman again, but her eyes were drawn to him like filings to a magnet. The woman had started back toward the hotel, but Andrew didn't immediately follow her. Instead he seemed to be waiting for Elena to glance his way. He wasn't smiling, but Elena imagined his face had a look of appeal. Elena's heart gave a lurch before she shifted her gaze to the trees and the sky, anywhere but at Andrew. Her imagination was running away with her. He hadn't given her any kind of special look. Not even a hint of a smile.

At the hotel, Elena's mother wanted to go to their room to freshen up before going to the dining room. Elena started to follow them, but General Dawson stopped her.

"Can I have a word with you, Miss Elena?"

When her mother gave her a look, Elena's throat tightened. Had her mother made some kind of arrangement with General Dawson without telling her?

"Of course, General." She pulled in a breath and smiled as she went with him out onto the veranda, mostly empty now since it was the dinner hour.

"Let us stand over by the railing where we can have a little privacy."

"If you wish." She let him escort her over to the wooden railing. She grabbed it to hide the tremble in her fingers. She wasn't sure she could make herself say yes.

He stared out toward the horizon for a moment before he spoke. "I saw you looking at Andrew."

That wasn't at all what she expected him to say. "Andrew?" She acted as if she wasn't sure who he meant. When he simply looked over at her without saying more, she went on. "Oh, yes. Andrew Harper. I did see him in the crowd. With a lady. Is that his intended, Gloria?"

"His intended last summer."

"Oh. Do you know Mr. Harper well?" She tried to keep her voice casual, but the old gentleman seemed to see through her pretense.

"I have known Andrew for years." He smiled a little at Elena before he turned his gaze back to where the sun was sliding lower in the afternoon sky. He was quiet for a moment. "The question is do you know him?"

"I can't really say that I do. I met him on the stagecoach on the way here."

"Ahh. The same one where Mr. Frazier heroically stopped the runaway horses."

259

"You heard about that?"

"Here at the Springs, nothing much stays secret for long."

That made Elena remember the whispers she'd heard from the women in the crowd. "I guess except who Vanessa really was."

The general waved his hand in dismissal. "In time, that will be discovered."

Elena looked behind them to be sure no one was close enough to hear. "Do you think she was poisoned?"

He hesitated a moment too long before answering. "Dr. Graham doesn't think so. As a doctor, he should know. I think it's best that we trust his superior knowledge in this. The local officials have agreed with his findings."

Elena nodded. This conversation wasn't at all what she expected. First asking her about Andrew and then appearing to be uncomfortable talking about Vanessa's death. She supposed that was to be expected, but why had he asked about Andrew? Had Andrew told him about meeting her in the gardens? She pushed aside her questions and waited for whatever the general had to say.

The silence stretched between them. A few other guests came out on the veranda, perhaps already finished with their dinners. When General Dawson finally spoke, his words again were unexpected. "The artist, this Kirby Frazier, what do you think of him, Elena?"

She felt a rush of warmth in her cheeks. "He's an interesting man. I admire his artistic ability."

"True. And he's a strong figure of a man. I can understand if you are attracted to him."

Elena studied her hands on the railing. She could feel him watching her. Why was he asking her about Kirby? Did he think Kirby was his competition? "Kirby Frazier is not someone I can be interested in except as an artist."

"Because of your mother?"

That surprised Elena too. She looked over at him and decided to answer honestly. "Yes."

The general actually smiled as he stared out at the lawn again. "Juanita has been scheming since she arrived here, but she is somewhat blinded by all her machinations. I think she wants to be a general, but she has no army."

"She has Ivy and me. Especially me."

"True, that she does." He gave her a quick look and then stared out at the horizon again as he went on. "My dear wife used to accuse me of being a matchmaker. She would laugh and say that was not a job for an old general." He chuckled. "She, of course, was right. The dear woman was always right. But here at the Springs I rather enjoy watching the matches being made between this or that lady and gentleman. This is a great place for romance."

"I've heard others say the same. Unfortunately for my mother, I don't appear to have a talent for romance."

He turned to look at her then. "My dear Elena, you sell yourself short. I think, should you open your heart and arms, you could have your pick of men."

"Are you one of those picks, General?" She couldn't believe she spoke those words aloud. What would the man think of her?

When he threw back his head and laughed, she wanted to sink through the veranda. "Do forgive me for being so forward, sir." Her cheeks were on fire.

"There, there, not to worry. I like a young woman not afraid to ask the pertinent questions. No need tiptoeing around what needs saying."

That wasn't an answer, but Elena didn't dare ask him anything more.

He reached over and patted her hand as she gripped the railing. "I knew Juanita had that in her plans, but rest easy, my dear. It is not in my plans. I would much rather have you as a daughter."

"You mean . . ." Words failed her.

"I mean my matchmaking has your mother in my sights."

"Mother?"

He shrugged a little. "She's a lovely woman, and I hope to convince her that I can be a suitable match once her mourning time is over."

Relief flooded Elena. She wasn't going to have to say yes to a proposal from the general. Her mother could do that. "She may think she has to play the widow role for a year."

"Play the widow role?" He laughed again. "Are you saying she is not sincere?"

"No, not at all. I chose my words poorly. It's just that Father left us in a rather precarious situation, and she has some resentment of that."

"Yes, I know about your situation."

"Mother told you?" The general was full of surprises.

"While Juanita was asking about me, I did some asking about her."

"Then you know that we are pretending to be something we are not."

"I wouldn't say that at all. Juanita has made no secret of the fact that she would like to make favorable matches for her daughters. She is not the first parent to come to the Springs with that in mind. Your financial situation would become clear before any final matches were made."

"I see. Then it could be that Mother will not be able to make a favorable match for me."

"Perhaps. But it could be that I can be a better matchmaker than her."

"With Kirby Frazier? He has no interest in me."

The general frowned. "I might have thought that myself before I saw your portrait today. You did look at it, didn't you?"

"Of course. Not that it looked much like me."

"Maybe not as you see yourself, but it was as he sees you. Every line of that painting had love in it."

"Love of his art, perhaps." The man was talking nonsense. At least about Kirby. It was wonderful that he planned to propose to her mother and not her. The general as a father figure was much more attractive to consider.

"That too, no doubt. However, I do not think he would be your best choice."

Elena smiled and shook her head. "You are being very kind, General, but I don't truly believe I have choices."

"I saw you looking at Andrew." The general stared straight at her then with no hint of a smile. "And I saw him looking at you. The same as Kirby Frazier is not your best choice, Gloria Collins is not Andrew's best choice. Keep that in mind in the days ahead. That is all I ask. I am very fond of you both."

Elena didn't know what to say. She wanted to believe the general, but she had seen the beautiful girl clinging to Andrew. That morning, she had heard the sadness in his voice when he spoke of her. Whether General Dawson thought she was best or not didn't really matter. It was what Andrew thought was best.

The general turned away from the railing. "There's your mother and Ivy looking for you." He started across the veranda toward them. "Perhaps we can find a table together in the dining room."

Elena stayed where she was for a moment. The sun sank below the horizon. The night bugs began chirring. A whippoorwill sang its name. And Vanessa in her beautiful princess dress would be covered with dirt. Elena didn't want to go in to dinner. She wanted to walk down off the veranda and along the paths through the late afternoon shadows.

"Elena, are you coming?" her mother called.

With a sigh, she turned toward her. "I'm coming."

32

Kirby watched for Elena after the funeral. He was disappointed when her mother and Ivy came in the hotel without her to head up the stairs, but that might be better. The mother had yet to smile his way. She could definitely spoil his chances with Elena.

He waited close to the door as people streamed inside and toward the dining room. She didn't come in. A couple of older ladies tried to get him to join them. Normally, he would have smiled and gone along, but this evening he was determined to talk to Elena.

With the promise that he would find them later, he stepped away to peer out a window. Elena was next to the veranda railing with General Dawson. What was it with that old man and Elena? Did he think his money could buy him a young wife the way he'd wanted to buy Elena's portrait? Kirby probably would have a pocketful of cash if he'd let the general have it, but sometimes it rankled when a man with money thought he could get whatever he wanted.

Besides, he liked the portrait. He shouldn't have freed her hair from those tightly braided buns, but it seemed somehow necessary. Elena had liked it. He knew she did, even though she had never seen herself that way in a mirror. Today he had been her mirror.

The old man hadn't wanted to buy it because he liked it. Instead, something about the portrait, something about Kirby, bothered him. Another reason not to let him buy the painting. He might have destroyed it somehow. Still, money was money. He couldn't remember ever refusing to sell one of his paintings. He once even sold a portrait he'd done from memory of his little sister. He could always do another. That was true with Elena too. Especially if she agreed to marry him.

Marry him. He had come to the Springs to find a wife to finance his dream of going west. He needed the money, but what would he do with a wife? Ever since he left the farm, he'd been on his own and able to do whatever he wanted whenever he wanted.

Having a wife could change that. Most women wanted children, and want them or not, they generally came along pretty fast after a couple married. The idea of being a husband was shocking enough, but thinking about being a father was terrifying. How could a man roam the west if he had children?

He shrugged off those worries. He had always been able to figure out how to do what he wanted. Being married wouldn't change that. The only thing it would change was having the money to do those things. Besides, Elena seemed the adventurous sort. She might like roaming the west, and didn't women who went west figure out how to raise their children the same as they did here in Kentucky? Things would work out.

He actually felt a flame of excitement at the thought of marrying Elena. She had a unique beauty that he had captured in the portrait. To make it all even better, she was an artist. She would understand about the pull to capture images with paint. She would support him.

All he had to do was ask her as soon as he got that old general out of the way. She couldn't be considering anything romantic with him. Just as he thought that, the old man laughed and put his hand over Elena's on the railing. She was smiling. An easy smile. That didn't mean anything. Probably the old codger had told her some story he thought was funny and she was being polite. She wouldn't politely promise her life to him. Not if she could choose Kirby instead.

Her mother and sister called to her to go in for dinner. The general went first, but Elena hesitated a few moments as she stared out at the view from the veranda before she followed him.

Kirby headed toward the kitchen, where he would get one of the servants to fix him a plate. Dr. Graham could entertain his old ladies without Kirby's help tonight. He would eat fast and be back here to watch for Elena. It looked a perfect evening for a walk. A romantic walk. He wasn't waiting any longer.

· · · ·

After dinner, Elena's mother and Ivy were both ready to return to their room. Ivy was exhausted after the funeral, and Mother felt a headache coming on. Elena promised to be along shortly, after she went out on the veranda to enjoy the evening air. The nearly full moon was just coming up to spread silvery light over the grounds.

The general followed her out to tell her good night and ask her to promise not to wander alone on the grounds.

"Don't you think I would be safe?" Elena asked.

"I'm sure you would, but it's never a good idea for a beautiful young lady to step out into the dark alone."

"The moon is full. That will make it almost as bright as day."

"But there are shadows. Deep shadows." He studied her. "If you must walk, I will go with you."

"No." She could tell the general was tired. "I promise to stay on the veranda. You go rest, and tomorrow you can teach Ivy how to lawn bowl."

"Perhaps we can talk Juanita into giving it a try as well. She claims that when she was a girl, she was the best of all her friends at keeping her hoop rolling."

"She never told me that."

"I'm sure there are many things about your mother you don't know. That is how parents and children can be. Divided by years and expectations. But now that you are a young lady, the two of you can be friends as well as mother and daughter."

"I hope so."

"Sometimes we need to do more than hope. We need to add actions to that hope of friendship."

"I will keep that in mind."

He smiled and patted her arm. "Good night, Elena. Tomorrow will be another day. Just give thought to what I said earlier about Andrew. And you."

She watched him go inside. Even though he was tired, he still had a spring in his step that hadn't been there when she shared that first dance with him a few weeks ago.

And what about her own steps? She had changed too. Happy to have partners for the dance instead of dreading it as she had on those first nights. She was no longer afraid of the thought of romance. She had met men who might make her consider marriage. Of course, she had yet to hear even the hint of a proposal.

The general saying Kirby had painted her portrait with love had to be his matchmaking imagination. Not that he wanted her to make any kind of match with Kirby. He was pushing her toward Andrew. A place she would be more than ready to go, but even though General Dawson said Gloria wasn't the match Andrew needed, that didn't make it true.

She had sneaked looks across the dining room at Andrew and Gloria. She was beautiful with her honey-brown hair, her perfect nose, and bow-shaped lips. The way Ivy was. The way

Vanessa had been. No matter how Kirby had flattered Elena in the portrait he'd done, she did not have their beauty.

Andrew was very attentive to the woman. After all, she was his intended whether the general thought she was his best choice or not. The general wasn't the one making that choice. Nor was Elena.

Besides, she hadn't known Andrew nearly long enough to consider herself in love. So what if her heart had felt lighter when they were talking and she had matched his dance steps with ease? She had simply allowed herself to be carried away by his kind offer of friendship.

There would be someone else for her. Someone she might yet find before they left the Springs. If not, then after she returned home. She could stop hiding out in her father's rose garden. She was ready to begin life on her own. If not with a husband, then as a teacher or clerk or something. She needed to be something other than a spinster daughter with no future.

"Lovely night, isn't it, Elena?"

Elena jerked around to see Kirby. She had been so deep in thought that she hadn't noticed him coming up behind her.

"Sorry," he said. "I didn't mean to startle you."

"No, that's fine. I was simply woolgathering." She smiled at him and tried not to think about what General Dawson had said. No way could Kirby Frazier be attracted to her. "I was enjoying the moonlight."

"Would you like to take a walk?" He offered her his arm.

She thought of her promise to the general, but she wouldn't be alone. Not that he would approve of her escort or the fact that the two of them would be alone with no chaperone.

"It would be lovely to see the lake in the moonlight." She slipped her hand under his elbow.

"Then that is where we will go." He smiled down at her as he led her toward the steps off the veranda.

The trees and flowers along the walkway took on a different

beauty in the evening light. "Have you ever painted a moonlit scene?" Elena asked.

"I have, but never one with a lady wearing black. That would be an interesting study of moonlight and shadows." He looked at her as they moved past a pine tree's shade. "If you were to duck your head to hide your face under your bonnet, you might look like a shadow."

She stopped and looked down. "Have I disappeared into the gray of night?"

He laughed. "Not completely. The moon may be too bright this evening, but you do make a lovely shadow in the night."

"A shadow in the night." Elena echoed his words. "That could almost describe Vanessa. A shadow, but a bright one, that fell across our paths for just a moment and then was gone. Ivy and I wanted to honor her by wearing a symbol of mourning, although I do think Vanessa might have preferred we wear our brightest dresses instead."

"Will you continue to wear black?"

"Oh no. Black is a trial in the summertime. Summer needs light, bright colors."

"Men wear black or dark colors all year round." He seemed to be teasing her with that.

"True, but men can remove their jackets during the heat of the day."

"And roll up their shirtsleeves. Especially an artist wielding a paintbrush." He waved his free arm around in the air to demonstrate. "Part of doing ladies' portraits is the performance."

"I didn't notice you performing while painting mine today."

"You are right. I hoped to impress you with the actual art."

"I've never worn my hair like you painted it."

"That was a bit of artistic license that I perhaps should not have taken. I could paint it out and do your hairstyle more as it is now."

"No, no. That isn't necessary. I can't take the portrait, so it really doesn't matter if it resembles me that much." Better that it didn't, she thought. "Since I couldn't pay you for your work, you should have let General Dawson buy it."

"I could have, but I didn't. Men like him think everything can be bought, and that's not always true."

"Do you think General Dawson wealthy?"

"I would guess nearly all of the guests here are well off."

"I suppose so." Elena looked ahead down the path as she wondered if there were others here like her pretending to be something they weren't. Maybe it would be best to slide away from talking about money. "Do you have family, Kirby?"

"None to speak of. I've been on my own since I was sixteen."

"Always as an artist?"

"Yes, but I've done plenty of other things to get by."

"Such as ladies' portraits instead of painting something more creative?"

"You're very intuitive, Miss Bradford. Not that it doesn't take plenty of creativity to please those ladies you speak of." He smiled. "I don't think I even pleased you with yours."

"It was lovely and very creative. I have looked in plenty of mirrors."

He stopped walking and cocked his head to the side to peer at her. "But obviously with eyes too critical."

His eyes seemed to be seeing more about her than she wanted to reveal, just as he'd seen more about her while painting her portrait. It could be she should have told him good night and returned to the safety of her hotel room instead of agreeing to walk out in the moonlight with him.

Safety? Why did that thought come to mind? She was safe walking this pathway with him.

She let his remark go unchallenged. "What are some of those things you've done other than art? If you can tell me."

He laughed then and began walking again. "I have yet to rob a bank or anything like that, although some husbands have

thought my prices for their wives' portraits were highway rob-
bery."

"But the wives were pleased?"

"I learned early who needed to be pleased." He was quiet
for a moment before he went on. "Have you ever had a dream?
Wanted to do something so much that you would do almost
anything to find a way to make it happen?"

Everyone seemed to be challenging her view of her future.
Did she have any dreams? Any hopes? The memory of Andrew sitting among the hollyhocks with her flashed through her
mind. If that was a hope, it had vanished like mist at sunrise.

Could Kirby Frazier be a hope? She had thought so when she
walked with him in front of the stagecoach horses. He was so
good-looking. So manly and yet an artist. She liked him. She
truly did, but something was missing. Then again, she had considered a life with the general. While she had never been able
to imagine loving General Dawson, she could imagine loving
Kirby. She didn't now, but surely she could.

He watched her as he waited for her answer.

"A dream," she said. "I suppose most women dream of marriage and family."

"Most women? Does that not include you?"

"I don't know. Maybe if I met the right man. My mother
says I never tried to find whomever that might be."

"Could it be you were wishing for something better?" he
asked.

"Wishes don't always come true."

"I believe they can if we wish the right things."

They had reached the lake. She freed her hand from his elbow
as they stopped to admire the still water kissed with silvery
sparkles by the moon. Frogs added bass notes to the trill of
katydids and crickets. In the distance, an owl hooted.

After a moment, she said, "But I hear in your words you

do have such a dream. That something you would do almost anything to make happen."

"I can draw maps."

Elena glanced over at him, not sure why he mentioned maps. Perhaps he wanted to change the subject to keep from talking about his dream.

But then he went on. "So, I talked a surveying party into taking me west with them. They were desperate since the man they had lined up to record their journey and make those maps did something to get arrested. They figured taking a chance on me was better than trying to break him out of jail."

"I'm sure you had no problem drawing their maps."

"I learned as we went along. By the time we got to new territory, I could make the maps they wanted, but I saw so much more to record. The country out there is incredible. That was ten years ago, and I've been working for a way to go back ever since."

"Ten years is a long time."

"I know." He kept his gaze on the lake. "I had a room full of paintings I planned to sell earlier this year, but the hotel where I was staying had a fire. Everything was destroyed."

"That's terrible." Elena touched his arm.

When he captured her hand, she didn't try to pull away, but she didn't feel the lightning flash she'd felt that morning when Andrew took her hand.

"You would like the west."

He put a finger under her chin to turn her face toward his. She had the feeling that if she took a step toward him, he would draw her into an embrace. She didn't take that step or speak. She had no idea what to say.

He traced her cheek with the tips of his fingers. "You could sketch the flowers you see."

"Are there flowers?"

He looked a little puzzled by her question. "Aren't flowers everywhere?"

"I suppose so, and I've read that cacti have blooms, and sometimes after a rain, the desert explodes in flowers."

"It's not all desert. There are amazing things to see out there."

"Amazing things for you to paint and perhaps flowers for me."

She didn't know why she felt let down. She did sketch flowers. She wasn't the artist he was, but had he even noticed a flower while he was in the west? Of course, he would have been only a little older than Ivy then. A boy didn't always appreciate the beauty of flowers. He was seeing mountains and rock formations and canyons, perhaps even the boiling pools and geysers she'd heard about.

"It will be perfect for both of us. All I need is a stake."

"A stake?"

"Enough money to get me there and keep me going until I start selling some of my work."

"I see." And she did see.

She almost laughed as she realized he thought she could supply that stake. That her family was one of the well-to-do guests here at the Springs. That she had money.

She stepped back, away from the touch of his hands. She started to tell him how wrong he was but decided to wait. Too much had already happened on this day. Tomorrow she would find words to let him know he would have to look elsewhere for that stake.

"I better go back to the hotel. Mother might be worried." She wouldn't be. She'd be in bed asleep by now, but he wouldn't know that. She turned to start away from the lake.

He caught her arm to hold her there for another moment. "You will think about it, won't you, Elena?"

"Of course." She doubted if she'd think of anything else. Unless it was Andrew.

33

Elena didn't sleep well. How could she with all that had happened in the last two days? Vanessa coming and so tragically dying on the same day. Her funeral. Finding out General Dawson wasn't interested in her but in her mother. Feeling drawn toward Andrew only to see him with his once bride-to-be. Seeing that portrait Kirby did of her and hearing the general say love was in its lines.

Then Kirby the same as proposing marriage because he needed a stake for his westward dream. Thinking she could make that happen. She didn't know whether to laugh or weep. Certainly sleep wasn't easy.

All of it was enough to make her go back to thinking about the peace of a spinster's chair in her sister's house someday. She could sketch Ivy's children or at least the flowers they might bring their old aunt.

No wonder she had never entertained the idea of love if this was how it made one feel. Confused. Unhappy. Hopeful. Distraught. Uncertain. Wishful.

Even before she knew Kirby was looking for a rich wife-to-be the same as her mother was looking for a rich husband-to-be for Elena, something didn't feel quite right. She was attracted to him. What woman wouldn't be? But . . . There shouldn't be a *but* in her thoughts if she was truly ready to go west with him.

She could have said yes. She could have stepped into his embrace. Perhaps even been kissed. Wasn't it time she was kissed to give herself something to remember if she did end up in that spinster's corner? Of course, when she revealed her lack of money, he would be looking elsewhere.

Still, there in the shimmering moonlight by the lake, she could have let romance overrule common sense. She could have pushed thoughts of Andrew away. She needed to do that anyway now that Gloria was back in his arms.

And she was ending up in no man's arms. Not even the general's. What tricks life could play on a person.

When Elena got back to the room last night, Ivy had stirred from sleep and asked where she'd been. For a moment she had thought about telling her, but she needed to think it through first. Ivy would tell her to say yes to Kirby and not worry about money or the lack thereof. She would think romance should rule. Elena did hope it would for Ivy.

Now with the first light of day creeping in their windows, Elena slid out of bed without waking Ivy. She had laid out her day dress last night. Even her corset. The one lacing in the front that she could do on her own. As she put it on, she wondered if the women out west wore corsets. Surely they did. If they were ladies.

Maybe she wouldn't have to worry about being a lady in the west. She could forget about corsets and waists squeezed so tiny it could be hard to breathe. She started to take off the offending garment. Did she care about being a lady? But then she pulled the laces as tight as she could before tying them. She wasn't in the west. She was at the Springs, where a woman was expected to be a lady.

She might have broken rules for ladies last evening walking

out into the moonlit night with Kirby. She might be the subject of more whispers. Thinking that made her remember the whispers she'd heard at Vanessa's funeral. *Poisoned drink.* She needed to warn Ivy again about looking at anyone with suspicion.

Whatever had happened to Vanessa might never be known. Elena couldn't do anything about that, but she wanted Ivy to be safe. She still wished her mother would send Ivy back to Lexington instead of thinking Elena was worrying over nothing. Maybe that was true. She fervently hoped so as she picked up her sketchbook and slipped out the door without making a sound.

Outside, the gray of night lingered while the coming of the sun was naught but a faint glow along the eastern horizon. She should have stayed in bed. Tried to sleep instead of being on this fool's quest. Andrew wasn't going to be searching for her among the flowers this morning. He had found someone else.

Andrew wasn't the only reason she wanted to be in the gardens. She needed time to think about Kirby. He hadn't actually proposed, but he had to know she wouldn't go with him unless they married. Not that it mattered. Once he knew her family had no money to finance anything, she was sure he would lose his desire for her to go west with him, but what if he didn't? She could go with him. She didn't love him, but she liked him. That could grow into love.

And wouldn't her mother be surprised? Everyone would be surprised. Maybe most of all herself.

She went by the lake and remembered Kirby's touch on her cheek. She didn't look over to where his easel stand waited for a new canvas. Instead, she kept her eyes on the ducks floating out on the water and found a new path that led through the willows and up among some blooming bushes she didn't recognize. She needed a flower book.

The path led out of the trees and bushes into a wide-open space. The shooting range. Deserted now but someone might come to practice their shooting skills before breakfast. It wasn't the place for a solitary female.

Elena melted back into the trees where she stepped off the path when she caught the scent of roses. Her shoes and dress hem got damp in the dewy grass, but she didn't care. They would dry. She didn't always have to stay on the beaten path.

That made her think of going west again. That would certainly be an off-the-usual-path destination for her. If only she wanted to seize that opportunity instead of lingering here in hopes Andrew would be somewhere in these gardens hunting her.

All at once she heard angry voices. She pulled in a breath and stopped still behind a thick line of evergreen bushes. While she had wanted to find Andrew, she had foolishly given no thought to the possibility of stumbling across others. Perhaps men who weren't gentlemen. Elena couldn't see anyone through the bushes. She didn't want to see anyone. Most of all she didn't want the men to see her.

"You killed the wrong girl." The man sounded furious.

Whoever it was had to be talking about Vanessa. Elena's heart started pounding so hard, she thought the men on the other side of the bushes might hear it. She took tiny sips of air to stay as quiet as possible. She wanted to run away but was afraid to move.

"I didn't kill anybody." The second voice sounded scared. "I only put a little stuff in that drink. 'Tweren't supposed to do anything except make the lass do some heaving. Not die. I wouldn't never kill nobody. Specially not a girl. 'Tweren't my fault she up and died."

"But she did."

"Not from what I gave her."

"You think anyone will believe that? I don't even believe

that. You messed up. Wrong girl. Wrong poison. And then let that Bradford woman see you." The man sounded disgusted.

Elena put her hand over her mouth to smother her gasp.

"Nobody saw me. And even if they did, they wouldn't know me since I dressed up like a gentleman instead of wearing my servant's clothes."

"You think so, do you? But then you've been pretty wrong about everything else."

"I just did what you told me to."

"I never told you to kill anybody. You can hang for that."

"I won't hang by myself." The second man's voice rose.

"I ought to just shoot you and get it over with."

"You don't have the nerve. That's why you paid me to do your dirty work for you."

There was the sound of a scuffle. She could peek around the bush to see the men. That way she could identify them to Dr. Graham. No, better to seize this opportunity to get away without them knowing she had overheard them.

Without looking behind her, she stepped backward and tripped over the cat. She tried to catch her balance, but her feet got tangled in her skirt. She fell with a heavy thud. She had wanted to see the cat again but not like this. It yowled and streaked away.

The men came around the bushes as she scrambled to her feet. She screamed as one of them shoved her back down onto the ground. He clamped one hand over her mouth, pressed down her shoulder with his other hand, and put his knee hard on her middle. He wore a servant's shirt. The other man in a frock coat and top hat stood to the side, his face turned away.

The man holding her down stared at her. "Best stay quiet if you want to keep breathing, lass."

She grabbed at his hand over her mouth and pushed it away to scream again.

"Oh, for the love of—" The other man leaned down to stuff a handkerchief in her mouth. "Get her on her feet."

With her tongue, she pushed the handkerchief out of her mouth as the first man jerked her up and pinned her arms behind her. She only managed a yelp before the other man grabbed the handkerchief and tied it tightly around her head and mouth to gag her.

She kicked at him, but her feet got tangled in her damp skirt and petticoats. She would have fallen again if the man gripping her arms hadn't kept her upright.

"It will go better for you if you stop fighting," he said.

She couldn't listen to him. She had to get away. The man in the hat looked straight at her and without a word punched her in the stomach. Elena slumped back against the other man and tried to keep from passing out as she fought for breath.

The man who hit her spoke to the man holding her. "Take care of her, and then I never want to see you again."

"This will cost you extra."

"I could just put bullets through the both of you." The man's eyes tightened as he reached for his pocket.

"Go ahead. They'll know it was you. The doctor won't cover for you again."

The man swore and jerked some coins and banknotes out of his pocket and threw them on the ground. "Just do what needs doing and be gone from here." He turned on his heel and stalked away.

Elena couldn't help it. She started crying. She wasn't going to be that spinster in her sister's house or go west with Kirby or ever see Ivy or her mother again. Or Andrew.

"There, there, miss," the man said after the other man disappeared through the trees. "I'm sorry he punched you. He's a sorry sort. I shouldn't have never teamed up with him."

She tried to say something but she couldn't make recognizable words, only sounds.

"I won't hurt you so long as you don't try to get away. I've never killed nobody. Not even that pretty lass the other night at the dance. I did put something in her drink, but 'tweren't enough to make her fall down dead. It's just like the doctor says. She danced herself to death."

Elena nodded. Her only hope was that the man meant what he said. She couldn't escape. She could barely breathe.

He pushed her back against a tree trunk. When he jerked up her skirt, she gasped.

"You don't have to worry none about that either. I'm just getting a piece of your underskirt." He kept his shoulder pressed against her as he ripped off the strip on the bottom of her petticoat. He pulled her hands behind the tree and tied them tight. "I'm not leaving that money here to be carried away by squirrels."

She shut her eyes and tried to swallow. She couldn't get sick. She could choke if that happened. Better to stay very still and breathe in and out slowly. This man said he wasn't going to kill her. She had to focus on that as she opened her eyes to watch him snatch up the money.

He muttered under his breath. She only caught a word now and again and nothing that made sense. If only she could talk to him, she might convince him to let her go. She would promise to stay hidden here until he had time to get away. She would promise almost anything to get this gag out of her mouth.

She strained against the fabric tying her hands together. It felt loose enough that she might be able to work one of her hands free. When he looked over at her, she let her arms go limp.

Her hope of sliding her hand free died as he came over to her. "Can't leave you here. Too close to the firing range. One of them shooters might have a call of nature and come trotting over this way." He untied her and then pulled her hands behind her back again. This time he pulled the strips of fabric much tighter as he tied the knots. "Just do what I say and all will be fine."

She nodded. If he'd take the gag off, she wouldn't even scream.

At least not right away. She'd say how she could tell he was a good man who hadn't aimed to hurt anyone. How she hoped he would get away from that other man and that she was glad he'd gotten the money.

"There's an old shed over a ways where I can stash you. They'll search for a pretty girl like you and find you before long. But plenty long enough for me to get my stuff and be gone from here."

Again she nodded. He held one of her elbows as he guided her through some bushes and down a hill to an open field where daisies bloomed. She had always loved daisies. The blooms looked so cheerful, but now they brought tears to her eyes as she wondered if she'd ever see flowers again. She thought of her sketchbook that she dropped when she fell over the cat. Princess Cinderella. And now Elena was going to be locked in a dungeon. Would a prince show up to rescue her?

She must be verging on hysteria to think such silly thoughts. She stumbled along beside the man. Walking with her hands behind her was clumsy. More than once, the man caught her to keep her from falling. He was still muttering, but she didn't try to hear what he said. She just concentrated on putting one foot in front of the other and not getting sick.

The sun was up, spreading fingers of light across the ground that was rougher now. Not clipped. Briars snagged her skirt. The area looked deserted except for the shed the man pushed her toward.

He pulled the bar up that fit across the door. He held on to her with one hand and tugged at the door with the other. Weeds grown up in front of it made it hard to open. No one had been in this shed for a long time.

After he stomped down the weeds and finally yanked open the door, he peered through it. "It won't be so bad. I don't see no snakes." He brushed down some cobwebs with his hand and pushed her inside.

She didn't fight against him. Better to save her energy and keep her wits about her. He could still hurt her. She hunched up one shoulder toward her mouth. She begged him with her eyes as she tried to say "off."

"I don't reckon it could hurt none. Nobody around to hear was you to scream."

He took a knife out of his pocket. Elena's eyes widened as she stepped away from him. He grabbed her. "I told you I wasn't gonna hurt you. Stand still." He turned her away from him and sliced through the handkerchief on the back of her head.

She pushed the gag out of her mouth with her tongue and coughed.

"I'm sorry for all this, but you shouldn't have been sneaking around listening where you had no business being." With that, he stepped out of the shed and banged the door shut.

Elena heard him put the bar down, and then he must have wedged a rock against the bottom of the door before he walked away. If only he hadn't left so quickly. She might have been able to talk him into cutting her hands free too.

The light in the shed was dim in spite of sunlight pushing through a few wide cracks between the planks. When she moved around, dust rose up from the dirt floor. The building was small and empty except for a block of wood in one corner. She didn't see anything she could use to get her hands free. She jerked against the fabric but it held tight. She could wiggle her fingers but couldn't reach the knots.

She sat down on the wood block and bowed her head.

"Dear Lord," she whispered, then hesitated. She'd been taught that every prayer should start with praise. The Bible said to be thankful in all things, but how could she find anything to be thankful for right now with her hands bound behind her and no one to hear even if her mouth wasn't so dry that she wasn't sure she could yell for help?

A rustling at the other end of the shed made her freeze.

What if it was a snake? Or a rat? Or who knew what kind of varmint? But then coming out of the shadows was the cat that must have followed them across the field.

"Hello, Princess."

The cat pushed its head against her skirt.

"I can't rub you, poor thing."

The cat didn't seem concerned. It jumped up into her lap and settled down. When it started purring loudly the way it had yesterday morning, she felt a ridiculous surge of hope. She had little reason to hope. She was in dreadful trouble, but the cat had found her.

This very unusual cat could be her praise, even if it had tripped her earlier. "Dear Lord. Thank you for this cat in my lap. Thank you that I am still alive. Thank you that the man took off the gag. But please help me get my hands free, and send someone to look for me. Please."

She thought of Ivy waking up to find her gone. She wouldn't worry right away. She would see that Elena had taken her sketch pad, but she would miss her eventually. Dear Ivy. She hoped Jacob would answer Ivy's letter and that someday they would marry and be happy together.

She hoped her mother would lay aside her black dresses and take General Dawson's hand in marriage. She hoped Kirby would find a way to go west and become a famous western artist. She hoped Andrew—

Here she stopped. She didn't hope Andrew and Gloria would be happy. She could say it, but it wouldn't be true. What she really hoped was that Andrew would seek her in the gardens and find her the way he'd promised when they were dancing. But he wouldn't look for her here. No one would look for her here.

If only she had a drink. She would even drink down a glass of that unpleasant-tasting spring water without the first complaint.

She moistened her lips and tried to forget being thirsty as

she leaned back against the wall and let prayers without words rise up inside her. Then the words General Dawson had shared at Vanessa's funeral were there in her mind.

Yea, though I walk through the valley of the shadow of death, I will fear no evil: for thou art with me.

34

Andrew went first to where he'd watched Elena sketching the roses in the garden. She wasn't there.

All night he had lain awake trying to decide what to do after he saw her walking in the moonlight with Kirby Frazier. More than walking. They had been standing close together at the lake when he turned away. He hadn't wanted to see them kiss.

His thoughts were in turmoil when he got back to the hotel. The last person he had wanted to see then was Gloria since he had told her after dinner that he was no longer in love with her. That he wasn't sure he had ever actually been in love with her.

She must have been shocked by his words because she had merely glared at him as he followed Elena outside. He'd wanted to explain about Gloria. But then she walked away with Frazier.

After following them and seeing their near embrace, he wanted to be alone, out of sight of everyone. But Gloria had been waiting for him, demanding they talk. He told her there was nothing more to say and started toward his room. That was not to be. Some things couldn't be avoided, and a scene with Gloria was one of them.

She stepped in front of him. "I won't accept this, Andy. You can't throw away all we've had together as if it means nothing." She went from anger to distraught tears.

"I didn't ask you here, Gloria. I didn't leave you last year. You left me." He kept his voice low and calm.

She grabbed his hands. "I told you I would make it up to you."

"I don't want you to make it up to me." He jerked his hands free.

"It's that Elena person, isn't it? I can't believe you would leave me for someone like her."

"It isn't anyone else. It's you and it's me."

She smiled then. "Us. The way it's supposed to be."

"Not any longer. There is no us. No we. You can stay or go, but I won't be escorting you around. I'm sure you won't have trouble finding someone else to carry your luggage."

"I don't believe you." She lifted her chin defiantly. "This melancholy has you not thinking straight."

He simply looked at her a moment before he moved on toward the stairs.

That time she let him go. "You'll be sorry," she called after him.

For a moment as he walked away, he had wondered if she was right. Elena seemed to be choosing Frazier. Not him. But then he knew that even if that was true, he wouldn't be sorry he no longer had to try to please Gloria.

When she left him last summer, he had felt betrayed, broken. Useless, just as his father had always said he was. He had done everything Gloria wanted and failed at love, or so he thought. But had he ever really known love?

He'd expected love to be like thunder and lightning, something demanding and impossible to ignore. Gloria was that with her emotional storms. She had drained him and left him empty. Here at the Springs he had found new life. Dr. Graham would say the spring water had healed him, but Andrew thought it was a girl among the flowers.

When they touched hands the morning after Vanessa died, he had felt that lightning jolt he had expected from love but never felt with Gloria. They talked the way he never had with Gloria. They danced as though they knew each step before it was taken. He wanted to be with her, and he thought she wanted to be with him. Until he saw her with Kirby Frazier at the lake.

As daylight filtered through the window curtains after his sleepless night, he knew he couldn't simply give up on the feelings he had for Elena without at least talking to her. That was why he was out at daylight looking for her even though he had no idea whether she would be in the gardens at sunrise or not. He hoped if she was, she would be glad to see him. Perhaps he had imagined he had seen more in the moonlight than he had. Either way, he needed to know for sure. No more hiding in the shadows instead of facing whatever must be faced in life.

He looked among the roses. He went to the lake and searched through the willows. He stepped through the hollyhocks and thought of the cat that had appeared out of nowhere the day before.

As the sun leaped over the horizon, his heart sank. She wasn't out here to watch the sun come up. Perhaps that told him all he needed to know. He would still talk to her, but he was losing hope that she would want to talk to him. He sat down on a rock and watched the sun spread its rays across the grounds.

He was on the rise above the hotel not far from the rifle range. He didn't feel like eating. He wanted to avoid another scene with Gloria. So he stayed where he was, trying not to think about Elena. Instead, he remembered his grandfather's morning saying about the day being one the Lord had made and how they should rejoice in it. He wondered if his grandfather had been able to rejoice in the days after Andrew's grandmother died. In his own way, he probably had by planting the rosebush in her memory and then more rosebushes every year.

No rosebushes were in sight here, but he caught the sweet fragrance of roses in the air. After a while—he didn't know how long—he got up, but instead of heading back to the hotel, he walked on toward the shooting range where some men were practicing their aim. He didn't have a rifle with him, but he could watch the others. Someone might even let him take a shot with one of their guns. He wasn't a marksman, but the blast of a gunshot might drown out the unhappy thoughts in his head.

He strayed off the path to take a shortcut. Strange, there near an evergreen bush, the grass was mashed down and the ground torn up in a few spots. Two animals fighting perhaps. He walked closer out of curiosity at what sort of animals might be on the grounds. Could a horse have gotten out of the stables?

Odd, he spotted something that looked like a book under the bush. It was a book, damp with dew. When he picked it up, the pages fell open to a sketch of roses. Elena's sketch.

What was it doing here? Had she met Frazier in this isolated spot and then forgotten her book in the excitement of their tryst? That didn't seem possible, but something had happened. The book was here and she wasn't.

He tucked it under his arm and headed down the rise toward the lake. He would confront the man.

• • • •

Elena was gone when Ivy woke up. She wished they could have talked last night, but Ivy hadn't been able to keep her eyes open when Elena came to bed, patted her shoulder, and whispered for her to go back to sleep. Mother was up already at the little desk.

Ivy climbed out of bed and stretched with a yawn. "Are you writing to the boys?"

Seeing her mother's ink and paper made Ivy feel guilty, but in the next instant her heart sped up a little when she wondered if Jacob had read her letter by now. She couldn't wait to go ask Mr. Frazier if the letter was delivered.

"Yes. I do hope they are behaving themselves." Her mother blew out a weary breath. "Did you talk to Elena last night when she came in?"

Ivy shook her head. "I was too sleepy."

"That girl is in and out like a whisper of the wind. What does she do so early in the day?"

Ivy looked around. "She took her sketchbook."

"Of course she did." Her mother sighed again and dipped her pen in the inkpot. "Do you know why the general wanted to talk to her before dinner yesterday?"

"No, I haven't had a chance to ask her, but I don't think he was proposing."

Her mother turned to look directly at Ivy. "Proposing?"

Her mother's frown surprised Ivy. "Isn't that what you wanted? Him to propose to Elena?" Ivy began brushing her hair. "But I don't think he did. Elena did seem upset, but not at the general. More at Andrew Harper—you know that other man on the stagecoach—and that woman he was with. Somebody said they were getting married." She stuck a comb into a cluster of curls to hold them back from her face.

Her mother didn't seem to be listening as she stared out the window. Ivy shrugged and dressed quickly. "I'm going to find Elena."

Her mother came back from her reverie. "When you do, tell her I need to talk to her."

Ivy watched for Elena in the lobby and then on the paths as she went straight toward the lake. If Kirby was painting, she might be watching him. At least, he might have seen her.

But he hadn't. He was preparing his paints when Ivy got to the place he'd claimed for his easel.

"I saw her last night, but not this morning. Why? Is something wrong?"

"I guess not. She's probably in one of the gardens and has lost count of the time while she's sketching something. That's all."

"She should show me some of her sketches."

"She's very good. We have some of her paintings of roses on the wall at home."

"Do you think I can get her to do a sketch of me?" He grinned at Ivy.

"Maybe. You should ask her."

"I did ask her something last night. I asked if she wanted to go west."

"Go west?" Ivy stared at him. "Why would she do that?"

"Why not? I'm sure there are flowers out there. And I'm going."

"Mother would never approve."

"Your mother doesn't have to approve. Elena does."

Ivy had been sure Kirby was attracted to Elena, but she hadn't expected this. For him to want to take her west with him. She might never see her sister again. "Did she?"

"Did she what?" He kept his eyes on the paints he was mixing.

"Approve."

"I'm sure she will." He looked up at Ivy. "Don't look so tragic. You want her to be happy, don't you?"

Ivy blinked back the threat of tears as she nodded.

"Wait." He put down his palette. "I've got something to make that sad face disappear. Dr. Graham's man brought my supplies this morning and he had something for you." He reached in his pocket and pulled out an envelope to hold out toward her.

She snatched it and tore it open. There were only a few words. He must have had to write it fast while the man was waiting. But they were the right words.

Nothing could ever make me stop loving you. Come home soon. Jacob.

She hugged the letter against her chest and spun around.

"Good news, I'm guessing." Kirby was smiling at her.

"The best." But then she remembered Elena. If Elena loved Kirby the way Ivy loved Jacob, she should want her to go west with him even if Ivy could hardly bear the thought of her being so far away. She folded Jacob's letter and put it in her pocket. "I need to find Elena."

"When you find her, tell her I'm waiting for an answer."

"I'll tell her." It seemed everyone wanted to talk to Elena. Ivy started to head back toward the hotel. She stopped when she saw General Dawson coming down the path. "Oh look, here's General Dawson. Maybe he's seen Elena."

35

Not the general again. Kirby was beginning to wish Dr. Graham's medicinal water hadn't given the old gentleman a new spring in his step. Better if he was one of the old folks happy to stay on the veranda instead of always showing up to poke in Kirby's business.

He clamped down on his irritation and managed a smile. "Good morning, General. Early to see you down this way."

"Good morning, Mr. Frazier. Miss Ivy." The general's face brightened when he looked toward the girl. "Where is your sister?"

"I don't know. I'm looking for her. You haven't seen her this morning?"

"She wasn't in the dining room or on the veranda."

"I can't imagine where she could be for so long. She usually comes back to the room after the sun is up." Ivy looked a little worried. "Were you looking for her too?"

"I actually came to talk to Mr. Frazier." The man's eyes tightened as he looked at Kirby. "About Elena. Someone told me the two of you went for a walk last evening."

"A walk in the moonlight isn't a crime."

"A young woman has to guard her reputation," the general said.

"He asked her to go west with him," Ivy burst out.

Kirby shouldn't have told the girl. She wasn't one to keep a secret. Not that he'd told her to keep it under her hat, but he hadn't expected her to spread the news before she talked to Elena.

General Dawson didn't even glance toward Ivy as he frowned at Kirby. "I feared that might be your purpose."

"I can't see how what I do or what she does is any business of yours. You're not her father or any relation."

"Not yet, but I have grown fond of Miss Elena. I won't stand by and let you ruin her life."

"Marrying me would hardly be ruination for her. I think she might find traveling west an exciting adventure."

Ivy had her hand over her mouth as she watched them with wide eyes.

The general, ramrod straight, kept his eyes zeroed in on Kirby. The command of his soldiering years was plain on his face. "Did she agree to this adventure?"

"Not yet, but she will. A lady like Elena has to think things through."

"I don't think you've thought things through, Mr. Frazier." The general reached in his pocket and pulled out a banknote. "I'm prepared to give you two hundred dollars if you pack up and leave the Springs. Alone."

Had he heard the man right? Two hundred dollars? That was more than twice what he had hoped to raise with the paintings he'd lost in the hotel fire. He could reach out and take the banknote and be on his way west by the first of next week with plenty of supplies. He could even get a horse. A good horse. He glanced at his easel. He wouldn't have to do another portrait of an old woman who thought she looked younger than she did.

All he had to do was say goodbye to Elena. Never see her

again. Never see those children he didn't want but now felt sad to think about not having. He had felt something last night by the lake that he hadn't felt in a long time. Not since his little sister had died. The desire for someone to love. The need for family. Elena could give him that.

He didn't have to be bought. Elena would have enough to get them west. Then he could sell his paintings to keep them going.

He kept his hands by his side. "Keep your money. We can make it without anything from you."

"I regret to inform you that you have overestimated Miss Elena's family fortune."

"What do you mean?" Kirby looked from the general to the girl.

"They have no fortune." General Dawson looked over at Ivy too. "Tell him, Miss Ivy. I can see he won't believe me."

When the girl kept her fingers over her lips, Kirby said, "Ivy?"

She sighed and made a sad face as she dropped her hand away from her mouth and stared down at the ground. "It's true. My father got loans on our house before he died. Too many loans. Mother doesn't have any way to pay them back. We could lose our home."

Kirby frowned. "Then what are you doing here? You need money to stay at the Springs."

Another sigh as she peeked up at him and then lowered her eyes again. "Mother found a way for us to come somehow. I don't know how. She says our only chance to stay a family is for Elena to fall in love with someone who has the means to get us out of debt. Mother says it doesn't matter about love, but I think it does."

Kirby stared at her, then at the general, and back at Ivy. He didn't want to believe what he was hearing.

The girl looked up, her lips trembling. "If she doesn't find such a husband, Elena and I will have to find positions as maids, and Mother will be forced to beg one of her relatives in Mississippi to take her in. I don't know what will happen to my brothers. It's all so sad. And now if Elena has fallen in love with you and wants to go west, we have no hope at all. Unless someone wants to marry me, and it won't be anyone I can love because I desperately love a boy in Lexington. And he loves me too, but he doesn't have any money either."

Kirby laughed. He didn't know what else to do. This had to be some wild story that Ivy had seen in a newspaper. Maybe something written by Charles Dickens.

"I don't know what you find amusing, Frazier," General Dawson said.

"Only me, General. Only me." He turned from the general to look at Ivy. "It seems my plans have gone awry the same as your mother's, Miss Ivy."

How could he have actually fallen in love with a woman in more need of financial help than he was? He had been foolish to let love come into play.

"I'm sorry, Mr. Frazier," Ivy said.

He looked at the paints on his palette drying into uselessness. Everything was useless. All his plans.

"My offer is still good," the general said.

"Your offer." Kirby spit out the words as anger flooded through him. "You make me disappear and then convince the poor girl to marry you? A man more than twice her age."

That made the old man laugh. "Not at all. She isn't the Bradford I plan to wed." Ivy's eyes got wider before the man went on. "Or you either, child. I plan to marry Mrs. Bradford as soon as she thinks such a union proper after the death of your father."

"Oh." Ivy's face lightened. "That would be wonderful. I can't wait to tell Elena. She told Mother a week ago that you were attracted to her."

"So, that's settled, or will be as soon as Juanita agrees to our plans." The general looked back at Kirby. "You can still agree to the plan I suggested for you."

Kirby met his eyes and, without blinking, turned him down. "I won't be bought."

"Very well." A slight smile touched the man's lips as he slowly folded the banknote.

As he put it back in his pocket, Kirby thought he'd probably just done the dumbest thing he'd ever done in his entire life. But he wasn't sorry. At least, not very sorry. A man had to have some pride, and his stash of cash from doing the portraits was growing. Plus, there was Elena. He didn't want to give her up, even if she had no family fortune.

He had been so focused on the general and Ivy that he didn't see Andrew Harper until the man was right in front of him, his face red, his hands balled into fists. Kirby didn't think things could get any stranger, but they did when Harper tried to slug him as he yelled, "What have you done with Elena?"

· · · ·

Elena had no idea how much time had passed. She counted to sixty, then to one hundred. It didn't help her gauge the time. Her shoulders ached, and her fingers felt numb. The cat, as if sensing her agitation, stood up in her lap and put its front paws on Elena's chest to sniff her face. Then the cat rubbed its head against her chin.

"That's nice, Princess, but it would help more if you'd gnaw through the fabric tied around my wrists."

The cat stared at her and meowed as though it knew she was in trouble. Then it meowed again. Maybe this time to tell her to stop sitting there like a bump on a log and try to do something. It jumped down out of her lap.

But what could she do? She struggled to her feet. It was hard to do anything with her hands tied behind her. She looked around. Maybe she could find something sharp enough to tear the bindings since the cat didn't appear ready to bite through them.

The cat watched a moment and then went to the back of the shed where she'd first seen it. She followed and felt like crying when the cat crept through a hole along the bottom of one of the planks.

"I'm sorry, Princess. Don't go." She stared at the hole, wishing the cat back.

"Here, kitty, kitty," she called.

The cat didn't come. It might not have had any way of really helping her, but the cat had kept her from feeling so alone.

She turned to look around the small shed. Why was it out here in the middle of nowhere? There was no workbench, no feeding troughs. Nothing except a small, dusty space with plank walls holding her captive.

The wood was weathered and old. Maybe if she shoved her shoulder hard against the door, the board that had slapped into the brace to hold the door shut would break. She tried again and again, but it didn't give an inch.

She winced when she leaned her bruised shoulder against the shed's wall to peer though the crack between the planks. With her bonnet bill in the way, she had to twist her head to the side to get close enough to see out. Nothing but green grass.

After moistening her mouth as much as she could with her dry tongue, she yelled. The wood seemed to absorb the sound and not let it escape the shed. She screamed louder and yelled until her throat hurt. Nobody came. Not even the cat.

She started kicking every plank in search of one that might be loose. One did seem to give a bit. Perhaps she could push the plank aside and squeeze through the opening that would make. When she kicked the plank again, something jabbed her foot. She slipped off her shoe and felt with her toes. Her stocking snagged on a nail almost at the bottom of the plank.

She stared down at it. The nail might tear the fabric of her bindings, but to reach it she'd have to be almost flat on the ground. If she couldn't free her hands, she might struggle to get back up. She didn't want to lie in the dust and wait to die. Better to stay on her feet if possible. Where there was one protruding nail, there might be another.

She struggled to see in the dim light, and the bonnet shading her eyes didn't help. She scraped the bonnet's bill against the side of the shed until it fell to the back of her head. The ribbons still held under her neck, but at least she could see better. Two planks over, she spotted a nail up higher. She would have to scoot down but not all the way to the ground.

When she turned to feel the nail with her fingers, it didn't feel very sharp. Still, if she could poke it through the ties around her wrists, she might rip the fabric.

Dear Lord, please let this work.

She scooted down with her back against the planks and felt for the nail. She tried to position the material holding her wrists against the nail. She felt a little victory when she got her hands in the right place, but then when she tried to poke the nail through the strip of petticoat tying her hands, it pushed back into the wood. She could no longer even feel it with her fingers.

Tears slid down her cheeks as she sank down to sit on the ground. What difference did it make if she couldn't stand up? If nobody found her, nothing would matter.

She wished the cat would come back. When she thought about praying again, she couldn't think of the first praise. Just the word *please* over and over.

Maybe the man would tell someone where she was. He hadn't seemed evil. Not like the other man. He thought someone would find her. He hadn't wanted to kill her, but it could be he had anyway. Just as he hadn't wanted to kill Vanessa, but she had died. Been buried.

Elena shook her head. She couldn't think about that. Being covered in dirt. She sucked in air in fast breaths as she thought about dirt falling in on her.

She forced herself to stop and breathe slowly in and out. If she died, she wouldn't be here or in a box being buried. She'd be in heaven. With her father. With Vanessa.

But she wasn't ready. She wanted to live. To see her mother and Ivy. To hear more of the general's stories. To wish Kirby well on his trip west. She wouldn't be with him. Even if she was rescued from this shed. That was his dream and not hers. He wasn't her dream.

She shut her eyes, and Andrew was there in front of her. He reached for her hand. She flexed her hands behind her back as she remembered the feel of his palm on hers.

Her fingers dug down into the dirt behind her. She touched something hard. Not a knife, though that would have been a sweet answer to her prayers. It felt like a shard of a crock.

She held it between her fingers and tried to push it against the fabric that held her captive, but her fingers couldn't reach high enough. Again she forced herself to breathe in measured breaths. She needed to think. Find a way to use what the Lord had put in her hands.

If she could jam it into the crack between the planks behind her, that might work, but the crack was too wide. The shard needed to be tight in place to keep it from sliding out of reach the way the nail had.

She held the shard in one hand and twisted the fingers of her other hand around to grasp a fold of her skirt. She raised one hip off the ground to jerk the cloth up high enough to wrap around the crock piece. Very carefully she shoved it back into the crack. She tested it with her fingers. It felt tight.

With a fervent prayer for the Lord's help, she pushed the fabric binding her wrists against the sharp edge of the shard. The material tightened and then gave the slightest bit.

She held her breath and pushed against the shard again. This time she heard a rip. With all her strength, she pulled her hands against the cloth. More fabric tore. When she relaxed her hands, the bindings were looser. She squeezed her fingers together to make her hands as narrow as possible and jerked one hand out of the bindings.

Sharp pains stabbed her shoulders and elbows when she brought her hands around to the front of her body. The skin on her wrists was raw, but none of that mattered. Her hands were free. Praise God. She scrambled to her feet without thinking about pulling her skirt loose from where she'd jammed it into the crack. When she heard it rip, she didn't care. She threw out her arms and whirled around.

She was still locked in the shed, but at least her hands were free. She untied her bonnet, jerked it off, and threw it on the ground. Some of her hairpins fell into the dust with the bonnet. She stared at them a moment before she took out the rest of the pins and combed her fingers through her hair to let it fall loose down on her shoulders. She wasn't sure why, but that made her feel better.

She pushed an eye tight against one of the cracks. No one to be seen, but she yelled anyway. Someone could be out there close enough to hear. She peered through a crack on the other side of the shed. Still nothing but grass and bushes.

Even so, she kept yelling until the shed echoed with her voice. No one came. Not even the cat.

36

Rage had surged through Andrew at the sight of Kirby Frazier. He dropped Elena's sketchbook and ran at him, fists up, ready to smash in the man's face.

Frazier blocked his punch and shoved him back so hard, Andrew almost fell. "What is wrong with you?" The man glared at him.

Andrew regained his balance and went at him again. Somebody grabbed him from behind. "Easy, Andrew."

General Dawson. Andrew took a deep breath and stopped fighting to get loose.

The general kept his grip on his arms. "This isn't a fight you can win, son. Not this way."

He was right. Frazier was bigger, stronger, a man who looked as if he knew about fighting, even if he was an artist. Frazier picked up the palette Andrew must have knocked out of his hands. Blue paint smeared his sleeve. He laid the palette aside and turned to face Andrew, his fists clenched and ready.

Backed against a tree behind the artist was Elena's little sister. She looked scared. But of what? Him? He felt ready to fly apart, but something about how the little sister stared at him made him pull in another breath to calm himself. Frazier continued to watch him with wary eyes, and General Dawson kept a grip on his arms.

He glanced around. Where was Elena? If she'd made her choice for Frazier, Andrew couldn't change that by fisticuffs, but he would make her tell him to his face. He wouldn't accept it as true until she did.

"Do you have yourself under control now, young man?" The general slightly loosened his hold on Andrew. "Are you going to act like you have some sense and tell us what has you acting the fool?"

Andrew nodded, and General Dawson dropped his hands away from his arms. "I can't find Elena," Andrew said.

"Seems nobody can." Frazier stared at him. "But why are you looking for her? What about your lady friend? I heard you were marrying her."

"Were. Not am."

The man smiled so knowingly that Andrew barely kept from charging at him again. "And now you're after Elena, are you? Well, you're too late. She's going west with me."

"She hasn't said yes," Ivy spoke up.

"But she will." Frazier sounded as if it were a sure thing.

"Then I'll wish her the best." Andrew had to force out the words. "Both of you the best, but I want to hear it from her."

Frazier shrugged. "Suit yourself. Where is she anyway?" He looked around. "She seems to have gone into hiding."

"You should know. You were with her this morning. I found her sketchbook where she left it." Andrew pointed to where he'd dropped it.

"I don't know what you're talking about." Frazier frowned. "I haven't seen her today."

Ivy ran to get the sketchbook. She hugged it to her and began crying. "Something has happened to her. She would have never

302

left this." She turned toward Frazier. "If you know where she is, Mr. Frazier, please tell us."

"I haven't seen her, Ivy. Not today." Frazier looked genuinely concerned. "I don't know what you're thinking, what any of you are thinking, but I wouldn't do anything to hurt Elena."

The man obviously did care about Elena. Andrew's heart sank, but just because Frazier cared about her didn't mean Elena was in love with him.

"We will find her." General Dawson took charge. "Ivy, go back to the hotel to make sure she isn't there. There could be a reason she lost her sketchbook."

Ivy shook her head. "I don't think so. What if it has something to do with Vanessa?"

"Vanessa?" Andrew frowned.

"With me seeing the man who gave Vanessa the poison."

"The doctor said she wasn't poisoned." The general didn't sound very sure of his words.

"What if he was wrong?" Ivy's voice was small, uncertain. "What if whoever did give Vanessa that drink before the last dance knew I saw him but thought it was Elena instead of me? She might be hurt because of me."

"We shouldn't panic, Miss Ivy. Your imagination is running away with you." The general sounded like he was trying to convince himself. "This surely has nothing to do with Vanessa."

Frazier spoke up. "She could be right. A few days ago, I overheard two men arguing over some money. The man trying to get the other to pay up threatened to harm his daughter."

"Why didn't you say something?" Andrew demanded.

"That was before this Vanessa was here at the Springs. Then no one has claimed to even know her, much less be related to her. I couldn't see how those men could have anything to do with the young woman's death," Frazier said.

"Nor can I," General Dawson said.

"They could have given the drink to the wrong woman." Ivy's voice wasn't much more than a whisper.

What if it was true and Elena was in danger? Andrew's heart sped up. He wanted to run in a dozen different directions to find her, but where to start?

"Who were the men?" the general asked.

"I didn't see them. Just heard them, but one of them was Carson Sanderson. I recognized his voice."

"Carson. Dr. Graham's nephew." The general frowned. "I think we best go talk to the doctor but first make sure Elena isn't at the hotel." He looked at Ivy, who nodded and took off up the path.

"You go talk to Dr. Graham. I'm going to keep looking," Andrew said.

Frazier looked at Andrew. "So am I."

"No." The general had command in his voice. "Both of you are going with me to talk to Dr. Graham. If it turns out a search of the grounds is necessary, we will need to enlist more help and come up with a strategy to cover the area. The Springs has more than a hundred acres."

Even though he knew the general was right, Andrew was reluctant to follow him. Frazier looked even more loath to go toward the hotel.

All the way there, Andrew hoped Elena would appear on the path in front of them. She did not. Nor was she on the veranda when they reached the hotel. Nobody had seen her.

Where could she be? His heart thumped with worry as Dr. Graham took them into his office and waved away their concerns. He dismissed the idea that her absence could have any connection to the mystery woman's death or to the conversation Frazier had overheard between the two men.

"This is a big resort," the doctor said. "Miss Bradford must have gone for an ill-advised walk by herself this morning and gotten confused on her way back. If I understand you correctly, she's only been missing a few hours. She will find her way and show up on her own. With that in mind, I see no need in alarming all the guests by organizing a search."

When General Dawson started to protest, the doctor held up a hand to stop him. "At least not yet. Hear me out, Clive. Mr. Frazier's story about my nephew may be true. Carson has had his struggles, but I can't see how it can relate to Miss Hasting's death or to Miss Bradford's absence now." He turned from the general to spear Frazier with a stare. "Why didn't you report this earlier, Frazier?"

"It was none of my business. I didn't know the men. I am here to paint, not police."

"Then why are you telling it now?"

"Now it may matter to whatever has led to Miss Bradford's disappearance." Frazier didn't shrink from the doctor's glare.

"But it most likely does not. Carson is known for coming and going without bothering to inform me." The doctor had sent a servant to fetch Sanderson, but the man was nowhere to be found. "If Miss Bradford doesn't show up in the next couple of hours, we will determine if more drastic steps need to be taken to find her."

When General Dawson started arguing with the doctor, Frazier moved over beside Andrew to speak close to his ear. "Let them argue. Take me to where you found the book. We can start there."

Andrew nodded. While they might be rivals for Elena's affections, they both wanted her safe.

They met Ivy in the hotel lobby. Her eyes were red from crying. She hadn't seen Elena. Her mother hadn't seen her. She had never gone off so long before.

"We'll find her, Ivy." Frazier patted the girl's shoulder.

"We will," Andrew added. "You tell General Dawson we've gone to look for her up toward the rifle range, where I found her sketchbook."

He felt odd walking with the man he'd wanted to pound into the ground only a little while ago. They moved fast with a united purpose.

Frazier surprised him by asking, "Do you have money?"

Did he want money from Andrew? "My grandfather does."

"You don't?"

"I work for him with the horses. I have enough."

"Enough. I've never had enough. Never had money."

"That can be difficult," Andrew said.

Frazier looked over at him with a laugh that was anything but happy. "You with your comfortable house, comfortable family wealth, can have no idea. I guess you stand to inherit plenty."

"Money doesn't make everything easier."

"Maybe not. I wouldn't know. I do know without it, everything can be hard."

"Is that why you want to marry Elena? For her money?"

Another short laugh. "You are as blind as I was."

"What are you talking about?"

"Thinking Elena comes from money. General Dawson just let me know her family doesn't have two coins to rub together. Ivy says they came to the Springs for the sole purpose of Elena finding somebody to marry who was rich enough to keep them out of the poorhouse."

"Then why would she pick you?"

Frazier blew out a sigh. "I didn't say she did. I was the one to pick her."

"Thinking she had money."

"Yes. Life can throw a man some curves."

"You love her." Andrew looked over at Frazier.

"I think I do." Frazier blew out a breath and met Andrew's look. "Not something I planned on. How about you? You in love with her too?"

"I barely know her."

"Maybe so, but you've got her snuggled down in your heart.

After all, you must have thrown over that woman who came here hunting you, and you were ready to beat me into the ground because of Elena. Wouldn't have happened, but looked like you were going to give it a try." Frazier pulled in a breath and blew it out. "Might as well admit it. We're both after the same woman whether we think we should be or not."

"I'm not worried about her not having money, if that's what you mean."

"I don't guess I'm worried about that now either. I just want her to go west with me."

"Is that what she wants?"

Frazier smiled. "I guess I'll have to see what she says if we find her."

"Don't say *if*." Andrew's heart froze at that word. Frazier was right. Whether he'd known Elena long or not, he did love her. Or at least knew he wanted to.

"Right. Not if. When." Frazier clapped his hand on Andrew's shoulder. "I wouldn't have thought it possible, but I think I like you, Harper."

At the place where he'd found the sketchbook, the grass was still mashed down in a few places, but they couldn't see a trail leading away. They decided to split up. Frazier went up toward the firing range. Andrew headed in the other direction. He stopped now and again to search for something that might indicate the best way to go. He didn't find anything, but he kept moving. Kept hoping.

• • • •

Every five minutes, or what she thought might be five minutes, Elena yelled until she was hoarse. Her fingernails were broken and her hands sore from pushing on the boards to see if she could loosen them. The shed might be old, but it had been well-built. There was no escape.

She peeked out of the cracks to try to determine how much time had gone by. The shadows showed it was past midday. She had to have been missed by now, but no one would ever look for her here.

She didn't know how far the man had dragged her along. She'd been trying so hard to stay on her feet and not get sick with that gag in her mouth, she'd hardly noticed anything else.

The cat was suddenly coming toward her from the back of the shed again. "Hello, Princess. I hope you brought help."

The cat dropped a dead mouse in front of her as though it were a gift. Elena laughed then clapped her hand over her mouth when she noted a hint of hysteria. She pulled in a slow breath to calm herself. "Thank you anyway, Princess. I'm not quite that desperate yet."

But how long before desperation did seize her? The cat stared up at her with those beautiful blue eyes as though it knew all about desperation. Then it turned, stepped over the dead mouse, and disappeared back out its hole.

She stared down at the mouse. She didn't like mice. Alive or dead. With a piece of the cloth that had bound her wrists, she gingerly lifted the mouse by its tail and held it far out in front of her to carry to the back of the shed. She dropped it in front of where the cat came in.

37

Andrew came out of a stand of trees into an open area. The grass hadn't been clipped here. Daisies spotted the field. He stopped and stared at the flowers.

He should go back. She wouldn't have gone this far. Not by herself. But what if she wasn't by herself? What if someone was forcing her along? The mashed-down grass back where he found the sketchbook might be due to a struggle and not the lovers' embrace he had imagined.

"Please, Lord, show me which way to go. Help me find her." He whispered the words as he took a few steps out into the field. He stopped. It was useless to keep wandering without direction.

He stared down at a thick patch of flowers. Daisies. Just as he started to turn back, he noticed a broken stem and then several more that seemed bent. Some of the grass seemed disturbed too. A cow or a horse could have nibbled at the daisies. Or a woman's long skirt and petticoats could have brushed against them.

Stem by stem he followed a faint path across the field, but then the daisies were replaced by blackberry briars and weeds. All at once, a gray cat streaked out from under a blackberry bush to run in front of him. Not any cat. *The* cat. The one with eyes the same blue as Vanessa's.

The cat pounced on a grasshopper. That was what might have broken the daisies. Not Elena at all.

"Harper."

Andrew looked back the way he'd come. Frazier was at the edge of the trees. Alone. But he might have found her and come to tell him.

"Did you find her?" Andrew yelled back.

"No. You find something?"

"I don't know. Maybe."

Andrew was almost sorry when Frazier ran across the field toward him. He wouldn't understand about the cat. Andrew didn't understand about the cat, but he couldn't shake the feeling it was there in front of him for a reason.

When he knelt down, the cat left the grasshopper to push its head into Andrew's hand. When Frazier came up behind Andrew, the cat skittered a few feet away before it stopped to stare at them.

With his hands propped on his knees, Frazier leaned over to catch his breath before he said, "A cat? That's what you found."

"Not only a cat." Andrew explained about the trail through the daisies.

"Could have been anything walking through here." Frazier straightened up and looked around. The cat slinked back toward them to rub against the man's legs. He gave it a push away with his foot. "Never much liked cats. Always under your feet trying to trip you."

When the cat came back over to Andrew, he stroked it head to tail before he stood up. "This isn't just any cat. It came out of nowhere to find Elena in the garden yesterday morning."

"Are you saying it's Elena's cat?"

"No, but it hopped right into her lap. Elena thought the cat's eyes looked like Vanessa's."

310

"The mystery girl. The dead mystery girl." Frazier frowned. "Now you're sounding a little weird."

"It does have blue eyes."

"A cat is not going to lead us to Elena. Cats are useless except to catch mice, Harper."

Andrew picked up the cat that settled contentedly in his arms and started purring at once. "I don't know. It found Elena yesterday. Maybe it can find her again."

"Out here in the middle of who knows where? This cat is hunting for something to eat."

The cat twisted in Andrew's arms and jumped to the ground to streak away.

Andrew sighed. "You're probably right, but at least it's a possibility. You can go back, but I'm going to go at least to the top of that little rise." Andrew pointed across the field.

"The cat didn't go that way."

"Cats don't always go in straight lines." Andrew shrugged and started walking. He didn't care whether Frazier followed him or not. "Do whatever you want. I just have a feeling."

"A cat and a feeling." Frazier trailed along behind Andrew. "I guess that's more than I've got."

At the top of the rise, the cat was nowhere in sight. The grass didn't show any sign that anyone had been this way. All Andrew could see was more field with a small building down the way. Nothing to make him think his feeling was leading him toward Elena.

Andrew was glad when Frazier didn't say anything as they stood there looking at nothing. All at once Andrew had the crazy impulse to shout Elena's name. It was foolish, but then hadn't he already foolishly followed a cat? A cat that had disappeared.

"Elena!" he shouted.

Frazier surprised him by saying, "It'll be louder if we shout together."

"Elena!"

The name seemed to hang in the air.

• • • •

The cat came out of the shadows from the back of the shed again. Elena was glad it wasn't carrying another mouse.

"Back again, Princess?" She squatted down to stroke the cat. "I wish you'd bring help. Something besides a mouse."

The cat pushed its head against Elena's hand and purred louder.

Elena jerked her head up. She thought she heard her name. She must have been imagining things. She stood and went to peer out one of the cracks. Nothing, the same as every time she'd looked. But then, she heard it again. Her name. Not close but somewhere.

"Help." That wasn't loud enough. She yelled the word again. Still not loud enough. She stood up straight, clenched her fists and screamed. Not a word. Just a desperate screech.

The cat yowled and ran for its hole out of the shed. Elena screamed again.

• • • •

Kirby put his hand on Harper's shoulder. The man looked ready to fall apart. He really did love Elena. But so did he. They might be rivals for her affection, but they were united in wanting to find her. Perhaps Dr. Graham was right and Elena was fine.

That didn't explain why she dropped the sketchbook and left it. Not something an artist would do, but there could be a reason. She could have run from a snake or spider. In her fright, she might have strayed off the path and taken the wrong direction. But she wouldn't have ended up way out here. She might be at the hotel by now while the two of them were wandering around on a fool's errand. Following a cat.

Without speaking, they turned back toward the Springs. Suddenly Harper threw up his head and stopped. "Did you hear something?"

"I didn't—" Kirby started but Harper stopped him.

"Listen."

"What?"

Harper held up his hand for silence. A scream split the air. They both turned and ran toward the sound as another scream sounded. From the shed.

The cat raced across the field away from the shed. Kirby was going to have to change his opinion of cats.

"Elena," Harper yelled.

They could be wrong. It might be some kind of bird. A guinea hen could scream like that, but it sounded like a woman. He got to the shed a step before Harper and lifted the bar holding the door. There was Elena, her face dirty, her hair down and in disarray, something like he had painted it in her portrait.

She walked out the door straight to Harper, who held his arms out toward her. "Elena." The man breathed her name like it was a prayer. An answered prayer.

For a long moment, she stayed in Harper's arms as if there was no place she'd rather be. But then she pushed away from him and reached a hand toward Kirby. A hand. Not her arms.

"Kirby. Andrew. How did you find me?"

Kirby looked at her. He didn't try to pull her into an embrace. "I think it was a cat." He squeezed her hand slightly. "And love."

She turned toward Harper. "You saw Princess?"

"Cinderella."

Kirby had no idea what they were talking about, but she had plainly chosen Harper over him, as hard as that was to believe.

"What about Gloria?" she said.

313

"She's not important." Harper reached to stroke Elena's face. "Are you hurt?"

"I don't think so. Not badly. A few bruises, but I am so thirsty."

"What happened? Who put you here?" Kirby asked.

She looked back at him. "I heard two men arguing. About what happened to Vanessa and about Ivy. I tried to sneak away, but I fell over the cat."

"The cat," Kirby echoed.

"It didn't mean to trip me, but then the man in the hat told the other man—one of the servants, I think—to get rid of me. He gave him money. The man said he wasn't a killer. That he hadn't poisoned Vanessa. He just put something in the drink to make her sick. He locked me in here to give him time to get away. He said someone would find me." Her face crumpled. "But I didn't think anyone would. I thought I'd die here."

"Shh." Harper smoothed some of her tears away with his fingers as a few tears wet his face as well.

Kirby gave Elena his handkerchief. Harper was going to need his himself.

"Thank you." She turned from Harper toward Kirby. "Thank you both."

When he reached toward her then, she let him embrace her. He didn't look at Harper as he held her close for a moment before he gently kissed her forehead and let her go. Back to Harper. His heart felt heavy, but it was for the best. He could travel better alone. The west would heal his heartache.

38

Elena held her face up toward the sun and sent up a prayer of thanksgiving. For these two men who had found her. For the man who hadn't killed her. For the cat she called Princess. For freedom. For the sun on her face.

She supposed she should go back in the shed and get her bonnet, but she couldn't step back through that door. Besides, she liked the breeze ruffling her hair. She couldn't remember how long it had been since she had been outside with her hair loose around her shoulders. Something like Kirby had painted it.

Kirby. He had embraced her with a kiss and then released her. Given her to Andrew. She'd felt him saying goodbye even though he wasn't leaving. Andrew hadn't kissed her, but it was his love that Kirby had meant when he said the cat and love had found her. She had felt love in his embrace and in his tears. Kisses could wait.

"I can walk," she said when she heard them talking about going for a horse. They looked at her as if unsure. "Please. I need some water. I'll even drink the spring water."

That made them both smile. A good thing to see. Andrew had looked so tragic and Kirby so sad. Who would have ever thought that she, a woman who had seemed destined for a spinster corner, would have two men wanting her love? Two such wonderful men. She wanted to take both their hands and run back across the field to the Springs.

"If you get tired, we can carry you," Kirby said.

And he could. So strong. So capable.

"Yes." Andrew reached for her hand.

He might not be as strong as Kirby, but he had a different kind of strength. That of a good man who, when he loved, would love with all his heart.

She didn't doubt that Kirby thought he loved her, but the west called to him more than family. She needed family.

Back at the hotel, Ivy ran to meet them on the path, tears wetting her face. Dear Ivy. Her heart stayed full to bursting with emotions. General Dawson waited at the steps up to the hotel. He grabbed Elena in a tight hug. Another man who loved her, although in a different way. It would be good to have him as a second father.

People on the veranda and lawn seemed to sense something unusual happening and edged closer to get a better look. General Dawson let go of Elena and barked an order at the curious to be on about their own business. Then he rushed them all inside to Dr. Graham's office. The doctor was behind a desk that practically went from one wall to the other. Mother was the only other person in the room. The general shut the door behind them.

Her mother's eyes widened at the sight of Elena. "For mercy's sake, what have you done to your hair? Where is your bonnet? And your dress. It's filthy."

Elena pushed some loose strands away from her face. "I suppose I do look a bit disheveled."

"A bit?" her mother started, but the general hushed her.

"Don't fuss, Juanita. She is beautifully alive."

"Oh, my dear girl." Her mother stood then and held out her arms to Elena as she burst into tears.

Elena hugged her. She didn't know when she'd hugged so many people. "I'm all right, Mother. Don't cry." She'd seen her mother dab at tears now and again but never sob like this.

Her mother dropped back down in her chair. "I'm so sorry, Elena. This is all my fault, expecting you to save us."

"It has nothing to do with that. It was about Vanessa, after all."

"We need to hear the whole story," Dr. Graham spoke up.

"Let her at least sit down," Kirby demanded.

The doctor gave Kirby a hard look but then merely nodded.

"Please, may I have a drink?" Elena eyed the pitcher of water on the doctor's desk as Andrew pulled a chair over for her. She hoped it wasn't spring water, but if it was, she'd drink that too. "The gag dried out my mouth, and it was so dusty in the shed. And then I kept yelling and hoping someone would hear me."

"Gag?" Her mother looked near a faint.

"Please, Mother. I am all right." Elena sat down and took a drink of the water Ivy brought her. Spring water, but she was so thirsty, she drank it all. Everyone watched her, waiting. She'd have to tell it all again. Andrew and Kirby stood behind her chair like two guards daring anyone to bother her. That made her smile.

She told it as succinctly as possible. Dr. Graham made notes but waited until she was finished to ask, "Did you recognize either of the men?"

"I'd seen the one dressed like a gentleman at the dances, but I never danced with him. I think the other man was a servant, but I didn't remember seeing him before."

"A servant didn't report for work this morning, and Carson is gone." The doctor sat back in his chair. "So, it seems both men have left the Springs and will no longer be a danger to you, Miss Bradford. The local sheriff can take over the search for them. If you or your mother or sister need anything, anything at all, I will see that you get it. A maid will bring you fresh water."

Out in the lobby, Ivy and her mother headed toward the stairs. Her mother looked back at Elena when she didn't follow them. "Come along, Elena."

"In a minute."

Her mother seemed ready to demand she come right then, but instead, she tightened her lips and turned toward the stairs.

Elena wanted to thank Kirby and Andrew again. Andrew was beside her, a silent source of strength. She looked behind her for Kirby. General Dawson had stopped him.

"I admire a man who can't be bought." The general pulled something from his pocket to offer it to Kirby.

Kirby didn't take it. "She made her choice. It's not me."

"I see that." He pushed whatever it was toward Kirby and went on. "Take it. Consider it an advance. For two paintings you do out west."

"Of what?"

"Whatever you want to paint. A rock. A canyon. A bubbling pool in the Yellowstone area. And if you've changed your mind about that portrait, I'll pay extra."

"I'll take the commission on the western art." Kirby took what looked like a banknote. "But I'm keeping the portrait."

"I thought you would." The general pointed toward Elena. "I think she's waiting to speak to you."

Kirby lowered his voice, but Elena still heard him. "He won't break her heart, will he?"

Andrew stiffened beside her.

"I suppose that remains to be seen." He reached into his pocket and pulled out another card to give Kirby. "Here's my address. Let me hear from you, and if the unexpected happens, I will write you to see if you want to come back for a second chance."

Andrew muttered something about meddling old men.

"He is that," Kirby agreed as he stepped up beside them. He gave Andrew a long look. "Just one thing, Harper. You're a better dancer than a fighter."

When Andrew laughed, Elena gave him a puzzled frown. "I'll tell you about it someday," he said.

Kirby was smiling too as he turned to Elena and smoothed back her hair. "I knew you would look like this with your hair down."

"Thank you, Kirby, for the portrait. For rescuing me today. For being a friend."

He dropped his hand away from her hair. "Goodbye, Elena." After another glance toward Andrew, he turned and walked out the door.

Somehow she knew she'd never see him again.

"Are you all right?" Andrew asked.

"As long as you don't say goodbye like that too."

"My goodbye will be only until next time. I'll expect to see you at dinner if you feel up to it. At the next ball. Among the flowers in the morning." He smiled. "But maybe we shouldn't do the hiding and seeking."

She smiled. "That would take all the fun away, but I will stick to easy-to-find places next time. Actually, I was looking for you this morning."

"And I was looking for you. I found your sketchbook but not you."

"You found me when it mattered." She smiled. "Did Princess really tell you where I was?"

"Close enough. That is one amazing cat." He put his hand on her cheek. "And you are one amazing woman."

She put her hand over his for a moment before she turned to follow her mother and Ivy up the stairs. She would see him again. And again and again.

39

The next morning Andrew slipped out to the veranda in the first gray light of dawn. If Elena went out before sunrise, he wanted to be sure to see her. He hadn't wanted to let her out of his sight since they opened the door of that shed and found her there. Of course, he had. She'd gone to her room. She'd been to the baths. But he was continually watching for her, thinking about her, wanting to be beside her.

Gloria had confronted him with another unpleasant scene the day before. He had listened without saying a word as she accused him of betrayal. All the time she was talking, he kept thinking about Elena and how she'd come out into the sunlight and straight into his arms. Then she'd walked back to the hotel without complaint or concern for her unkempt hair, torn dress, or broken fingernails.

"This woman, this Elena, is just a flash in the pan for you. You'll come crawling back to me, but believe me, I won't be waiting. You have lost your chance."

She was still talking when he walked away, leaving her alone. She didn't stay alone long. General Dawson reported she left late that evening with a man named Harrison. A good match for her, the general said with some pleasure.

"I didn't know you were such a matchmaker, General."

He had smiled. "An old soldier has to have something to do once he can't ride out to battle anymore. But Gloria was never right for you, son, not even when you thought she was."

"Is Elena right for me?"

The general's smile got broader. "That's for you to find out."

"We really don't know each other that well."

"I suggest you use the next few weeks here at the Springs correcting that."

"Will she be here that long?"

"Dr. Graham has told Mrs. Bradford that she and her daughters can stay as long as they like. Until the end of the season if that is their wish. Without charge, to make up for his unfortunate reluctance to organize a search for Miss Elena."

"Has his nephew, Sanderson, come back to the hotel?"

"Not as yet. I rather doubt he will."

"Will the officials find him or the other man?"

General Dawson's face hardened. "I have my doubts about that too. A man can disappear in this country if he chooses to do so."

"Could they have really caused the mystery lady's death?" It was all so difficult to believe.

"Miss Vanessa's?" He looked thoughtful. "The man would have no reason to lie in the conversation Miss Elena overheard. He intended someone ill, but not death. However, he could have gotten his poisons mixed up the same as he was confused about his intended victim, or perhaps the poor girl had some problem that made the concoction more deadly for her." He shook his head. "I doubt we will ever know."

"Or who she really was?"

"That surely will not stay secret forever. Her identity will come to light in time."

"If it does, do you think her family will want to move her body from here to their own graveyard?"

"Another question we cannot answer. Perhaps. Or perhaps they will want her to stay here where she had her last dance." The general patted Andrew's shoulder. "Don't concern yourself with questions you can't answer. Think more on the answers you can discover."

That was what he hoped to do as he watched for Elena in the early morning light. He had no assurance she would come. She might need to rest after the events of the day before. She hadn't come to the dance last night. Her sister told General Dawson they all needed some quiet time to recover.

Even so, he hoped she would be out to see the sunrise. As the horizon began to warm to a golden pink, she did come out of the hotel. He didn't call to her. Better to follow and pretend to find her as he had promised to do at the dance on the night the mystery lady had died.

He trailed her, but not close enough for her to notice him. She went straight to the lake where Frazier did his painting. A finger of doubt poked Andrew.

Was she hoping to see Frazier? She had been in his arms beside the moonlit lake two nights ago. She had embraced him yesterday after they found her. Frazier had kissed her forehead and perhaps had kissed her the night before.

Andrew hadn't kissed her when she walked into his arms, but that was his hesitation, not hers. He tried to quell his jealousy. There was no reason to guess at what she was feeling. He would ask. Whenever she stopped.

She slowed and glanced over at the shade tree where the artist worked, but then went on. Andrew looked that way too as he passed. Frazier's easel and stool were no longer there.

When he looked back at the pathway, Elena had disappeared. A moment of panic seized him before he noticed a few weeping willow limbs by the lake moving in the still morning air. She had found her hiding place.

She laughed when he ducked through the willows after her. She was backed up against the tree's trunk. "It's good you were following me or I might have had to whistle some birdsongs to help you find me this morning."

"Can you whistle birdsongs?"

"Only a bobwhite." She demonstrated. "Although the female only does the white, and the male says the bob with the white."

"How do you know that?"

"My father told me." She smiled a little sadly. "He loved birds as well as roses. He was a good man in spite of making poor financial decisions." She hesitated a moment before she went on. "That is my way of telling you my family has no money. Only debts."

"Do you think I care about you having money?" Andrew frowned.

"I don't know. Some men would."

She had to be talking about Frazier. Something he didn't want to do, but he needed to know what she was thinking. "Did Kirby Frazier know you weren't well to do?"

"Not when he asked me to go west with him. Ivy said she told him yesterday morning. That General Dawson insisted she make our situation clear to him." She gave him a curious look. "Did you hear her?"

"No, it must have been before I tried to fight him."

"Fight him? You didn't!" Elena's eyes widened as she stared at him.

"I did." Andrew shook his head. "Fortunately for me, the general was there to stop it. Frazier would have made short work of me."

Elena twisted her mouth to the side to hide a smile. "He is bigger than you."

"And surely more skilled at throwing punches."

"That could be. What I have a hard time believing is that he still searched for me after he knew I wasn't a wealthy heiress." She had a look of wonder.

"That surprises you?"

"It does. He and I were both here for the same reason. He to find a wife to finance his trip to the west and me to find a husband to save my family from poverty. Such pretense on both our parts." She shook her head sadly.

"I think he truly loves you."

"And going west would be a grand adventure." She sounded as if she believed that.

"I suppose it would be." Doubts kept poking him. "Why didn't you go with him, then?"

"He would have tired of having family. Besides, I couldn't go with him." She smiled a little.

"Why is that?"

"Because I do truly want to love whomever I marry. I didn't realize that until my mother pulled me out of my spinster corner and insisted I find a husband. A rich husband. She made sure I knew that requirement. Of course, that left out Kirby even had I fallen in love with him."

"I see." Andrew wasn't sure what he should say, what answers he needed to find.

"Do you?" She didn't let him find an answer to that question before she asked another. "Why are you here at the Springs, Andrew? Because Gloria broke your heart?"

"My heart was wounded. I felt betrayed by her and by my friend who ran away with her."

"That's understandable." Her smile was completely gone. "The two of you could have renewed your promises to each other when she came here."

"We could have."

"But you didn't. Why is that?" She asked him the question he'd asked her moments before.

"Because the same as you, I do want to truly love the person I marry. In the time since Gloria left, I have discovered that is no longer her. If it ever truly was her."

"You surely thought you loved her when you asked her to marry you."

"I did, and we would be married a year now if she had gone through with the wedding."

"I don't know where that leaves me." Her brow furrowed in a frown.

"What do you mean?"

"I mean that I have fallen in love with you, Andrew Harper." She searched his face a moment before she went on. "And I don't know if you think you might fall in love with me."

"I do think I could." Why couldn't he just say he loved her? Still, he'd known her such a short time. Did he feel love or merely attraction? But then, what about his panic when he thought something had happened to her? Surely, that was because of love.

"Love. Such a little word to be so hard to say at times. So hard to trust." Her gaze drifted away from him to study the willow branches shivering in the morning air.

He wanted to trust his feelings, but he hesitated to speak them aloud.

She looked back at him and spoke first. "I've always wondered why people call it falling in love, but now I understand. It can be like walking along through life doing what has to be done when suddenly someone shows up among the flowers to talk to you. Somehow, you know that this is a conversation you never want to end. You've fallen off a cliff into a whole new place where feelings matter more than sensible thinking."

She didn't give him time to say anything as she took his hands and went on. "But if you haven't fallen off that cliff, I understand. I can go back to my spinster's corner now that the general wants to marry my mother. I no longer have to search for that rich husband to save us."

"Spinster's corner?" That made him laugh. "No spinster corners for you." She was smiling now. A beautiful sight. "If I haven't already fallen off that cliff into love, I am tottering on the edge."

"I'm glad, Andrew."

"May I kiss you, Miss Bradford?"

"I am sure Mother would think it scandalous to hide among the willows to steal a kiss, but a former spinster can dare a little scandal." She lifted her face toward his.

He dropped his lips to cover hers just as the first sunrays streaked across the lake to sneak in between the willow branches to touch them. He felt himself falling.

40

June became July and then August. Each day better than the last as Elena met Andrew every morning at dawn somewhere on the grounds. They spent the day together, and Andrew even convinced her to drink at least one glass of the spring water each day. A small glass.

At night, they danced until the wee hours of the morning. Not always with one another, for changing partners was part of the dances at the Springs. But Andrew always found Elena for the last dance.

The first week in August, Elena, her mother, and Ivy went home. General Dawson followed them to buy their house, which let them settle their debts. He met the boys, who didn't have to be told to call him sir. They just did from the first.

Elena's mother stopped wearing black but continued with purples and browns. Although her smile came easy whenever the general was around, she wouldn't agree to marry him until a full year passed after Elena's father's death. But the promise was made.

They went back to the Springs for the last week of the summer season, taking the twins with them. General Dawson even convinced Jacob's parents to let him go along. Ivy danced on air and never stopped smiling except when she went by Vanessa's grave.

No family showed up looking for the mystery lady. Carson Sanderson was arrested in New Orleans for mistreating a woman there. The other man, the servant, was not found.

Elena no longer felt fated to belong in a spinster's corner. She had found a man to make her consider marriage. More than consider it. To desire and hope for a life with him. She loved Andrew the way she had never thought she would love anyone.

Andrew's melancholy disappeared like mist in the morning. Dr. Graham gave the credit to his spring water. Elena gave the credit to love.

After the summer season ended at the Springs, Elena visited his grandfather's horse farm and learned to ride, much to the envy of her little brothers. But Grandfather Scott said that next summer the twins could come work for him and Andrew to learn more about horses.

In January, Elena's mother and General Dawson married, and they packed up to move to his grand house in Madison County. When the general found Elena walking sadly among her father's roses before they moved, he offered to have someone dig up the rosebushes to take with them, but the January ground was frozen. She feared transplanting them in such cold weather would kill them. Besides, the roses seemed to need to stay where her father had planted them with such care. She did catch her cat, Willow, to take along.

As for the cat Princess, it had disappeared as completely as Cinderella in the fairy tale when the clock struck midnight. She and Andrew searched for the cat at the Springs without success. Others did claim to sometimes see a gray cat near Vanessa's grave, but no matter how Elena watched for a silvery cat with vivid blue eyes, she never saw it again.

In June, Elena became Mrs. Andrew Harper in an outdoor

wedding near Grandfather Scott's rose garden where Andrew had planted a yellow rosebush like the one he had called Elena's rose on that morning he had found her sketching. In spite of being so newly planted, it was in full bloom on their wedding day.

After the wedding, General Dawson gave her a package from Kirby, saying it was a wedding gift. He had long before sent the general the two paintings he owed him. One of a buffalo and the other of a canyon that seemed to have no bottom.

Elena wondered as she undid the parcel if it would be the portrait he'd done of her, but instead it was a painting of a cluster of yellow flowers growing up out of ground so dry that cracks showed in the bare dirt around the plant. But the flowers bloomed profusely.

The letter inside had only one line.

I told you there would be flowers.

Andrew looked a little worried when she laughed and read Kirby's message aloud. "Do you wish you were there to paint those flowers?"

"No, Andrew." She stepped into his embrace. "My dance will always be with you."

"And mine with you." He kissed her.

"I think I hear music." She smiled up at him.

"So do I. Beautiful music."

And their forever dance began.

Author's Note

Graham Springs here in Kentucky was considered the Saratoga of the West in the first half of the nineteenth century. It was owned by an amazing man, Dr. Christopher Columbus Graham. Born in 1784, he lived to be 104 and was said to have known every important man in the United States during his long lifetime. He was also considered the best offhand rifle shot in the country.

He claimed his spring water could cure many afflictions and also believed in the benefit of exercise. That included dancing at the many grand balls held at the Springs. In the early 1840s, a young woman did come to Graham Springs alone and claim to be a Louisville judge's daughter. She was said to be beautiful. That night she danced every dance and died in her partner's arms during the last dance of the evening. The judge had no daughters. The woman had nothing in her room except the dress she'd worn that day. When they couldn't find out who she was, she was buried on the grounds.

To this day, her life and death are still a mystery, although various theories have been advanced, one of which involved a relative of Dr. Graham. A city park is now on part of what was once Graham Springs. The dancing lady's grave is well-tended there and has an inscription that reads, "Hallowed and Hushed Be the Place of the Dead. Step Softly, Bow Head."

Through the years, many stories have circulated about the dancing lady, including how some claim to have seen a girl in a fancy ball gown during the midnight hours near her grave.

And now I have added another story about the dancing lady at Graham Springs. I changed her name and added details to her day in my fictional account, but I didn't solve the mystery of her identity or her death. *No one will ever know.*

Read on for an excerpt
from Ann H. Gabhart's

The

SONG *of*
SOURWOOD
MOUNTAIN

Available now
wherever books are sold.

1

When Mira Dean left her rooms for church on Sunday morning, she had no idea that she would hear a proposal of marriage before she returned for her midday meal.

"I-I don't know what to say." Her hazel eyes widened with shock at Gordon Covington's words. She barely knew the man watching her with what seemed the polite smile of someone who had said nothing more than "Good day."

Perhaps she misheard him. Surely she had misheard him.

He glanced around at the people lingering in the church and kept his voice low. "I suppose I should not have been so direct."

When she had approached him after his message to compliment him on his work, he pulled her aside for a private word. Had she any idea what he intended those private words to be, she would have smiled, disengaged her arm, and hurried out the door.

Now she stared past him at the stained-glass window and let those words run through her thoughts again. *"Would you consider marriage, Miss Dean? To me."* She moistened her lips, but he began speaking again before she could give him the only possible answer. No.

"I did not mean to unsettle you, but I have discovered in my time of service to the Lord in the hills of Kentucky that it is nearly always best to plunge forward whenever the Lord prompts me, Miss Dean."

She obviously had not heard wrong. He not only had said the words, he was implying the Lord wanted him to do so.

She pulled her gaze away from the window to peer at him from under the brim of her hat. He was head and shoulders taller than her, but then she did lack appreciable height. Petite, her mother always claimed for her. A prettier word than *short*.

His coat hung loosely on him as if he might have missed too many meals since she'd known him when they were teens. Not well, although they had attended the same school. At the time, she had her life planned out. Marriage to Edward Hamilton. A houseful of children to love. She had no need to consider other pathways then. That was before Edward contracted tuberculosis and went to a sanatorium.

For over two years, she had stormed heaven with prayers for him. The Lord had to heal him, but her prayers weren't answered. Edward had not recovered and instead died without ever leaving the sanatorium. Quite suddenly, or so it seemed to Mira.

This man, Reverend Gordon Covington, with the intense dark blue-gray eyes little resembled the classmate she remembered. That boy was the first out of the schoolhouse to get to the ballfield. She had been interested in seeing him again when she found out he would be visiting their church to talk about his missionary work in the Kentucky Appalachian Mountains. He'd spoken with passion about the church and school he hoped to establish there.

His words touched her heart. When he talked about the mountain children who had no school, tears had filled her eyes.

How terrible it would be to have no way to learn to read. She could hardly believe such a thing was possible here in 1910. All children in Louisville had public schools they could attend, were even required to attend.

She had led many students along a learning path since she began teaching while praying for Edward to regain his health so they could marry. When that did not happen, she had given her life to her students with the thought that they would be her only children.

She had no desire to marry. Besides, even if she were so foolish to dream of love again, at her age she would be unlikely to find a husband. After all, she was twenty-five years old. Gordon was a year older than that, but age mattered less to a man when it came to marriage.

Marriage. The word crashed into her thoughts again. This was absurd. But she was a lady. A mature lady. She could handle this with grace.

"Did the Lord prompt you to be so forward, Mr. Covington?"

She didn't know where those words came from. They weren't at all what she had intended to say. She had meant to step away from him with a murmured refusal to end their uncomfortable encounter. At least she was uncomfortable. Her heart pounded so hard it thumped in her ears. He, on the other hand, looked completely at ease.

"Yes, I do believe that is true. I've prayed with diligence and hope for someone to share my work among the people in Sourwood. The children there need a teacher." His eyes on her were intense. "I need a helpmate."

"I will join my prayers to yours that the Lord will answer your prayers." It was time to make her escape from this impossible conversation. As she started to turn away, he caught her arm.

"But can you not believe you already are that answer?" His gaze didn't waver. "I have no doubt the Lord led us both here on this day. At this very moment. The children need you."

He didn't grip her arm, merely touched it, but his words froze her in place. She did feel a tug at her heart. Not for the man staring at her, but for the children he mentioned. Children with no teacher. The force of his calling seemed to go from his hand to her heart.

"I barely know you."

Her head was spinning. If not for his hand on her arm, she might have swooned. She never swooned, but now it seemed his touch was all that kept her grounded. Or perhaps not him. Perhaps his talk of the Lord. Yes, that was what she should cling to. His mission for the Lord. A mission he was inviting her to join.

When he didn't say anything, she added, "You barely know me."

"The Lord knows us both and he knows the need. A need you and I can fill in Sourwood. You wouldn't be a teacher hired by the county. Ours would be a mission school with our own rules for the position of teacher. A teacher chosen by the Lord." Now he did tighten his fingers on her arm the slightest bit. "I think you feel the calling too. Think of the children you will help."

"I already teach here in Louisville."

"City children have many teachers. In Sourwood they have none, but we have faith the Lord will provide the perfect teacher for the schoolhouse we're building." He leaned closer to her. "And here you are."

She felt captured, not only by his hand, but by his mission. "The need for a teacher doesn't explain your—" She hesitated before continuing. "Your proposal. You do know that teachers are required to be single."

A flicker of a frown tightened his face, but only for a moment. "A foolish policy, in my opinion. Don't you agree?"

"I-I have never considered it, as I knew it would not apply to me."

"You never thought of marriage?"

"Not after Edward died." Even now, years later, simply saying the words made her heart clench with sorrow.

"I was sorry to hear of his passing. A good man lost to the world." His face softened as though he understood her grief.

"So much lost," she murmured. This man could not know how much. The emptiness, the barren feeling that settled deep within her.

"But the Lord has another plan for you now. Come to the mountains with me. As my wife. The mountaineers will accept you sooner that way and trust their children to your instruction."

"I can't marry you. I don't love you." She looked directly into his eyes. "You don't love me."

"But I love the Lord. You love the Lord. I believe he will honor that love, and with a common mission in both our hearts, the Lord will grow love between us as he did so many of those he brought together in the Bible."

"We are not people in the Bible."

For the first time since he'd pulled her aside, he smiled fully to transform his face. He looked more like the boy she remembered from school, someone everyone liked. She felt her own lips turning up in an answering smile despite the complete disarray of her thoughts.

"We are not, but I believe the Lord still works through people in our day the same as Bible times. He knows the plans he has for us and he opens up paths to let us accomplish his purpose. He sent me to the mountains to minister to the people there. Could you have ever believed that possible when you knew me years ago?"

How could she answer him? At that time, she could have never imagined him becoming a preacher. "I don't know. I suppose I could have if I had considered the possibility."

He waved away her words with a laugh. "Now, now, Miss Dean, I think you do know. You can be honest with me. Honesty is important, even vital, in a marital relationship."

If he wanted honesty, she could give him honesty tempered with kindness. "I think it is important not to pretend, Reverend Covington. I am intrigued by the idea of teaching in your mission area. Sourwood, did you say?" When he nodded, she went on. "But I have no intention of marrying you or anyone."

"Nor did I have intentions to be a preacher or, once I did surrender to preach, to go to the mountains. But the Lord can change our intentions."

"The Lord may have spoken to you and given you a mission. He has not spoken to me." When she stepped away from him, he dropped his hand to his side. The strange urge came over her to move back toward him in the hope he might claim her arm again.

"Are you sure? You did come to hear my message. You seem sympathetic to my plea for help."

"This is the church I attend regularly. I put a gift in the collection they took for you." Her words sounded stiff.

"Such funds are much appreciated, but you have so much more to give." He pinned her in place with his gaze. "Will you do me one favor?"

"I cannot marry you." As he had said, honesty was best.

"I have asked that, and it would be a fine favor, but this is a different request."

"Very well. What is it?"

"Will you pray about what I've asked? Will you let the Lord put that intention in your heart if it is meant to be? As I think. As I hope."

"I will pray for you and for your mission." That seemed a reasonable answer to his request.

"I do covet your prayers, but will you also pray to be open to what the Lord wants from you? I do not believe he ever demands more than we are able to give, and I, should you accept my outrageous request, would never demand anything you are not ready to give with an open heart."

"I will pray for you," she repeated.

His eyes looked sad then, as he nodded slightly. "Thank you. Your presence here was a gift and so will be your prayers for me."

As she turned away from him to find her way out of the church, she wondered if she would ever see him again. For some reason, that thought bothered her. Not because of him, she was sure, but because of her sympathy and concern for his mission.

Under her cloak, she touched her arm where his hand had held her. Despite the frosty chill in the January air, her skin still felt warm. She jerked her hand away and pulled on her gloves. She would pray he would find the teacher he sought.

Acknowledgments

First and foremost, I thank the Lord for granting this country girl the desires of my heart by giving me the joy of sharing stories with readers like you. Writing a novel sometimes feels a little like magic when characters spring to life in my head. No, magic isn't the right word. Inspiration given by the Lord is better. I am thankful for each story and for you readers who go down story roads with my characters and me.

Once the story gets rolling along the publishing road, there are many who have a hand in guiding it through the channels to become a book. My editor Rachel McRae has a wonderful ability to see ways to improve a story to make it better. I appreciate the care she gives to each story to make it the best it can be. Many thanks as well to Kristin Adkinson, who carefully goes over the story to keep the words flowing along and to catch those things that can slip by an author even after a dozen read-throughs.

I appreciate Laura Klynstra and the art department for how they always come up with gorgeous covers that invite readers into my stories. I am blessed with my whole Revell team as they take my story through all the steps that go into making it a book for readers. Thanks especially to Karen Steele and Lindsay Schubert for always being just an email away when I need help and for finding great opportunities for me to share about my stories with readers.

My agent, Wendy Lawton, is the best. She's always ready with advice and encouragement when needed. I'm grateful for her support through the years.

Last, but certainly not least, I thank my husband, Darrell, and all my family for cheering me on as I wrote yet another story. Oh, and I can even thank my dogs, who never let me forget it's time to take a walk, even if deadlines are looming.

Ann H. Gabhart is the bestselling author of *The Song of Sourwood Mountain*, *When the Meadow Blooms*, *Along a Storied Trail*, *An Appalachian Summer*, *River to Redemption*, *These Healing Hills*, and *Angel Sister*, along with many novels set in a fictional Shaker village. She and her husband live on a farm a mile from where she was born in rural Kentucky. Ann enjoys time with her family and taking her dogs, Frankie and Marley, for walks. Learn more at AnnHGabhart.com.

Dear Reader,

Thank you for selecting a Revell novel! We're so happy to be part of your reading life through this work. Our mission here at Revell is to publish stories that reach the heart. Through friendship, romance, suspense, or a travel back in time, we bring stories that will entertain, inspire, and encourage you. We believe in the power of stories to change our lives and are grateful for the privilege of sharing these stories with you.

We believe in building lasting relationships with readers, and we'd love to get to know you better. If you have any feedback, questions, or just want to chat about your experience reading this book, please email us directly at publisher@revellbooks.com. Your insights are incredibly important to us, and it would be our pleasure to hear how we can better serve you.

We look forward to hearing from you and having the chance to enhance your experience with Revell Books.

The Publishing Team at Revell Books
A Division of Baker Publishing Group
publisher@revellbooks.com

Revell

Meet
Ann H. Gabhart

AnnHGabhart.com